RODE

J. ADAMS

An earlier version of "Quack" was previously published in the *12 Gauge Review*. An earlier version of the Martin section appeared in *Genre* magazine.

ISBN: 979-8-9856972-1-6 (paperback)

ISBN: 979-8-9856972-2-3 (ePub)

Interior design by Booknook.biz.

In memory of W. Wagner
(and everyone else up there)

CONTENTS

QUACK

There weren't any ducks the first time we came. Just us. Me and Skelly, skipping stones. Ripples across the pond. That whole Sunday seeming like it was never going to give way. No matter if it did, besides, with so many more spreading out in front of us. Classes had only been in session a few weeks, and we were still in the beginning part of getting to know one another, when she asked me to meet her that morning in front of the chapel.

Then she brought me here.

Along with some cheese, crackers. Wine poured into paper cups. Seemed like the only difference between us and church was the cheese, and when I mentioned it, she looked at me like I'd had some sort of epiphany.

Of course, it was a lot easier to impress her then. Easier to impress myself.

This morning, I came alone. Looking for a place to lie down. Imagined me all bucolic and laid out among the grass blades. Maybe some tweety birds in the piñons. I hadn't thought to incorporate a herd of ducks into the scene, but here they are. Honking, splashing, generally having their feathers all flapping, fighting with the occasional pigeon, getting chased by dogs. Not the ideal place to try to get some sleep, it turns out. I should probably have stayed up in Santa Fe last night like I was supposed to. I had reservations for Ren's couch, but I guess I hadn't been quite ready to go. It seemed like if I spent the whole night out I might be able to get my fill but all I got, really, was tired.

I throw down my pack for a pillow and stretch myself out on the damp ground. A chill soaking into my spine. I've got visions of waking with a beak clamped to my nose, but I manage to keep my eyes closed.

Next thing, the bell on the upper quad's chiming nine. Might have dozed off for a bit, but I doubt it. I'm usually quick to dream, and I wasn't dreaming anything, just a break taken from the glare of the world, and my thoughts drifted far enough away so I could get some leave of them.

It seems quieter now—hoisted up on my elbows and squinting in the bright light—with the dogs gone, having calmed the ducks. Something close to peaceful, and I'm wishing it would keep on like that when I hear the first voices of the students coming down the path.

All the science classes are still over here, according to Skell. I remember giving her my initial opinion on that subject, about halfway through the bottle of wine.

"So you science freaks have been keeping this pond hidden over here for yourselves?"

"It's hardly a secret, Jack. Maybe you should try to get out more."

"I've been getting out plenty," I told her. "I can already name two bars I can get into and that was with minimal facial hair." It sounded defensive, and it probably was. I didn't like being on my back foot with Skelly and took my time finding a near perfect skipper among the rocks and pebbles scattered along the embankment. Then I sent it jumping across the water.

"Nice throw," she said. "That's the best one so far."

"Thanks," I said, feeling like I was in position to push my luck, "but don't you think certain humanities scholars could be getting more inspiration from having this near North campus?"

Skell nodded politely, maybe hoping I'd leave it at that.

"Think Frost. Think Walden. Do you suppose Socrates could have come up with a single brilliant idea if he'd spent his days crammed between parking lots?" I could see her struggling with the flaws in my logic, but she still didn't say anything. What else could I do but follow my argument to some demented conclusion. "I say drain it. Drain it and move it to North campus immediately."

The redness in her face, which had been gathering in color, finally flushed in with her freckles. "And I suppose you think scientists have no need of contact with the natural world."

"Precisely," I said. "I'm glad we're in agreement on this." Then I gave a quick salute and plunged sideways into the water. When I came up, I let out a holler and looked over to see Skell laughing.

"You know, I was this close to pushing you in."

"I know," I said, laughing back, "I thought I'd save you the trouble."

Students are descending onto the lawn now. They collect in groups under the trees, by the bridge, chattering and joking, not seeming all that distressed about having classes in July, although it's still early. In the month. In the term. Half the time I'd been enrolled here, it seemed like it was too hot to think straight, but it's hard to remember exactly how things are when you're no longer on the inside of them.

When I asked how she felt about being back in school again, Skell thought for a moment and said, "It's more like a job now." I was straining to find a note of regret or even resignation in her voice, but I just don't think it was there. She was happy with what she was doing. Career-wise, at least, she felt like her life was moving forward.

Myself, I couldn't imagine being confined to another lecture hall. Actually, I had imagined it, a number of years back when I first applied to grad school. At the time, it seemed like a harmless next step, but I'd already soured on the idea even before I'd been accepted. Wanting to believe I'd been built for better than knees cramped behind more desks, debates without end, drinking too much at faculty parties. Presumably,

I would've gotten my degree this past spring and found myself pretty much where I am right now. Wondering what I was going to do next.

That was one benefit of being in school. Rarely having to make up your mind about anything important. Freedom without consequences. And while I was still attracted to the loose energy scattered across campus—all that potential in no hurry to be converted—the students themselves seemed barely aware of it. At least, that was the impression I got from the trio of undergraduates I found myself hanging out with earlier this morning.

The pretty blonde who, between sips of coffee, eagerly described the parts of her anatomy she liked best. Her maybe/maybe not boyfriend. Their third wheel, a bubble-headed girl named Nancy. Personally, I was enjoying the blonde's attempts at being provocative, but Nancy seemed to grow increasingly uncomfortable as her cohort began to elaborate on the topic of female genitalia and was soon pleading with me to take her across the street from the Pancake Palace to the Allsup's for a pack of cigarettes. I suspected she was probably used to these antics by now but agreed to go anyway. Feeling the increasingly easy pull of other people's lives.

When we got outside, Nancy asked if we could take the motorcycle over to get the smokes. She was hoping we could go for a spin around town afterward, and even if that's what I'd been mostly doing since the late movie let out, I couldn't say I was opposed to the idea.

I was trying not to think about it too much. How it was going to be with the bike all locked up in storage. Buried in the back of Ren's shed, somewhere in between the broken air conditioning unit and his brother-in-law's Camaro engine. Anchored to its center stand, primed to gather dust. Tank full, but the battery disconnected and oil drained out.

Sure, another cruise was fine by me, so I undid the helmet off the back of the bike and handed it to her. Then I pulled the bootlace from around my neck and selected the starter key.

"Is that a necklace?"

"No, it's not a *necklace*."

"Well, what is it?"

"Like a chain, I guess."

"But it's leather."

"I don't know. I just wear it so I don't lose track of my keys." Plus, it gave me a good feeling having them right there against my chest when I wasn't riding, but I wasn't about to tell her that.

"I like it," she said.

"I'm glad. Now, where did you want to go?"

"Anywhere," she told me.

So we hopped on and drove up Central, then shot along Tramway hugging the base of the Sandia Mountains. The sky was starting to brighten. The bike's single headlight fading into the pavement. I looked out over the city, then further west beyond the interstate to the horizon, where I caught a glimpse of something so strange that I had to check the road and look again. But it appeared only more real the second time. Streaks of fog had spread up thick from the Rio Grande Valley, and I swear I was staring at the ocean out there—soft waves and gray water—drifting restless in the distance. You could almost believe that sometime during the night California had finally fallen into the sea, and with such force that it had managed to drag Arizona and a sizable chunk of New Mexico right along with it.

I pulled over to show my riding companion.

"Check this out," I said. "It looks like the Acoma Pueblo's got beachfront property."

The follow-up line on that was supposed to be "at least, until the government figures out a way to make a claim on their land," but unfortunately, I didn't get a chance to share my political views, because Nancy didn't really see what I was talking about in the first place.

"It looks kind of . . . cloudy," she said. And then added, "I guess."

I outlined the picture again with my finger, but she wasn't following it. So I backed off and tried to salvage the stop as best I could. "Anyway, that's where I'm gonna be headed. All the way to the Pacific."

"Oh my God, to California?" Zero to sixty in about two seconds; I hadn't guessed she'd be the excitable type. "On your bike, that's so cool! Do you think you'll go to Hollywood? No wait, Venice. Venice would be so cool!"

I'd stopped nodding. "I'm actually taking the bus," I told her.

"Oh," she said, "that's kind of sad. Why are you doing that?"

Why? I thought. *Because I don't want the responsibility, right now, for anything besides myself.* "Because the bike needs a rest," I said.

"A rest," she repeated, nodding her head slowly. Then she opened her mouth partway and held it there, like she was trying to figure something out, before she dropped it all the way open and said, "Wait, your bike's not broken, is it? I mean, it's not dangerous?"

I fielded the easier part of the question. "No, I've been taking great care of the bike. It may well be in the best shape of its career."

"It does sound really smooth," she agreed, her confidence seesawing back. "I don't see why you don't take it. Or at least fly. That's be better than riding in a grubby old bus."

"Yeah, but sometimes airplanes get you there too quick. I want to feel the miles roll out from under the wheels. Appreciate the distance, you know what I mean?"

She didn't. "So you're trying to save money?"

"The bus isn't that much cheaper."

"I can't believe that. I always thought to myself if I ever really wanted to get out of here—and I was desperate—I could at least afford the bus."

"Well, it isn't that expensive. They have student discounts. I bet you got enough in your purse to buy a ticket right now if you wanted."

"Oh, no, I can't. I mean, I don't have enough money for sure." She held her purse tighter. "And don't you think we ought to be getting back? Because my friends are probably wondering where I am."

It sure doesn't take much for misunderstandings to crop up between people. Of course, I hadn't been suggesting she take off on the next bus out of town, let alone take off with me. And I definitely didn't have any designs on her purse. All I'd been hoping to point out was that if she wanted to go to California, or anywhere else for that matter, it really wasn't very hard to get there.

I probably shouldn't have pulled the bike over to begin with. Just stayed driving, with that ocean view kept to myself.

On the way back down Central, though, I got to thinking how if Skell had been with me, she would've been sure to see what I was talking about. And even if it meant something to her to have a cushion between herself and the sea—something solid before the land fell off—I still think she would've enjoyed the image. She had a great eye, picking up everything from ladybugs on your jacket, to exit signs on the freeway. Combined with my kind of kaleidoscopic way of looking at the world, we'd managed to get around well.

It's hard to believe we had dinner together last night—that memory already feels like a relic from that same bygone era of Sunday wine—with her telling me she was finished with her lesson plan mockups as I was heading out the door. It was pretty clear she was up for going out, but I just couldn't handle running through the whole Last Night Together routine, so I said goodbye after dinner. Then stayed out, carousing around like I had nowhere to go.

After dropping Nancy back off with her friends, I headed over to the Frontier for yet another cup of coffee. Frontier was one of the brighter stars in the constellation of all-night restaurants that kept the city going after the early close of the bars, that city being Albuquerque, New Mexico, aka the Double Q. Skell came up with the name our sophomore year in retaliation to the lame "Burquee" tag that was being bandied about. Albuquerque wasn't a cute town, she said, and besides, how many places could claim a single Q in their name, let alone two. You just couldn't take things like that for granted.

In addition to having a handy nickname, Albuquerque also possessed a kind of low attitude cool, although, I have to admit, I hadn't been completely taken with the idea of moving back to our college town. It was right after Thanksgiving when Skell first brought it up. We'd been living at a celebrity chef's ranch north of Santa Fe, taking care of an arkful of animals, performing medium to light duties in exchange for trailer housing and a small monthly stipend. Skell had more of the responsibility with me still working twenty-four-hour shifts in town, and she'd had a lot of time to think. After a long stint in landscaping, she was ready to be having a more direct impact on people. She wanted to teach.

I admired her for it. Knew she'd be just the kind of teacher you'd want popping up on your class schedule. So I put aside any misgivings I might have had when she homed in on the graduate program at UNM. They offered the fastest accreditation in the state—you were out in the field your first year—and that meant taking courses in the summer. It all sounded reasonable, except I hadn't planned on having unemployed myself by the time we moved in.

It was just supposed to have been a pivot—from city firefighter to wildland firefighter. There shouldn't have been any looking back. Maybe I read too much of a sign into that little brush blaze up at the ranch, but there'd been a simple satisfaction in knowing we'd been able to put it out with boots, shovels, dirt. A feeling I rarely got riding around on the engine in town, where the lack of action had been bothering me for a while. The idea about switching got stuck in my head, and once that happened, it was only a matter of time before I did something about it.

Ren had been more cautious about the change, but, still, he'd made a call for me. To his cousin, Tito, who headed a crew out of Cimarron. It should have been a lock, but right after I got out there, one of the guys who'd retired at the end of the previous season changed his mind and decided to come back. My connection had no business overriding the seniority and it didn't. I was able to test for and get my red card while

I was there, but that just continued to sit in my wallet doing nothing. We were still under the spell of an El Niño, and the snowiest winter in years had turned into one of the wettest springs, but with no one believing the rain around here, I kept hearing the same thing: *You'll be good with that red card, bro. Just wait till the middle of the summer, the fires'll get going.* It wasn't an ideal position to be in, rooting for drought in a part of the country that suffered far too many of them, and at a certain point, I stopped not only believing the job was going to happen, but even wanting it to.

Until then, I'd done my best to be patient. Dutifully checking the messages at the end of every day to see if one of the crews I'd been waitlisted with had called me up. I passed the time gathering futile information online, with library books, dollar movies at the San Mateo 8, crossword puzzles, and games of Scrabble with Skell. I took the bike cruising, north to Madrid, east to Santa Rosa, south to Carlsbad and White Sands. I changed the oil, polished the frame, swapped out the windjammer for a bigger one, installed new saddlebags, and took it in to Bobby J's for a full tune-up. After getting the bill on that, I decided to cool it on the expenditures. The balance from my former PERA account was only heading in one direction, and with no word yet from the Forest Service, I considered doing a little part-time work to tide me over. I made a couple of inquiries, but didn't follow up, thinking I could be called out any day.

Finally, I succumbed to the "easy money" ads on the back page of the *Alibi*. I sold my blood, my plasma, and was seriously contemplating the triple by offering up my sperm, but Skell put the kibosh on that idea real quick. "If you're selling it to anyone, you're selling it to me" was her first response. I was waiting for her to lighten up about it, and eventually, seeing my reaction, she did. "I'll pay double whatever the going rate is," she smiled, "and I won't make you use a cup." All I could think was, *You don't want my DNA; the kid'll probably get panicked after a few months in the same womb and need to relocate somewhere else.*

For years, the more time Skelly and I spent together, the better things were between us. The progression was nearly effortless. With hanging out at school becoming hooking up at school becoming hooking up after school had ended. Of course, we were both going to stay in New Mexico. Of course, she'd be spending the night occasionally, regularly, getting her own key. The timing always seemed right. And I never felt crowded in.

Admittedly, some of that had to do with her allowing me to pursue other relationships along the way, but I really don't think that explained everything. The first woman I'd taken up with had infuriated her, but by the time I'd bailed on the second, Skell had become, in many ways, more clearheaded about my prospects than I was. With me still thinking every time this was going to be The One, and her kicking back and waiting for the inevitable break-up. Then it would be just Skelly and me again, stronger than ever.

When we moved out to the ranch, I'm not sure either of us fully realized what we were signing up for. Our nearest neighbors were monks, but with their monastery five miles upriver and their habits unsurprisingly reclusive, we rarely saw them. Living in relative isolation offered us a new kind of intimacy, and at first we embraced it. We felt at home in each other's arms at the end of the day. Took pleasure in the projects we'd seen through. But as our friendship continued to deepen, it didn't seem like there was enough else to accompany it. It was difficult to ignore the feeling that we were roommates—with benefits, sure—but roommates nonetheless.

By spring, it was clear something was missing.

I wonder what ducks think about the whole thing, relationships and the rest. One of them has waddled over by my feet and seems to be carrying on about something. If she does have an agenda, I can't quite make it out. It's possible she wants to be fed, or that she wants me to move out of her way. The longer she goes on quacking, though, the more I feel like I'm getting a reprimand. I've heard that ducks mate for life, and she might well have some strongly held views on the subject. Skelly would know about it, I'm sure. She's the one with the biology degree.

When we were packing up the trailer, I tried to be casual when I mentioned that I wanted to start seeing other people again. It had worked so well before, hadn't it? No, I didn't have anyone in particular in mind, but we were going back to the city, and even if it was a small one, I felt like we both ought to have the opportunity to explore some more. "Especially you," I said. "Think of all the time you'll be spending alone when I get called up."

Skell was folding a pile of clothes, and she waited until she'd finished before speaking. "It's been a while since we've done anything like this, so let me remind you what I've said in the past. I want you to be the most important person in my life, Jack. If you think we should see other people again, then I need to know I'd still be the most important person in yours."

The fact was, there hadn't been anyone who'd had a more positive impact on my existence than Skelly. She brought out the best in me and made it seem like the best was normal. She knew things about me that other people didn't, had seen more of my faults, and still wanted me around. She was upbeat, savvy, and easy to wake up next to in the morning. I couldn't imagine anyone taking her place and I told her that.

So we arrived back in the Double Q with freedom to spare. I never did anything with it besides flirt around, but still, it wasn't enough. With my job prospects dimming, the town was closing in around me, Skell was becoming more and more a part of the town, and I honestly couldn't tell where the one ended and the other began, because the tension was coming from inside. Trying to keep down the feeling that I was getting off track. But damn it, if I could name even one time in my life when I'd been able to change course after suspecting a wrong turn.

When I told Skell that I needed to get out of town, at least for a little while, she didn't seem all that surprised. She'd watched me get increasingly irritable in the flat, had sympathized with my frustration without giving in to it. We were still making each other smile every day, but it was getting harder, and I couldn't see waiting around for that to disappear.

Skelly accepted my leaving the way she'd accepted so many other things, but the question was, where was the limit?

I couldn't figure it out.

Maybe she thought I had something to get out of my system, one final childish kick before I would grow up and come back to her. Or maybe her love for me was so strong that she was prepared to support me no matter what, willing to let me go even if that meant I might stay gone. Either way, she offered to drop me at the bus station.

12:04

Rain falls hard from the night sky but I'm not getting wet, under the ledge of this building. There's room enough to move. To pace, along the narrow strip of sidewalk covered by the overhang. But when the wind blows, pelting the drops toward me, I stop. Press myself up against the building.

I've got my back to the wall. I've got some change in my pocket. There's a payphone not far from here—at least there used to be, I haven't been by the park in a while—and as soon as the rain lets up, I'll take a walk in that direction. Meanwhile, the only thing crossing the intersection of 17th and Church is the cabled wire strung out above it.

I stare at the traffic signals. Not knowing when they're about to turn. It's better not to know . . . the minor suspense . . . but before long the timing's become as predictable as the colors, running over and over empty streets that can't tell the difference between coming and going.

Finally, a vehicle approaches from 17th. The light's just gone red, and the car comes to a stop. I can see the shadowed figure of the driver inside. Lean up to the windshield. Slouch. Lean up to the windshield again. The light's still red. No traffic. The wipers are shifting back and forth.

"What are you waiting for?" I want to yell. "Just go."

The driver glances to the side like he's somehow heard me. Maybe he sees me, I don't know, but when the light turns he floors it. The sound of wheels spinning on wet pavement slashes through the rain, skidding the car a few feet into the intersection before the treads get a proper grip, pulling it away clean.

There's more room for error in a car, that's for sure. That same move on a motorcycle and it wouldn't take much to find yourself spilled over onto scrapes or a busted leg.

No, it'd be a crappy time to be out on a bike.

Not like that makes me feel a whole lot better about where mine is tonight. Over at City Cycle, but it might as well be a thousand miles from here.

Jack **missed the bike** already and they hadn't even crossed outside the city limits. The jerky starts and stops getting on the highway. The plodding speed. Leaving the driving to them was going to require some effort. More than he would've guessed, considering all he really needed to do was think like luggage.

In Grants, they picked up a handful of people, and by the time they'd finished loading in Gallup, the seats were full. All except the one next to Jack. He chalked up the vacancy to a combination of his sprawling size and luck, allowing himself to relax a bit, when the doors closed. Maybe he'd be able to get a nap in.

Inching away from the building, there was a banging sound on the side of the bus. The doors opened and closed one final time, and when a man came teetering down the aisle, Jack knew exactly where he was headed.

The guy was drunk. Very drunk. Giving off a stench that said hello and sat down before he did. Jack slid over to make room. Kept his nose hovered over the window vents while the guy settled in. Eventually, the smell dissipated into the background and he was able to wean himself off the AC. That left only a mild case of claustrophobia to contend with.

Jack reached into his pocket and pulled out a copy of his itinerary, scanning down the list of scheduled stops. The next break was in Flagstaff, but that wouldn't be for four hours. Or three, depending on the time change, he couldn't remember if there was one.

"Strange town you're going to."

He looked over to find the man staring at the ticket. He would've been hard-pressed to call it an invasion of privacy since there was so little to offend.

"Strange town," he repeated. "Even stranger than people say."

Jack nodded. "Might be. But I hear the weather's supposed to be good. How about you? How far you going?"

"Gehenna, I'm afraid. And they're making me pay full fare to boot."

Jack debated whether to encourage him any further. "You taking the local or the express?"

"That I couldn't tell you." The man leaned back in his seat.

Jack put away his ticket and did the same. Every time he managed to nod off, though, he was interrupted by a pudgy-faced boy who kept running back to the bathroom. The kid would repeat a word every time he passed, louder every time he said it: dog, Dog, DOG, DOG! DOG!!

At one point, he emerged from the stall and yelled up to his mother that he'd broken something; she told him to get back in his seat and stay there. He trotted by waving the latch in his hand, leaving the door to rattle, flap like an injured wing. Every time the bus braked it swung wide open, then slammed shut again, pushing another blast of foul air into the cabin. Jack figured someone in the last row would at least stick their foot against it, but that didn't happen.

His seatmate was slow to respond with exaggerated sniffling noises. "Can you believe that shit?" he asked, jerking his thumb backward, indicating the distance that lay between someone else's stink and your own.

"It's pretty bad," Jack agreed.

"Damn right it's bad." He wiped his brow with a soiled handkerchief. "Just like every other thing in this godforsaken place."

Then he began to elaborate.

For a while, Jack tried to hang with what the guy was saying, but after a few honest tries, he'd given in to ignoring him. Fixing his stare to the window where, outside, the light was fading. Faster through the tinted glass. If he'd been on the bike, he might have pulled over. Swapped out for the clear shield on his helmet. That always gave him a little boost—the sudden brightening at dusk—as if he'd just managed to add some time to the day.

He closed his eyes, trying to find the hum in the wheels, but his neighbor was continuing to talk over it. *Why won't you people pay attention? Don't you see what's happening here?* He was indignant. Still rambling on about the same things. How the country had lost its way. Sold its soul to the lowest bidder. He would tick off a grievance or two— *You wanna know what a sin is? I'll tell you what a sin is*—then return to his favorite refrain, that things were bound to get worse if people didn't *wake up and smell the donuts.* Jack couldn't help but snigger at that one; it got a little funnier every time he said it. *You think this is funny? Well, you better wake up and smell the donuts!*

Meanwhile, the couple in the adjacent seats were beginning to grumble and the driver had already called back twice telling him to pipe down. Feeling somehow responsible, Jack turned to face him again, doing his best to maintain eye contact. That seemed to calm the man. Twenty minutes later, he passed out on Jack's shoulder.

Almost immediately, the man's odor began to ripen. As if in slumber he'd given up a previously unsuspected control of his pores, releasing something deeper and even more unyielding. It seeped from him with abandon. All humor from the encounter drained. He was snoring out a thick string of mucus and Jack couldn't look away. It stretched down from his nostril toward his upper lip, then was yanked back in again, like a worm trying unsuccessfully to escape.

Nearly convinced he was rotting, Jack fought the temptation to push the man off him. To push him aside and make his way to the front of the bus and tell the driver to stop and let him out right there. He ran the scenario through his mind several times, but that's as far as he got with it. Hitchhiking didn't strike him as a particularly bright option, and wherever they were, it couldn't be that far out from Flagstaff. He'd at least get a breather there.

Jack eased himself back against the window, careful not to disturb the man's head. Then waited on the impending darkness.

The man stayed with him through morning. Tipped his hat and made his way off, leaving plenty of space. But as Jack twisted and turned, trying to get comfortable, it was like the man was still there, wheezing in his ear.

The bus was late getting into San Bernardino. Jack missed his transfer and was stranded there for the day. Then the 7:10 overheated in the parking lot and he was told it would be hours before they got a replacement.

The driver's announcement woke him in Bakersfield. Some dark of the morning hour, the slow stirrings of the other passengers. He needed to take a leak. Felt only the thinnest film of consciousness over that. Enough to direct him inside the station to the urinal. And then after, to confront him as he stood facing the mirror. With the reflection of a man who wanted to get away from getting away, and not by going back either.

The sudden severity of the thought. The water still running.

He looked down at his hands—the stream slipping through his fingers—then dried off quickly and returned to the bus. He stayed awake the rest of the way to San Francisco.

Jack was anxious to put some distance between himself and the Greyhound terminal. But with the street names indistinct and the buildings nearly featureless in the fog, he was having a hard time getting his bearings, so he ducked into a diner. A bell jingled when he opened the door, but no one looked up. He sat by the window and ordered some lunch.

When the food came, he took his time with it, unsure of his next move. By the time he was scraping the bottom of the plate, though, he realized how tired he was. When he went to pay the tab, he asked the guy behind the counter for a tip on a cheap motel.

"You could try the Chase, that's not too far from here." He handed Jack his change. "A couple ladies run it. Real friendly, I hear. I bet they got room for one more."

Jack had no trouble finding the place, sandwiched between Tex-Mex take-out and a pawn shop that looked like it had gone out of business. Inside, he found himself at the foot of a long, red-carpeted staircase, which he followed up and around as far as the office. Seeing the *Back Soon* sign taped to the window, he put down his pack and took a seat on the floor beside it.

For a while he tried to read. But even with the pages held steady, it was no better than on the bus, when the same bloom of a headache had caused him to give up on the idea. So he set the book aside, and let his eyes wander over the carpet, which stretched out everywhere, crimson thick. He thought it was kind of classy at first, but then noticed how many stains it had taken in and almost completely absorbed.

There was a decent amount of traffic through the building, but what he saw of it was mostly glimpsed through the stairwell entry, bodies shuffling their way past to a higher floor. The only person to step into the hall was a guy with military fatigues and a limp. Frowning suspiciously as he made his way by. Maybe he had some information as to the whereabouts of management, but it didn't seem like it'd be worth the hassle to ask him about it.

There was definitely something off about the place, but that only helped it to fit right in with the rest of the trip and how that'd gone so far. Jack decided to wait on what little promise was left in the *Back Soon* sign. If no one showed by two o'clock, he was out of there.

A couple minutes later he heard the door open below. A cough came pounding up the stairs, followed by footsteps. Then a pair of unlaced high tops standing in front of him, filled by a young guy in jeans and a T-shirt. Unshaven face. The same Raiders cap Jack was wearing.

"Nice hat, man."

"You got a good one, too."

"Waiting for the office guys?"

"I was," Jack told him, getting up from the floor. "I've about had it."

"I don't know where Ali is, but Ari's probably banging his chick up in 412. He should be down any minute, he usually doesn't last long."

"He must be making a pretty good run of it today. I've been here since one."

"I bet he fell asleep is what happened. He's a fine piece of work, you'll see." He held out his hand. "I'm Eddie."

Jack gave his name, shook.

"So you're needing a place to stay, right?"

"Looking for one."

"You're welcome to stay with me if you want. Don't seem to be much point in giving those guys your money."

"Oh, yeah? Thanks." Jack wasn't sure what to make of the offer. It wasn't like the guy had looked at him funny; in fact, he'd barely looked at him at all. "Yeah, you know I'm wondering if I even got the right place. I was expecting a couple of ladies to be here, some guy told me they ran this hotel."

"Oh, you mean Susie and Bee. Sure, they used to run it, but they adopted a kid and moved out about six months ago. Then we got these fools."

There didn't seem to be much else to say about it. "Well, maybe I'll at least go back and check out what the rooms look like."

"Whatever you want, man. Follow me."

Eddie's room seemed barely large enough to accommodate one person.

It had an unmade bed, a dresser, television. Some stereo equipment. Microwave and a small fridge. A few clothes scattered around.

"Housekeeping hasn't been by this week," Eddie explained, picking up a shirt and tossing it on top of the dresser. "So you here for a while?"

"A little while, yeah. Maybe longer."

"Well, you can stay here for a little while. You have a sleeping bag?"

"Not with me."

"That's all right, I got some extra blankets you can use. Yeah, you can stay on as long as you don't try to steal my stash." Eddie laughed. Took his cap off and ran his hand through his buzz cut. Put the cap back on his head. "Just kidding."

"Just kidding you've got drugs?"

"No, just kidding you'd think about stealing them. Hey, you're not a cop, are you?"

"No."

"You sure about that? You kind of look like a cop."

"Seriously, man, don't sweat it."

"But you wouldn't tell me if you were a cop?"

"I wouldn't have to, no."

"How d'you know that if you're not a cop?"

It probably wasn't the best time to mention he used to work with the police. "You seem to have it all figured out and you're not a cop. Are you?"

"Hell no."

Jack grinned. "You sure about that?"

"All right, wise guy. I believe you, but the fact is you're out of place around here, and that gets my attention. Don't get me wrong, I can deal with the cops. I just don't want them staying in my room." His laugh trailed off into another cough. "This cough sucks."

"Yeah," Jack agreed. "Drag." He looked around the room again, pressed his fingers to the wall. Not quite the poster guy for Just Off the Bus.

That first afternoon, Eddie seemed like he had it pretty well together. Jack was surprised to learn the guy was thirty-four—he'd thought they were closer in age—but he supposed that didn't matter. They shot the shit for a while and then Eddie told him he'd be working late at the club where he deejayed and needed to grab a few z's. Jack lay back on the floor and tried to do the same.

When the alarm went off, Eddie didn't react until Jack called up to him. He muttered something in return, reached over and ripped the cord from the wall, then lay in bed another few minutes before getting up. While he was changing his clothes, he told Jack to make himself at home, to help himself to whatever he could find in the fridge.

"Keep the door locked, all right. And if anyone knocks, don't answer it." Then his tone softened. "I'll be back late, but it'd be nice if you wait up for me."

With that, Eddie walked away down the hall, whistling. Jack stood there for a moment before, slowly, turning the bolt. Then he walked over to the window. Spreading the curtains farther apart, he could see the fog had lifted, the street below almost empty. He tried hoisting the window higher. Got it to move a couple more inches before it stuck again. When he saw Eddie come out of the building, he drew back.

Eddie had taken him in awfully quick, he knew that. But wasn't he prepared to handle all kinds of friendly? Eddie's paranoia about him being a cop seemed like more of a concern, but then again, Jack had never had a stash of drugs to protect before, probably he was just being smart about it. Probably, too, Jack was feeling the effects of being overtired, making everything seem more sketchy than it really was.

He wasn't hungry but decided to have a peek at what was in the fridge anyway. Half a sandwich and some milk. There was also an opened package of Pop-Tarts and he picked those up. Skimmed the label before putting them back. Then settled onto the floor where he stayed, reading mostly, while night filtered in. The pages were getting harder to see, and the last thing he remembered was wanting to get up and switch on a light.

The sound of keys jangling and a lock turned woke him, came in from the far side of the room. He was just putting it all back together—about where he was, what'd gotten him there—when the door opened. The person standing in the doorway was Eddie. "Hey, I picked up some porn. You like porn, right? Everyone likes porn." He flicked on the light. "So, what kind of porn do you like?"

Jack squinted, yawned like he was still half asleep. "Any kind, I guess."

"You into women?"

"Yeah, of course."

"No worries. I got you covered."

He wondered what Eddie thought about women. He wanted to ask, but he was all clammed up, not wanting to appear too interested in anything.

The porn got him over that shyness . . . once the clothes came off and the actors stopped pretending to be something besides flesh. There were three of them on screen at first, two men and a woman taking a hike in the woods. Then, after a water break and an accompanying smorgasbord of activities involving the woman, the action shifted to the two men. *Smart pick*, he thought.

Jack's hand rested on the thigh of his pants. Beside him, he heard the unambiguous slide of a zipper. He didn't look at Eddie right then, but when he finally did, he saw something in his eyes give way, and he never looked back at the screen.

The sun came early through the window and onto the pillow, with Jack feeling pretty good about the place where it had found him. More interested in trying to remember how things had gone than in covering them up. Nothing definite he could say about it. Seemed like sometimes he was getting off on being with another guy—armpits, stubble—and sometimes he was just getting off. It could have been with anyone, skin touching skin.

The strangest part of the encounter had to have been when he was tonguing Eddie's nipple, hard, and all he could think of was that perfect little bump of a clit on Skelly. Like he could almost taste her there—salty sweet—but then she was gone again, melted back into the sweat. At the time it had made as much sense as anything else, but now it was tugging at him, asking for an explanation.

It was true he'd never messed around with another guy before, but he'd thought about it. Not a lot, but enough, lately, to know that he hadn't come here for the weather. Once, in high school, he'd had a pretty steamed up dream about a guy. Woke up sweaty, wigged out and stayed that way for a couple of days. But when he didn't find himself with any sudden urges to re-decorate his room, he figured it for a fluke, and hadn't given it much attention since.

Then a few months back a buddy of his had been visiting at the ranch. Skelly was inside making dinner. They were outside, crouching, checking out all the stars, and when the guy reached over to give him the binoculars, his elbow dropped onto Jack's lap and stayed there for what seemed like one moment longer than necessary. He'd popped a boner, Johnny on the spot. It would've been easy enough to dismiss, he supposed, since he got hard if the wind was blowing from the right direction. But there hadn't been any wind that night, and he wondered if there wasn't something more to it.

Jack had lost count of how many relationships he'd cut off at the first sign of trouble, and while he and Skelly were still hanging in there, that was hardly a ringing endorsement of their situation. She was in Albuquerque, he was in San Francisco, and even though when he asked to open up the relationship he hadn't planned on opening it in this direction, he supposed he had paved the way for it. There was his request to see other people, there was the stargazing episode, and then there was the Forest Service job falling through at the last minute, and suddenly Jack had all sorts of time on his hands to toy with thoughts like, *Hey, I've never broken up with any of my guy friends before.* And, *Maybe it wouldn't be that big a deal to give it a try* and, *Wouldn't it be something if it turned out I could be more committed to a guy?* Now, less than twenty-four hours after arriving in the city, he was on his way to finding out.

The longer he lay next to Eddie, however, the harder it was for him to ignore the case of morning withdrawal setting in. And while there was something reassuring in its familiarity, Jack was mostly disappointed with how quick and typical it had come. Normally, this would be a sign that the longer-term prospects weren't good, but then this hadn't been a typical hookup, and he wasn't sure what to attribute his feeling to. Possibly, Jack wasn't as comfortable with the situation as he initially thought. He wanted to be, though, so he got out of bed before the feeling could sink in any further.

While he was getting dressed, he kept his eye on Eddie, but he still hadn't stirred by the time Jack was ready to pack up his things. He considered whether to leave some of them behind—it'd be nice not to have to carry everything around—but, in the end, he decided to take it all. He wasn't sure whether Eddie's offer about staying would stand the daylight, and even if it did, he wasn't sure he should be taking him up on it.

He left a vague note saying thanks, he'd try and stop by later.

On the way out, he noticed the lights in the manager's office were on, the window partially open. Inside were a couple of seedy-looking characters with slicked black hair, unbuttoned shirts, and gold chains. Jack put his head down and tried to move straight past, but they nailed him a few feet short of the stairs.

"Hey. Hold on there, buddy."

Name's not buddy. Jack kept walking.

"Hey, you on the stairs. You gotta pay."

He stopped and turned around. "Pay for what?"

"Pay for the room." It was the shorter one talking.

"What room?"

"The one you stayed in last night."

What, exactly, did he know about last night, Jack wondered, feeling exposed. Guilty even. He was pissed at himself for that. Pissed at the guy for bringing it out in him. "I stayed with a friend, what's it to you?"

"I don't care if you were staying with your sick mother, it's twenty bucks for every extra person in the room, and you were an extra person, so you gotta pay." He slid the window all the way open and held out his hand. Jack considered telling him where he could stick it. It was tempting, but he knew that would have effectively ended his career at the Chase. Even though he wasn't sure what the story was going to be with Eddie, he wanted to try to keep his options open. He had the twenty bucks and he paid it.

Jack headed out of the hotel and followed the first cable car tracks he saw up, up, and somehow up again, into the sky, cresting in the most outrageous views of the city. In every direction, and he was still greedy for more, wanting to see four ways at once. So he slow-spun around, then let himself drop down the other side of the hill in anticipation of the water below.

By the time he'd reached the bottom, though, the view to the bay had become blocked by a line of knick-knack shops sprawled out along the boardwalk. Metal gates were being pulled up, doors unlocked, people with maps in their hands were starting to gather. A place to be avoided, most likely, so he decided to keep going until he found a series of run-down-looking wharfs. One of them was deserted and he walked out to the end of it, breathing the salt from the air.

In New Mexico, about the only thing he hadn't had access to nature-wise was the ocean, and even with the wild rivers and man-made lakes, he hadn't been quite comfortable without it. When he left the small

Eastern coastal town where he'd grown up, Jack had taken something of it with him, the rush and ebb of the tide. But he'd been gone a long time and couldn't always remember the rhythm.

It was a good place to think, next to the water. Something hopeful in the fluidity. The reassurance that not everything in the world had to be defined in solid for it to hold together. Gazing out across a huge body of it, you realized that even if you couldn't figure everything out, or even one single thing, there was still plenty of room to keep swimming.

He spent the rest of the day poking around the nearby neighborhoods, but by noon he'd already fallen for the city. San Francisco was a charmer, sure—he kept catching glimpses of the water or running right into it again—but whenever he glanced down, he also realized how grungy it was and he liked the mismatch. There was a certain precariousness to the buildings, the preposterous steepness of the streets, that made the entire town feel as if it was on the verge of toppling. But then again, it wasn't. Hanging on by whatever invisible thread ran through and cinched it together.

His only real complaint was that everything was too damn expensive. The supermarket had corner store prices, and the corner store had already upped the ante. At the register, he noticed the "take a penny leave a penny" container was being employed as an ashtray. And when he asked the guy behind it for some hot water to add to his cup of noodles, he was told it would cost him another buck. For hot water. When he protested, the guy had schooled him. *The water does not heat its own self, yes?* Fortunately, the diner next door was feeling more generous.

On the curb outside, stirring up his food, Jack came to terms with the fact he wasn't going to be able to tool around for very long without getting a job. Something short term, maybe, but he could hammer all that stuff out later. His more immediate concern was about where he was going to spend the night. Even though his funds were technically limited, he did have enough to get his own room, but he wondered if he shouldn't head back to the Chase and see if Eddie was still up for having him stay there. Saving money was an attractive idea, but not a decisive one. And while he wasn't opposed to getting in the guy's pants again, it felt like more of a hypothetical than anything he wanted to do right that minute. After a close to perfect day, he was feeling depleted of that thing inside him that was always pushing for more, and what he was really in the mood for was something a bit familiar. Eddie was at least that, and having half-disappeared on the guy already, Jack realized he didn't want to disappear completely. Now that he had some space around him, it was obvious the only thing to do was go back and at least check in. They could take the rest from there.

When Jack reached the top of the red stairs, he could see the door to the office was open. The guy who'd given him the speech that morning was there, alone this time. "What's going on?" he asked, right off like there was already a problem.

"Just wanna see if a friend of mine's around."

"Which friend?"

"A friend," Jack repeated.

"Let me ask you something, buddy. Are you a registered guest at this hotel?" Jack just stared at him. "Because if you're not, then you're going to have to tell me who you want to see here or you're going to have to leave."

"His name's Eddie."

"Eddie what?"

"I don't know." Jack heard the edge go out of his voice.

"What room number's he in?"

"I don't know the number. Come on, man, you remember me from this morning. I paid you twenty bucks to stay here last night. It was down the hall, last room on the right."

"That's room nine. And no one's in."

"Are you sure?"

"Not in. That's what I said."

The whole thing was past not going anywhere. He would go to another hotel, just so long as it was someplace this clown wasn't working. "All right, then just tell him Jack stopped by," he said, not really expecting the guy would deliver the message, but figuring he could straighten things out with Eddie another time.

Then he launched down the stairs and ran right into Eddie.

"Hey. Where've you been?" Eddie asked.

"I was out looking around. Man, that guy at the desk is an ass."

"I didn't think you were coming back."

"Didn't you get my note?"

"Yeah, but I couldn't tell what you meant by it."

That's because I wasn't sure what I meant by it either. "Listen, Eddie, I'm sorry. It's just that I knew you'd gotten in late and I didn't want to wake you."

Eddie took off his cap, held it with both hands in front of him. "You eaten yet?"

"Could always eat again."

"Why don't we get some dinner."

Over enchiladas, they worked out the living arrangements. Eddie restated his offer about staying, and Jack told him he'd like to take him up on it, at least until he found a job. Eddie said he'd talk to the guys at the front desk so Jack wouldn't have to worry about forking over the extra twenty. "Then we should split the rent," Jack told him, but Eddie's response—"When I asked you to stay, I didn't say anything about paying"—seemed firm and Jack didn't push him on it.

The next day he woke with the sun again, slipped his book into the bed and finished it, finally. *Ceremony.* A story about how you can't separate the sickness inside a person from the sickness in the community where he lives. How one can't heal right without the other. It was the kind of book he would like to have talked to someone about, but only Eddie was around, and he was still asleep. Maybe he'd mention it to him later. Or at least find out if he was into reading.

He climbed out of bed and grabbed the towel off the floor, hoping there might be a clean corner to it. It was dry, at least, so he wrapped it around his waist, took out his shaving kit, then headed down to the bathrooms.

The building was quiet. Leading him to think he was the only one up, but on the way into the john he felt the door connect with someone on the other side. It turned out to be the military guy from the first day, now in full uniform. He glared through the apology, then stepped past him into the hall.

"You better watch it next time."

"Hey, take it easy, man. It was an accident."

But the guy just shook his head. Turned and limped down the hall.

Jack had a long shower thinking about it afterward. Wondering about the guy and whether he'd muttered *fairy* under his breath before turning the corner.

Eddie hadn't made it out of bed yet, but at least his eyes were open. Jack began getting dressed.

"No reason to put your clothes on so quick."

"Yeah, well . . ." He tried to come up with a good reason for why he needed to go. "I was gonna head out now but—hey, you wanna come out and spend the day with me. You know, show me around. I'll buy you lunch."

"My sightseeing days are over. Why don't you meet me back here around five?"

"Okay, sure." He zipped up the side of his pack. "Mind if I leave some of my stuff?"

"Go ahead. You can take one of the drawers, if you want. No, wait . . ." Eddie reached for the phone. "I'm gonna get us some more room here.

I should've taken care of this a long time ago." Then he dialed and gave Jack a thumb's up.

"Hi, Gerald. Hi, Sweetie. I need you to get your shit out now, Gerald . . . No, tomorrow it's all gonna be litter on Market . . . No, this isn't a negotiation, Gerald. You've got nothing to . . . Okay, okay . . ."

Eddie covered the phone and lowered his voice. "There's an extra key on top of the fridge. Use it whenever you want, just make sure you return it when you get back here."

Jack got the message. He took the key and left.

Walking back into the room at the end of the day, Jack noticed that one of the dresser drawers had been pulled out and emptied. He didn't know if this meant Gerald had removed his stuff or Eddie had, and frankly he didn't want to know. Anything more about Gerald, in fact. He put a few things into the drawer and closed it.

Eddie looked up from the desk he was hunched over. "Glad to see you using that." Then he turned his attention back to the project he'd been working on. He'd placed a small square mirror on the desk, and now he poured some whitish powder onto it. After examining it, he decided to pour out some more before resealing the packet. "I only snort it," he explained as he began to break it up with a credit card. "I never smoke it, that just makes people crazy."

Jack nodded, not in any position to be debating the point. It seemed like Eddie was definitely over his fear of Jack being a cop.

"You ever do this shit?"

"Not that shit," Jack told him, not exactly sure what he was sniffing. Probably coke.

"You should give it a try."

"Yeah, sometime maybe."

It wasn't that Jack didn't have any reservations about continuing to stay with Eddie but that they weren't enough to prevent him from doing it. Occasional drug use didn't seem like it should be disqualifying for anything—Jack had been around that kind of thing before—and as far as Eddie's other quirks went, well, everyone had quirks. Jack was mostly worried about himself. He wasn't sure he was capable of distinguishing the mild discomfort he'd been feeling around Eddie from the discomfort he might be feeling toward being with a guy, any guy, in general. And until Jack was confident he wasn't just dealing with his own same-sex hang-ups, he felt like he needed to see things through with Eddie.

Monday morning, and Jack was late for his first interview. "Office assistant with a focus on filing." *Lame,* he kept repeating to himself on the way over, wondering why he'd even bothered to set it up in the first place. After waiting so long to get a callback from the Forest Service, Jack had to admit it had been a relief to have someone respond right away, but it turned out his enthusiasm for the job had peaked with that conversation. He supposed the original attraction had something to do with the fact the work would be temporary, and yet he wasn't sure if he, himself, would be leaving anytime soon.

After being directed to Human Resources, he took a seat in the too-small chair he'd been offered and immediately remembered how much he disliked sitting in one. Once he'd been called in for his interview, he apologized for not being on time, but it was obvious the whole thing was headed for a nosedive no matter what he said. Five minutes into it he was asked to "characterize" his alphabetizing skills and then, soon after, to demonstrate them. On the pop quiz, he rearranged all the words in the wrong order, skipped the math problems, and walked out. Adolescent behavior, he realized about two blocks away, which depressed him even more.

Employment-wise, it wasn't going to be easy to find something exciting after working for the fire department. And even if it was only going to be temporary, Jack realized a 9-5 would represent too abrupt a change. What was the point in acing an interview when he could already taste the disappointment first morning in front of the water cooler? There had to be something else—something that went better with the territory there in San Francisco—and the more he ran it through in his mind, the more convinced he became it was just a matter of finding out what it was.

Maybe Eddie would have some ideas. He seemed like the type.

Eddie had ideas all right. He opened the door, pulled Jack over to the bed and started sucking him off. He came in less than two minutes, then two more times, and was feeling more than a little sore when Eddie tried to coax him up again. No way he thought he'd ever complain about a blowjob going on too long, but it looked like there was going to be a first time for everything.

"Hey, Eddie, can you, uh, ease off a little bit down there." No response, so he held him back. "I can't take it anymore, man."

Eddie squinted up, coughed. "What you need to do is spend some time with my friend, Tina. Then you'd be good to go."

Tina? Jack stared in confusion for a moment before realizing that Eddie must have been talking about meth. *Shit, that stuff is supposed to be the worst.* He remembered not quite laughing along with the other guys during a medical training as they'd looked over the pictures of the users. Smiling cheerleader in one photo, toothless criminal the next. The whole thing had seemed so unlikely, made up. But now it was making him nervous. When a knock came on the door, Jack bolted off the bed, pulled up his pants, and tried to look somehow occupied.

"No reason to be so jumpy," Eddie told him as he stood to answer it.

It turned out to be the girl from upstairs, the one Eddie called Bad Luck Joanne. Jack had only met her a couple times, but he could tell it was her right away. She had a giggle like she was hooked to helium.

"Yes, Eddie. I just wanted to tell you that . . . that . . ." she burst into fresh hysterics, "that I think you dropped your panties in the hall."

Before Jack could peer around to see what, if anything, she was referring to, Eddie told her, "I don't wear panties, Joanne," and proceeded to shut the door in her face. Then he said "bitch" but not too seriously and not too loud.

Joanne lived with her boyfriend. Skinny guy tattooed within an inch of his life. Like the rest of the people who came through there, they seemed to be customers of Eddie's.

That Friday night, Jack took the F down Market to check out the bar where Eddie worked. The Rack was crowded, ninety percent guys. Jack grabbed a drink and tucked himself away in the corner by the pool table, watching this one guy run his shots against the other players. There was a routine sort of atmosphere around the place, but then, when Eddie's set started, things really seemed to bump up a notch. The music had been mostly a drone before that, soulless beats, repeating. But Eddie mixed in everything, hip hop to rock, layered the songs so that almost every cut was undetectable. All the hints of the upcoming track transformed into it while you looked back across the place he'd sewn it up, trying to find the tear.

When the ringer at the table finally missed, he came over to introduce himself. Jack didn't let the conversation go on for too long before asking if he knew Eddie.

"Eddie Flynn? Are you kidding?" He glanced up at the deejay booth. "I grew up on that man."

Jack was beginning to feel some pride in the guy he'd been staying with, and the feeling was growing on him. When the bartender waved at him, he went right over. It turned out Eddie wanted him upstairs. "So you're hanging with Eddie now," he observed, pouring another beer. "What a hot little package he used to be. And he could dance like you wouldn't believe, you should ask him about it."

Jack said he would.

Up in the booth with a great view of the crowd, Eddie was jamming with headphones so fat it looked like he might tip over with the weight of them. Jack tapped him on the shoulder. Eddie held up a finger and then, after another minute or so, turned and slid the phones around his neck. "How's it going down there?"

"Fine." Jack told him. "You sound really good."

"Good enough so you want to blow me?"

"Not that good." Jack smiled.

"Well, how's about I blow you then?" he offered, tugging on Jack's belt, and Jack realized Eddie was being serious. He guessed he had flexible arrangements there at work.

"I don't think I'm really up for that."

"No one would notice."

"I would," Jack told him, at which point Eddie put his phones back on and turned around.

In the cab, he continued to heap on the praise for Eddie's set, but Eddie said he thought it sucked. "Unlike some people I know," he added.

It was hard to tell if he was really upset about the lack of action, but his music had put Jack in a good mood and he wanted to keep it light. "Hey, so I hear you're a pretty good dancer."

"Says who?"

"Says the bartender."

Eddie shook his head, "I don't know what that whore's talking about. I never liked to dance."

That took care of the conversation for the remainder of the ride.

Back in the room, Eddie asked Jack if he wanted to beat off.

"So we're asking now?"

"I'm asking you. I want to watch. You want to do it or not?"

"I don't know about 'want.' " He looked to Eddie for further clarification.

"Would you do it?"

Jack still wasn't sure how he felt about it. He'd had plenty of practice, sure, but not on demand. Or request, it seemed. Maybe it was because he was feeling like he'd already let Eddie down, or maybe it was because he couldn't come up with any reason not to, but he decided to go for it. "So you just want me to stand here and whip it out?"

"However you want to do it."

It took Jack a little while to get warmed up, and he waited until he was fully hard before pulling himself from his jeans. He was afraid to break his concentration now that he was this far into it, but eventually he managed a glance over at Eddie, who was sitting on the bed. "Hey, you decided to join me."

Eddie didn't smile, and that's when Jack noticed he was only half-heartedly stroking himself, showing about as much interest as if he was peeling a potato.

"That's all I got right now." Eddie stopped abruptly. Then he took his pants the rest of the way off. "I'm going to bed."

Jack stood there—dick in hand—trying to determine whether he should continue. He wanted to finish himself off but . . . *shit.*

He got in bed beside Eddie and lay on his back, staring at the ceiling. He wondered if Eddie was on something. Maybe he was always on something, it wasn't like Jack would know the difference. He really didn't know much about Eddie at all, and was just weighing how much that mattered, when Eddie startled him by rolling over and wrapping his arm and leg around him, squeezing him tight. They'd never been affectionate with one another before and Jack didn't know what to make of it.

Then Eddie started talking. Nonstop. Unloading about how everyone at work was trying to cheat him out of his paychecks, trying to take his job, someone had been stealing his albums, so he was going to have to stop leaving them in the liquor closet. This, that, the other. It was hard to figure out what was scratching at the bottom of the pile but the underlying sadness in his voice was impossible to miss.

Even if Jack had any guidance to give, he didn't sense that Eddie was looking for it, so he just stroked the back of Eddie's buzz cut, trying to convey the idea that everything was going to be all right.

While he was warming up coffee the next morning, Jack decided to ask Eddie about one of the job ideas he'd been tossing around. It no longer seemed as farfetched as when he'd first read about it, and now, fully five weeks into his job search, it seemed like it was time to pull out all the stops.

"You ever heard of this place called the Cage?"

"Yeah, what about it?"

Jack noted the scowl on Eddie's face but pressed on. "Well, do you know what you have to do there? I mean besides dancing. It looks like they pay pretty well."

"You're not doing that."

Jack reddened.

"I don't want you out there on display," Eddie added.

What, did you slip a ring on my finger while I was sleeping? "Listen, Eddie, I'm not interested in you telling me how I should be buttering my bread. I was just looking for a little advice here."

"What I'd like to know is where this idea came from. Did you suddenly wake up and decide you're ready to become a stripper? Because it doesn't seem like you've got a problem showing yourself off in public unless it happens to be with me."

"I really dug your music, Eddie, I was glad to be there with you. I just didn't wanna feel like some groupie."

"No one would have seen us."

"Right."

Eddie considered this for a moment. "And I'm just trying to look out for you, is all. Trust me, the owner of the Cage is not someone you want to be working for."

"Maybe not, but it'd be nice to have something to help me pay the bills."

"What bills? I've been fattening up Ari's weekly bag so this place shouldn't be costing you a dime."

Bingo! "Okay, but I thought you were being cool because I just got to town and you know I'm trying to get on my feet here."

"I am being cool."

"Which I appreciate, but I still need to earn money. There's day to day expenses. Food. I've got to do something, man."

Eddie put his index finger to his chin, tapped it there a couple times. "Why don't you go over to the firehouse. You know they've got one here that's just for fags."

That stung twice. "Shit, you just don't stroll in there when you want a job. They have times when they hire. It's a long process. And besides, I don't want to work for a city anymore. I'm going in with a wildland crew next spring to fight forest fires. This is just a little downtime in between."

"All right, all right, settle down. Look, I can get you a job if you want."

"Where?"

Eddie sniffed a couple of times, then shrugged his shoulders. "It's good money."

"I don't wanna be selling drugs, Eddie. No one would buy from me anyway, I look like a narc, remember."

By the time Jack reached the piers, he'd half gotten the anger out. He could actually feel some regret replacing it when he thought about the previous night and the way Eddie had opened up to him. He could have held Jack even tighter then and it wouldn't have suffocated him anywhere near the way his words just did. It was too bad, because even though they didn't have much in common, there was something he admired about the guy. The niche of a life he'd made for himself and the music he filled it with. Still, there was no getting around the fact that, one way or the other, he was under obligations in that room. The price paid for not having insisted on splitting the rent from the get-go.

When he tried to give Eddie some cash, he didn't want to take it. "Why are you starting in with this now?"

"I've been here for a while. Longer than I was planning on."

"I didn't know you had any plans."

Jack was all too aware of his current lack of direction but didn't like having it pointed out by Eddie, whose own life seemed in such disarray. "I'm just gonna leave it on the fridge, then."

Eddie continued to sit in his place on the floor in front of the TV. He was done talking about the subject, obviously, and Jack decided to climb on the bed behind him and try to follow along with the program. "Hey, when did that guy's hair go grey?"

"A long time ago. You don't know much about television, do you?" He sounded sympathetic.

Jack was thinking how he hadn't seen any morning game shows since he'd been home sick from grade school. Eddie reached back and started rubbing Jack's foot while he was trying to counsel one of the contestants. "Pass the showcase. Pass the showcase!" Once his advice had been followed, Eddie seemed to relax. He'd clearly been onto something, as the original prize package of appliances and living room furniture was soon overshadowed by one with a new car and a trip to the French Riviera.

When a commercial came on, Eddie turned around and started massaging Jack through his jeans. Then he undid Jack's button-flys and grabbed him through his underwear. His face looked so intense, it reminded Jack of the first night they met. But when the game show host's voice came on again, welcoming everyone back to the program, Eddie's head snapped around like it was on a leash.

That was the moment Jack got clear on something. He never would've let this go on for so long if he'd been hanging with, say,

Edwina, and not just because of the scary-sounding name. Jack almost certainly was carrying around some low-grade homophobia, but he was working through it, and the chance of that being all that was behind his inability to connect with Eddie was getting slimmer by the minute. That didn't mean that the sex, itself, hadn't been enjoyable; that he hadn't learned anything from it. But continuing to play around with a guy he should've just been friendly with risked souring Jack on what had otherwise been a positive experience. What he needed to do was get serious about finding his own place. Making his own plan.

The Tenderloin was Eddie's neighborhood, but Jack wasn't ready to concede the area just because of the way things had gone down between them. He liked the location, and after looking around the city, he knew the rents there at least approached something affordable. So he expanded his search to include all nearby housing units, ringing buzzers on any doors with signs in front, until, finally, he found a deal on an apartment. The building wasn't the greatest, but the manager, Liz, was nice, and seemed grateful to have a prospective tenant with the respectable background he presented. She told him she'd just concluded an unpleasant eviction that morning and was hoping to avoid a repeat. He left her with a small deposit, and she agreed to hold the place while he pulled together the rest of the money. Then he went back to the Chase, prepared to handle any mood Eddie might confront him with.

Eddie was standing over the bed, putting some things into his messenger bag. He raised his hand without turning around, then explained he needed to take the bus crosstown to the clinic. He hadn't been able to shake his cough and wanted to get some medicine for it.

"I'd like it if you came along with me. *If* you're not doing anything."

"You think it's still open?"

"It stays open till six," Eddie informed him.

Jack figured he could talk to him about moving out while they were on route. He wanted to leave things on good terms. Give him his new address, tell him he'd definitely be by the club to hear him play. He wasn't planning on mentioning the job he'd taken at the Cage, but as it turned out, they got split up on the bus, and he didn't have a chance to go over any of it.

They were dropped off in front of the clinic and took the elevator up to the fourth floor. Eddie pulled a number from the ticket dispenser, which unwound deli counter style, while Jack tried to find a place for them to sit. He didn't see any empty chairs, but what he did notice was how unhealthy everyone looked. Not that they should've been looking well—it was a clinic, after all—but it was the way they were looking unhealthy. Jack looked closer. A bruise on a guy's neck. Another guy's hand. *Lesions! Oh man, no. No way.*

He told Eddie he was going to wait outside.

Across the street, he bought a pack of cigarettes. Started smoking them, one after the other. He was sure Eddie had more than a cough. A lot more. Suddenly, it all made too much sense. His taking Jack in off the street, comments people had made at the Rack. He was going over every move he'd ever made with this guy—every time they'd touched—and the worst part about it was, he wasn't even one hundred percent sure what it meant. How risky it had been. It was more than embarrassing, not being sure. All the information he'd been given, from the fire department right on up to the brochure he'd gotten the last time he gave blood, and all he could come up with was, *Use a Condom When you Fuck or Don't Fuck at All.* Well, what about all the messy ground in the middle? How about cum in your eye. Or the day your dick got so raw from a marathon blowjob that the skin ripped.

He couldn't believe he'd waited to have a conversation with himself until now, but he'd never thought about it once with Eddie.

Sure, the flip side of San Francisco's gay mecca reputation was that it was also a place that a lot of people had gotten sick, but that was just it, he'd gone there knowing what sick looked like. In his district in Santa Fe, they'd had a few regulars with AIDS. One of them, in particular, used to call the ambulance whenever he got in trouble. Sometimes they could stabilize him, sometimes they had to take him to the hospital, but either way it was plain to see the kind of shape the guy was in. And then the calls stopped coming. Could Jack really have allowed himself to believe that was the whole story?

By the time Eddie came down, he'd smoked away a quarter of the pack.

"How'd it go?"

"Fine." he said. "They gave me some meds, no problem."

"Glad to hear it."

"When'd you start smoking?" he asked, but Jack didn't answer him.

Back at the hotel, he followed Eddie into the room, then closed the door behind them.

"Just tell me one thing, Eddie, are you sick? I mean are you really sick?"

"What d'you mean? I've got a cough, that's all." He coughed. "See, cough cough. Now if you'll excuse me, I also need to urinate." He opened the door again and headed down the hall.

Jack stood there for about thirty seconds unsure of everything, and then his head turned toward the messenger bag, to the piece of paper sticking out of it like he knew it'd be there. He only hesitated for a moment before swiping it out and scanning down to the doctor's notes section, *HIV+ patient with upper respiratory* . . . He crumpled the paper. Gripped it in his hand, looking up at the ceiling. Then uncrumpled it and read it again. When Eddie walked into the room, he flung it at him. "What about that, huh? What am I supposed to make of that?"

Eddie looked down to where the paper had landed, then back at Jack again. "So you went through my shit. This is the thanks I get for letting you stay with me."

Jack could barely swallow, the spit thick in his mouth. He knocked Eddie across the face.

Eddie didn't look the slightest bit surprised staggering back, just put his hand to his jaw, touching it lightly. "You never asked," he said. "You don't know the rules around here."

Jack wanted out of that room. He began to cram the stuff into his pack while Eddie continued to talk.

"I thought you were different but you're like all the other guys. You don't care. You don't care about me."

"If you say one more word . . ."

And he didn't say another word. Until Jack was halfway down the hall, when he called out, "I could've pushed it a lot further, you know. You're lucky it was me and not someone else."

Jack put every bit of willpower he had left into getting himself down to the Greyhound station, where he bought a ticket for the next bus leaving town. Bound for Los Angeles, but he didn't care, he'd work out a transfer when he got there. He sprinted outside and tagged onto the end of the line that was just disappearing into the bus, followed it to the back, to the last row, where he sank into the seat, closed his eyes, and didn't open them again until they started to move.

He was coming back, he knew that much. He was coming back, but not without the motorcycle. He should never have left that behind. Always more dangerous when all he had to take care of was himself, didn't know why he couldn't get that through his skull.

He had this picture in his mind. Coming off the hill at the end of Geary where the road flared out wide and down in a deep curve, red cliffs falling alongside on the left, and right, the Pacific stretched across forever. Sea and rock and land and sky, tilted, in a single unbroken horizon, and they were racing after.

And how about a clean blood test, pal, maybe you'd like to bring that along, too? And how about some fucking common sense.

He couldn't stand sitting there with himself. Everything inside. The sweat that wouldn't break. So sick with it, he was probably converting his cells right then, if they weren't already screwed up.

The city was driving by outside the window, but he wasn't watching. Just knocking his head slightly into the glass, trying to understand what had been going on inside him, what he'd been thinking. Because it didn't matter if it was God or if it was only Eddie that sent that cough up the stairs the first day. He'd been the one to hear it. And he'd been the one to let it ride.

12:38

I can't believe my bike's still in the shop. That it's been fixed all this time and I haven't been able to pick it up yet. It's off the street, at least. Inside where it's dry.

Something's gonna have to give there soon. Don sounded serious on the last message he left. Said he couldn't keep storing it, that he needed the space. Which I can understand, but then he took the extra step of offering to buy it off me. I know he was just trying to help out—not like there's a bundle to be made off a beater with a record of unpaid traffic citations—but still, it ticked me off. His asking. I didn't want him getting it in his head like that, even a little bit, so I tried to put some assurance in my voice when I called him back. "Relax," I told him, "I've almost got the money."

Just like I've almost got it a dozen other times since the work's been finished. In a rubber band, under the couch. Problem is, all it takes is one night to blow what you've been saving for six. Or you need a little for this or that, and suddenly you don't need that rubber band anymore.

The bike should be running great now. Almost like new, is what he told me, although I'd like to see for myself. I wonder if he'd let me take it out for a spin. Just a test drive, around the block a few times. Maybe if this storm clears, I'll go by in the morning and ask him.

"So you came all the way back here just to get the bike? Just decided to hop on the bus and come all the way cross country again?"

"Cross country? Christ, Vasquez, it's only two states away."

"I don't care what you say, it's still far." Ren pulled the lock off the shed, then slid the aluminum door halfway open before turning around. "Now, you're sure you thought this through. I mean, from the bike's point of view. Because I can guarantee you, this desert-raised son's gonna rust riding around out there." He disappeared into the shed.

Jack called in after him, "Hey, things are supposed to rust, you know. It's messed up around here the way metal keeps on shining . . . Not natural is what it is."

Ren poked his head back out. "Now that's just the kind of thinking you *pendejos* from the coast can never get out of your system."

"All right, let's go ahead and take it from the bike's point of view. Bike's got two choices: One, cruising along some drop-dead gorgeous cliffs with waves breaking down below, or two, sitting on its rust-free ass accumulating dust."

"Don't think you've been doing me any favors by leaving it here. Nothing but setting a bad example for my bike, as far as I can tell. I haven't taken it out once since you left."

"Well, we'll definitely get a ride in tonight."

Ren began to fumble through the clutter inside. The sound of metal scraping, something falling, a box of nails maybe.

"Need some help in there?"

"I wouldn't recommend coming in, this place is booby trapped all to hell. Should probably be condemned. Like the Academy tower, which, you're not gonna believe, the city officially closed last week."

"No way, they finally shut that sucker down?"

"They did. There's no more training there for now, but they're supposed to start construction on a new one soon."

Jack looked on as the front wheel popped out of the shed, followed by the rest of the frame. His feeling at seeing the bike was strong. And acutely conflicted. He wanted to put his hand to the tank, let it rest there till he felt the coolness rise up from the metal through his fingers' skin. The way he liked to do before starting it in the morning. But he was tentative, as well, not quite able to overcome the accusation of neglect hanging over him. The bike looked smaller, and even standing before him now, abandoned. He held back as Ren kicked out the side stand and leaned the bike onto it.

"Wanna know why?"

"Why what?"

"Why they're putting in a new tower."

Jack was still staring at the bike; he watched as Ren brushed some cobwebs off the seat.

"Because the old one was a piece of shit."

"Yup. And because they're getting ready to recruit another class."

Jack looked up. "You're kidding."

"Don't worry, you've still got time. They're talking about maybe the spring, probably not before May."

Jack nodded.

"But I say, if you're gonna come back, the sooner the better. Think of your brothers down at Station 1. Suffering without all that fine gringo cooking of yours."

"Yeah, right."

"No, really. I heard Ricky even tried to make pancakes the other week in your honor, but I guess he burned them up. Set off the alarm at his own goddamn station."

"The man can't heat a tortilla without torching it. Don't know what he was thinking trying to handle a pancake."

"That's exactly what I told him. Anyway, while you're working on extricating your head from your ass long enough to see clear to moving back here, I figured you might check out a lead I got on a job down in Florida. Jessie was telling me the Forest Service runs all winter down there. Lots of controlled burns. It'd be a good way to get some experience."

"So would you say this is a better tip than the one from your cousin in Cimarron?"

"Easy, brother, that was just bad timing. There was no way of knowing that guy was gonna come back and bump you."

"Yeah, I know." Jack realized how ungrateful he sounded. "To be honest with you, I was feeling like I needed to get out of town anyway."

"If you were that disappointed about missing out this summer, you should be pleased to hear about this, no? If that's what you're still trying to do."

"It is what I'm gonna do. I just figure I'll wait to do it in the spring. Back here in New Mexico. It's good to know about, though, thanks. Tell Jessie thanks. Or I'll tell her myself, I guess, if she's free tonight."

"She'll be free. She said she couldn't stay late, but she's gonna meet us. You owe her a beer. That's the other thing I was supposed to tell you." Ren looked down at the bike. "You ready to bring this machine back to life?"

"Yeah, let's roll it back up on the center stand before we put the oil in." Jack grabbed onto the bars and hopped on. "You wanna give me a hand here."

Later that night, they drove over to the Long Bar, where they spotted Jessie holding one of the tables in the back. Jack ordered a round of beers, and he and Ren carried them over to the table. Ren elbowed Jessie in the ribs after he sat down.

"He missed one heck of a good fire last week, didn't he?"

She looked perturbed. "This guy still doesn't seem to understand there's no such thing as a good fire. Maybe you've smartened up since you're been gone."

Jack shook his head. "I doubt it."

"So how are things going for you out in California?"

Jack took a quick swig of his beer. "All right."

"That's the full report? I come all the way into town on a day off for 'all right.' "

Jack tried to thread the needle between saying too little and having them suspect something was wrong and saying too much and having them know there was. "It's been a lot of adventure, that's for sure."

"Seems to me you two had plenty of adventure around here."

"True." Jack exchanged a conspiratorial look with Ren. "How about you? You had any adventures lately?"

"Yeah," Ren jumped in, "I heard she got her toenails clipped last week."

"Funny you should mention it, I *did* get a pedicure recently."

"What's the point of that? No one cares what your feet look like."

"I wouldn't expect *you* to care, Ren."

"Who does care? Your cats?"

"Your kids?" Jack ventured.

"As a matter of fact," she began, big grin, her head weaving from side to side.

"As a matter of fact," Jack repeated, imitating her motions, "what?"

"Yeah, what's been up with you lately? Practically floating around the station like you've been getting laid. But that can't be it."

She grinned even bigger.

"Uh-oh." Jack shook his head. "I think she met someone."

"It's not right. You waiting till Jack comes back to spill it."

"Aw, quit your boo-hooing. I was getting ready to tell you anyway. I just didn't want to jinx anything, introducing him to all you fucknuts before we had to a chance to make it solid. But he told me he was bringing over his own toothbrush later tonight, so I'd say that makes it official."

"So you're taking off on us just so's you can go home and brush your teeth with some guy?"

"I don't think we'll be doing much of that, thank you very much."

"Oh, I see how you are. Making up for lost time, huh?"

"You better believe it."

"So, how did you meet him?"

Jessie sat up straight and folded her hands together. "The personal ads."

"The personal ads? Holy shit, our girl's found herself a man in the goddamn newspaper." Jack finished what was in his glass. "I may need another one so I can ponder this latest development."

"Uh, Jess, the personal ads are for losers."

"Yeah, and senior citizens," Jack added. "Couldn't you have at least gone online?"

"You can say what you want, but, as you know, I hadn't had much success in my previous attempts in this area. I didn't see what I had to lose besides a little pride, and there really wasn't much of that left. Besides, I was getting tired of sitting around and complaining about it all the time."

"There wasn't anything you weren't complaining about for a while there." Ren turned to Jack. "She just about bit my head off Fourth of July weekend when I forgot to put the toilet seat up."

"If your aim was better you wouldn't have to worry about what position the toilet seat was in. Now, where was I?"

"You were gonna tell us about what a great guy he is, no doubt."

"Oh yeah. Definitely a keeper. Nice. Considerate. Makes me laugh. He's a few years older, but I figure that just means he's already been through all the kid play." Jessie took a drink. "He turned forty-four last week, but like he said, it's better than being with a couple of twenty-two-year-old twins. Still hot, but twice the experience."

"That's probably just the kind of thing you say when you're forty-four, but I'm gonna let him get away with it," Ren raised his glass. "To Jessie and . . ."

"Mike."

"To Jessie and Mike, then."

They all clinked glasses.

"Before I forget, I want to make sure Ren told you about that firefighting opportunity in Florida. Mike's from there, that's how I heard about it."

"Yeah, he told me." Jack was sorry to have the subject change back to him. They were both looking like they expected him to say something more. "Thanks. Maybe I'll check into it."

"Or maybe you won't," she said.

"Don't understand that, bro. You're not seeming like you're gonna go for it. With your red card and everything."

"Didn't I already break this down for you? I'll be coming back here in the spring. Where there's actual forest to worry about burning. Not some palm tree."

"Seriously, Jack, just watch yourself if you're going back to California. I spent some time in Santa Cruz when I was about your age. Did the surfer chick thing for a year longer than I should've. It's easy to get sucked in. You better have a plan if you want to keep yourself out of trouble there."

"Who says I wanna stay out of trouble?" Jack forced a grin.

"I'm not talking about trouble with a small t."

"Hey, do I need to take notes on this? Because I forgot my pen."

"You think this is a lecture? Please. You should see me with the kids. Well, you have seen me with the kids, you know I don't enjoy doing this."

"Oh, yes you do."

"Mother Fucking Hubbard is what it is."

Jessie smirked. "Well, Ms. Hubbard is feeling pretty unmatronly at the moment. Do you know Mike told me I've got the best ass he's seen in years? Said he couldn't get it up for all those skinny girls."

"He best be getting friendly with your ass," Ren chimed in, "cause he's gonna be bumping into it all the time."

Jessie smacked him across the back of the head, they all busted up, and for a precious few moments, Jack felt like he'd never left.

He spent the weekend at Ren's helping clean up and then plaster the garage, which Ren's stepdad was converting into a workshop and office space. Knowing Jack's financial situation was tight, Ren had set him up nice, overpaying him for under-skilled labor, which meant he'd more than bought his right to slag him about the job performance.

"Hey, I think you got more plaster in your hair than you do anywhere else."

Jack looked down from the ladder, then put the joint knife back to the ceiling. "At least I'm working and not yapping."

"I can work and yap at the same time."

"Seems like you're just yapping to me. Besides, I'm just getting warmed up here."

"For three hours?"

"Look, a man's gotta find his own pace, all right?"

"While you're trying to find yours, I'm gonna break into these sandwiches."

"What'd she make us?"

"Mom's special. Turkey, jack, and green chili . . . make that turkey, turkey, and green chili."

"Gobble, gobble." Jack came down and grabbed a sandwich, sat on the bench across from Ren and began to eat.

"You know if you wore something on your head, you'd save a lot of trouble later trying to get that stuff out of your hair."

"Hmm," Jack mumbled through the food.

"Where's your Raiders cap?"

Jack stopped chewing—a hazy image of himself throwing it in the trash in L.A.—then finished what was in his mouth. "I lost track of that a while ago."

"You had it before you left."

"I don't know. I don't have it now."

"Must've fallen apart from overuse."

"Probably."

Ren tossed him a soda.

"So you must be feeling all warm and fuzzy inside, being so close to your Raiders now."

"They're not my Raiders."

"What are you talking about? You like 'em."

"Nah, I just co-opted them when I moved out here. I figured I had to get a little interested in a team this side of the Mississippi. It was never anything deep."

"Uh-huh. So what happened, you go ask if you could be towel boy and got turned down."

"Why don't you keep your fantasies to yourself, *vato*."

Ren laughed. "Whatever you say, man, but they're looking good this year. It's not a wise time to abandon ship. Any bets you wanna place against them, just let me know."

"I'm not much into gambling these days."

"You can't have changed that much in two months." Ren shook his head. "I guess this means you won't be in for a little poker tonight. Richie's having a game."

"Don't tempt me, brother. I told Skelly I'd be down there in time for dinner anyway."

On the way out the driveway, he pulled up beside Ren. "Thanks for everything, Lorenzo, I really appreciate it."

They hit their palms together and shook.

"No problem," Ren said, and then added, "Rust or no rust, I'm glad to see you going out of here on the bike. Dropping you at the bus station last time was a real downer."

"For both of us," Jack agreed. "Believe me."

He took the back road down to Albuquerque, meandering his way along 14 past the State Pen, through Cerrillos, then into Madrid. It was an unfortunate series of dominos that had fallen whereby getting the bike had meant seeing Ren and seeing Ren meant having to see Skelly. Whether he was ready to or not. He hadn't made any progress on his explanation for why they wouldn't be sleeping together, and he was tempted to stop for a beer in Madrid to try to come up with something. As he approached the Tavern, though, he realized he'd only be procrastinating further. The only good explanation was the truth, but he wasn't going to give her that.

It was his stupidity he was ashamed of. And that's what she wouldn't forgive him for if she knew what had happened. She'd always assumed he was smarter than he was, rarely calling out his recklessness, as if she believed he was constantly weighing risks and then deciding to move forward anyway. But he didn't think things through all the time, and the less she knew how much he didn't, the better. Their relationship needed her confidence right now, and he didn't want to lose it.

Skell would be moving out to Fort Wingate in another week. To teach at a school that enrolled a lot of kids from the surrounding reservations. It was funny how you passed through those reservations all the time but never really knew what went on so far back from the road. Back from gas stations and tobacco stands, the bells and whistles of the casinos. She'd mentioned one nearby the school that was hiring blackjack dealers. He wondered when he saw her if she'd bring it up again.

He'd been gaining in speed on his way into Cedar Crest, and then, picking up the highway east of the city, he decided to gun it, the inevitability of the situation finally pushing his desire forward. The 40, the 25, Central, and finally the two quick turns onto Gold Street, where he parked the bike in the dusty lot behind the flat. Crossing it, he remembered the troubles he'd had there while waiting for the Forest Service to call—the aimlessness, the boredom—troubles with a small t.

When he reached the side entrance, he saw that only the screen door had been left shut. The strip of wood surrounding the mesh shuddered when he rapped on it.

"Hey!" Skelly came toward him, wiping her hands on the sides of her shorts. "What's all this knocking about, your name's still on the lease."

"Well, you know me, all protocol and courtesy." He waited for her to open the door.

"Hey," she said again, softly this time, and he kissed her, felt the warmth behind her lips. She was the last person he'd kissed—the night he left— and in a way, kissing her still felt more intimate than anything he'd done with Eddie. With the tingly sensation heading directly south, he pulled back and sniffed.

"Wow, something smells good back there. What you got cooking?"

She smiled. "Well, the smell part's going fine, I'm just not sure what's going to happen with the taste. I'm trying a *mole* on the chicken."

"*Mole*, huh. Doesn't that have chocolate in it?"

"Don't tell me you've given up chocolate."

"No, but I generally like to keep my entrées separate from my desserts."

"Well, we can have it for dessert if you want, just think of the salad as the main course."

He brushed his hand past her ear. "See how you're always one step ahead."

She leaned into the bend of his fingers, resting there, both of them comfortable for a moment. Then his gaze tipped slightly over her shoulder.

"Come on," she said, reaching up and taking his hand into hers, "you must be famished."

Dinner had gone nicely, the food filling and delicious. He listened to her talk about the comings and goings at school, the latest news from her family, deciding, through successive glimpses, that she looked more attractive than he'd ever seen her. He kept having to tamp down on the voice inside him saying simply, *Don't leave.*

"Well, I'd have to say that *mole* is welcome to the table any time." He wiped his face with the napkin, then put it on the empty plate. "I'd even consider it for breakfast."

"I don't know if I'd go that far, but I'm glad you liked it. Should I make some coffee?"

"No thanks," he said, getting up to clear the plates. She stood to help him, but he shooed her back. "No way you're having anything to do with these dishes."

"Great. I'm gonna finish boxing up some stuff, then." She stopped in the doorway to the backroom. "Jack, you are sure you don't want to take the laptop?"

"Positive. You're going to be doing something useful with it. I've got the bike back now and . . . enough to keep me busy."

He put the stopper in the sink and filled it with water. Then he began to wash, trying to keep his mind on the task at hand but his thoughts drifted. Placing the last pot in the drying rack, he felt her hand on his arm. He flinched.

"What's the matter?"

"I don't want to talk about it."

"Talk about what?"

"Nothing. It's weird being back here, that's all." Which was true. But what was really seeming weird at the moment was everything outside their door, and it had just managed to find its way in. "Just so you know, I don't want to fuck around tonight."

"That's a lovely way to put it."

It did sound poor, but he didn't even want to think about that now. And he didn't want her too, either.

"Whatever, Skell, I'm just saying it like it is. Maybe it's not a good idea we sleep in the same bed."

She looked incredulous. "You want the couch? That's fine if we don't make love, but if your plan is to sleep on the couch, if you're just going to drop in here like some sort of . . . houseguest, I want you to know that's really going to hurt. I'm trying to give you all the space you need, Jack, but you're really pushing me."

"I don't mean to be."

"We're only going to be together one night . . . unless . . . I don't suppose you've changed your mind and decided to stay longer?"

"No, I gotta get going. In the morning. I mean, if you really want me to stay and help you pack . . ."

"That's all right. I'd like the help, but you'll make me pay for it by being a grouch all week. So, no, it's not worth it."

He didn't argue with her.

They tried a round of Scrabble after dinner, but they were both preoccupied and called it before the game was finished. He told her he wanted to read for a while and waited till he thought she was asleep. Then he slipped into bed. He lay there with his chin on his hand, elbow on the mattress, watching her breathe. He could feel all the tenderness he'd denied her earlier flowing in, and he struggled to contain it.

He left early the next morning, heading west on 40, the heat thick off the pavement as soon as the sun hit. It was an open stretch of road, but he felt closed off to it, not sure if he was doing the right thing by leaving. His guilt only intensified when he passed Fort Wingate where Skelly would be living, by herself, for the coming school year. He could at least have stuck around to help her move. Not like his remorse was doing her any good—or him, either. It wasn't going to change anything.

The next exit was Gallup, the place where the drunk had boarded the Greyhound during his first ride out. He would probably be sticking to much the same route the bus had taken, hopefully covering it with better memories.

Crossing the border into Arizona, he began to feel some relief. His speed, which had been steadily increasing, finally felt fast enough, and he gave himself over to it. To the momentum. The sense of getting out in front of things: relationships and test results and new recruiting classes. If he felt some uncertainty trying to creep in, all it took was the slightest turn of the throttle to feel that rush forward, the burden sliding off his back. With the wind coming across, refreshing him.

The only interruption came when he had to stop for fuel. Early in the day, he made short work of it. Filled the tank, cleaned some bugs from the windjammer, then back out onto the highway. In the afternoon, he hustled into the station for a snack, a cup of coffee over ice, wolfed down a sandwich. But as the day wore on, the trip started to take its toll. The wind and heat began to wear, feeling like something he was up against. His vision narrowed, no longer taking in the landscape around him. And as dark settled in, when he pulled over for gas, he knew it was going to be for the last time. The muscles in his legs ached. A dull depression settled over him. He would ride a little longer, then park by the side of the highway, under a bridge, then crawl up the embankment with his pack. Lying there, exhausted, he could feel the road rumbling beneath him. And he continued to follow it, escaping still, into his dreams.

12:55

It's been a while since I've been on any kind of road trip. For obvious reasons, I guess, but even if I did have the bike, I'm not sure where I'd go.

I remember the first time Don asked if I wanted to take a ride with him and a few of the guys from the shop. Seeing as I'd never been up to Mount Diablo before, I agreed to tag along. I even had a good time. But I didn't go again.

It wasn't just worrying about who was ahead of me or behind. Pacing myself with the other riders. It was more the difficulty I was having appreciating the journey as a social occasion. I tried to explain this to Don the next time he invited me and, at first, it seemed like he understood. But then he reflected on it some more and said maybe the problem was it wasn't social enough. "That's why some of the boys take their wives," he told me. "Maybe you ought to have someone in the saddle with you." And I pictured how it could be. Two people coordinating their movements, leaning—hard—to the left or right. Together, extensions of the bike, steel into bone, chrome skin. Sure, with the right person, it could be more than just logging miles or sharing the scenery passed. But when you've got both hands gripped to the bars, when you're the one driving, how can you be expected to hold onto someone like that?

For a while, it was enough just having the bike. Every day he'd venture out, getting a better feel for the streets of San Francisco. Learning how seriously the cars took yellow lights (not at all), how bold the pedestrians were (not extremely). One ways mattered now. The condition of the pavement. What was left of it, anyway; there were enough cracks, bumps, holes, and sinks to make most every ride a challenge.

He noted the routes that stretched farthest across the peninsula, the ones with the least number of signals. He discovered idiosyncrasies, like how on Valencia, if he picked a single red light to ignore, he could avoid having to stop for the next four. He clocked how fast he could haul through the Presidio tunnel, and along sections of Geary, Sundays at daybreak, when there was little traffic. On foggy days, the lights were easy to miss. And even on clear ones, it was wise to approach every intersection with at least some caution.

He tested himself on the crookedness of Lombard Street. Once. It was slow and extra hell on the brakes, more a novelty than anything else. For the sheer thrill of vertigo, his favorite was Jones Street at night. Crossing California, where the road only revealed itself as he passed over it. No bends, just straight across Washington, Clay, down the dip at Sacramento. Nod at Grace Cathedral and then over. Just shy of airborne. The lights spreading out below. He'd coast until he reached the turn at Ellis, and then he was home.

Once he began to get familiar with the city, he left it, for Route 1 and the coastline. South to Santa Cruz, north to Stinson Beach, Point

Reyes, and beyond. But with every trip, as he had to pass by more and more of what he'd already seen to get to what he hadn't, he found his thoughts turning inward. Returning to the same question. *Now what?* He didn't know. He tried to outpace his uncertainty with the usual turn of the throttle; but there, in the face of such beauty, his haste struck him as a kind of sacrilege. He slowed down. Imagined what it would be like to share the ride with someone else. That would make it new again. For a while, at least.

He hadn't been keen on getting to know people real well after what went down with Eddie. He was pleasant with his neighbors, and especially the building manager, Liz, who'd held onto his studio with just a phone call and then, later, a wire from his bank in New Mexico. He spent time at the public library downtown, and was on a first name basis with Louise, one of the librarians who was always suggesting new titles to him. At the gym, he would nod at some of the regulars, occasionally giving a spot. But that was about it. His job was taking up most of the social energy he had handy, anyhow.

When he'd gotten back to the city, they'd still had an opening for him at the Cage and he'd taken it. For the same reason he'd applied in the first place—he wanted to try something different. Dancing around half-naked in front of a group of strangers—sometimes on a caged platform suspended from the ceiling—seemed unreal to him. And, he had to admit, awkward. He hoped the feeling would pass, but even as his fears of being out in front of an audience began to subside, he realized he was going to remain a reluctant exhibitionist.

Still, the job had its benefits, and they weren't just financial. He liked having an excuse to walk in the door. To be able to observe what was happening around him without having to interact with anyone directly. Available to be seen, but not to get involved or get burned. Unlike many of the guys he worked with, he rarely mingled at the bar afterward, and he never went home with the patrons.

Most of his co-workers were nice, but the only one he had any kind of rapport with was Bishkey, a Bronx native with a reputation for being tough that he didn't take very seriously. Jack enjoyed reconnecting with his East Coast roots. Appreciated the guy's directness, calling things out for what they were. The only real problem he had with Bishkey was that he was a Yankees fan. He owned a vast supply of Bomber propaganda, in the form of T-shirts and muscle shirts and sweats, at least one of which he always started out the night wearing. To balance things out, Jack took to wearing a Mets cap, even though his loyalty to the team had wandered.

The two of them had gone for drinks after work, but Bishkey usually couldn't stay long, he had a girlfriend to get back to. He was helping put her through school, which was the reason he gave for working at the Cage. Jack wondered if she knew about the guys Bishkey sometimes left early with. And he was curious about rumors that Bishkey could suck himself off. Was it size or just a matter of angles? But he didn't end up pressing him on either one, as they quickly fell into a pattern of dissecting the day's sporting events, recapped on the multiple monitors spread throughout the bar. For Bishkey, it was a step down from the club he said he needed before heading back to see his girlfriend. For Jack, it was beer and company, and after a while he realized he wouldn't mind having a little more.

He considered checking out some of the chat rooms online, but that meant going to the library or a cybercafe, and he didn't like the idea of leaving his back exposed to any number of passers-by. The only person he'd ever known who used the personal ads had been Jessie, but she seemed to have had excellent results, so he figured he'd give it a go. Even if he didn't think he was looking for romance, long term or otherwise.

He got a stack of papers and began by searching under the "Just Friends" category in each. But the entries there—"racquetball partner needed," "looking for someone to share season opera tickets"—were a little too specific. So he delved into the regular ads, focusing on the men and women who'd emphasized friendship.

The format had turned out to suit him better than he expected. He liked the idea that he could start slowly and work his way in, remaining at a distance for as long as he wanted, just examining the ads, listening to the voice recordings. It's true he nearly got stuck in this phase of the operation. Actually, he did get stuck. But not having had close contact with anyone in months, it already seemed intimate enough to read what people had written about themselves, and especially to hear what they had to say about themselves. He didn't know if it was technically stalking to keep calling back the same recordings at odd hours, but it had started to feel similar enough that he finally forced himself to move on.

The ad Jack chose to respond to was one of the shortest. He was attracted to the straightforwardness of it, and to the analytical tone of the guy's voice on his audio profile. When the beep came on indicating it was time for Jack to leave his message, he figured he would be a pro after listening to so many other recordings, but he kept screwing up the simplest phrases, like stating his name. Finally, after a lot of deleting and re-recording, he came up with something he liked. He hit save and exited the system.

It was past lunch and Jack was out of peanut butter. He stuck his finger in the jar and swiped it around the sides, then licked what little he'd been able to recover while he did a further inspection of the kitchen: one crust of bread, two eggs, no deli meat, no yogurt, and, incredibly, he was running low on cereal. None of this was acceptable. So he grabbed some cash from his tip drawer and headed downstairs.

Crossing the lobby, he could hear a woman at the entrance. She was yelling into the intercom, demanding to be let in. If someone had been talking to her, they'd apparently said all they were going to say, because there was only static on the other end. He sensed a confrontation coming and wasn't the least bit happy about it. He didn't want to be keeping anyone out, but he didn't feel comfortable letting them in either. Mostly, he didn't want to have to play hall monitor during these not infrequent encounters. Having to deny a human being standing directly in front of him, obviously suffering under a matter of utmost (though likely drug related) urgency, to protect what? The tenants in the building. The building itself. His own place, which consisted of a mattress and some books. Protect it from who? Loud street people who were generally harmless, and almost certain to be having a worse day than himself. Of course, one of them had taken a crap on the lobby steps the previous week. Liz had witnessed the end of that little demonstration and had to clean it up. The memory of her weary face as she looked up from squeezing the mop was enough to buck him up against this latest interloper.

He opened the door. The woman turned toward him, her face peeking out hopefully from the hood of an oversized ski jacket. He nodded at her, but as she reached out to hold the door, he pulled it closed behind him. Then he muttered, "Sorry," a kind of general apology that was meant to cover everything from his potentially misguided perceptions of her, up to and including the general state of affairs that allowed for such regrettable interactions between people. He was sure she had nothing but contempt for him now, and as he stepped out into the light drizzle on Ellis, he could still feel her eyes on his back.

He hoped she wouldn't be there when he returned, and she wasn't. He carried his groceries inside, then balanced them against the lobby wall while he checked his mailbox, which was empty. He took the stairs up and made his way along the hall. Outside his door, he could hear the phone ringing. He dropped the bags, opened the door, and hurried over to answer it.

"Hello."

"Is this Jack?"

"Yes, it is."

"This is Martin Richards. You responded to my personal ad."

"I sure did. How's it going?"

"Good. Do you want to meet me later this afternoon?"

"Today?"

"If you're not too busy."

Jack thought they should probably talk a while first, get to know each other a bit. But who knew, maybe this was how things were supposed to go. He didn't really have anything planned, didn't have to work until late.

"Sure, why not. What'd you want to do?"

"I don't know."

Jack tried to think of a suggestion but came up short. "Well, I'm up for anything."

"There is this movie I've been wanting to see."

Except that. Jack generally avoided going to the movies with other people. It was like saying, let's spend some time together so I can forget about you. Still, he didn't want to make things difficult. "What movie?"

"There's a new documentary on Derrida. *The Three Faces of Derrida.*"

A documentary? That might work. "Do you know where it's playing?"

"No."

"Hold on, I've got the weekly right here."

So they made the arrangements to meet. Jack hung up thinking the conversation had been a little stilted, so he flipped through to the back of the paper where Martin's ad was circled with exclamation points next to it. "24 y/o male into discussion, philosophy, reading, and music . . . looking for some calm in the noise." *Looking for some calm in the noise.* Jack really liked that. A lot more like the women's ads, which were generally better about describing what was going on with the person, their thoughts and interests. All most of the guys wanted to tell you about was the shape of their ass, but he could see that walking down the street. He put the paper down, freshly convinced he'd made a good choice.

Then it dawned on him he might have gotten himself into a little predicament. On the message he left Martin, he'd emphasized his philosophy background, thinking by the time he might decide to return the call, he'd be able to brush up on his studies from school. It was something he'd been meaning to do anyway, and seeing the ad had given him just the incentive he needed to follow through. He'd gone to the library and found Durant's *Introduction to Philosophy* to get him back in the swing of things. The problem was, while he was waiting in line to check out, Louise had slipped him two new fiction titles, and when he got home, it was those books that received his attention.

Now, not only had he failed to follow through on the philosophy reading, but he was about to see a movie on Derrida, a contemporary philosopher he didn't know much about. He considered running back to the library to pull a biography on him, but then decided he should probably stick with what he had. Maybe he'd be able to draw some parallels between the classic material in the Durant book and the film they were about to see.

In any case, he still needed to get the groceries from the hall, so he brought those in. Took off his sweatshirt, damp. Placed it over the radiator, lukewarm. Then set himself up on the floor with the book, a notepad, and a pen. He was just getting started with the first chapter when the phone rang.

"Hello."

"Hello, Jack?"

"Hey, Martin, what's up?"

"Hi. I was wondering, did you say the Lumiere?"

"Yeah, you know where it is, right?"

"I know. I thought that's what you said."

"All right, see you there."

"Wait, Jack?"

"Yeah?"

"Do you think ten minutes will give us enough time? Suppose it takes us a while to recognize each other?"

"I'm really tall, Martin, I doubt you'll miss me. But if you wanna make it quarter of, why don't we do that."

"Quarter of four?"

"Right."

Martin didn't seem especially self-confident, but Jack didn't bother himself with it too much. He had work to do.

Twenty minutes later, he was getting frustrated. It wasn't that the reading was difficult, but he was disappointed he didn't remember more from school. He thought seeing the material again would trigger some responses, but there hadn't been many. It was like he was back in Plato's proverbial cave. So he decided he should take a break and make himself a sandwich. He was just washing it down with some milk when the phone rang. There was no possible way it could be Martin again.

"Jack, it's Martin. Do you know I didn't realize it's raining out? And I don't have my umbrella. I left it at my friend's house."

"Well, did you want to wait and go another day?"

"Do you have an umbrella?"

"No, rain doesn't tend to bother me much. I was just out in it, it's pretty negligible."

"I guess I can manage it then."

"You sure there's nothing else on your mind?"

"No, that's it for now."

Okay, so Martin was a little peculiar. It was probably best to face up to that fact before starting to raise too many false expectations. Still, Jack tried to put things in the best possible light. Maybe he was one of those super brainy types who went around bumping into walls, not sure what day it was, but had all sorts of interesting views on the world. That's what he hoped, anyway, but there was no point in trying to overanalyze the whole thing, he'd find out soon enough. So he picked up the Durant book and fought to make it through to the next chapter. He didn't quite get there, though. He kept getting distracted looking over at the phone, thinking it was going to ring again, but it didn't and then it was time to go.

He got to the theater and set himself up between the movie posters on the outside wall, trying to look as conspicuous as possible. After about a minute of kicking back and trying to make quick eye contact with anyone who appeared to even remotely resemble the description Martin had given of himself, he was conscious of the fact that it was beginning to feel a lot like work. He didn't know how else to act, though; it didn't make much sense to be hiding.

At one point, a crowd of people approached—he'd been scanning left and right—and by the time they passed, Martin had been deposited directly in front of him. He took one look at the guy and thought, *Genius. He's gotta be a fucking genius.*

Martin was inhabiting the most alarming combination of apparel Jack had ever seen.

Bright red corduroys for pants, flooded. An OP plastic windbreaker, orange. So many layers of intermingled undergarments it was hard to tell where one ended and the next began. There were at least two collars poking through the top of a gray V-neck sweater, and besides that he had another sweater wrapped around his waist.

Jack could see he had a pleasant-looking face, although that was mostly covered with a thick coat of facial hair that appeared to be a coarser prototype of the close-cropped, but somehow tangled variety on his head. His tiny nose barely held up a pair of extra-thick eyeglasses, and he'd already adjusted them twice before Jack finally acknowledged him.

"So you must be Martin."

Martin nodded, seemingly unfazed by the scrutiny, instead explaining that he wanted to get inside right away so they could sit close up. While they were waiting in line to get the tickets, Jack tried to put the guy's unusual appearance into some context. He reminded himself that he didn't know squat about clothes. That this was the main reason he wore the same thing every day—so he wouldn't confuse himself trying to get dressed in the morning. Still, it was hard not to wonder. Was the guy so smart that he just didn't care what anyone thought, or was he part of some uber-hip circle of people who tried to outdo each other with the most hideous get-ups? Jack hoped it wasn't the second explanation, because he couldn't see how if Martin spent that much energy un-coordinating his outfits, he would have any time left to be making insightful observations about life.

He followed Martin down the aisle to the front of the theater, where they settled into the seats. Martin removed one of his layers and put it in his lap. Then he turned to Jack.

"You don't look like a philosopher," he declared.

It wasn't very enjoyable having the spotlight turned his way. "Yeah, well I mostly freelance these days. Besides, it's hard to pull that sort of thing off until you're like seventy." Martin didn't smile, just continued staring at him. "I should probably start growing a beard now so I can have it down at my feet by the time I get to a respectable age."

"I don't know many living philosophers who have beards."

"But you know some dead ones."

Martin looked puzzled. "Are you making a joke?"

Apparently not. "No, you're right. They are in short supply these days. Philosophers with beards. Philosophers and beards, actually, and, uh . . . jokes."

Jack was feeling kind of clammy, so he went to take off his sweatshirt. Just as he was pulling it over his head, Martin slipped in another question.

"So who's your favorite postmodern theorist?"

Jack drew a total blank. He knew he should have prepared himself better. Fortunately, he was in position to take cover under his sweatshirt, which he did, flailing his arms a bit in an attempt to convey the appearance of being trapped. A few names were coming to mind, but the problem was, he couldn't be sure if any of them were considered "postmodern." He'd always hated that word. Probably because he'd never gotten a good grip on what it was supposed to mean; it seemed so definitive and yet so impossible at the same time. He was pretty sure Derrida was postmodern, but it would be too obvious to reference him. One thing he was certain of was not being able to hang out under his sweatshirt for the remainder of the afternoon, so he finished pulling it off, stuffed it under the seat while announcing, "I really don't have a favorite." Which was true enough as far as it went. "Who do you like?" he added quickly.

"Derrida's good, but I prefer Baudrillard."

"Oh, yeah?" Jack glanced up at the screen where they were still flashing a series of slide ads. He wished they'd get on with it; at this rate, he was never going to make it to the opening credits without being exposed.

Martin proceeded to launch into a whole speech on Baudrillard, which was hard to follow, partly because Jack didn't know what the heck he was talking about, but mostly because his attention had been diverted by a building anger toward the philosophy department at UNM. Cultural Studies that included the likes of Baudrillard had hardly been in vogue there. In fact, his advisor had gone so far as to say that he considered the material "nothing but eurotrash suitable for childish malcontents." Jack suspected if he'd been offered a more well-rounded curriculum, he would probably have already gotten to the crux of this whole postmodern conundrum. Still, he couldn't really fault the department for his having skipped grad school so he could end up working in his freakin' underwear.

Martin was still talking, which was good. The pressure was off for the moment. Jack made an effort to grab on to something he was saying, ". . .which is just another example of the whole repetitive nature of culture. We're not just recycling plastic."

Okay, that sounded reasonable. *Wait, what?*

"So what do you think of Baudrillard?"

Jack panicked. What was he going to do, fake it? No way, he decided, he had no back-up whatsoever. He was in over his head as it was. "I'm actually not that familiar with Baudrillard," he admitted, and then waited for the fallout. It was a little too dark to tell if Martin was looking at him like he was dense, but his next statement left no doubt about what was on his mind.

"Do you think IQ is important?" Martin asked. "Because some people would say if your IQ is 78 then you aren't very smart."

Jack couldn't believe it. What a jerk, not even giving him the courtesy of a smile to go along with the mockery. And all because he didn't know Baudrillard.

Then, as the lights were dimming out, finally, he found Martin's scruffy face nuzzling against his neck. This is why, Jack told himself, he should've stuck to his old rule about going to the movies alone. And his new one about no more personal ads.

The movie turned out to be worthwhile, although it started off on unsure footing: a bunch of clunky American filmmakers who seemed like they were utterly invading the life of this elegant French thinker. It was funny how Derrida kept repeating how impossible it was for him to be natural in front of the camera, and yet when he'd forget the crew was there, he would reveal some very candid aspects of his life. It was as if the camera was intrusive only to the extent that he acknowledged it, and Jack ended up being pleased with the director for preserving this unique person he otherwise wouldn't have had an opportunity to meet.

He compared notes with Martin on the film, and the discussion was so engaging they decided to continue it at a Chinese restaurant down the street. That's where Martin informed him he was autistic. At first, it was hard to believe the guy wasn't bullshitting. But when asked why he would make something like that up, Jack couldn't think of a good reason. It turned out Martin was the one with an IQ of 78, which would hardly be the first example Jack had seen of how arbitrary that measurement was. According to Martin, he was operating at one of the highest functioning levels, and while he was explaining this, Jack stretched back to grade school, trying to remember his experience in the classroom they had for autistic kids there. Mrs. Eringos, the teacher he'd had a serious crush on at the time, asked if he would be willing to help out in the "special" classroom a couple times a week during recess, and he was like, "When do I start?" From the first day, though, it was tough. Making contact with the kids, even having them acknowledge he was there to begin with. There was one little blonde girl who used to surrender a smile, but that was rare. Smiling at all. Every afternoon he'd leave wishing he could have done something more useful than clean up building blocks.

Of course, he was also trying to focus on details from the past, because he wasn't quite ready to deal with the looming question in the present, which was whether he might be doing something wrong. Martin had moved his hand onto Jack's leg, and it seemed to be inching closer toward his crotch. And so there he was, as seemed to be happening a little too regularly lately, nearly convinced he was just waiting around for someone to wake him up. Before things could get any more complicated, he excused himself to go to the bathroom.

While he was on the can, he was thinking about the expert piano players and mathematicians he'd seen once on a PBS special, that guy in *Rain Man* and all the unusual abilities he had, and when he eventually made his way back to the table he asked Martin if his being autistic meant he was especially gifted with counting spilled toothpicks, or playing a musical instrument, or anything like that. He didn't know if this was the right topic to be inquiring about—*so I hear you're autistic, can you do any tricks?*—but Martin told him it was a good question. He wasn't a savant, he said, but he was in a band. He seemed pretty excited about it, actually.

"What kind of band is it?"

"Postmodern."

Jack held back a smile. Barely. "What does that mean to you, exactly?" he asked, hoping to get to the bottom of things once and for all.

"It means we argue a lot."

Jack let go and laughed. "You're pretty funny, Martin, you know that?"

He didn't quite smile, but Jack thought he'd taken it as a compliment. At least, he hoped he had.

By the end of dinner, he'd gotten a really good feeling about Martin. He had his own way of approaching things, sure, but he seemed so uninhibited about it, so honest. Jack felt like he could trust him. He wanted to show Martin he was someone who could be trusted as well, but that was going to take some time. When they walked out of the restaurant to say goodbye, he asked for the third time if Jack was going to call him, and for the third time Jack assured him that he would.

A few days later, they met for coffee. Martin had already explained that he didn't drink coffee, and Jack had already explained that meeting for coffee didn't necessarily require you to order one. Martin went for a cream soda.

"You know what?" Martin began.

"What?"

"You remind me a lot of my brother."

The fact was, Jack got uneasy when a new person told him he reminded them of someone they knew. Especially when that someone was a family member or an ex-boyfriend. There was no way he was interested in trying to live up or down to someone else's reputation, let alone getting caught in some Freudian web. In general, it just seemed like an opportunity for all sorts of trouble, but with all that was going on with Martin, he decided this probably shouldn't be his biggest concern. So he tried to go with it.

"Older or younger brother?" he asked.

"My twin brother."

"Your what?" Jack responded, far too loudly, nearly knocking over his cup of coffee in the process. He lowered his voice. "What do you mean, your twin brother?"

"We're fraternal twins."

"Oh . . . right." *Chalk up another one for Martin.*

It turned out he was the second kid in line. The one who went from breech birth to the incubator, and the theory was that something unusual had happened along the way. He explained that he was "seconds from being normal" like his brother. Jack wasn't sure if the phrase was something he'd repeated often or not—seconds from normal—but he said it so matter of factly, it made it sound like it really wasn't tragic.

His brother was a mechanic who'd just gotten married. Martin said he was tall, just like Jack, and then wanted to know how tall Jack was exactly. It was funny, but for the first time since he was like seven, he wasn't irritated to hear the question.

When he told him the answer, Martin seemed impressed. "My brother's only 6'3. He's not as tall as you are."

"Well, almost. So are you close to him?"

"He lives in Pasadena."

"I mean, do you guys like each other, do you get along well?"

"Oh yeah, we get along. He's a really nice brother. I bother him sometimes, but we get along."

Bother him, huh? And this from the brother who was only seconds from not normal. It wasn't like Martin was asking for it, but Jack couldn't help but feel a little protective toward him.

They saw each other a few more times that week. He'd take the bike over to the western edge of the Western Addition, where Martin always met him, waving, at the curb. "Martin, I think I know where you live now," Jack told him, "I can use the buzzer." But he insisted on coming out, like he was still afraid of being passed by.

Once inside, Jack listened to him talk; Martin definitely had a lot of ideas on his mind. His philosophy of life was mostly an abstract amalgam of the things he'd read, and while it was difficult to see how they had any direct impact on his day-to-day existence, they seemed important to him.

He also showed off his collection of stamps, his comics, and his baseball cards, all of which were expansive, although, as he flipped through the albums, there didn't seem to be anything but the most perfunctory satisfaction with them. And that only came when he explained the various systems he'd used to catalogue his collections, rather than from any particular excitement about the items they contained. A shortstop seemed to hold no more interest for him than a man who could travel time. Jack had never been much into that stuff as a kid, much less now, but he asked questions, trying as best he could to get a sense of where Martin was coming from.

If he had any doubts about continuing to hang out with Martin, they were erased the day Martin accidentally discovered that his motorcycle had been stolen.

"Are you okay?" he asked, before Jack had even gotten the phone properly to his ear.

"Fine. Why?"

"Well, what happened to your bike?"

"My *bike*?"

"It's all scratched up, Jack. The leather bags are gone. The . . . the . . . the windshield's missing. And there's some colored wires hanging out near the place where you put the key."

"The ignition you mean."

"Why won't you tell me what happened to your bike?"

"There's not much to tell, Martin. I needed new brake pads. The bike's in for servicing. Over at City Cycle."

"No, it isn't. I just saw it on McAllister."

"You're seeing things, pal," Jack told him, "I dropped it off yesterday."

And he said back—solemn, even by Martin standards—"I know your bike, Jack."

At which point, he remembered Martin wasn't one to joke around.

"All right, where *exactly* did you see it on McAllister?"

"Between Broderick and Divisadero. I can meet you there and show you if you want."

So Jack went over to check it out and sure enough, there it was, a little banged up, but still in one piece. He had his extra keys and he stole it back.

It turned out the mechanics had somehow forgotten to take it in the previous night, and by the next day it was gone. The owner, Don, had been in a bit of a panic when he discovered the bike had been taken. He wasn't sure if one of his guys had been involved, debated about whether to call the police. Afterward, he explained all this. That he'd put the word out and was just giving it till the end of the day to see if it brought the bike back to him.

Boy, was he surprised to see Jack ride up on it. And sincerely sorry about what had happened. He wrote a personal letter apologizing, then not only fixed everything better than it was, but promised plenty of free repairs in the future.

"For how long did he promise you?" Martin wanted to know.

"I don't know, what does it matter? Point is, I got something really good out of something really bad and it's all thanks to you, man."

There was no way he was going to turn his back on Martin after that. The bike gods had shone through him, and Jack felt like he owed him more than he'd ever be able to repay. He would look out for him and do what he could to make his life better. He was on a mission.

As it was, other people's lives always seemed easier to deal with than his own. Not like he had anything to complain about at the time: he had an apartment, a job, had set up a routine for himself. But it didn't feel very substantial and he wasn't sure what to do to change that. He wasn't even sure he wanted to change it, too much, but at least he could make himself more useful in the meantime. He would be ready to respond the next time Martin called.

"Jack, I can't have cream soda with you anymore. I've got almost no money left and my disability's not going to make it till the end of the month."

This sounded serious.

"I think we better talk about this in person, Martin. I can spot you a soda, it's not a big deal."

"No, that's not how I want it to go."

"Well, you can sit and have a glass of water, can't you?"

Jack expected he'd have to think about this for a moment before answering, which he did.

"I guess that would be okay."

"All right, I'll meet you at Bodie's in thirty minutes."

Parking the bike in front of the restaurant, he saw Martin slowly working his way down Fillmore. That gave him an idea, so he dropped it back in gear and scooted over to him. Martin seemed to be hugging the sidewalk a little.

"I know something we could do that doesn't cost any money."

"I can't hear you," he said, sticking his fingers in his ears.

Jack cut the engine.

"I said, I've got something we can do that doesn't cost money." He spread his hands over the bike in a kind of *voila* motion.

"What?"

"This, here, is what is known as a free ride."

Martin still looked bewildered.

"Come on, man, me and the bike want to take you for a tour. As a way of saying thanks."

"No!" he practically shouted this. "I went on a motorcycle once with my brother and that was the last time."

"Well, I didn't necessarily mean right this second. Come to think of it, I'd have to rustle you up a helmet, anyway."

"I don't want to go. Now or any other time."

Jack shook his head, thinking how funny it was that Martin should have been the one to find the bike. "Okay. But if you change your mind, just let me know and we'll set something up." He turned the key, then moved his hand to the starter.

"Wait, Jack?"

"Yeah."

"We could go back to my place."

"We could . . . play some cards or something, sure."

"Are we ever going to sleep together?"

It was going to be difficult to pretend for much longer that this wasn't a problem. Every time Martin had indicated a physical interest, Jack tried to brush it off as an anomaly, but a series of anomalies were probably better described as a pattern. The thing was Jack hadn't found himself attracted to Martin in that way. He got a nice feeling when the guy was around, just not a chubb. It was certainly easier like that because he didn't have to think about the implications of sleeping with someone who was autistic. Well, of course he did think about the implications, but at least he didn't have to think too carefully about them. He'd like to have believed he would have just gone for it. What did autistic even mean anyway? Martin was a functioning, independent citizen. But since he wasn't into it in the first place, he wasn't about to make a point of testing himself on the issue.

"Uh . . . I really don't think that's a good idea, Martin. Why don't we go inside so we can talk about what's happening with your finances?" Then he cranked the engine, before adding, "I just gotta park."

Inside the restaurant, Martin was looking none too happy over his water.

"I'm not getting any work, Jack. And I spent all my money on those ads. I can't keep living like this."

What a heartache of a story that was turning into. Martin had been to school for massage therapy, which was maybe an unexpected choice, but he seemed to know what he was doing. He'd given Jack a short demonstration on his shoulders, and even though Jack hadn't been particularly comfortable with it, he felt like the right spots were being hit, some of the kinks worked out. Very professional. The problem was, about six weeks before, he'd lost his bread and butter position when the computer firm he'd been servicing moved their entire office up to Seattle. So at the same time he placed his personal ad in the weekly, he also decided to pay for a massage ad in one of the queer magazines.

His difficulties began when the calls started coming in. The guys wanted to know if he played around, whether he had big muscles or a big cock or both. And even if they were only interested in a massage, Martin seemed unable to convince them he was the right man for the job. Jack had been there once when he'd taken a call, and it required a good deal of restraint not to grab the phone out of Martin's hand and broker the deal himself. Martin didn't try to build himself up at all. He spoke in his usual monotone, kept his responses to the absolute minimum.

"Martin, couldn't you jazz it up just a little when people call. I mean, you don't have to tell them you're a professional body builder but couldn't you, I don't know, sound more enthusiastic."

Martin was doubtful. "But what happens if they show up. Then they're going to see who I really am."

"Who you are is someone with the full range of skills you've been advertising. Now if you could just throw in some enthusiasm when you're talking to people, and maintain it when they show up, you'd be all set."

"No, I don't think so. Massage just isn't one of those things that makes me enthusiastic. I like to do it but that's all."

A week later, Martin had gotten only one new client. Combined with the two people he already had it just wasn't cutting it.

"I think I'm going to have to put an end to my practice."

"Are you sure, Martin? You should wait and see if you get any more calls. Isn't the ad supposed to run for another week?"

"People have stopped calling, Jack."

It was times like these he wished he had a circle of friends that he could've sent to see Martin, at least once in a while, maybe it would have been enough to get him through. He'd given an abbreviated explanation of the situation to Bishkey at work, and he said he'd try to send his girlfriend over as part of an anniversary package he was putting together for her, but that obviously wasn't going to be enough to turn things around. And Martin wouldn't take a loan. He'd already made himself quite clear on that point. Of course, Jack admired him for it, but still, he wished he could've accepted it as a temporary solution. He decided to take a chance and mention the offer again.

"Jack, no, I don't want to borrow money from you or anyone else. It's bad enough I have to take my disability."

He could sure be stubborn. Jack was starting to see how his brother might find him difficult, at times.

"So what are you going to do?"

"I'm going to have to find another job."

Martin called a few days later.

"Jack, you're never going to believe this!"

"Try me."

"Well, we've all been feeling like the band is ready to perform, and so our cymbalist talked to his friend at the Bluelamp and they're going to let us play there next Tuesday. If they like us, they said they'd start paying for a regular gig."

"Wow, that's great, Martin. You guys must be excited. Are you gonna be able to make it money-wise till they start paying you?"

"Well, it's not definite that we're getting paid. That's only if they like us. But that's okay because I think I found another job."

"Fantastic, Martin, what is it?" He thought how life was so often like this—either everything was working or nothing was.

"There's an opening at T.A.F., the Telefund AIDS Foodbank."

Just hearing the acronym was enough to make Jack suspicious. "Are you sure that's not a volunteer position?"

"It's paid. I picked up the application yesterday."

"Well, did you fill it out?"

"Yes. Yes, I did. Most of it. But I'm worried about my references."

"Do you have any?"

"Yes. I have them but they're mostly friends of mine."

He weighed this information. "Well, that's probably okay. Did you put me down?"

"I haven't known you long enough, Jack, you know that."

Martin was so right on most of the time. What else could he do but cross his fingers for the guy.

The next night Martin called, sounding more than a bit agitated.

"They already called my friend. I didn't think they were going to call so fast."

"Who called your friend, the Telefund office?"

"Yes."

"Well, you've got to expect they were going to check your references. That's what you want to happen, that must mean they're interested."

"I know, but they asked her what my most negative characteristic was."

"And what'd she tell them?"

"She said I was gullible."

Jack hesitated before starting in, thinking how this might affect his application. "Well, being gullible isn't necessarily a negative thing. I mean, if that's your worst characteristic, you're probably doing something right." He was feeling more confident about it by the second. "No, Martin, there's no reason why that should hurt you on the job. You're just talking on the phone with people, right?"

"Yeah, that's all."

Gullible. He knew it wasn't Martin's style to imply anything, but still. He was constantly trying to determine if he was taking advantage of the guy, somehow leading him on. He knew it wasn't completely right between them. The way a relationship tends to be when only one of the people in it is really getting what he wants.

"Jack, can I ask you something?"

"Sure."

"Do you think I'm attractive?"

Oh brother, here we go. "Yes, of course I think you're attractive. Why, did someone say something to you?"

"No, I just want to know if *you* think I'm attractive."

"Yes, Martin, I do."

"Well, why don't you want to sleep with me then?"

Jack took a deep breath. "I find a lot of people attractive, but it doesn't mean I should be sleeping with all of them." He hadn't even made it three quarters of the way through that remark before he was ready to disown it. How weak. Like he'd never been one to compromise himself, and for a lot less. Where was the inspiration for some more worthwhile response, he didn't know. He wanted to explain to Martin he barely had any experience with guys as it stood, but that seemed beside the point. "Martin, the important thing is that you stay focused. You've got a lot of good things happening right now. The show's coming up with the band. And it sounds like they're seriously considering you for this job. Now when are they supposed to let you know if you've got it?"

"By next week. Well, that's if they want to interview me."

"Okay, you let me know as soon as you hear anything."

Martin got an interview for Friday. Jack was actually starting to feel good about his prospects, but when he called up afterward to find out about it, Martin sounded terrible.

"I don't think the interview went very well."

"I'm sure it went fine."

"No, it didn't go right. I tried to answer the questions as best I could, but I'm not sure."

"Well, did you know the answers?"

"I think so. I mean, they were mostly about why I wanted to have the job. I told them I was really looking forward to intervening on their behalf. Do you think that sounded enthusiastic enough?"

"Intervening?"

"Yeah, what's wrong with intervening?"

"Well, I mean usually . . . nothing. Listen, I'm sure your responses were fine, Martin.

Martin?"

Martin had dropped the phone. There was a small commotion on the other end, followed by the sound of pages flipping. A dictionary, he could almost guarantee it.

"Oh no. Oh no, Jack, you're right. Intervene's got like five different meanings and none of them is how I used it. I'm sure he took it *all wrong*."

"Martin, it's not like—"

"I know I've heard 'intervene on your behalf' before. I saw it in a book or on television or maybe someone told me. I swear to you, Jack, I thought it meant to help out."

"It's okay, Martin. It *is* like helping out. Come on, you're hardly that far off the way you used it. You've got to stop being ridiculous, here. They're not going to penalize you for slightly misusing one phrase. People never speak perfectly in interviews, anyway, everyone gets a little nervous."

"You wouldn't get nervous."

"That isn't true at all. Now listen, I'm sure they saw what a responsible guy you are. They've got your references to back it up. The ball's in their court now. Just hang in there with this, all right?"

"Okay. I'll try."

"Now will you let me buy you a cream soda?"

"No, Jack."

"Hold on. Will you let me buy you a cream soda if you agree to help me out with some Baudrillard? I picked up one of the books you recommended and I'm having some trouble with it. I could seriously use some tutoring, Martin, no b.s., who else is going to talk to me about this stuff?"

Martin considered the idea. "Which one'd you get?"

"Uh, I think it's the . . . hold on . . . *The Ecstasy of Communication.*"

It was easily one of the most overwrought titles he'd seen in a while, but of all the books that were sitting on the shelf, it was also the thinnest. He figured he'd better ease his way into the postmodern world.

"Oh, that's a really good one. All right, I'll meet you. But it'll have to be a little later, there's something I want to do first."

Jack was at the restaurant, rereading some of the passages he'd underlined in the book, when Martin arrived in a state. There was something almost guilty about him, an emotion Jack didn't realize he was even capable of; he barely glanced up from behind his eyeglasses when they shook hands.

"Is everything all right, Martin?"

"I went back," he blurted.

"Where?"

"To the Telefund office."

Calm, calm. Keep calm, Jack told himself. *It might not be anything.* "Why'd you do that?"

"I wanted to tell them what I meant by 'intervene on their behalf.' "

"Oh Martin, I really wish you hadn't done that."

"I know. I knew it as soon as I left the office. I should have listened to you."

Maybe you shouldn't have even met me, Jack was thinking. He'd been the one to get Martin started with all that "be enthusiastic" baloney.

"Well, there's no point feeling bad about it now. All you can do is sit tight and see what happens."

"Do you think I should go back to explain to them why I wanted to explain to them about intervening?"

"No fucking way, Martin!" He was cowering but Jack couldn't stop. "Now you're just gonna have to wait and see what they say, but whatever you do *don't go back* there. And don't call either. You've gotta learn to trust yourself more."

Martin nodded his head slowly. "You remind me a lot of my brother," he said.

"You told me that before," Jack reminded him, deflated. "Right after we met." It seemed like an unquestionable sign of failure. He thought he was going to be able to offer him something different than his brother had. That Martin had been looking to him for that. Maybe there was still a way.

"I bet your brother doesn't read Baudrillard."

"No. He doesn't read anything."

"See? So why don't we talk through the book like we were planning on."

Martin adjusted his glasses. "It wouldn't hurt, I guess."

So they spent the next couple of hours debating the finer points of the book. Jack thought it had turned into a thoroughly enjoyable afternoon.

Martin didn't get the job. And to top it off, his band had been disinvited from coming back to the Bluelamp. Jack could only imagine how things had gone, since Martin had asked him not to come at the last minute, telling him it might "negatively affect" his performance. Which made

Jack feel like a criminal, but what else could he do besides respect his wishes. As a consolation, Martin had given him a one-man sample of how the show would go. The concept was basically the band would riff for a while on their various instruments, and then they'd do some spoken word type stuff. Self-referential phrases like, *Yeah, we always save the best song for last. It's like the orange icing on the carrot cake. Baby.*

Martin was the primary vocalist; he didn't write the stuff, but he had the perfect deadpan voice for it. Jack thought he would really have dug seeing him perform, not to mention wishing he could have been around to help provide some support. Supposedly, the audience hadn't been real friendly.

The fallout hit two days later. Martin called to deliver the news.

"Jack, the band broke up."

"What happened?"

"You know how badly the show went."

Not really, he thought. "Maybe it wasn't the band," he told him. "Maybe the audience was just a little slow on the concept."

"I doubt it. We just aren't very good at connecting."

"Yeah, but Martin, you're just starting. It can take a while to build up a rapport."

"But what's the point?"

"The point? I don't know. I thought you really liked playing with those guys."

"I did," he said, about as sad as Jack had ever heard him. Martin's heart was reeling, that was for sure. He was so sad, in fact, it was the one time Jack actually considered messing around with him. He just felt so hopelessly out of suggestions, he didn't know what else to do. Of course, it was a lousy idea that would only have made things worse, but it didn't stop him from thinking about it. Thankfully, they were on the phone at the time.

The last call he got from Martin he'd been dreading about as much as he'd been expecting it. The bottom line was he was giving up his practice and his apartment, and would be moving out on the thirty-first, back to live with his parents in Pasadena.

Expecting it hardly made Jack feel any better about it, though. It just seemed like such a defeat. The guy had been out there for over a year, on his own, and he'd managed to pull through the whole thing right up until then. It didn't seem fair. If only he had . . . Christ, bigger biceps or something, he probably could've kept going.

Jack realized there wasn't much point in trying to argue with him. Still, he felt like giving it a whirl. At least for old time's sake.

"You know, Martin, I'm sure if you keep looking you'll find something here."

"I don't think so."

"Can't you just do some temporary work at a restaurant or something. Just for a little while?"

"I'm not a waiter, Jack."

And so he reached the point where he understood that something was going to happen whether he wanted it to or not. Nothing he could do about it, or nothing he was willing to do, so he got down to the business of accepting the situation.

"Well, you've got my number in case you come back to town."

"I don't think I'm coming back."

"Well, do you have a number down there? I could give you a call if I'm ever in the area."

"I don't really think I can give you my parents' number."

"Well, okay," Jack said, thinking, *have a nice life then*. He tried to keep the disappointment out of his voice. "Stay smart, Martin," he told him.

"I will," he said. "Bye, Jack."

Jack hung up the phone shaking his head. He couldn't believe it. His first queer friend in the whole city and he was already out of there.

Like that. He'd been hoping to convince Martin to go to the aquarium with him next week. It was free the first Tuesday of the month.

Jack missed having someone to check in with on a regular basis. He tried to carry on his cultural theory studies without Martin, but it felt increasingly pointless. It seemed like he was too traditional for most of the ideas. He liked taking things apart, but then he wanted to be able to put them back together afterward, hopefully better than they had been. The postmodern approach seemed too satisfied to just leave all the parts out there on the table, mocking you. He decided to take a break from the books and redouble his efforts at the gym.

Working out had a lot to recommend it. He could do it alone. He didn't have to think very hard. There was a simple correlation between input and results. It had always been his go-to after a bad call at the department—a way to keep feelings in check—and he justified his continued efforts by maintaining that a better body would help bring him more tips at the Cage. But that reasoning had started to feel more than a little shallow the night he found Bishkey waiting for him after work. Shivering under an umbrella and looking scared.

Bishkey had missed his last couple of shifts, so Jack knew something was up, and agreed right away to grab a coffee. At the diner, Bishkey broke the news that he'd been confirmed positive for HIV. He said he'd done something he shouldn't have for a lot of money and there was nothing to be done about it now. His girlfriend was still healthy, though, and his main concern seemed to be about her, whether she was going to leave him, whether he was fucked up for wanting her to stay. At one point he started to cry, and Jack didn't know what to say to him after that. It hadn't been that many months since Jack had been careless with himself, too, and even though all his tests had come back clear, he suspected it could have been him.

Once they'd parted ways, Jack did think of some things he could offer besides *Sorry, man,* but Bishkey didn't pick up his phone, nor did he return any of Jack's messages. Except for the last one, when he said he appreciated the check-ins but was going to need some time. It sounded like a goodbye for now.

With no one else to call, and feeling somewhat fatalistic by this point, Jack started going out to the clubs. Something that felt vaguely social but was mostly an exercise in being alone in a crowd. He'd sit at the bar, nursing a drink. Fragments of conversations all around him. If someone said hi, he tried to think of something to say besides hi back, but nothing worthwhile came to him.

1:31

Getting close to other people hasn't usually been a problem for me. It's staying close once there's been a move beyond friendship. Someone suddenly needs their space, wants time to think. It's not always me. Carrie says the best way to get ahead of that curve is not to get involved in the first place.

I sure hope she's around tonight. That she'll be there to pick up the phone. If she was a normal person, she'd be home. In bed. Asleep. But if she was that normal, she probably wouldn't be into someone calling at this hour. Especially if that someone was looking for a place to crash.

Carrie's not the easiest individual to get hold of, but you never know. She always said people could find her if they really wanted to.

He **spotted her** in the middle of the dance floor at Devotion. Everyone dreaming her dream, like she'd conjured the deejay from the darkness. When she yelled out, it went through him like a shiver. He had to grin bigger, yell back. It wasn't as if he was the only one to join in when her voice tracked the music, pumping toward some spectacular crescendo, but he was the only one to pass her an opened bottle of water when he noticed her jaw start to lock. Her tongue sweep the top of her lips. Again. She smiled into him, took a long drink. Then sent it along to some other outstretched hand. He kept his eyes on her.

When the crowd began to change, Jack took off on his motorcycle—nowhere to go, just a cruise around town, by the beach—wishing he could feel the wrap of her legs around him.

Next week she was back. Still mixing it up with everyone in the place, still looking like she was with no one. He was feeling good. Good enough that he only small-talked it with her for a little while before asking if she wanted to get together sometime. She didn't seem to comprehend his proposal, but he raised his voice as if she hadn't heard it. "I mean do you want to go out, you know, sometime, maybe later in the week or whenever?"

"Oh," she said, "you mean like a date? Oh, that's so . . ."

"So yes, or so no."

"What d'you suppose we'd do?" she asked, finally.

There was nothing flirty in the way she said it.

He wanted to tell her, *I'd just like to drive you around, anywhere you want for as long as you want*, but his confidence was flagging.

"You're too *healthy*," she said suddenly. "I can smell it."

What was she talking about? He watched her wave at someone across the room. Then she made the following suggestion:

"We *could* see a movie, I guess. That would make it an official date, wouldn't it?"

Her tone wasn't even condescending, which would have made it better somehow. He was on the full defensive by now.

"I usually see movies by myself," he told her.

"Does that make you a loner, or someone who hasn't found the right company?"

"What's the difference," he shrugged, and she finally stopped looking around the club long enough to seem interested.

The truth was he had been feeling lonely, and once he'd used the word with himself, the acknowledgement had come as a kind of backhanded relief. All the solo bike trips he'd taken during college, after college, and he'd always had to get back to school or work long before he'd reached the point of actually missing anyone. People talked about missing each other like it was the most natural thing, and he'd wondered if maybe there was something wrong with him.

Well, it turned out he wasn't completely immune. Living in the city had shown him he had his limits, and even if it took him longer to reach them, he guessed he was probably no different than anyone else once he did. Starting around the holidays, he'd been more and more tempted to check in with people in New Mexico—which is why he forced himself not to do it very much—and even though he brightened when the phone rang and it was Skelly or Ren on the other end of the line, hanging up the phone afterward always left him with a bit of a hangover. He preferred whatever loneliness he was feeling over that, but what he really wanted to get back to was no loneliness at all.

He met Carrie at the Lumiere later that week. She hadn't mentioned the name of the film they were going to see; it seemed she'd picked the theater based on the fact that her friend, Christophe, was an usher there and would let them in for free. Once inside, she headed straight for the bathroom, and then, coming out with a smile, grabbed Jack's hand and pulled him along after her as she peeked in on a couple of features before choosing one where there were no people watching.

Unusual approach, he thought. He felt like it might even be an excellent one, but he was still unsure of her intentions. Once they'd settled into their seats, though, he realized how nice it was having the place to themselves. Lounging around like they lived there, talking when they wanted. Christophe came in once to check on how they were doing, explaining it was the end of the run for that particular film and wondering what they thought about it. Jack was somewhat embarrassed that neither of them had much to say, and after Christophe left, the conversation continued to taper. Seeing as they hadn't been paying much attention to the screen, it was too late to pick up the story, and when Carrie let out a serious yawn, Jack didn't want to wait around for the sequel.

"Hey, why don't we get going?" he suggested, and she raised her eyebrows while nodding her head up and down.

On their way back through the lobby, they stopped to talk to Christophe, who was sweeping behind the concession stand. He wasn't quite as friendly as before, but Carrie didn't seem to notice. She asked what he was going to do with all the leftover popcorn.

"You're gonna throw it *out*?" she said.

Like almost every inspiration Carrie would ever have, this one took at least a small cue from reality. She imagined a full-on feed-the-streets campaign. Courtesy of the Lumiere. Lining up the needy after the last picture show for popcorn distribution. She was especially attracted by the low-calorie aspect of the idea, and he tried giving her some hell about her diet for the food insecure. She wouldn't take any of it, though.

"What I meant was," she explained, rolling her eyes at him, exasperated, like he hadn't understood a single word she'd been saying, "popcorn's *good* for you."

So they ended up walking out with a huge Hefty bag slung over his shoulder, Santa Claus style. Passing out popcorn to everyone they saw. She filled shaking coin cups, the palms of open hands before there was even a chance to say no. She left piles of it on benches, on the blankets covering sleeping bodies, which the wind must have carried away, maybe before they even turned the corner. When it became obvious they had way too much to give out, she began to throw it in the air like confetti.

Jack could barely keep up with her, not something he was used to having to do with anyone. He remembered one woman he'd been seeing a couple years back and the morning-after talk about how she wished he'd Slow Down when they were out and about. She said she already worked out plenty, and she had a point about that, so he'd resolved to do better. Carrie made no such efforts. With her long legs pulling her forward in an ongoing rush, her hair constantly wired—the black strands tight up in coils, sometimes striking out in a dozen different directions—she was a force. But if it was a challenge to try to match her steps, Jack felt he was up to it, and by the time they finally came to rest on the curb in front of the taxi stand, he felt more exhilarated than exhausted.

"I think I actually enjoyed myself tonight," she told him, once they'd reached the front of the line.

He grabbed hold of the cab door and held it open for her. "Don't sound so surprised."

"I like being surprised." She leaned up and kissed him behind the ear. "Hope to see you around."

"Good night," he said, smiling to himself as he closed the door.

That was a victory of sorts, right? He was already analyzing the kind of kiss it had been. Like, definitely not grandmotherly short, but then again it wasn't really a long smooch either. Maybe it wasn't worth parsing too much because it obviously hadn't been on the lips, but it mattered to him.

From the beginning, there'd been no question how attracted he was to Carrie, which normally wouldn't have made front page news, except for the fact she was the first woman he'd had that strong a feeling toward since coming to San Francisco. He hadn't realized until he felt it how much he didn't want his feelings toward women to be erased, how he thought guys would make a better addition than substitution. And yet it wasn't clear that maintaining this attraction was of any benefit to the female population at large. Or, for that matter, to himself. He'd built up a lot of hurt inside from all the hurt he felt like he'd caused with past breakups, and despite all evidence to the contrary, he just didn't picture himself as the love 'em and leave 'em type. Even though Carrie had flirted with him a bit tonight, he wasn't foolish enough to think he'd gained the upper hand. She had it, she'd probably always have it, and he drew an odd comfort in believing that if there was anyone likely to be hurt in the relationship it was him.

Jack began to write a series of poems about her. Seeing as he'd never written poems before, he thought this was significant. Probably they weren't even poems—more like a series of sentences, really—but whatever they were, he was happy with how easily they came. He kept them in his pocket and handed one to her every time he saw her out. She always crinkled them into her purse like gum wrappers. He couldn't be sure she was reading them, though, until one night when she confessed they were starting to bother her.

"It's mostly nice what you write," she explained, the piece of paper still held between them, "but you've got to take it easy on me. You're making me sad, and that's not something I'm interested in being." But she ended up taking the paper anyway and didn't ask him to stop. Instead, she mentioned that she sometimes wrote poetry too. Like her last poem, for example, "The Day the Medicine Stopped Working."

When she told him about it, he was kind of leery, thinking the title might have been the whole story there, but she didn't give any more details about it that night.

For the moment, the idea of making a move on her seemed ill-advised. She still hadn't given him enough of an indication she was interested, and he was worried she'd either laugh or stop talking to him, neither of which he wanted to happen. If only he could get her on the bike, maybe that would improve his odds.

So he waited until the night when, saying goodbye, she gave him an extra-long hug, and then took a chance and asked if he could give her a ride to the club the next week.

"Next week I won't be here," she said.

"Oh, okay. Some other time, then."

"I'm going to Resonator. Eddie Flynn's playing."

Jacked tensed. "Eddie Flynn?"

"He's only the absolute best deejay. You've usually got to catch him in the Castro, jammed between all these sweaty guys."

Jack nodded vaguely.

"You should go."

"Maybe I'll see you there," he told her. But he knew he wouldn't be going.

1:53

I pull the collar up on my jacket and step out into the street. Barely aware it's even raining anymore if it wasn't for the puddles. They catch the drops like pebbles tossed from the darkness. Handfuls of them, at first, windblown, then fewer and fewer until the last ones seem to disappear into the water without disturbing it.

When I reach the park, I skirt along the perimeter until I see the payphone. There are two of them, actually, side by side. I pick the receiver off one, put the coins in, but no matter what buttons I press, I can't get past the dial tone. Then I pull the coin return, but nothing comes out, like playing cold slots.

I thrust my hand back into my pocket. Grasp and pull out the loose change, counting across my palm, just to make sure there's enough left. I try to be extra careful using the second phone—taking my time with each coin, listening to the dull clink dropping into the box before I insert the next—hoping this will improve my odds. And it works. I enter her digits and the number goes through.

The only problem is, Carrie's not answering.

It figures. She keeps the volume off half the time, and even though she's got it set to like a thousand rings, she's just as likely to ignore them unless she needs something. I told her she should at least glance down every once in a while, just to be sure. You don't want to miss an important call.

I hang up before her voicemail comes on. Tense up waiting to see what the coins will do. When they fall through, I'm quick to retrieve them.

Okay, so it's hardly a lost cause at this point. She could be dancing by the speakers and not caring about anything except the music coming out of them, but sooner or later, she's gonna need to step outside for a cigarette. Or she could be all tweaked up and not wanting to deal with anyone, and then she could change her mind on a whim and grab for the phone and scream, "Hello!" Or she really could be home doing her version of sleep, which never amounted to much. So I keep on calling back, and I keep letting it ring. Imagine the ringing—in her apartment, on her mattress, against her jeans—and feel connected by the sound of it.

She'd gone up to Oregon. To do some camping, according to one of her friends, although no one seemed to know when she'd be back. Jack kept going to Devotion, Sundays, hoping she'd be there. Finally, one night, waiting for a game of pool, he heard that scream, rising above the crowd. Pure joy, if there was such a thing. And he followed the sound of it over near the deejay booth where he spotted her communing with the deejay. Determined to dance his ground until she recognized him, he got lost in the music, and the next thing he knew she had her face about an inch from his.

"Hey, it's my favorite poet!"

"Come on, how many poets do you know?"

"Lots and *lots*!" she yelled. "I *thought* that was you, but then I thought it couldn't be you, busting out all those moves." She pointed at his feet.

He laughed, "Well, I gotta do it for work. I figured I might as well get out here and enjoy myself once in a while."

In fact, that had been his biggest accomplishment since she'd been gone. Thinking she was bound to be back at some point, he was determined to impress her when she returned. The guys at the Cage were good, some of them really good, but this one Brazilian dancer was the best, and one night Jack had gotten up the courage to ask him for some tips. "You are so right, my friend, you need some help. Let me show you."

And then he'd gotten behind Jack, which put him immediately on edge but with the larger goal in mind he'd gritted his way through the demonstration. "You have a lot of energy I can see in there hiding, this is good, but it is not making it out to your hips." He tried swaying Jack. "You need to relax, or you are going to be always having this problem." There had been a few moments when Jack had able to focus on the music and relax, and it was those moments he'd gathered up and tried to put together that night on the dance floor in front of Carrie.

Carrie looked outrageously good. She'd put on weight, curved out nicely with it. Her breasts seemed perkier. Her whole body did, in fact, like it might finally be able to hold up against the currents of energy coursing through it.

"So how was camping?" he asked, after watching her spin a series of dizzying twirls.

She raised her eyes, her head nodding up and down.

"That good, huh?"

"It was. I needed to get out of here, it was getting a little out of control." She slid her purse off her shoulder, scrounged around inside and came out with a lollipop, which she popped into her mouth.

Then she started to tell him about it.

The rivers, all the trees up in Oregon. How green everything was there. "It was so green," she said, "you could almost forget it was raining all the time."

"Wow, that sounds incredible."

"I'm already missing it in a way."

"Maybe you could set up a tent in your apartment."

"We didn't use a tent. My friend has a cabin."

"I thought you went camping." He wondered who this person was, friend or "friend," but then decided it really didn't matter.

"So do you think it's a good idea that I came back?" She was looking at him, serious all of a sudden.

"Good for who?"

"For me, of course. We know everyone else benefits when I'm around."

It was hard to find much argument in that.

"Well, it's looking pretty righteous on you at the moment. You could always go back if it starts getting too weird again."

"True. But it was a lot harder getting out of here than I thought." She looked worried for a moment, then brushed it aside with a shake of her hair. "It doesn't matter anyway. I'm staying. I was getting bored, I'm so bad, I know it." She bit down on the lollipop. "And I was getting fat, too. Yuck."

Was she nuts? What did you say to people, he wondered. "You mean less emaciated."

"I wish. Hey, that's the end of Ruben's set, let's go outside." She took his hand, led him over to the waterfall, where he moved a few of the half-emptied beer bottles off the concrete stones so they'd have a place to sit.

"So can you really see me up there? Taking walks under the stars, hugging trees and all that." She was looking at him closely again. This time like she was conveying something important and wanted to know if he was getting it. He did get it. He could picture her there. He tried to send as much spark back into her eyes as she was giving out. And with that kind of feeling ricocheting between them, it was hard for him not to believe they would be getting together sometime soon.

The next night, he met her at the Red Vic. The movie was *Microcosmos*, this amazing documentary showing glimpses of the world of the tiny, mostly insects and smaller water creatures. They were in the third row, their legs flung over the seats in front of them, totally absorbed in it, and then these snails started to embrace with the most unbelievably sensuous expressions and sounds, and they pulled in their legs, grabbed for each other's hands in the dark. She said, "Oh God," and he said, at the same time, "Oh my God." It was so intense it blew right past all the usual suspects: tricked-out effects, the conspiracy of camera angles and weepy violins. There was something so passionate in the embrace. Something so human . . . even more than that, it was . . . snails, for Christ's sake.

Afterward, they walked around the Haight, swapping their favorite scenes from the flick, although neither of them mentioned the snails again. She showed him the place where she worked, and then said she was ready to go home. When he offered her a ride, she told him she'd been counting on it.

He gave himself a nice pat on the back for having purchased an extra helmet for the occasion, but when they got back to the bike, she didn't want any part of it.

"I can't put that on," she insisted.

"Why not?"

"Because I'll get claustrophobic."

"Yeah, but there's a law here."

"Is there? Well, seeing as we're not breaking any other ones at the moment . . ."

He hadn't expected this and needed a minute to think it over, so he bent down and began to examine the wear on his tire. Back in New Mexico, he wasn't required to use a helmet, which left him to make the decision based on any number of factors: the length of the trip he was taking, where he was taking it, weather, mood. Ren said the choice was really between whether you wanted an open or a closed casket, but regardless of the amount of truth in that, he'd never taken on a passenger without one. If he told her that, though, she'd probably want to take the bus back home or try to find a cab. And then if he insisted no, he'd make an exception, she'd see how quick he could be to break his own rules.

Fortunately, Carrie had a suggestion.

"How about this?" she said, pulling the scarf from her neck while Jack looked on, explanation pending, as she proceeded to re-wrap it around her head like a turban. "This will keep the hair out of my eyes, at least."

"Which is the main reason people use helmets."

"Now, there's no reason to be sarcastic."

She looked endearingly absurd with the scarf bulging out in various places, clumps of her hair poking through the bottom. He certainly couldn't accuse her of being unwilling to make a fashion sacrifice.

"Aw, hell," he relented, "that'll work," re-locking the helmet onto the back of the seat. He thought about not using his, either; he sure didn't want to be the only one protected in the event of an accident. Plus, it had been more than a few times cruising around that he felt so stifled, he just wanted to rip the thing off. But then he decided he didn't want either one of them to have to crap around with trying to hold onto it. Besides, maybe with her hood of hair, in the dark, they'd pass for legit if no one was looking too close.

He got on the bike and started the engine. She got on behind him, and they took off down the street. Within no time, it was feeling like everything he'd imagined, having her there with him, arms, legs holding tight, her chest pressed into his back. He was torn between getting back to her place as quickly as possible, and staying out half the night, but he kept up with her directions until just after they'd crossed Cesar Chavez, deep in the Mission. That's when they got pulled over.

"Damn."

Carrie just laughed. "I so don't feel like we're doing anything wrong right now."

Maybe not. But he'd heard the fine for not wearing a helmet was stiff. Plus, he'd managed to finagle a California plate and registration without ever following through on switching his New Mexico driver's license. He'd just pulled out his wallet, trying to remember what story he'd come up with to explain the mismatch, when a flashlight shone onto them, then into his eyes, where the cop held it for a moment before dropping the beam to the ground.

"Everything going all right tonight?"

"Fine," Jack told him.

"Do you know how fast I clocked you going through that intersection?"

"No, I don't."

"Two miles under the speed limit. But I'm sure you realize that's no guarantee for your safety, and I see that your lady friend here isn't wearing a helmet. Now, I'm sure you wouldn't be very happy if something happened to her, would you?"

"Of course not, but—"

"Officer, can I show you something?" Carrie had already begun to unwind her scarf. Popping out all that wild hair of hers, which she proceeded to shake. For emphasis, she explained later, when they were rehashing the evening. "Now, Jack, could you please take off your helmet."

His instinct was to make eye contact with the cop to try to somehow convey his innocence in this current enterprise, but he realized he'd be consorting with the enemy, so he just followed instructions, undoing his chin strap and removing the helmet. "Do you see this?" she said, scruffing the back of his buzz cut. "And do you see this?" she said, gesturing toward the cop's head.

The officer hadn't changed his expression, which was none at all.

Then, somehow deciding she hadn't gone quite far enough, she stood up, and not only touched the cop's hair, but ran her hand through it. Jack squirmed, envisioning the assault charges that were likely being added to their list of offenses.

Carrie continued. "Now you can see my friend here was thoughtful enough to bring me a helmet"—she pointed at exhibit A— "but honestly, officer, to try to get all this hair into the confines of that tiny space . . . it's simply too much."

Jack waited, along with the officer, to see if there would be more, but Carrie sat back down and was apparently resting her case. Nobody said a word for at least ten seconds. It was all up to the cop, now, who was either too pissed to speak, too confused, or mulling over the best way to ask for her number.

"All right," he said, finally, "this is going to be a verbal warning. Lady's walking from here, though. Unless you can get her to put that helmet on." He walked back to his car without even asking for Jack's paperwork. "Don't let there be a next time, folks."

Carrie squeezed his side, then jumped off. "Come on," she said, waving the scarf at him.

It turned out they were only a few blocks from her apartment. He found a space in front, parked the bike and followed her inside. In the elevator, he counted aloud with each passing floor, and at the door he leaned into her playfully while she was trying to open it. So that when she turned the key and the lock clicked, they both fell through, down onto the floor, where they stayed for a good while.

When he woke up, he found himself alone. Glad to be there but feeling a little off at being the one left in bed. So he got right up, wrapped the comforter around him, and went looking for her.

She wasn't in the bathroom. And it didn't seem like there were too many other places she could be unless it was under one of the massive piles of clothes scattered on her floor. He actually stuck his toes into one of them on the way by, but ended up finding her outside her window, on the fire escape, smoking.

"Hey."

"Hey," she said, like he'd just walked up off the street.

"Everything all right?"

Carrie sighed, "I don't want you to take this personally, but I think you ought to know that sex generally disgusts me."

"Oh, yeah?" He nodded, letting that sink in. It seemed this hadn't been an exception.

"Did you want a cigarette?" She held out the pack.

He knocked one out, lit up thinking, *what the hell happened?* He didn't get it.

Carrie touched him on the shoulder. "Don't feel bad. It's not you that disgusts me. Really. It's just that I expected . . . I don't know what I expected. Look, why don't you finish your cigarette and come back to bed." Then she ran her finger provocatively down through the comforter and slid back inside the window.

Well, there wasn't much point whining about what a puzzle she was. Presumably, that was one of the reasons why he was there, to try to solve it. So he moved on to a review of his moves in an effort to figure out where he might have gone wrong. It was weird to think something that had felt so good at the time was subject to further interpretation, but some was obviously required.

One by one, he allowed the more awkward moments to filter in. The way she'd never let him touch her face for too long, his hands pulled away from their caressing. The way his kisses, too, had been reined in with her tongue, never let to wander far from her mouth. He'd caught a taste or two of her makeup—vaguely noting it as bitter—but he couldn't have cared less, that was the whole thing, he didn't care how much makeup she had on, or where it ended up, and he didn't see why she would have cared either.

But she had. She'd been trying to protect it, somehow. And that's when he realized he'd made pretty much the only mistake you can make during sex and that was to not pay enough attention when the other person is trying to make clear they don't like something. He hoped it wasn't too late to show her he'd gotten the message.

For the next couple of weeks, he mostly stayed over at her place. Dropping her off at work, picking her up again on the nights he wasn't working himself. They had a couple of late dinners out, he showed her where he lived, but mostly they hung out in her apartment where they'd painted the bedroom purple together. She didn't seem to be using, and even though she was less larger than life when she woke up next to him in the morning, calmer, softer at the end of the day, he liked it just fine. He was just never sure she did.

He knew she'd spent a year in college, a year in rehab, and a year in Nicaragua before coming back to the city, but when she originally told him, it had sounded like a line. Now he learned what she'd been doing in that country—teaching English in the village where her mother grew up—and how much it meant to her. She didn't say a lot about her American father, but it was clear something was wrong—possibly very wrong—there, and that she'd been happy to get away from him and into the welcoming arms of her mother's extended family. They fought over whose table she'd sit at for meals. They poured compliments on her for the way she'd connected with the children. Carrie said it didn't even feel like she was trying very hard. Still, they continued to follow her around both during and after school. Coaxed her to play tag with them at dusk. The morning she left, they ran after the bus shouting her name.

The night Carrie told him all this was the night Jack thought there might really be something between them. But then it became the night she announced there'd be no more fucking. It couldn't have been more than a twenty-minute turnaround, with him drifting off to sleep, vaguely aware she was getting increasingly restless beside him.

"*Everyone* wants to have sex with me, Jack. But you're the only one who's ever written me poems. And you haven't written any since I've been back."

He sat up. "Uh, I can fix that real quick." Carrie rolled her eyes. "No, seriously, I've had one here on the tip of my tongue, I don't know why I didn't bother to write it down." If he'd realized the gravity of the situation, he would have taken a moment to lament his utter lack of skill at improv, but he barreled ahead like nothing was really on the line.

"Okay, here goes. Roses are red . . ."

"This is no reason to embarrass either one of us."

"No, wait, listen. Roses are red, violets are blue, please don't kick me out of your bed. No wait, violets are blue, roses are red, please—"

"You're cute," she said. "But you're going to have to stay cute over on your side of the mattress if you want to keep staying over, because no more of this spumoni for you."

Jack hoped she wasn't serious, but later that night she made it clear she was done messing around. With the door to her apartment building shutting behind him, he wondered if he'd ever hear from her again.

2:04

The rings are becoming more distant, blurred together, so I hang up the phone. Reach into my jacket for a cigarette. There are three of them left.

If you're gonna quit smoking, you've gotta have strategies.

Keep a pack handy to help build your resistance. Only smoke at night. After meals or instead of them. Have a couple when you're drinking. Weekends. Not because you're bored or angry or upset about something.

I try to focus as I inhale. The way this bartender told me to do, making sure I'm aware every time I breathe in the smoke. Make the most of every cigarette, he said, and you'll smoke less. It made a certain amount of sense at the time.

I take a last drag, then crush the filter under my boot. My body's starting to feel heavy, so I take a seat. Lean back against the base of the phone and wait.

There'd been no word from her for nearly a month, but there she was, non-stop with the buzzer, then bursting through his door like she'd been trapped outside for hours.

"Are you *crazy*?" she said, "Why are you sleeping?"

"Because the sun's not up yet?"

She shook her head, dismissing the possibility outright.

He tried again. "Because I'm not on whatever you're on."

"Oh. That's true. You could be, you know." She started rummaging through her bag. "Look, at this!" she exclaimed, and pulled out a super-twisted drinking straw. It snaked up around a plastic eyeball—a bulging bright blue pupil that exploded into red blood vessels. The eye spun wackily when she waved it. "Can you believe this?"

"Pretty neat," he said, expressing about as much genuine enthusiasm as he felt was possible toward a straw.

"Do you realize how much money could be made off these? Hawking them down at The Rexx. I could take around a bunch on a tray, you know, strap 'em to my chest like a Peachy Puff girl." She shoved her tits toward him like they were something she was carrying, not her. "Automatic sale," she said.

He fumbled around the mattress for the smokes. "So where'd you get it?"

"Taco Bell." She motioned for a cigarette. "You know Sebastian's a manager down there. I already talked to him and he said he's willing to pull out all the eyeballs from the Happy Taco Meals and sell them to us for next to nothing."

"I didn't think there was an us."

"We're still friends, you dope. I thought you'd be finished being pouty by now."

He considered it for a moment. He was finished being pouty, yes? Hadn't he heard everything he needed to hear? "Okay, well, I still don't see my part in this plan."

"Investment, of course. This is a prime financial opportunity."

After leaving her apartment that last night together, he'd ridden around on the bike, running through all their best moments strung together like some cheesy movie montage, though it hadn't felt cheesy at the time. He hadn't been able to shake the feeling that he'd lost something important, and by the time he pulled up in front of his place, he'd only become more convinced he wouldn't be getting it back. But it didn't take much more than some solid sleep for him to realize that he'd swapped out the big picture for a bunch of smaller ones, and the big picture was that he'd put a decent amount of effort into trying to make things go well and it hadn't paid off. He'd even tried cooking—once—although she'd never seen the results of that little experiment. Maybe someone else could've pulled it off, but he couldn't seem to make up for the lack of drug-taking, and even though he never got the sense she was craving anything, it was probably still too many flat notes for her, coming from an instrument that was used to being tightly tuned.

Time had slowed when they were together. It had slowed even further when they were apart, with the days' edges increasingly dulled and his nights off spent reading, the occasional times he ventured out less out of curiosity than a lack of better options. Pride would have continued to keep him off her doorstep, but when she came to his, underlined the fact she wanted to stay friends, Jack had become persuaded—maybe as much as Carrie—that he was ready for them to speed up again.

She started calling him, dropping by whenever she felt like it. He never reached out to her because he didn't feel like he needed to—things seemed good between them and he was already getting more socialization than he required. It wasn't like he hadn't gone out to clubs in New Mexico, but things tended to be quiet earlier in the week, and what struck him here were the hordes of people waiting on the other side of the curtain Monday and Tuesday nights. Didn't these people have jobs? Or maybe they had hours like his and had just repositioned their weekends. Whatever the case, Carrie always knew where to find them. Moving through lines quickly or avoiding them altogether to get beyond the door. She seemed to be on good terms with all the gatekeepers, and recognizing the value in that, Jack had insisted on taking care of the cover. It was pocket change compared to the drinks inside, but he liked this minor, unspoken, settling up of things. So did Carrie. After that first night, she never reached into her purse again, and it didn't take him long to realize she had an interesting relationship with money.

Of course, he'd agreed to finance some of those straw purchases, and of course, he'd never expected to see the money again, but just when he'd all but forgotten about it, she paid him back in full. Plus an extra seven dollars. Funny thing was, he didn't ever see or hear about her selling the straws and he never questioned her about it. That was probably because she said, "Here. You made seven dollars. Don't ask me any questions." Carrie, it turned out, didn't like debts going in either direction. And even though, like pretty much everyone else Jack knew, she never seemed to have enough money, she rarely complained about it. Instead, she tended to help herself to things.

Never quite stealing, she'd pull it out from under you. Offer her a cigarette and she'd end up with the pack. Usually the lighter too. "Don't act like this is precious merchandise, Jack, you can get more at the store." Food on the counter was vulnerable, food in the fridge, T shirts, boxer shorts, candlestick holders, everything overstuffed into her monster bag and she'd be out the door. To go shopping or to go to work, although with her it was sometimes hard to tell the difference between the two.

Carrie bought and sold clothing for Seconds in the Haight, where she would have done well if she didn't take out half her pay in used fashions, which continued to pile up in her apartment: nine times out of ten when you walked in, you couldn't even see the bedroom floor. Carrie also designed her own clothes and Jack got the idea that she must be pretty talented because any time they went out with Carrie wearing something she had made, the opening five minutes of any conversation would be spent with gals and sometimes guys cooing about how amazing she looked. He already knew that. He asked her once if she ever saw any career potential in it for herself, but she'd given him the look she used to remind him he really didn't know her very well. "You'll be sure to know if I ever turn ambitious because I'll move to L.A." It sounded like a threat and he didn't mention it again.

No, as far as he could tell it wasn't drugs that kept her short on cash; she had too many friends willing to help her out in that department. It was the clothes. And it was the makeup. When she explained what she paid for one tiny compact case, Jack was sure she was exaggerating, but then she showed him the sticker. She was obsessed with the stuff, used it to plaster her face morning, noon, and night. It was the olive color of her flesh and it smelled like cement.

One night it took Carrie a full ninety minutes in her bathroom—the sound of products banging on the counter. The sink on and off. On again. Jack couldn't stop himself from knocking on the door a couple of times, asking if she was almost ready. Her only response was a high-pitched humming noise, which he took to mean he was bothering her. He waited awhile before knocking again.

When she came out, he didn't notice anything different from when she'd gone in except she was in a better mood, but it was worth waiting for. She was worth waiting for, even if they weren't having sex anymore.

They were supposed to be meeting some people at Vertigo. Carrie walked into his apartment, took off her coat, and settled down on the floor next to her purse—the one she took with her to go clubbing, not as bulky as her other bag but still plenty big. Then she withdrew a genie-shaped bottle, purple with white lace around it. She explained there was bubble bath inside.

"It's a present," she said, pushing it into Jack's stomach.

"Great," he said, *I only use the shower.*

"Well, aren't you going to try it?"

"Sure."

"I mean now."

"Are you serious?"

She bugged her eyes at him.

"Okay, but I thought we were going out."

"That can wait."

"So you want me to take all my clothes off right now."

"That's up to you. As long as you get in the bath with the bubbles."

He nodded, not quite convinced of the necessity of the operation.

"Trust me, you're going to be transported. The bubbles are enormous, and it smells like a forest. It's beyond. Oh, and you're going to need this." She reached back into her purse.

"I hope you're not fishing for drugs in there."

She looked up at him, seemingly perplexed. "What else would I be looking for?"

"Well, don't you remember . . ."

He could see her spinning her wheels. It bothered him a little that it didn't come to her right away. "Oh, that. You're just never gonna let me live that down, are you?"

It had been months now since she'd walked back into his life and become a semi-permanent fixture in it, but that first morning when she woke him up with the buzzer, he still wasn't sure how things were going to turn out. They'd ended up spending the whole day out together, with him not wanting to miss a single moment with her, and consequently taking every one that had been offered. He'd gone along to Sign of the Psychic, watched her try on a dozen different outfits at Macy's, to a bunch of other places, and still she was thinking they were somehow going to go out that night. When he told her he'd need coffee—a lot of it, and even then he wasn't sure how long he'd last—she made a suggestion. *It's like coffee, only better.* He'd barely hesitated before agreeing to take the bump.

It wasn't immediately obvious he'd made a mistake. But over the course of the evening it began to dawn on him. He found himself overly engaged in the most minute details of conversations, and yet never once feeling even remotely connected to anyone he was talking to. Even Carrie. It was like something icy was running through his veins that wasn't blood. And even though his interest in music had reached a new peak, the one time he caught himself in a mirror at the back of the club, it had taken a moment to recognize the zombie dancing. On the plus side, it had kept him up—Carrie had been the one who said she was done for the night—but the next time he saw her he told her he never wanted to do meth again.

"Anyway, that's not what I brought." Then she produced what appeared to be a joint.

He looked at it.

"Don't tell me you haven't smoked before."

"Yeah, but. . ."

"Then you're all set. I brought a deck of cards to play with. Go ahead, I'll be right here."

He took the joint, figuring he didn't have to make up his mind about using it right away, and brought it into the bathroom where he placed it on the counter along with the bubble bath. Looking at the tub, he wondered if the drain plug even sealed. Well, might as well find out, so he put the stopper in and turned on the water. It seemed to be holding. Then he put down the toilet cover, sat on it, and picked up the joint again.

It had been years since he smoked, since before joining the fire department, but it wasn't like he was being drug tested anymore, and at least he knew what he was getting into with this one. It wasn't that he thought pot was a big deal, but rather that it wasn't a big enough deal for the price you paid when you smoked it: losing track of your thoughts and simply feeling tired. He supposed he could always go home early if he got in a funk. Besides, Carrie had actually brought him something, and he'd begun to question whether he would actually get into the tub unless he was stoned anyway.

Jack lit up and took a hit. He could tell right away it was strong stuff; he'd need to pace himself. Steam was filling the room, making things seem exotic enough, and he watched the tub fill.

His first deep thought was that Carrie had become inseparable from the city itself. A place he'd tried to make his own, before realizing it didn't belong to anyone. The peninsula was barely attached to the rest of the country, and she was like this perfect ambassador for it, beautiful, with hints of something less attractive underneath. Not judgmental—at least about some things—but then again maybe not caring enough. That wasn't necessarily a negative. Caring too much about things could get you in trouble. Which led to his second deep thought and that was that maybe the two of them weren't so different. He tried to think of ways that might and might not be true, but got sidetracked processing the transitive property, by which his having things in common with Carrie meant he had things in common with the city, too. *Interesting.* Except the tub was almost full and he'd forgotten to add the bubbles. *Better let some water out.* Then he wondered if he should read the directions first. *No wait, that was ludicrous.*

He sprinkled out some of the powder and watched the bubbles beginning to form. They were intense smelling, just the way Carrie said they'd be. Like a forest after rain. He let the water run until foam had risen above the sides, and then slid out of his clothes. It took a while to get situated, but once he'd sunk in and closed his eyes, he didn't want to leave. Who would've guessed what a great asset the tub would be? As far as he was concerned, he was on vacation, and didn't know when he'd be getting back. "Hold all my calls, please," he yelled, to no one in particular. *Wow, maybe I shouldn't have taken that last hit.*

Carrie came in, all excited. "It's great, isn't it."

"So great."

"I told you. Now we have to go."

"But I've only been in here five minutes."

"Try half an hour."

"No way." He wiped some bubbles from his chin. "Any chance you want to come in?"

"None."

Then she proceeded to grab his arm and drag him up, his feet slipping and scrambling on the tub floor.

"All right. Relax already."

"You see, it's no fun being disturbed when you're in the bathroom and you're on drugs."

He looked at her through a haze, dripping. "Wait. Are you saying this was all some sort of elaborately plotted revenge?" He was pretty stunned at the possibility.

"No, no, no, no. No. I came over here tonight with nothing more than the thought of your prospective pleasure at taking a bath. Now I'm very happy to see that you've had a good time, but we've got to go."

It was a toss-up, but he believed her.

Carrie smoked the rest of the joint while he dressed. They decided to skip going to Vertigo. Instead, they headed straight for Release, a seven-block walk that she managed to turn into an hour expedition. It seemed like every dumpster had a snag of potentially valuable furniture sticking out, so they kept stopping to investigate, diving in if it looked really good. Carrie jumped out of one toting a gigantic curvy green lamp, and from nowhere a shopping cart appeared. It just rolled right up next to them, there was no one even close by. Carrie was so happy, she screamed. Hugged the lamp, then put it in the cart. She pushed it along, piling in more items as they went, before abandoning the whole project in an alley behind Market.

And still it continued to happen around her.

Crossing Natoma, two guys in hoodies approached them. Jack pulled his hands from his pockets expecting trouble, and then felt like a jerk in about two seconds when they started to sing to Carrie. "Unforgettable." In harmony. In the middle of the Mission. One verse after another, they followed behind them the rest of the way to the club. Carrie giggled smoke out through her nose and gave each of them a cigarette before stepping inside.

Downstairs, where the ceiling was too low, all he did was smile at some guy, but that was it, she was already making introductions. After a few minutes of cordial chat, the guy excused himself to get another drink.

"You mind telling me what that was all about?"

"I was just thinking you don't seem to have any male friends here."

"I don't really have any friends here period, besides you and Bishkey."

"But I think you've got a problem with guys."

"Why?"

"Because the ones I've introduced you to think you're a little standoffish."

"Like who?"

"Like Christophe."

Man, people constantly surprised him. The couple times he'd seen Christophe at the Lumiere, he thought things had been pleasant. "I like Christophe, it's too bad he feels that way."

She shrugged.

"What about you, I barely see you talking to women when we're out. More like tolerating them."

"That's because I've got a problem with women. See? I know."

"I don't think you do. I've always had good guy friends."

"Have you ever slept with any of them?"

"My friends? No."

"Or any guy?"

Even though Carrie knew where he worked, she'd never brought this up before, and he'd been thankful for it. For the fact that it hadn't mattered enough for her to ask.

"I've had a few encounters," he told her.

"And?"

"And I don't think they're going anywhere."

The guy pulled his pocket inside out, shook a pile of condoms onto the floor. "Check it out, I've got tons of them. All colors and styles. There's some lube in there too."

There was something either appealing or annoying about the way the guy had been handling himself since they got back to the apartment. Jack couldn't quite get a grip on it.

"I see you come prepared."

"That's so *you* can cum prepared." The guy laughed. Jack liked it better at the bar when they were staring more and talking less. It had seemed like such a good connection, but that had been after a couple of beers that were now in danger of wearing off. He looked down at the pile and grabbed one. Neon Magic. The guy grabbed a pack of lube, like they were drawing picks in a card game.

"I'm really glad I met you," he said, catching Jack's eye directly. *Sexy, no doubt about that.*

Jack was a little nervous, but glad, after all, to have him over. He'd waited this long. Obviously, his guest was super safe. He leaned in toward him.

Ten minutes later the guy grunted. Squeezed. Then arched his back, shooting his load up under his chin—*that was impressive*—then stopped moving.

He pushed Jack out of him.

"Did you get off?" he asked, looking at the wall.

Jack was confused. Yeah, it had felt good, but he hadn't cum, no. Wasn't that obvious? He shook his head.

"You wanna lose the rubber, and I'll suck you."

"Uh, no, that's all right."

"Mind if I use your bathroom, then?"

"Go ahead."

Jack pulled off the condom; it sprang from him with too clean a snap. Walked over and tossed it in the trash.

He didn't really know what he should be doing with himself in the meantime. It felt like he was in someone else's apartment. He glanced at his clothes, wondering if he should put them back on. He was tempted to, but that would probably be rude. The guy's clothes were still sitting there. The shower was running. He supposed he should wash up, which he did, using dish soap. Drying himself on the towel, he wondered if the whole thing even happened.

The door to the bathroom opened, and the guy came across the room toward him.

"That was really great," he said, reaching for his pants.

Jack guessed he was leaving. Well, it wasn't as if he'd been expecting him to spend the night. He really hadn't thought it through that far.

Now the guy had his pants on, was reaching for his shirt. Jack was still naked and definitely uncomfortable. He walked over to get his stuff. Put on his underwear, jeans. Then stuffed his hands in his pockets. It didn't seem like there was anything else to do but watch him dress. Even though he could see the guy was proceeding as quickly as possible, it still seemed to be taking forever. Finally, the double knot on the last sneaker was tied. He stood up.

"That was really great," he said again.

Jack nodded. Extended his hand.

It was knocked with a fist. "Catch you around."

"Yeah, take care."

Jack followed him to the door, then closed it behind him. Turning around, he surveyed the apartment. Stray packets of condoms and lube remained scattered on the floor. He went over and began to collect them in his hand. Then took them into the kitchen, where he shoved them into the back of one of the drawers.

Trying to fall asleep that night, he could still smell the guy on the sheets. He figured it would be a while before he'd bring anyone back to the apartment again.

2:15

There's a squad car crawling along the outskirts of the park. Could be trouble but probably not. I should just wait and see what . . . yup, he's stopping. I give a quick wave but the driver's motioning me over. Better go and see what he wants.

The cop's an older guy. Weathered, square face. "The park's closed," he says.

That, I couldn't care less about. "I'm trying to make a call."

"Looked like you were sleeping to me."

"With my eyes open?"

"All right, I got you. Let's see some I.D."

I fumble for my wallet, find my driver's license and thrust it at him. Such bullshit.

"New Mexico, huh?"

"Yeah."

"What are you doing here?"

"Visiting. Look, am I breaking any laws right now because I'd appreciate it if—"

"Why don't you sit tight while I run this through the computer."

I stand there, looking around at nothing. I suppose I'd been half hoping I'd piss him off enough to get myself hauled in. Just to have someplace to go. But it wasn't worth it. Now, I wish he'd just get on his way.

There's some chatter on the radio, a brief exchange. He turns his attention back to me.

"Looks like you got some outstanding violations." I nod. "On a motorcycle with a California registration. Seems like you've been visiting for quite a while."

It's maddening having a complete stranger know so much about me. So much access, so quick.

"Yeah, well I stayed a little longer than I was anticipating."

"Where's the bike?"

"I don't have it anymore. It's already been impounded. In the shop. If I could afford to get it out, I wouldn't be stuck here right now." The cop sighs. "Look, I know you've heard it all before, but there was a mix up tonight, and I'm having a hard time getting hold of my friend where I'm supposed to be staying. I'm really trying to get myself together to leave here and . . ." I listen to myself rambling, realize I don't want to hear any more of my excuses either. When he stares at me, I don't look away.

"All right, here you go. Don't suppose I need to be writing you up for having a bad night." He hands me back the license. "You need a ride somewhere?" He chuckles. "Besides New Mexico, I don't think I could take you that far."

"No," I tell him, thinking how easy I've had it with the police. "Thanks, though."

"Make sure you pay those tickets up before you leave town. They just keep getting more expensive, you know."

"Yeah, I know. I will."

I walk back toward the phone, a mixture of gratitude and anger for feeling it. As if another human being could really pardon my actions. Like when I'd go to confession, and any relief I might have gotten never lasted for very long afterward. Still, I seem to keep going. Explaining myself to the next person with authority, having already lost most of my own.

I look over my shoulder. The strobes still flashing, silent. The glisten in the pavement washes over red, then blue.

Even if it was the streets. The way they came at you, in waves. Like the Pacific had swept across the city from the Sunset to Mission Bay, rippling the pavement, leaving the traffic sounds to skip along the crests, or become lost in the undertow. Even if it was the wild bends in the streets, or how narrow they could get, with the wind coming through sharp, whistling your ears full. Even if it was all these things, it still didn't seem like enough to explain how many near wrecks he'd been in lately. And it definitely didn't account for how many of them had been with fire department vehicles.

Two ladder trucks and an ambulance.

After the first time, he hadn't thought much about it. It hadn't been that close a call. Nor had the second, but by then he was already trying to find some further justification. Reminding himself that sirens were particularly susceptible to distortion. You would hear them growing louder, but without any corresponding sense of where they were coming from, never certain if they'd be crossing your path. More false alarms than not, and with the high volume of emergency traffic that traversed the small peninsula, it was hardly practical to stop every time you heard one.

The last time had been the worst. Racing toward the bottom of Portola where he'd caught the sound of the siren late. Too late to come to a complete stop, to any kind of stop at all he realized, once he'd gotten closer—the engine turning onto Market blocking his descent, oncoming traffic holding on the left, the green light in front of him meaningless. His only chance was to make the sharp turn onto Castro. He tried to take off as much speed as he could without locking the brake, then waited till the last possible moment, one final tamp down, before veering off. Still, the turn was too tight for the momentum of the bike, and he lost the cut about three quarters of the way through, skidding into the side of a Volkswagen bus in the far lane, bounced off it, straightened up, and then held on till he was able to bring it to a rest, a few hundred feet down the road. *Holy shit.* He looked behind him, the engine gone from sight, the VW turning the corner. On the sidewalk, a few of the pedestrians were expressing their disapproval. He squeezed his eyes.

Three times. It was beyond coincidence at this point. It had been an easy read right along, actually, if he'd only bothered to look. Flip through the calendar and there it was. In little more than a month it would be May, when they'd be making their first selections for the new recruiting class back in Santa Fe. Until then, Jack was still on an unofficial leave of absence. A kind of charm he'd kept with him since he shook hands with the chief the last day, one which he could take out and rub any time he wanted to wish himself back to his old life. But for the most part, Jack had been trying to forget it was there, hoping the deadline would hurry along and pass. To put out of his reach, once and for all, the ability to change what remained a potentially bad decision.

It was as if all his misgivings about leaving had gathered themselves together and were mounting a final blitz—somehow coordinated with local traffic patterns—to make sure he was alert to the fact that time was running out, and he had better make sure he knew what he was doing. Well, he didn't know what he was doing, really. Wasn't following some well-thought-out plan. Maybe it was time to face up to the situation. To go over things one more time, and either get behind his decision, or admit he'd made a mistake and try to fix it before it was too late. He dropped the bike into gear.

Coit Tower was allegedly the city's monument to firefighters. He'd seen it from hundreds of angles at a distance, and as he drew closer, curving Lombard under the shade of the overhanging trees, he was certain he was headed to the right place. But when he reached the top, the parking lot was mobbed, tourists grouped by nationality. He looked among them for some plaque, some statue, something. Talking to the vendor outside, he learned the real memorial was over in Washington Square park. He got the directions, but his mind had been set on this place, and eventually he found a nice spread of grass behind the tower that was mostly empty. He settled in there.

It was amazing how quickly things had changed. He'd finished up his departure interview, walked out of city hall, and then it was over. He was nothing but a guy with a bunch of paperwork in his hand and a line for his resume. One that stood out as a potential liability, the fact that he had left seeming more important than his holding the job in the first place. How different it was from that first morning on shift, on his way into the station, knowing he was a rook, but he didn't care, he could hardly wait. He glanced at the clock and realized he was far too early, so he decided to stop for some coffee. Then, standing at the checkout—the uniform scratching new, but still feeling like his own— the lady behind the counter wanted to comp him. And he realized she didn't know one single thing about him, how green he was, whether he was last week's hero or last week's goat. Nothing except that he was dressed and ready to go to work, and that was enough for her to say thank you. And now, after he'd fought fires and dropped IV lines and airways, helped to save lives, it felt further away from him than that first morning when he hadn't done anything besides order a coffee.

He'd been on the med that night, just a few months on the street. Cruz was driving, on the way back from the hospital, when the call came in: shooting on the east side. So it was bullets on his brain the whole way over. Running through his possibles, protocol on puncture wounds, remember to check for an exit, oh yeah, make sure the scene was secure before he did anything; well, Cruz would make the final decision on that.

Pulled up and right away he could tell it was going to be crazy. Neighbors gathering, someone was yelling, not sure if the gunman was still around, they staged on the street. PD was fresh on the scene, they were signaling them down, no wait, another two officers were there already, talking to a guy in the driveway, one of them holding a rifle. He grabbed his medic bag, oxygen, still not knowing where the patient was. Cruz was going over to talk with PD. There was a truck on the lawn–*damn!*—the truck had crashed into the house, into the adobe, cracked it, he was moving quick across the lawn, there was a guy half in, half out of the truck, torso through the driver's window, waving, throwing his hands away from himself, trying to disperse the crowd. "Everyone go home. Everyone get your asses home."

Jack reached the vehicle. There was blood running down the guy's face. "Hey, take it easy, man."

"Who the fuck are you?"

"Sir, you need to settle down, you've been in an accident."

"Who the fuck are you?"

The windshield's cracked, he's gotta stop moving around. "Sir, you've got to stop moving around. It looks like you knocked your head. You're bleeding."

Cruz was beside him. "There was no shooting. Did you get the O$_2$?"

"Got it."

"Hey chief, it's Cruz."

"Who?" The guy squinted his eyes. "Hey Cruz, Cruzer, what are you doing here?"

"I was just about to ask you the same question."

"Cruzer, someone's trying to kill me. I'm driving along and some guy starts taking shots at me."

"Chief, look around you, man, you just drove into his house."

"Wha–?" He looked around. "Oh, God." He slid back into his seat. "What a mess. What a shitting mess."

Cruz put his hand on the guy's shoulder. "So you had a few tonight."

The guy held up some fingers. "Only two."

"All right, let's get a look at you. Let Jack here work with you. Jack, meet my old Battalion Chief, Chief Collins."

"Who's this guy?" Collins asked.

"Rook."

"Rook, huh?"

"He hasn't killed anyone yet," Cruz smiled.

"Great."

"Sir, I just need to get this collar on you."

"Oh, not fucking c-spine. Not that piece of shit. My head's fine, I can't feel a thing."

Cruz's voice got dead serious right then. "Chief, you know how lucky you are no one got hurt. Now relax, and let's get through this."

Going to put on the collar, Jack noticed the empty passenger seat; he'd forgotten to look around for anyone else, maybe someone crawled away. "Sir, were you alone tonight?"

"Of course, I'm alone, can't you see that?"

"Relax," Cruz said again.

And then the guys from the engine were there. Ricky getting into the back of the cab to hold c-spine, Rodriguez talking to Collins. "You want me to call your wife?"

"Negative."

"Right."

Jack opened the medic bag, took out the blood pressure cuff, and when he looked up again the whole scene was starting to color in around him, people's voices no longer disembodied, PD directing the neighbors back to their homes. With the background quieted, he could hear the blood rush out from under the cuff. His vitals were looking good, pupils equal and reactive to light.

Cruz gave him the once over. It seemed like he'd just hit his head on the steering column, not the windshield. He should still be going into the hospital, though. "You know we gotta take you in, right?"

Collins seemed resigned to it, disappearing into his own thoughts. Jack helped Pete and Ricky load him onto the gurney, then followed them down to the med where Cruz was waiting. "Fuck, man, the owner was watching TV with his girlfriend when the truck plowed into the living room wall. Scared the shit out of him. He came out firing shots in the air, didn't know what the hell was going on."

Jack looked back at the house again, shook his head. It was hard to believe even with the remains of the scene still around them. Then he hopped in the back with the former Battalion Chief and the door closed. According to what Cruz said later, he'd been an ace BC.

In the med, neither of them said much except to trade question and answer for medical history, drug allergies. Jack took another round of vitals. Then, as he got up to call in his report to the hospital, Collins grabbed him on the arm.

"Listen to me."

"Sir, you've got to watch that cannula." Jack attempted to readjust the nose piece.

"Fuck the cannula, you're not listening."

"Yes, sir."

"Don't ever retire, you understand me?" And then he squeezed Jack's arm tight against the bone.

Jack smiled uneasily. "I don't think I've got to worry about that anytime soon."

"Right," he said. "Right." Then he patted him on the arm. Looked up at the ceiling and closed his eyes. "Keep up the good work."

He still felt like a sell-out for even mentioning it. They'd asked, sure, but he could've said he'd been a dishwasher during college or bartended right after it. He could've told them he'd driven cab. To shore up his rookie pay while better learning the streets in Santa Fe, although he wouldn't have had to explain his reasons. He could have made something up. When the interview consisted of him stripping down to his underwear and turning around a couple of times, it wasn't like they were going to be checking his references. Still, they'd asked what he'd been up to and he told them, figuring it wouldn't hurt his prospects, knowing full well he couldn't dance for shit. Because he wanted the work. The money and the hours. The ability to look in on a world he was trying to understand. He told them and he'd gotten hired, without ever stopping to think that when you use something to help you open the door, you don't always get to drop it when you walk into the room.

He'd done his best to tune it out. The commentary, a seemingly endless parade of badly punned descriptors about him that ran the range from hot to smokin', with nothing better in between. "Let's hear it for everyone's favorite firefighter"—*not everyone's, not a firefighter*. The closest he came to battling a blaze these days was trying to put out the cigarettes he'd become increasingly fond of; a once occasional vice that had begun to smell a lot like a habit.

Still, that's how things continued to go. And what was he supposed to do? It was too late to take back what he'd said. He tolerated the job all right, the money was good. He'd learned how to adapt to the situation—to the crowds—offering the minimal amount of interaction required. But then, after about a month of work, he'd gotten called into the manager's office. Late one night after the club had closed.

"So, how's everything going for you, Jack?"

"Fine, thanks, Tony. What's up?"

"Well, we were just talking, and you know what we thought would make you more of a draw—you'd make more tips for yourself, too, naturally—is if you'd wear this." Then he turned around in his chair and spun back with a fireman's helmet in his hand—brand new, definitely the real deal. "You know, just some nights, but we think it would be fun."

Jack would like to have said he couldn't believe it, but he could. There was no way.

"I can't wear that. I'm sorry."

Tony didn't try to disguise his anger. "Well, of course, you can wear it. It's just a hat."

"Look, it's been hard enough with the introductions you guys make for me. I'm not a firefighter anymore. I haven't been one since the last fire I fought, can't you understand that?"

"Well, you're not a baseball player either, but I noticed you wore a Mets cap tonight."

"Come on, that's not the same thing." *Why was he even bothering to argue with him?* He looked over to the assistant manager, Sid, for some help, but he was busy with a calculator and paperwork at his desk. "I can't do it, Tony."

"Do you know it wasn't easy to get hold of this. I had to pull some strings, and the whole time we were thinking how much you'd like it. This was supposed to be a surprise."

It was everything he could do not to rip the helmet out of Tony's hand and knock him with it. Right in the chest, he'd like to hear some air gasp out of the guy. Instead, he looked down at the floor.

"It's your job, Jack, do you want it or not?"

"No, I guess I don't then." And he'd walked out of the office, back to the lockers to clear out his stuff. The tiny room was empty, everyone else had gone home. He slammed one of the lockers with his fist. Felt some satisfaction in the wildly echoing reverberation. So he hit it again. He was just starting to turn the numbers of his combo when Sid walked in. Jack nodded at him.

"I just want you to know I'm very sorry about all that. We should have talked to you first. I should have spoken up. I had a feeling it was . . . not such a good idea."

"Don't worry about it. It's not worth going over the whole thing again, really." It was hard having Sid there in such close proximity to the rawness of his feelings. Sid, who'd been such a good guy to him. He was beginning to think maybe he'd overreacted, trying to protect something that probably wasn't even his to protect anymore. He had rent to pay. That was serious. And here he was making a big deal about having to wear a stupid hat, when everything else could be such a game. Even at the department, some days.

"There's no need to clear out your things. I talked with Tony and we'd like to keep you on. It's been good up to now. We don't think there's any reason to change that."

Jack looked at Sid. He seemed nothing but sincere.

"As far as we're concerned this never happened." He held out his hand for Jack to shake. "I hope you can put it aside, too."

Placing his hand into Sid's, Jack didn't feel like he was sealing a victory or a defeat, just acknowledging the way things had fallen out at the end of a long night.

"Forgotten," he agreed.

"Good. Oh, and one more thing. Tony said to tell you to try to be on time from now on. Actually, he said for you to *be* on time, but I told him I was sure you'd make the effort."

He'd left for Station 1 later than he had on any of the previous shifts, but still thinking there'd be no problem getting there by eight. What he hadn't counted on was the exponential jump in traffic during the extra ten minutes he'd taken, and he arrived at the station two minutes after. It was non-stop for the rest of the day.

"Rook thinks he can come in when he wants."

"Enjoyin' the old lady and couldn't tear yourself away. You can bring her down here with you, homie, we like her, we're all friendly."

"Hey, lay off him, man, you can see the guy needs his beauty sleep."

Jack figured he was too green to be throwing back lines after a slip-up, that his standard excuse—"I'm eventual, not punctual"—wouldn't fly there. So he just nodded and took it. All through the morning, then into the afternoon when, just sitting down to lunch, the buzzer had gone off for a seizure on the plaza.

"Hey, Rook, you look hungry, why don't you eat first. You can meet us at the scene a little later if you want."

"A few minutes won't make a difference, don't worry about it."

Fucking relentless, he thought. And it stayed that way till late that night, returning from a cancel with Cruz.

"So how long do you think it'll be before I stop getting shit for being late?"

"You mean if it doesn't happen again anytime soon?"

"Right."

"By the start of next tour, probably," he laughed. "Someone's bound to screw up something more interesting than that between now and then. You're not gonna get to keep the limelight for long."

"Uh-huh."

"Don't let it get to you too much. It happens. But seriously, being on time's one of the simplest things you can do to make things go smooth around here. And being early's better. After twenty-four everyone's burnt, and you'll see how many calls come in at quarter of, ten of, right at the changeover like clockwork. It's much better if you can send out someone fresh."

That was the last time Jack had been late. He'd had things put in perspective for him, realizing that when people show their disappointment in you by making jokes about it, they make sure you don't forget, while reserving the space you need to be hardest on yourself. Keeping things light, so there wasn't an awkward transition when you were ready to get back on board.

At the department, there was little that couldn't be laughed at and it usually was. The anything-but-practical jokes he'd taken part in and fallen for. From his first day, given instructions to go down and check the med, when every electrical device had been set up to come on with the turn of the key, until near the end, when four of the guys had managed to pick up and move his motorcycle from its parking place, Jack finding it missing, running back up the stairs, *who the hell would steal a motorcycle from the fire department?*, phoning up and explaining everything to dispatch, the woman there finally breaking the joke.

He'd been out at Mezzanine, standing by the bar, when the kid next to him had collapsed onto the floor. The people nearby didn't seem to notice for the most part, and he had to look down twice to make sure it had happened. The guy was still lying there. "Hey, man, are you all right?" He bent down. "Hey." He touched him on the shoulder. No response. Eyes stayed shut. He could feel a nauseous lurch inside him, the shift in gears to one rusty with lack of use. He yelled over to the bartender, "Call 911!" and then took a breath and threw himself into it. *Watch the head.* He got the kid's neck between his legs, held it there. *O.D.? Diabetic?* Leaned in; he was breathing. Fast, but good breaths. The smell of alcohol. His pulse strong and regular at the radius. *What was going on?* Shit, he should've asked someone to help him. He looked up. There were people making a sort of half circle around them now. "Anyone know this guy? Anyone know if this guy has some kind of condition." He heard someone snicker, no one said anything. "All right, you. Yeah, you. Can you get down here and hold him like I'm holding him? Right, just keep his head steady, don't let it move, *I need to take a look . . .*" He was just getting ready to palpate the body, head to toe, when the kid opened his eyes. Smiled. "Hey, aren't you gonna give me mouth-to-mouth?"

What? "Are you okay?" *What was he saying?* Then he heard a couple people above, laughing. "Steve, you can't even get a kiss to save your life." He looked back and forth between the faces. "Why don't you ever strip for us here, Mr. Fireman?" Then he began to get a sense of what happened. What he deserved, really, for forgetting to give the guy a good hard pinch on the shoulder to further determine level of consciousness. If he didn't get out of there quickly, he was going to take a swing at someone.

Jack got to his feet and looked down at the guy who probably wasn't more than a couple years younger than himself. "You are seriously messed up, kid. I mean seriously." Then he pushed his way to the door.

What ended up staying with him most about that night, though, was how alone he'd felt as the scene unfolded. It was the first time he'd ever tried to handle something like that without a team in place around him, and he realized how much harder it was without one.

Of course he was biased, but about halfway through his first year, Jack had taken enough overtime around the department to realize he'd been working for one of the best teams. The tone was set by his captain, Rodriguez. It's true there were other captains out there who possessed more technical expertise with either fire or medical. But he'd noticed that sometimes those individuals, while gifted, tended to tunnel into the scene when it was their specialty that was on the line. Suddenly, you had two engineers or two lead paramedics for one crew, causing a breakdown in the chain of command, with no one sure exactly what he was supposed to be doing anymore. Rodriguez could step in if he needed to, and did when the situation warranted it, but his strength lay in his intuitive sense of how to stay out of the way, keeping his eye trained on the entire scene. You could feel his presence without worrying about tripping over him. More than likely, he'd be the one to tell you to watch out, as you hustled down the stairs with a code on the gurney, your mind on everything but where your feet were, that you were just about to stumble over a laundry basket someone had left on the landing.

Rodriguez's personality was tuned to the right key, laid back but on top of it, and it was mirrored in Cruz, Pete the engineer, and the rest of the crew. When fuckups happened—and they were going to happen—that's when it really came into play. A scene starts going to hell, and a blow up by anyone would only lead to more chaos. Maintaining your cool was the best chance you had of getting back on track and minimizing the damage. Anything that needed correction could be talked about later and was.

He missed his crew for other reasons, as well; in the way he missed pretty much everyone in the department—the women in the front office, the guys in fire prevention, the firefighters on other shifts. Even the chief. He'd gotten used to the quality of an extended family that ran through the place. He'd never once considered leaving.

It all started with a couple of the guys getting friendly with a couple of the cashiers down at the grocery store. Pretty soon the ladies were stopping by the station, which seemed harmless enough, but one night one of the wives had walked in at an inopportune moment. She'd raised the expected hell, then stormed out and proceeded to call up the wife or girlfriend of every other guy on shift whose number she could get hold of. Then she'd called the chief. At first, all that happened was the crew was required to use checkout lines with male clerks, which had resulted in a minimal amount of inconvenience and a lot of jokes. But then, a couple weeks later, the word had come down that the team was getting split up. Rodriguez and Cruz gone, each to different stations and shifts, and there was nothing more to be said about it.

It was a tough enough loss as it was, but to compound the problem, Jack clashed with their replacements. The new medic seemed laid back enough, initially, but ramped up fast during even moderately challenging calls, pointing fingers, and making it hard for Jack to keep his concentration. With the medic thinking Jack cut too many corners, they were never going to be able to rely on one another. And the captain, well, he knew his job, you couldn't accuse him of being untalented or lazy, but when it came to everyone else, at least, he was 110% by the book. In a way that lacked heart for a profession that demanded it.

Until then, the only items of interest Jack had in his employee file had been letters of appreciation sent in from locals and visitors who'd been happy with the treatment they'd received from his team. But by the end of his third tour with the new captain, he already had two oral reprimands—both documented—for doing things as he'd always done, but apparently, not in a way that had been spelled out in the regulations manual. And he could see this was only the beginning. The next week, he'd been informed that his hospital reports weren't detailed enough and that his handwriting, while legible, could be better. When that didn't improve to the captain's satisfaction, he'd been told—on a shift when the med had been slammed, ten calls and on his way out the door to the eleventh—that he'd need to redo all his paperwork.

At four o'clock that morning, he finally had a chance to catch up. He sat at the table, alone, remembering how it hadn't been unusual to find Rodriguez up at this hour, pacing the balcony overlooking the park, smoking a cigarette. Sometimes Jack would join him, and they'd talk for a bit. Then the captain would get the coffee started before returning to his room. Jack did his best to work through the reports, trying to keep his eyes open, grumbling to himself how he didn't recall good penmanship as being one of the requirements for the job. By five he had them finished and in the captain's box. Then he went to his bunk and passed out.

Next thing he knew, someone was tapping his ankle. He looked up; the captain was motioning for him to follow him out. "Why don't you get the coffee going," he was told. Jack prepared the brewer, expecting a long discussion, but all the guy had to say to him was that, even though the reports looked better, he'd used red ink. He would have to do them all over again.

Jack's complaints seemed petty when he thought about them now. Even then, he must have had an instinct that he'd just need to develop the maturity required to deal with this different leadership style, because the personnel changes, by themselves, wouldn't have been enough to cause him to leave. There were the guys left over from his old crew he still enjoyed working with. And, as a number of people had pointed out to him, crews switched on a regular basis, and you just had to hang in there until another one came along and clicked.

But while he was trying to be patient, he found himself with more time on his hands to reflect on his career path. Not because the station was any less busy, but because he'd stopped wanting to hang out in living quarters. He'd be around for meals, then disappear down into the bay. Counting and recounting supplies on the med. Rearranging things. Sometimes he'd hang out in the mechanic's office and read his medical manual. Or just stare out the window.

When he'd joined the fire department, all he thought about doing was fighting fire. He hadn't even known they'd run the ambulance service until he'd gone down to the training center to find out more about testing, but he accepted it as an adjunct to the position he was hoping to secure.

But things hadn't turned out as he expected. Of course, he knew that Santa Fe was made, in large part, from adobe, but he'd never considered the fact that adobe didn't have a propensity to burn. Which was great for homeowners, but often made for slow days of smoke and alarm checks on the engine. In the past few years, there'd only been a handful of full-on fires, and there hadn't been anything major in months.

If you discounted the lack of high rises in the city, when fires happened, they could be just as dangerous as in any other town, and you were just as important. For the guys on the trucks, engineers on down, the ones who kept their knowledge on the tips of their fingers, the time between serious calls wasn't an issue, but unfortunately for Jack, his mind didn't work that way. He had a tendency to get sloppy when things were slow. He constantly had to be in the thick of things if he was going to do the kind of job he wanted to do, and that meant he'd found himself, more and more, riding the med. At his station, call volume was the highest in the city, and he'd eventually been able to get in something of a groove. He'd gone on to get his IV tech license and was starting to look ahead to the next year when he had a good chance of being selected for paramedic school.

And yet he'd never wanted to be a doctor.

Though that was the position he'd be mimicking to a degree if he continued to follow the path he was on. With medical procedures continually bumped down the ladder—from the higher to the lesser paid—from the doctors to the physician's assistant, from the physician's assistant to the nurses—it didn't take much to imagine the day when Candy Stripers would be dropping IV lines, and they'd be doing emergency bypass surgery on the med. He'd done well up until that point because he'd been dedicated to his team—not to the ambulance work itself—and without them he was sure his limitations were bound to show up more in patient care.

None of that had changed. Jack had been right about one thing, at least, he didn't miss riding around on an ambulance. But he did miss something. Something that, if he was going to be completely honest with himself, didn't have anything to do with saving lives or any of the other high-minded reasons for why he'd taken the job in the first place.

Every emergency call in the city was broadcast to every station and it was done the same way each time. Before the dispatcher's voice came on explaining the nature of the incident, there were two tones that went out. The first was always the same. It got everyone's attention. That was the lock. The load came with the second tone, the one that told you which station was going to get called out. The highest pitch one went with Jack's, and when he heard it, he could feel the adrenaline rushing in, that instant bump up, even if he was beat tired. Sometimes, multi-station tones went out if it was a particularly bad scene, or, as Jack was always listening for, a fire. But once you heard your tone, you knew you were on. And you would need to stay on from that moment all the way until the call had ended. Usually as a better version of yourself. Present. Focused. With the program. Jack missed that heightened feeling as much as anything else. And he couldn't see from where he was sitting now how he was going to get it back.

The sun had been working its way across the sky, the shadow from the tower long since fallen across him. It was getting late. For the first time since he'd given his notice, he was certain he wasn't going back to his old job, and even though it seemed like the right decision, that still didn't mean he had no hard feelings about it. He'd never really sat with them before—so quick to move on to the next thing—and he decided maybe he ought to sit with them a while longer before worrying about anything else to replace them. He got up and made his way back to his bike. There was one more place he wanted to go.

Company 3 was located near the corner of Post and Polk, just a few blocks from his apartment. It sat between Divas bar and San Francisco Cycles, a motorcycle shop. The station was on his way to the gym, but after passing it a few times, he'd made a point of avoiding the route.

The first time he'd gone by, the bay door had been open. A couple of guys were leaning against the engine, talking, and a couple of ladies were staging a piece of theater directly in front of them. One chasing the other, heels clicking to the concrete, hissing some accusation. Then the other one turning around, hands on her hips, explaining how it wasn't like that at all. Starting to move toward her costar threateningly. Back and forth, probably a half dozen times, all handbags at ten paces, while the guys ignored them or looked on with amusement.

This afternoon the bay door was closed. Jack positioned himself across the street. He'd gone there with the idea that maybe if he said a proper goodbye, he'd be somehow able to prevent further trouble on the road, but as he was trying to put together some final thoughts, he heard high heels approaching.

"Honey, you got a light?"

The woman was over six feet tall, with long legs that led up to the shortest, tightest pair of red shorts he'd ever seen. In most every way, she was managing to look more composed than Jack felt.

"Yeah, sure." He reached into his pocket and offered her the lighter.

"A gentleman generally lights a cigarette for a lady."

"Is that right?" he said, but looking more closely into her eyes he found mostly playfulness, with only a hint of attitude.

"My apologies," he said, and lit the cigarette.

She inhaled deeply.

"They're genuine heroes, you know," she said, nodding toward the station.

"Yeah," he muttered, "heroes."

"At least, that's what people say. As far as I'm concerned, they do enough good filling out their uniforms. If you know what I mean." Jack looked at her again and she batted a thick eyelash. "Yes," she said dreamily, "I can't think of anything better I'd like to do on a clear day than stand here and wait for them to come out."

Then she shook her finger at him.

"Just. Like. You."

"What was that?" He coughed, less from the cloud of perfume and smoke, than from embarrassment. He felt like he couldn't explain his situation fast enough, and then realized he couldn't explain it at all. He might as well play along. "Yeah," he nodded, "I'm hoping they come out soon." Then he bowed his head solemnly to the concrete. He heard her take one more drag.

"Well, I better leave you alone now." Then she goosed him and walked away.

He had to laugh. To himself, at first. And then out loud, harder and harder. "Hey, thanks," he called after her. *Thanks for not letting me take this whole thing too seriously.*

She turned and blew him a kiss.

He'd been foolish to think he could conduct some sort of private ritual in the middle of a heavily congested prostitution zone. And the idea of trying to exorcize the demons of near-collisions-past was clearly over the top. Still, he'd come this far.

It was another twenty minutes before he heard the buzzer go off inside.

There was a small delay before the bay doors opened, and then another before the truck emerged, slowly, with the lights flashing. It hooked the wide turn left, then began to move down the street.

He could feel a pull in his chest as he watched them drive away. Giving a couple blasts of the horn, nosing into the intersection at Van Ness. When the cars cleared, they continued threading their way along Post, finally disappearing over the top of the hill at Franklin. That left only the sound of the siren. It grew fainter, and fainter still, till he could no longer tell it apart from the city traffic.

The first call Jack made turned out to be the shortest—once he'd been able to get Delaney on the line. It wasn't like he believed his former chief had been hanging around waiting to hear from him, but with Ren having told Jack of rumors of his coming back—probably started by Ren himself—Jack wanted Delaney to know from him personally that he definitely wasn't. Delaney told him he appreciated the call, and Jack wished him the best with the new recruiting class.

The call to the ranger station was more complicated, so Jack waited another day before making it. Wildland firefighting should really fit him—it was all fires all the time—and he realized the only way he could accept his not pursuing it now was by telling himself that would only make him more eager to do it in the future. At least, that sounded right in theory. Ren wouldn't have been happy about the delay, but Jack felt like he would have understood his reason. All the hairy situations they'd gotten themselves into off-roading. So many times stuck in the mud, then unstuck, then determined to keep going even though that surely meant getting stuck again. Or that afternoon they'd followed an old logging road up into the mountains, the hairpin turns becoming increasingly treacherous until finally they approached one that looked so undoable that Jack made Ren's dog get out before attempting it. Ren wouldn't get out, of course, it was his truck, but they agreed if they did make it there'd be no more talk of turning back, because that's what you did when you were all in.

Jack knew he hadn't been all in when he'd first come to San Francisco, but having stuck around this long, he was thinking he should stick around a little longer. Nothing so far had felt meaningful enough to justify his being out there, and he was still hoping for something better than a twilight adolescence. And there was always a chance of something better. Toward the end of that day up in the mountains, he and Ren had eventually come across the most pristine little lake, pure snowmelt, and when they'd set up camp, cracked some beers and looked out over it, they'd both agreed it was nothing less than a slice of heaven.

Ren's cousin, Tito, wasn't there, but the district manager had taken his call.

"No, we just got a couple a guys up here now part time, doing some maintenance on the equipment. I'm sure he'll be stopping by in the next week or so, if you want me to pass along a message."

"Yeah, maybe you remember me from last spring. Got my red card with you, but one of your guys ended up coming back for the job. Name's Jack."

"Sure, I remember. You must be calling to find out about work this season."

"Actually—"

"Well, we got it for you. Having a tough time getting our guys through the pack test this year, it's a head scratcher. Maybe everyone had too much holiday cooking and here they are in March still trying to work it off." He laughed. "Of course, we never had pack tests back in my day and we did just fine, but you know how things are now." His voice was warm, decent sounding. One hundred and eighty degrees from his current boss. "So you gonna come down and help us out?"

He'd made it sound so simple. Like Jack could just hop back on the main highway, having made a detour of this past year. It was hard having the possibility back out in front of him again—tangible—and he hesitated.

Then came down hard on the tail of the hesitation, making it jump. "No." Damn it, he'd already made up his mind, free and clear. "No thanks, sir, I appreciate it. I've got other work this year. But I plan to check in with you again for next season, if that'd be all right. I just wanted to let you to know I'm still interested."

"As you like. If I recall, you've got your EMT license. That sure would come in handy around here."

That'll be expiring soon. "Well, like I said, there's a good chance I'll be around next year. Real good. Best of luck to you guys, though."

"We'll be all right."

Jack hung up the phone. He had one more call to make.

2:38

I wish I'd kept in better contact with people from New Mexico. Friends from the fire department. Ren. Jessie.

I wish I was still in touch with Skelly.

The problem is, the longer you wait, the harder it is to pick up the phone. Too many things have happened, you don't know where to begin. I wasn't very consistent about it that first year, and then after that, I really started to lose track.

Their numbers are mostly a blur in my head. Except for Skelly's, she's got an easy one. Unless she changed it. I don't know why she would've.

I press the digits, 1-5-0-5-, but I leave the phone on the hook, knowing I don't have the right to call. At this hour or any other.

"**Jack! I was just thinking** about you."

"Hope it was something nice."

"It was. How are you?"

"Good. Everything's going good, thanks." He wanted to ask how things were with her, but he checked himself, knowing he'd end up inquiring about all the details and avoiding the subject completely. "Listen, Skell, I just spoke with the ranger station, and I wanted to let you know I don't think I'll be coming back."

"They didn't have an opening?"

"No, it seems like they got an opening, but I don't think I'm gonna take it. Not this year, anyway." He waited for her to calibrate a response.

"I'm sure you understand that makes this harder to swallow." Her voice was measured, offering some hope for the rest of the conversation. "Have you thought about why?"

"I don't know. I guess, I feel like I need a little more time here."

"Time for what?"

"Just some time, that's all."

"I see. Are you trying to perfect a particular dance move?"

"Come on, don't be like that." It seemed his hope had been premature. "I'll be back for next spring. I told the guy to keep me in mind, and I'll probably take some refresher courses while I'm here, you know, see if I can keep up my EMT license . . . It's just another year."

"Just another year," she repeated, making it seem like he'd handed down a thoroughly unreasonable sentence. "Do you know how long it's been since we've seen one another?"

"Too long."

"I'm glad to hear you say that," her voice softened, "because I'm really starting to miss you."

Jack wasn't prepared to think about how much he might be missing her. He cleared his throat. "So what would you like to do about it?"

"I was going to ask if you had any plans with the Easter Bunny yet."

"Nothing formal, why?"

"Because I've been tossing around the idea of driving up to see you for break."

"You were? Well, how is it that you knew I was gonna be here?"

"Woman's intuition. Depressing as it is. Let's face it, I wasn't really expecting you to come back. Just hoping."

"Well, let's make it happen, then. When does your vacation start?"

"On the sixteenth. I think. Hold on, let me get my calendar."

Something was bothering him, and he was trying to figure out what. The easiest thing to point to was her driving up. Feeling like there was already enough pressure on the trip with them not having seen each other in so long. Suppose things didn't go smoothly. Then she'd have all those miles to drive back. Alone. All those miles to drive alone no matter what happened, and even if he could picture himself enjoying the solitude of the trip, he wasn't sure how much fun it would be for her. He made some quick budgetary calculations. When she got back on the phone, he offered to buy her a plane ticket.

"That's sweet of you, but I was thinking I might see Yosemite on the way."

"What a cool idea." He'd forgotten how independent she could be.

"You know, if you wanted, you could fly here and drive up with me."

Fly there? Wait, how'd that happen. "Uh, I don't know if I could get that much time off from work."

"Are you sure you're going to have any free time when I get there?"

"Of course. My days are free. Plus, I'm sure I'll be able to get one of my nights off for when you'd be here. I only work three nights, anyway."

"For the whole week?"

"Yeah, the club's only open Wednesday through Saturday." It did sound kind of feeble.

"And that's enough to live on?"

"More or less, yeah. It's not like I'm spending a lot here."

"What a nice schedule."

"Believe me, they're really long nights." Which was more a description of how they felt rather than how many hours they actually were. "I suppose I could arrange it so I could fly out there . . . but that would mean giving up Saturday night, which is when I make most of my money." The fact was he'd just cleared the way for another year in San Francisco and the last thing he wanted to do was leave. "Why don't you give some more thought to flying up."

"No, don't worry about it. Let's both do our own thing. I really hadn't thought about you coming with me till just now."

"You sure?"

"Positive. Just so long as I get to see you shaking that booty of yours up on stage."

"Did you just say booty?"

"Isn't that the proper term?"

"Not for you, it isn't."

She giggled. "All right, but I still expect front row seats."

The Cage wasn't set up like that, but she'd figure that out soon enough. "Only if I can get you drunk first so you won't remember it in the morning."

"Deal."

The sudden lightness in her voice made him wish she were there right then, that she'd just gotten there and they were about to do something fun.

"It'll be really great to see you, Skell."

Thinking about the trip over the next several weeks, Jack was in and out in terms of being excited about it. He'd compiled a list of all the things he wanted to show her, all the things they'd do together. Imagining her in the city was easy. He could imagine her pretty much anywhere. And yet, this visit would represent the mixing up of an old life with a new one and he wasn't sure they were going to gel.

Fortunately, when she called to tell him she was just coming through the toll at the bridge, he was in one of his more confident moods. He went right downstairs and was waiting on the sidewalk when he saw her dark blue Toyota, Miles, coming down Ellis. He waved. The truck stopped in front of him. She was in his arms before he realized he'd put them out.

She felt so buoyant. Incredible, really. All that energy after driving so far, and he spun her around, holding her to him. Then lifted her higher and kissed her.

"That was worth the trip right there," she beamed.

"I'll say, maybe you should pull back up so we can do it again."

"I could. Although you might start to notice I'm a little ripe."

"What are you talking about? You smell swell." He kissed her again, before putting her back on the sidewalk. "But *if* you want to wash up, I'll be happy to take care of Miles."

"I can wait," she said.

"In that case . . ." He opened the passenger door and held it for her. "So how was Yosemite?"

"Beautiful," she said. "But I only got to see the smallest part of it, I can't wait to go back."

She cleared some things off the seat before getting in.

He'd been given a parking space behind the gate for his bike, but it wasn't large enough to accommodate the truck, and as he began to look around for a spot on the street, he realized how good he'd had it. They were making increasingly larger circles around the apartment, and he was giving less than his full attention to Skelly's description of her trip.

". . . I don't know how they get up some of those rocks, but I'd really like to learn."

"You should."

"One of the guides told me there was actually some pretty extensive climbing in New Mexico."

"Really?"

"That's what he said." He felt a hand placed lightly on his leg. "You know we've passed several parking garages already. I'd be more than willing to pay for one, it's not even for a week."

"You're not paying for anything," he told her, a bit too adamantly, his frustration showing through. To his mind, parking garages were for tourists and suits. He lived there; he should know something simple like where to park a truck. "Don't worry, we'll find something soon."

After another twenty minutes of driving around, he felt compelled to make a suggestion.

"Listen, we're about to pass the apartment again, how about I give you the keys and you can go in and relax."

"As long as you're offering," she said, "I wouldn't mind using the bathroom."

He pulled over and handed her the keys.

"The silver one's for the building. Then it's up on the fourth floor, 413, end of the hall on the left. There's a kick-ass old-fashioned tub you can disappear into if you want. I mean, it's huge, I almost fit in it."

She gave him a quick kiss on the cheek. "That sounds great. Let me just get my bag." She got out, popped the seat and reached around behind it.

"Anything you want me to bring in?"

"Just the box in back."

When she closed the door, he breathed a sigh of relief. It had been an awkward start to things, but nothing they couldn't recover from. Now he just had to find a spot. He turned on the radio and begin flipping through the stations. It was great to be back in Miles again. The truck had handled all sorts of weather trouble the previous winter at the ranch. Even with that late blizzard, Miles had pulled them through.

It took another twenty minutes, but a Cadillac finally pulled out on Leavenworth leaving plenty of room. He parked and double-checked the signs. Then unlocked the camper shell, pulled out the box from behind the camping equipment, and locked it again. He patted Miles on the hood and walked back to the apartment.

His door had been left ajar, and when he walked through it, Jack heard some small splashes coming from the bathroom.

"Sounds like you found the tub."

"And the bubbles. I didn't know you liked bubbles."

"Yeah, well." He put the box down by the side of the door and went over to the kitchen to get something to eat. "Chef's making cereal, would you like to place an order?"

"No thanks. That box you brought in is yours, by the way, it's mostly things you left. Plus our old laptop. The school gave me one to use, and I know you don't have one so . . ."

He poured milk into the bowl and brought it over by the box. Then, curious, he set the bowl down on the floor and returned with a knife to cut through the packing tape. There wasn't much inside, mostly some old books and papers from college. He guessed he was glad to have them, although the symbolism of the act wasn't lost on him. It wasn't like it made sense for her to be holding onto his things, but there was something a little disconcerting about seeing them all laid out on the floor in front of him.

"Thanks for bringing the stuff," he called out.

"I figured I might as well."

He heard her standing up in the bath. Then, a few minutes later, she emerged with the towel wrapped around her.

"Don't get the idea that I'm kicking you out of my life or anything."

He nodded, looking at the tops of her breasts—the suppleness spilling over the towel, a piece of one nipple exposed. Water from her hair dripped down between them. He got up from where he'd been crouching and walked over. Put his hands to her face. Raked his fingers along her scalp, pushing the wetness through. The towel came down. They kissed . . . and kept kissing while he struggled to get out of his pants, finally realizing he needed to take off his shoes. He steadied himself on her shoulder.

"Hey, what's so funny?" he asked.

"You are. But mostly I'm just happy to be here."

He smiled. Pressed himself to her and held her tight. They began to rub up against one another, gently, at first. When he picked her up, he was struck by how easily she slipped on, but then, backing her toward the wall, he caught her eyes. Just long enough. He lowered her to the floor and stepped back. "I really should get a condom."

"But I'm still on the pill."

The surprise in her voice made it worse.

"Yeah, but I don't wanna take any chances. Give me a sec, all right."

He went into the kitchen, feeling sicker with every step, remembering how the condoms had gotten there. They weren't even his.

He opened the drawer, felt around in the back, and pulled out a packet of lube. Frustrated, he tossed it back in and located what he was looking for. He ripped open the package, fumbled to get it on, feeling another wave of blood drain from him. Why hadn't he planned ahead? He could have at least gotten a fresh pack, something special for the occasion. Unrolling the condom onto him, there was less and less resistance to pull against. His walked back over to her, his dick swaying uselessly in the latex.

"I don't think this is gonna happen."

She grabbed for his balls, but he caught her by the wrist.

"Seriously, not gonna happen."

She turned her hand to hold his. "Don't worry about it," she told him, as if there was a way not to worry about that. "We've got all sorts of time," she added, brightly. "And I'm kind of tired anyway. You know what I'd really love to do is take a nap."

She was being charitable, but he didn't feel like he deserved it. He walked over to retrieve the bowl of cereal, now thoroughly soggy. "Man, I slaved over this dish, and now it's ruined." Feeling a sort of glum half-smile attach itself to his face, he dumped the cereal in the trash, then put the condom in after it.

"If I know you, I'm sure there's plenty more where that came from."

He opened the cabinet, displaying a row of six or so boxes to show that something, at least, hadn't changed.

Lying next to her on the mattress, he couldn't decide whether he'd done the right thing by getting the condom. It wasn't like he'd done a lot to merit using it, but still, he'd done enough. All it took was one little slip-up.

She took his hand. "I'm sorry we didn't get to make love, but I'm glad you did what you did," she said, reading his mind it seemed. "I don't imagine there's any problem on my end, but it's possible. I haven't been in to see the gynecologist recently."

He nodded to himself. *Great. Thanks for that piece of information.* Well, what did he expect? That she'd be celibate for eight months? "So you've been seeing someone?"

"Just once, to see how it felt without you."

"And how did it feel?"

"I'm glad I did it. But like I said. Once. Draw your own conclusions."

She cuddled up against him, while he continued to stroke his fingers through her drying hair, long after she'd fallen asleep.

That night, he took her out to a nice restaurant, where they did their best to get comfortable with one another again, the mood helped by some wine and good food. Afterward, he suggested a club he'd picked out that was supposed to be swank. Skell seemed game for the idea, but while they were waiting in line to get in, she was already feeling uncomfortable.

"I think I'm overdressed."

"Hardly, no one cares about that stuff one way or the other here."

When they got inside, he asked what she wanted to drink.

"I'm not sure, yet. I just want to run to the restroom."

"All right, I'll be here."

He looked around, wondering what it was, exactly, he'd been so excited for her to see. That people were out partying on a Tuesday night? He'd thought it was a revolutionary concept just a couple of months ago, but now it didn't seem like much. The music was decent, but not as good as he'd hoped. The best feature was the crowd. When you looked around, one person didn't necessarily seem to be telling you anything about who they were standing next to. He wished more places were like that.

Someone tapped him on the shoulder, and he turned around to see Carrie's friend from the Lumiere.

"Hey, Christophe, how's it going?"

"Fine. You here alone?"

"No, a friend of mine's visiting. Carrie back yet?"

Christophe shook his head. "Who knows with her, but she said tomorrow."

She'd told Jack the same thing. Before taking off to some recently deceased great-aunt's house in Reno in hopes of salvaging the wardrobe before the Salvation Army got their hands on it.

"I didn't even know she could drive."

"I'm not sure she can, but she obviously convinced *somebody* at the rental company to give her that minivan."

Jack put his hands in his pockets. He tried to think if there anything else they had in common besides Carrie. "So, any good movies you've got to recommend?"

"People ask me that. All. The. Time."

His response wasn't exactly conducive to further conversation. And this coming from the guy who apparently thought Jack was too reserved. Still, he'd told Carrie he'd try to be more outgoing with her friends. So he mentioned *Microcosmos* to him, the movie he'd seen with Carrie a few months back at the rep house. "I doubt it's still playing, but it was really good."

"Yes, I saw it three times. You'd be surprised how much you miss the first go round."

Jack nodded.

"It's an extremely competent documentary. I understand the producer's working on another film on bird migration, which I'm eagerly anticipating. Jacques Perrin. French, as you might expect."

It seemed Christophe was still being a bit of a douche, but at least he was talking. Jack listened while he gave a little bio on each of the people involved with the film. He probably would've gotten to the gaffer if given enough time, but Jack had started to get concerned that Skelly hadn't come back yet. After scanning the crowd a few times, he realized he was going to have to interrupt.

"Uh, excuse me, Christophe, but I think my friend might've got lost. Maybe we'll catch you a little later on."

They shook hands and he left to search the club. He found Skelly sitting at the bar, talking with the bartender.

"I guess you figured out what you wanted to drink."

"Oh, hello Jack, nice of you to stop by." He looked back and forth between her and the barman. "Jack, meet Mario."

The bartender stuck out his hand. Jack shook it, confused.

"Skell, what's going on here?"

"Nothing."

"Well, why didn't you come back?" Mario asked if he wanted anything. He shook his head, aggravated at the intrusion. "Maybe you'd like to go somewhere so we can talk."

"But this is such a great place. Plus, I've just started my drink."

"All right, fine, I'll be outside then . . . whenever you're ready."

Jack bummed a cigarette from one of the girls chatting outside, then moved away from the group of them, further down the sidewalk. He'd only had a half a butt's worth of time to try to figure out what was happening when Skell showed up.

"Been smoking a lot since you've been here?" she asked.

"Not so much."

"Could I have a puff?"

"You can have the rest of it." He handed her the cigarette. "If you think that's appropriate behavior for a schoolteacher."

"Teacher's on vacation," she said, taking a quick drag and keeping her eyes turned out to the street.

"So, I'm not exactly sure what happened in there. It seemed like you were mad at me." She didn't say anything. "Well, were you?"

"Jack, let me tell you something. I came back from the bathroom and found you talking to that guy and I stood right there next to you. I stood there for probably five minutes and you never even noticed me."

"And that's what you're upset about?"

Her silence was in the affirmative. He couldn't believe it.

"Why didn't you say something, for Christ's sake?"

"Because I kept expecting you to look over and *notice I was there*."

Although he'd always been grateful for how little they argued, he had to admit, this time, it was kind of reassuring to hear the familiar tones of a bickering couple. Still, that didn't prevent him from looking at her like she'd lost her mind.

"That's nuts, Skell, the point is I obviously didn't see you. All you had to do was say hello or tap me on the shoulder. That's what that guy did to get my attention."

"I shouldn't need to get your attention."

"So, what, you conduct some sort of experiment to see how long it takes me to become aware of your presence?" She crossed her arms.

"Because if that's what you were up to, maybe you should go back and check your notes and verify the fact that I was scanning the crowd looking for you."

"Not right away, you didn't. And only briefly."

"Wow. You really were testing me." His affection for the argument had come to a quick end. "I don't understand why you'd do that. When all I was doing was killing time while I was waiting for you. It was a lousy conversation, anyway. I barely even know that guy."

"Where do you know him from?"

"He takes tickets at the movie theater, Skelly."

"Oh."

"Yeah, oh." He gestured for the cigarette back. "If you'd just let me know you were there, we could be enjoying a drink inside right now instead of standing out here acting like a couple of idiots."

"I'm sorry," she said, "it's just . . . I don't know anyone here. I feel like I've dropped in on someone else's party."

"We didn't have to come here. All you had to say was you weren't interested."

"Well, I thought I was."

"So, what do you wanna do now?"

"I'd like to get a cab, if you don't mind."

The rest of the week went by almost without incident, due in large part to how determined they both were not to say anything that would upset the other person. The politeness—the slight strain behind every comment—took its own kind of toll, though, and conversations tended to be kept short. Fortunately, there was a film festival playing and they purchased full-access passes, which they used daily.

It had always been easy seeing movies with Skell, as she shared every one of his habits: no buying snacks, no items passed back and forth, no hand holding, no chit chat, no crunching. It was only after leaving the theater that they let themselves go, discussing the lives of the characters they'd seen on screen, debating eventualities and choices made. But on this visit, as soon as anything started to hit too close to home, they were quick to back off.

Skell had wanted to see the children's science museum, so they'd gone there. It was fun, but Jack thought it would have been more so if they'd smoked a little weed first. Skelly's response was that it would have been better if they'd had kids with them. Trying for the compromise position, Jack said either option would have been fine, as long as they didn't try to do both together.

He took her to the botanical gardens and the aquarium, specifically to introduce her to Aqualung, the fish he'd become acquainted with during regular visits there. The lung fish had been sitting in the same tank for more than eighty years. Jack couldn't get over it. All the things that had gone down over the past century, and for this guy, maybe the most radical thing to have happened was the addition of a frond to his marine environment. Still, he'd probably seen plenty. With the millions of people that had passed in front of his tank, there wasn't much that was going to shake him up at this point and he seemed, inevitably, wise. At least, you were confident he knew you were there. If you stood around long enough, he'd slowly make his way over to the front of the glass, eyes bulged open, offering you a mild interest. Skelly gave him a similar appraisal but seemed to prefer some of the more colorful creatures in the other tanks. She said she wished the aquarium in Albuquerque had as much stuff for her students to see. At last, it seemed like a positive point for the city.

Encouraged by her enjoyment of the aquarium, he'd taken her to see the sea lions. At dawn, before the avalanche of tourists descended, which was the only time he ever went. The chill in the air stung the sleepiness from their eyes, and by the time they'd reached the piers, they were both happy to be out ahead of the day.

"Did you know they're highly thigmotactic?" he said.

"What?"

"A-ha. Looks like I got the science teacher on that one. Wanna take a guess?"

"Say it again."

"Thigmotactic."

"Well, it's got something to do with touch."

"That's part of it. It means they seek out lots of body contact."

Then he made the obvious play by putting his arms around her waist.

"It's a great word," she said. "Too bad it has too many letters for Scrabble."

"Yeah, I thought of that."

"They're certainly looking very thigmotactic this morning." She peered in closer. "They really are adorable."

It was nice to have Skelly around to be able to characterize them like this. Because they clearly were. Adorable.

"They're pretty calm at the moment but mating season will be starting soon. A number of the males don't even end up mating, actually, they just sort of form these bachelor colonies."

"So you're telling me the sea lions are gay."

"Well, you do get some interplay between some of the bulls and some of the adolescents."

"Gay pedophiles, then."

"I don't think they take it that seriously. Anyway, these guys aren't particularly queer. From what I understand, in a few weeks things will start getting testy with the really aggressive bulls fighting to claim their harems, while the rest of the guys kind of call it a day and end up loafing around together. But if you look at dolphins, or walruses, for example, now those guys can definitely be queer just for the fun of it."

She turned her head around just long enough to catch his eye. "Did you take me down here because you wanted to tell me something?"

"No, I took you down here because I wanted to share something I like to do here. These guys are like my best friends, besides Aqualung. Laid back, don't ask me any questions."

She was looking at the water again. "Jack, are you gay?"

He'd been prepared at different times to tell her no, and to tell her yes, before he'd come up with a response he liked.

"I'm gay enough," he told her.

"Meaning?"

"Meaning I've been with a few guys and I don't think it's that big a deal. Not like I really enjoyed it all that much. But I could. I could see myself liking it if the right person came along." He surprised himself with the last part. He hadn't planned on saying that.

Skelly pulled away from him and turned around completely.

"So you're looking for someone."

"I'm open to it, I guess. It's not like I'm actively searching."

"Because I can handle the fact that you're attracted to guys, in general. Just not any one in particular. Especially one you'd think about settling down with." She put her hands on her hips. "You haven't changed your mind about having kids, have you?"

"I didn't say I didn't want kids. I said I didn't want them now. And no, I haven't changed it. I've just been thinking, lately, that maybe this whole married with children thing is a little overprescribed. Especially when you consider how many people screw it up."

"In *your* family, you mean."

"I never should have told you anything about my family." He was hurt, but could tell right away she felt bad, too, so he didn't try to milk it. "Anyway, I checked out this book over Christmas and it was talking about all the different kinds of arrangements you find in the natural world. You've got your long-term hetero couples, sure, but then you've got your long-term homo pairings, ones that are only queer when they're younger, others only after they've mated. Some don't mate at all. Polygamy, tons of non-procreative sexual activity. Even ducks are a fairly promiscuous bunch as it turns out."

"And this is all documented?"

"Yeah. By a bunch of freaks who apparently get their kicks watching animals get it on."

"I think I would like to have the name of the book."

"Sure. It's not like I'm looking exclusively to the animal kingdom to see how I should be living. I mean, it's nice to have the validation, but I just like knowing there are all these different set-ups out there. It just makes things more interesting."

"And confusing."

"Yeah, well, that comes with the territory."

"I'm not sure what to tell you, Jack. You've obviously got a lot on your mind." He nodded. "I don't envy your position."

"I don't envy yours, either."

She looked at him for a moment—seemed to be wavering about something—and then decided to snuggle against him.

There was a lot they hadn't said, and he wasn't sure they'd be able to get away with avoiding the rest of it before she left, but things seemed peaceful for the moment and he wanted to capitalize on that.

"So how would you like to take the bike out for the day? I know this remote beach just north of Santa Cruz."

"That," she held him tighter, "would be great."

The trip down was perfect. The closest he'd felt to Skelly since she'd gotten there. With each piece of postcard scenery passed, a squeeze on his arm conveyed her pleasure and emphasized his own, reminding him how it used to be between them, before there'd been talk of sea lions and kids and the future of the republic.

They traveled along the Pacific Coast Highway until they reached the mile marker he'd committed to memory, then pulled off just beyond it into what seemed to be the middle of nowhere. The first time he'd come, he'd noticed a jeep there, and then, to the west, a lone surfer walking out through the high grass. He couldn't see the water but was sure there must be a trail leading down to it. He waited till the guy loaded up, then followed the path back, before it finally gave way to an expanse of beach that ran, deserted, for miles in both directions. He'd never seen anyone else there before and arriving with Skell over the top of the dunes, he was reassured to see the place was theirs. They walked barefoot, first south, then retracing their steps and moving northward toward an outcropping of rocks. There was an almost cave-like area ahead where the rock jutted out. When the tide came in, first only the largest, then practically all the waves, smashed up onto it, raining down onto the sand in successive waterfalls. Their timing couldn't have been better, and they waded into position beneath the overhang, where they yelled under each thundering crash, until their throats were hoarse.

On the way back from the beach, they swung by Miles so she could re-park in anticipation of the next morning's street cleaning. Pulling up alongside, they discovered that the truck had been broken into. It wasn't as bad as it could have been; only the camper shell had been hit, some broken glass in the bed, and the camping equipment—sleeping bag, tent, propane stove—missing. The theft had the feeling of necessity, someone trying to survive with, rather than fence, her stuff, but it was a violation nonetheless. One that Jack felt completely responsible for; he'd been the one to insist on leaving the truck in the street. She moved it to a garage after that, but the damage had been done.

Skelly was leaving the following morning, and Saturday night was the one they'd scheduled for her to go to the Cage. He'd warned her not to be upset if he didn't acknowledge her, and kept true to his word, turning in the usual, staring over the crowd to the nearest wall, which he tried to make out between blasts from the smoke machine. He'd gotten permission from Sid to leave early, and as soon as he finished, he changed quickly and grabbed Skelly at the bar.

"Let's get out of here," he told her. "There's a place around the corner."

They took a booth in the back lounge and ordered gin and tonics. He could see she had a pretty good buzz going already.

"So what'd you think?"

"It was a nice diversion."

"You had a good time, then?"

"I'm glad I went, thanks for letting me come."

"No problem. So what did you really think?"

She began to fidget with her napkin, turning up one of the corners. "Well, I did put a few thoughts together, if you're sure you want to hear them."

"Go ahead."

"This is obviously just a first impression, but—oh look, here are our drinks."

They both leaned back from the table as the drinks were dropped, then waited until the waitress had returned to the bar.

"You were saying."

"Well, I think it seemed a little . . . silly, and even, at times, depressing."

They both took gulps from their glasses.

"Yeah, it can be like that. Especially tonight, the crowd was kind of spooky."

"It didn't look like you noticed the crowd."

"Not while I was up on my block. But it can be fun to look around sometimes, you know. See who's there. We even get some bachelorette parties from time to time. They always have a blast—even if they do sometimes leave crummy tips," he said, mumbling the last part.

"What was that?"

"The tips women leave. Yeah, this really aggressive bachelorette requested private action from a buddy of mine, and when she held out the money, he was like, 'Lady, that's *a dollar*.' "

Skelly didn't seem to appreciate the story. "Well, I don't know about that, but at least the other guys didn't look like they were having their teeth pulled while they were up there. You, on the other hand, didn't seem to be enjoying yourself at all."

"Some people go for a standoffish look."

"Maybe. But how does it feel to be the one providing it?"

"I haven't gotten any complaints until now."

"I don't imagine you have, but I'm just surprised to hear that everyone else's good time is enough to sustain you up there."

"What do you mean?"

"I've never known you to put yourself out like that. Well, maybe that's a little severe but . . . what I mean is, the only reason I could imagine the Jack I know dancing up there was if he was having a good time. And anything the audience might be getting out of it would be a kind of fringe benefit."

"You think I'm that wrapped up in myself?"

"I didn't say it was a bad thing."

She was probably onto something. "Okay, I'll admit it was more interesting when I first started. It just seemed to . . . I don't know . . . fit the bill. But it has gotten a little repetitive lately. But, hey, do you have any idea how much money I cleared tonight?"

"No, I don't. I hope enough to buy me another drink."

The beverage had gone fast. He waved the waitress over for another round.

"I'm only giving you my opinion because you asked for it. It really doesn't matter."

"It does matter."

"Not really. As long as you're happy . . ."

As long as you're happy. People always said that when they suspected you really weren't. Well, he never said he was. "I doubt I'm going to be doing this forever."

"Then what are your plans, Jack?"

But his only response was to shrug and wait for the next round.

Two drinks later, he made the mistake of revisiting the question.

"An *escort*?"

"Yeah, you know."

"No, I don't, actually. Do you mean a prostitute?"

"Jesus, Skell, no, not a prostitute." He assumed there wasn't much difference but figured he might as well use the benefit of his ignorance now while he still had it.

"So what does an escort do, exactly? Are you like a companion for the evening?"

That sounded good. "Yeah, like a companion."

"With men?"

"Probably men, yeah."

She eyed him suspiciously. "But no sex?"

"Well, sex could be a possibility, I guess. I really don't know. I mean, I'm just investigating it. This guy came by the Cage and gave me his card and told me I should go down there for an interview." He reached for his drink. "That's all that's happened."

She put her hand on top of his glass. "Have you given any thought to how dangerous this might be?"

"Dangerous, how?"

She rolled her eyes. "What about *AIDS*, Jack? This is San Francisco, after all."

"I know where I'm living, Skell, thanks. It's not the only place that has it." He wanted to tell her there was zero chance of him getting caught off guard again, but that would mean letting her know he'd been caught off guard the first time. "Plus, HIV doesn't have to be a death sentence anymore. The treatments are getting better."

"You sure seem to know a lot about it."

"I know because my buddy, Bishkey, just started a new regimen and they think if he follows it, he's gonna be all right."

"Who is this Bishkey person? Someone you're sleeping with?"

"He's just a friend, Skell. I doubt I've had much more sex than you since we've been apart. And in terms of being careful, let's not forget, I'm the one who suggested we use a condom the other night."

"Believe me, I've already taken myself to task for that lapse in judgment. I don't need anything further from you on the subject."

"Fine."

"It's not fine. Nothing is. I don't feel like I'm getting through to you." Skelly looked like she was going to take his hand but then thought better of it. "Okay, how about this? Do you remember what you told me after you turned down grad school? What you said was, and I'm paraphrasing here, 'I don't want to sit around in a classroom talking about ethics, I want to do something ethical.' And I'll admit I thought maybe you were missing a good opportunity, but I heard what you said, and I believed in you, and when you joined the fire department, I got it, I really did. And then when you told me what you really wanted to do was fight forest fires—again, I had my reservations—you seemed so happy before your crew changed, Jack—and I wondered if you'd really thought it through, but in the end I went along with that, too. Even the way you've spent this past year, I thought you might just need some time to sort things out. But now . . . I don't see how you can justify this. To yourself or anyone else." She took another drink. "And it is dangerous. I don't care what you say."

How could he explain that it was the edginess of the job that he found the most attractive? She should know that about him. No, he wasn't going to fail to mention it.

"Skell, did you ever get scared when I was out in the field, fighting fires or on the ambulance or wherever. Were you scared at any time?"

"To be honest, no."

"Right. Because you knew I probably wasn't gonna get hurt and it was something I needed to do. You knew all the dumbass shit I did in college and how damn lucky I was nothing ended up on my record, and it was just simple math that I did less dumbass shit after I joined the department because most days I had all the excitement I could handle at work. I'm just built that way. I need an outlet."

"A positive outlet, yes, I understand that. But please don't tell me you're trying to make a comparison between working for the fire department and this thing you're thinking about doing. One is saving people's lives and the other is—"

"I'm not saying they're the same."

"I don't suppose it's really my business anymore, anyway. The point is, I'm really worried about you, what's happening to you."

"Well, don't be. Anyway, I didn't say I was definitely going to do it. I'm just considering it."

"Even the fact that you're considering it at all . . .You're changing, Jack."

It wasn't what he wanted to hear. He felt like he'd been acting more or less the same as always, but then again, he couldn't be sure. He didn't really have any other barometer besides himself, and he wasn't always the most reliable. He knew there was a part of him that had been wanting her to go along with the idea, that had been looking for her approval. Why else, really, would he have brought it up? She was right, she had been generous with her support of everything he'd done in the past, and her reaction was making him nervous. Still, he wasn't interested in having the brakes put on now.

"I'll probably just go down for the interview and take it from there."

"If you do this . . ." She shook her head. "I don't think I can go this far with you."

He looked in her eyes. "I never asked you to." Cold for the first time.

She was out of her seat and out the door before he could stop her. He settled up with the waitress before running after.

She hadn't gotten far. Down the next block, barely advancing along the sidewalk. Her hands clasped around the back of her head. Catching up with her, he confirmed the worst.

"Please don't cry, Skell, please . . ." He was having a hard time remembering the last fragments of their conversation. "All I was saying was, I don't want you to keep holding a place for me."

"Don't tell me what I can and can't do!" She stumbled ahead.

He caught up with her again. "Listen, will you stop already." He grabbed her by the shoulders.

She stopped. Held him fiercely. Then tried to push him away.

"What is *wrong* with you?"

Her fists were flying into him. He drew her closer to suffocate the blows. Then projected himself someplace far away, where he remained until her anger was spent. He felt her arms slide down his chest to hang, loosely, at her side. Her body not quite leaning against him.

Then she began to cry again. "I know you didn't ask me to save something for you but . . . you had to know that I did and . . . I really hoped you were coming back. You were supposed to come home, Jack."

He could feel all those months of disappointment coming out, sob by sob, and he hated himself more with every one. But he had no words of comfort to offer. For the first time, it seemed that they weren't going to be able to fix things. Not on this visit, and maybe not ever. That no matter how strongly they felt toward one another, it wasn't going to be enough to prevent them from going in different directions.

With her tears subsiding, she reached up to wipe her face. "I must look awful." Then she gave a quick smile. "I should try to get some sleep. I've got a long drive tomorrow."

The next morning, he woke to the alarm. Made some coffee, then headed down to the parking garage. He felt clearheaded and calm. The fear of losing her from his life knotted deep in his stomach where he could barely feel it. He would do what he needed to do to pull up the bridge behind her, and if things turned out badly, well, then better not to have any witnesses. He walked to the back of the garage where the truck was parked and unlocked the door. Getting inside, he noticed the faded scent of her perfume. The case from one of her favorite CDs on the dashboard. He sat there for a few minutes listening to the music before driving back to the apartment.

She was waiting on the sidewalk with her bag. He stopped the truck, and they traded places, pausing only to give one another a brief hug and kiss. Before pulling away, she mouthed I love you, but the expression behind the words was sad and defeated and somehow final, and the window had been closed.

He made an appointment with the Atlas agency for later that afternoon. The address was in Noe Valley and, after ringing the buzzer, he was greeted by a boy of no more than eighteen. Crew cut, chiseled. Soldier's posture. He said hi but didn't offer his hand. Then he led Jack down a hallway, before pausing in front of a living room where a couple of other young guys were hanging out, both with softer features, nearly as handsome. They glanced up but didn't look at him, then returned to whatever it was they were doing, one of them on the computer, the other lying on his back.

As they continued past the dining room and the kitchen, Jack realized the apartment was turning into a house. He'd forgotten people lived in those anymore. Eddie had his hotel room, Martin had left a small studio like his own. Carrie, at least, had a separate bedroom. Here was probably 1200 square feet of space and that was only on the first floor. They turned up the staircase, then walked to the end of the hall, where the boy knocked on the door, waited for a three count, then opened it. "This is Daniel," he said, motioning for Jack to enter.

It was getting close to comical by this point. The guy at the desk was another striking specimen, as if he, too, had been airbrushed in among the furnishings. Short, jet black hair. Black sweater which he filled out completely. As Jack approached him, he realized this guy was older, though, with lines around the edges of his blue eyes. Jack smiled and said hello. The guy's response was to look him over, briefly, then pick up the phone. "Excuse me one moment," he said.

It looked like the guy was going to be an ass. Jack figured he'd better gear up for it because he was prepared to do what was necessary to get the job. He tried not to pay attention to the message Daniel was leaving, glancing around the room from the neatly stacked piles of papers, to the back of the huge computer screen, to the wall behind the desk. Filled with printouts of faces, names in quotation marks underneath, "Steve," "Thomas," along with their proclivity for sexual positions, "Top" and "Versatile," respectively.

"Sorry to keep you waiting," Daniel's voice was deep and unapologetic, "but I needed to take care of that."

"No problem."

"You can have a seat. So Jonathan tells me you put on quite a show over at the Cage?"

Jack shrugged.

"Have you ever done anything like this before?"

"No."

"So what made you decide to come see me?"

"I heard the money was good. I thought I might give it a try."

"Why don't you take down your pants."

The request itself didn't bother him. He'd been expecting as much after his interview at the Cage. But it irked him the guy had asked him to sit down in the first place, the only reason for it seeming to be so he could have him get back up again. He stood and began to unbutton his jeans.

"Underwear, too."

He'd been able to keep those on when he applied at the Cage; he supposed this was progress. He pulled them down far enough to get to the point, then waited while the guy took his sweet time getting his opinion together.

"Not bad. Maybe you're a grower."

If you're expecting me to get hard, you can forget it. Relieved to find he had some limits, Jack pulled his pants back up. "So, are you interested?"

"Why don't you stand against the wall over there and let me get a shot of you. Then I'll need you to fill this out."

Daniel took a couple of pictures. Uploaded them onto the computer while Jack filled out his contact information. When he turned it in, Daniel skimmed down the page.

"It looks like you've listed a land line here."

"That's right."

"Is that all you have?"

Jack nodded.

"That won't do. We need to be able to reach you at all times. Everyone should have a mobile by now and you'll need to get one."

"Okay, sure. I could pick one up on the way home, if you want."

"Why don't you just wait until we see how you do on your first call. I hate for you to waste your money."

Jack had begun to develop a kind of grudging respect for the guy, at how adept he was at toying with him. He listened attentively as Daniel proceeded to reel off a bunch of rules and regs. What was expected of him, what wasn't. How after meeting clients, he was never to make contact with them on his own; how everything would get back to the office eventually. Jack nodded along with most of the points, which, on the whole, didn't seem unreasonable.

"I assume you're a top."

"Yeah." He assumed he was, too.

"Can you handle women?"

"You mean would I sleep with them?"

He tapped his fingers on the desk. "What else do I care about?"

"Sure, sign me up."

Daniel input the information into the computer.

"All right, I'm going to tell you what I tell everyone else we consider hiring. My advice is to think of this place as a used car lot. We've got all kinds of different models, but for our purposes, they're all the same price."

"So the rates are the same for everyone?"

"More or less." Daniel gave a proficient smile, flashing perfect white teeth. "Now, we've got our Rams, our Civics, a Lexus or two. Some are older, some newer . . . some have more mileage on them than others." He showed his teeth again. "So now you tell me, which one are you going to go for? Remember you're the client now, which model are you going to take?"

Jack hoped it was a rhetorical question, because he wasn't sure how to answer it.

"You're going to take whichever one you like. Now I could ask you about all those special qualities you have to offer, but then, I'm not the one who's interested in renting you for the evening." His iced blue eyes held Jack's to emphasize the point, but all Jack could focus on was the fact that you didn't rent cars from a used car lot. It was easier to be offended by his bogus analogy.

"We leave the evaluation up to the clients. We listen to what the clients have to say about you, and then we decide whether we want to retain you. You never get off probation, I want you clear on that. We're always comparing you to the other guys, and we're always looking to remove our least satisfactory employees, because there's always someone new wanting a job here." He paused, and then asked if Jack had any questions.

"How do I get paid?"

"The agency gets twenty percent of all calls. We keep a running tab between cash and credit card charges. If you owe us more than two hundred at any given time, you need to get in here and pay it. Immediately. If we owe you more than two hundred, then you can come in on Friday afternoons *only* to pick up the balance. Tips are yours to keep. Now do you have your own transportation?"

"Yeah."

"Good."

He buzzed the intercom on his desk. Then he opened the drawer and withdrew a business card, which he handed to Jack. "This is the doctor we use. Before you can get started, we're going to need to get you screened for STDs. It would be best if you could go over there right now. Is that a problem?"

"No."

"You'll have to sign a release to have the results reported to me."

There was a knock at the door.

"One more thing. If you want to succeed here, you're going to have to show a bit more personality than you've demonstrated today. I'm giving you a chance and that's all. Either I or my associate Benjamin will be in touch with you."

Daniel picked up the phone and the door opened. It was minion number two, the paper shuffler from downstairs. He showed Jack the way out.

First night on the job and he was running late. Late to see the priest. "We'll see how you do with O'Flannery," they'd told him, "and then we'll go from there." The address he'd been given was far enough out of town that it meant taking the highway, and taking it fast, if he wanted to make up for the delay. He snaked up the ramp at the bottom of Van Ness, then struck out against the open road with the full acceleration of the throttle, so it wasn't long before he was passing Candlestick and then onto his favorite stretch of the 101.

The road cut low and narrow through the bay there. During the day, the water spread out in a rippled glass, reflecting even the sparest light from the sky. Under darkness, it would lap up black and blend with the pavement, making you feel as if you were riding along its skimmed surface. At the moment, though, there was little pleasure to be taken in the scenery. The wind coming off the bay was as biting as he'd ever felt it, and combined with the speed of the bike, it had begun to push a chill through the leather of his jacket. By the time he'd crossed over to the airport, he was freezing. His chest, his legs, especially his fingers which were barely protected inside thin gloves.

He tried clenching and unclenching each hand in a fist, but already the cold had seeped into the joints making them fat and increasingly stiff. Figuring he could at least salvage his left hand, he brought it over above the throttle, then turned his right to pinch the material while he shook his way out of it. Then he took the glove with his freed hand, stuffed it into his jacket pocket, and stuffed his hand down the front of his jeans.

The results were immediately encouraging. And as the tingling sensation began to spread from his fingertips, he pushed his hand further down, past his lower abdomen, in search of warmer territory. He was just getting his hand cupped nicely around his sack, when he felt an odd knob of ice resting against his knuckle. Upon closer examination, he confirmed that this was, in fact, his penis. *Great*, he thought, now rather desperately trying to massage some feeling in there as well, *this should be one heck of an opening night.*

Approaching the outskirts of South Bay, he began to watch the exit signs more carefully, and when he found the one he was looking for, he got off going east. The road was mostly deserted. An empty commuter lot. A Shell station, closed. Two miles past it, a blinking yellow light marked the entrance to the apartments, and he turned into them thinking he was going to be on time after all. But after easily spotting the A and B buildings, he was frustrated to find the third in the row marked D. Naturally, C was the one he was looking for.

The last time he'd found himself in a situation like this was when he worked on the ambulance, where it seemed like the more urgent the call, the more likely there'd be some screw up in trying to find the place.

They'd be dispatched to something in the 700 block, and the street would dead end in the 600s. Or they'd be given 64 as the house number, and the mailboxes would jump from 62 to 66. There was always some explanation for the miss—that dead end road would reappear under the same name the next block down, that even-numbered address would turn out to be a stray located on the odd side of the street—but it seemed to take forever to solve these little mysteries, and the whole time you hadn't managed to do a single thing for the patient. Well, with tonight's call, at least, no one's life was on the line.

He found the C building soon enough, tucked away on the back side of the complex. He parked the bike, then made his way to the entrance, where he located the security keypad and punched in the four-digit code he'd been given. The immediate buzzing of the lock should have been a signal things were going smoothly, but as he pushed open the door he couldn't escape the feeling that he was breaking and entering, late at night with no one around.

He crossed the lobby quickly, then took the steps by twos in an effort to make like he knew where he was going. At the second-floor landing, he paused where the hallway split, then took a gamble left. A few doors down he found himself standing in front of C21. He unzipped his jacket, then decided it was probably best to remove it altogether, even though he was only just beginning to thaw out. He rubbed his hands together a final time before knocking.

If Jack hadn't already known the man who opened the door was a priest—or at least a former one—there would have been a pretty good chance of his guessing it anyway. He looked to be cut from the same cloth as any number of the Jesuits from Jack's parochial school back east. A little on the heavy side, pale skin stained red at the loose cheeks, white hair thin but covering his scalp, with a face both avuncular and stern.

"Father O'Flannery, at your service," the man introduced himself, "but you can call me Paul. And you go by what, may I ask?"

"Jason," Jack responded, extending his hand, wondering why he'd even bothered to come up with a fake name. They'd recommended it at the agency, but it was already feeling like a distraction.

He shook hands with the priest.

"Oh my, your hand's cold, Jason. How did it get so cold?"

It was an irritating question. Jack didn't want to talk about any of it, his trip over there, his motorcycle, or his temperature. He shrugged and offered a smile instead of an explanation while withdrawing his grip.

"No matter." Paul patted him on the shoulder. "You know what they say about cold hands."

Then he tried to take Jack's coat. But for some reason Jack didn't let go of it immediately, so that as the priest began pulling it toward him, the slightest bit of tug of war ensued, with Jack only releasing it the moment he fully grasped the problem he was causing.

"Oh, you'll have to forgive me," Paul remarked with the coat now in his possession, "I tend to lose myself around leather. Such a heady, such a heavenly scent. Don't you think?"

"Sure," Jack responded. *Whatever you say, man.*

"So what can I get you to drink, Jason. A glass of wine, or something stronger perhaps?"

"A glass of water would be fine."

"Water would be fine, but wine would be better," the priest said. "Do you prefer red or white?"

"Red, I guess."

"Ah, yes, the most civilized choice. Leather and red wine. Splendid."

Jack followed Paul into the main room. The apartment was rather large. Respectable looking. Standard beige carpeting throughout, with wooden furniture, antiques, laid out nicely. Shelves filled with books.

The priest was uncorking the bottle, when Jack remembered he was supposed to call the agency.

"Uh, do you mind if I borrow your phone? I'm supposed to call up the guys and let them know I'm here."

"Of course, I know the routine."

It seemed a rather odd procedure to Jack, but he made the call as he'd been instructed. It was Benjamin who answered, making note of the time, and asking if everything was all right. When Jack told him it was, Benjamin reminded him to call again when he was ready to leave and then told him to "have fun." Jack handed the phone back to the priest. "Sorry about that."

"Oh, that's quite all right. So tell me, Jason, what did you study in school?"

"Philosophy."

"Philosophy, oh my, I could see you were intelligent the moment I laid eyes on you. We'll have lots to talk about then. Philosophy and Theology are two sides of the same coin, you know."

For a moment, Jack got the rather preposterous idea that he could just hang out for a while, reel out his theory on Aristotelian ethics, and head home for the evening. He took a seat on the armchair and tried to look scholarly.

"Jason, don't sit all the way over there. Come sit beside me so we can hear each other better."

Jack obliged, moving onto the couch. Paul handed him the wine.

"Cheers," he said. "To you, Jason, and to the liberal, the very liberal arts." He laughed cheerfully and took a drink. Jack smiled along with him. "You know, all men of any greatness whatsoever have always admired younger men. And the admiration has been mutual. Plato was such an idealist, the boys loved him. For his knowledge, of course. Aristotle? A cold fish. Too uptight. St. Augustine is my favorite, but let's not waste time talking about him. Let's hear more about you."

Jack would rather have stuck with Augustine. Hadn't he been pretty much of a drunken playboy in his younger days before finally getting his act together? "Not much to tell," he said.

"I can't believe that, I'm sure you've led a remarkable life. Do you have a girlfriend?"

"Not at the moment."

"Must be waiting for the right one to come along."

"Yeah, something like that."

"So how did you get interested in philosophy?"

Jack could feel himself warming to this line of inquiry but wasn't sure how comfortable he wanted to get with it. "Well, I took one of those introductory courses my freshman year to fill a requirement and I got hooked." He could have left it at that. "I don't know, about halfway through the class I started getting really bent about the whole question of free will. I wrote this paper on Leibniz, ripping apart his explanation of it, but then I was having a hard time figuring out what to replace it with. I became sort of obsessed with solving the problem. I mean, so much seemed to be riding on it."

"And did you solve it?"

"Not exactly." Jack shook his head. "Not at all, really. Got the degree and still didn't figure it out."

"What a pity you had to struggle so. It's not nearly as difficult as you're making it out to be."

Jack knew this was why he'd bothered opening up in the first place. Just on the chance. The small chance. He looked at Paul hopefully.

"Undoubtedly, the Creator has designed the best universe possible. And the best universe would have to be a moral universe; that is, one that allows for free will. There's little room to equivocate."

Jack was disappointed. Of course, he should have expected it, he was talking to a priest, but he hated having God dragged into the whole thing so quickly. Still, he tried to stick with the conversation and responded in turn. "Well, you know how God has this reputation for being perfect, right?"

"It's more than a reputation, Jason."

"Okay, then would you say God had any choice in the matter of creating free will? Wasn't He sort of forced into doing it if it was the most perfect way to set things up?"

"I'm not sure what you mean. It's certainly not God's obligation to do so. Rather, it's out of His love for us that He grants us this greatest gift."

The guy was contradicting himself, which wasn't a good sign. And he didn't appear troubled about the possibility of God being a prisoner to perfection. If Jack had been given a choice between perfection and free will, he would have taken the freedom every time.

He tried another angle. "So, do you think since God is all-knowing, omniscient and all that, He's already figured out what we're gonna choose before He creates us?"

"Perhaps."

"Because it just seems like the worst sort of entrapment, where God is the one who's responsible for your existence, He knows exactly what you're going to do when He creates you, and then you're the one who ends up taking the fall for your actions."

"But He still allows us to make our own choices. That's what's important." The priest put his glass on the table. His tone suggested the discussion was over, and he underlined it by looking at his watch. "Now, Jason, I'm sure you're going to tell me what a fat cock you've got, aren't you?"

Jack felt his hand tighten around his wine glass, but at the same time he felt like laughing. The whole exchange had been a little too reminiscent of Little Red Riding Hood, although it wasn't clear in this scenario who was supposed to be the wolf.

"I'm sure you've got a nice one, Jason, you don't have to say anything. We'll find out together, now, won't we?"

Jack avoided his gaze.

"Let me ask you another question, then. Have you ever been hypnotized before?"

The one thing he hadn't wanted was for things to turn creepy. The possibility of getting hypnotized was definitely heading in that direction.

"No, I haven't," he answered. Actually, Jack had seen a hypnotist at a show once, but he'd thought the whole thing was a farce, with the guy relying on people's good nature for his act to succeed. For some reason, the audience members going up onstage seemed more willing to embarrass themselves rather than the performer. "I guess I did see a hypnotist once, but I wasn't one of the people who went up to do it. Although the guy did sort of this mass hypnosis thing on the crowd, but I didn't get much off it."

"Oh well, then you are in for a treat. Finish up that wine there. That's it. Why don't you have a little more before we start."

Jack could feel an anger brewing in him. He hated being told what to do and he really didn't want any more to drink. Still, he knew what he'd signed up for, and he held out his glass trying to look agreeable.

"Don't worry, I've done this with lots of other boys and they've all done just fine."

Jack nodded along with this reassuring thought. He took another gulp of the wine, then put the unfinished glass back on the table. "Okay, ready when you are."

"Very good. Now I want you to lean back and relax. There's no reason not to trust me, I want you to remember that. I have done nothing to you—nothing—that would ever give you the idea you couldn't trust me. Do you agree with what I've just said, Jason? That's a premise, you know. A premise that's fundamental you agree with."

"Yes," Jack affirmed as genuinely as possible, remembering that Paul was a regular at the agency.

"Excellent. Now I want you to close your eyes and try to clear your mind as much as possible. Put aside any thoughts that might be troubling you and merely listen to the sound of your breathing."

Jack closed his eyes. That part was easy enough. But how was he supposed to just stop thinking? Even if he could manage it, he wasn't sure it was such a good idea.

"You still look a little apprehensive, Jason. Take a couple of deep breaths . . . That's it. One . . . two. Good. Now, I want you to put yourself in a peaceful place. You have just come through the shade of some trees, but now you step though those trees and into sunshine. There is nothing but beach in front of you. Look as far as your eyes will take you, white sand and a long expanse of calm, blue ocean. Do you see the water?"

"Yeah," Jack acknowledged, feeling a vague tingle of interest.

"*Yes.* Yes, you do see the water." The priest cleared his throat. "You gaze at it longingly. It's the bluest water you've ever seen. Just the tiniest of waves rolling up onto the shoreline. You want to walk down toward the water, but there is something holding you back, something tense inside you . . ."

Of course, the priest was right. Jack hadn't exactly been able to let himself go.

"It's the tightness in your shoes, Jason, they're constricting your toes. Pushing them too close together. They are trapping your feet, making them sweat. The laces are binding. Positively binding."

Now that the priest had called attention to them, Jack had to admit his boots were a little snug. And as he waited for the priest to continue, he found them feeling even more so.

"Jason, I'm going to take off one of your shoes now. You are going to feel me touching your shoe." Jack could feel a hand resting on the top of his boot, followed by a slow pull of the knot. It felt good to have it untied. Then the priest began to loosen the lace, working his way down with such deliberation that Jack was tempted to reach down and yank the thing off himself. Finally, the hand slid under the tongue and around the arch of his foot. With the fingers dug in there, the priest managed to slip off the boot in one smooth motion. Jack hoped his feet didn't reek.

"You put your first foot tentatively into the sand. It isn't hot at all. Only warm. Pleasantly warm from the early morning sun. The warmth spreads up through your leg. You reach down to take off your other shoe."

The priest removed Jack's other boot just as deftly, only faster this time.

"Your other foot is free now. You place it into the sand as well, feel the tiny grains under your toes. Between them. You are walking in the sand, Jason. You can feel the warmth coming up through both your legs now. There is the slightest breeze, but it is balmy, tropical, it carries on it the scent of mangos. Do you know what a mango smells like?"

"Yes," Jack found himself whispering.

"The breeze is caressing your skin, running through your hair."

Jack felt the lightest touch of the priest's fingers on his hair, barely ruffling it. Then the weight increased. The priest began to massage Jack's scalp, sending shivers up and down his back. It reminded him of his barber back in New Mexico. The guy would dispense this odd-smelling tonic from a tall plastic bottle, one with a picture of an old-fashioned gentleman in a top hat. Then he would rub it into your hair. Especially if there wasn't a line, he would rub it in for a long time. Get you feeling all quivery like a dog scratched between the ears. Not wanting it to stop, not wanting to go anywhere.

The priest continued to knead Jack's scalp, his neck. He was getting goose bumps on his arms now. They felt large and exposed, the raised pimples of flesh.

Jack felt a tender squeeze on his right bicep. "You know you have lovely skin, Jason."

At this point, Jack realized the priest had gotten into his head somehow, and he decided to let himself go along with the whole thing. The guy obviously knew what he was doing. Besides, he told himself, it was his job to enjoy it.

"You are feeling hotter now, Jason. The sun is getting hotter. Your mouth feels dry. Your armpits are moist. A bead of sweat is running down your chest."

Jack felt his own hand move briefly in the direction of his stomach, as if to catch it.

"You see someone coming down the beach toward you. Just the silhouette of someone but they are getting closer. You would like to see who this person is. Sensing that they are very attractive, you stop and wait." Jack looked closer to see who was approaching. Long legs, long dark hair. It was a woman, carrying an armful of mangos. He couldn't make out any of the features on her face, but her arms were slender, her skin white in the glaring sun. Sweet smells and the ocean around her.

The priest continued. "The person is standing in front of you. Reaching toward you."

In Jack's mind, the woman remained at a distance. Unreachable. She had turned and was staring off toward the sea.

The priest slid his hand under Jack's T-shirt, pushing it up to his nipples. Then he began to pop the buttons on the fly of his jeans.

"The salt is collecting between your legs, the sweat, it's so very hot in there." Another breath and O'Flannery had his mouth around Jack. He moaned. With every motion, back and forth, he found himself wanting to thrust further into the priest, and the priest seemed willing to accommodate. Jack opened his eyes to watch it happening. Saw a flash of scalp through the thin white hair shifting below him, felt something unsettling in the barren flesh. As if sensing him there, O'Flannery turned his gaze upward, exhibiting a startling expression of vulnerability and fury. He held Jack apart from his lips. "Close your eyes," he scolded, "now."

Reluctantly, Jack closed his eyes again. He tried to remember the mangos. He could feel himself beginning to soften.

"Jason, I want you to start counting backward from a hundred. Quietly, to yourself. 100, 99, 98 . . ."

Jack knew just what the priest was up to and he was right to do it. Neither one of them wanted a slack dick right now . . . 92, 91, 90 . . . Jack found himself cursing, and then clinging to, the chain of numbers leading back out of the room. The priest had his hand around the base of Jack's cock now, was moving his mouth faster around it, lapping around the head . . . 84, 83, 82 . . . He could feel the blood rushing back in. He tried to get out of the way. . . 75, 74, 73, 72, 71, 70 . . . There was no need to count anymore. The tension had been pulled back down from his stomach and was now pulsing with the anticipation of release. Jack just wanted to get it over with.

"Don't cum on Father without warning him. You wouldn't do that I'm sure. Are you going to cum, Jason?"

Jack nodded his head rapidly. The priest pressed Jack's dick up against his stomach. Just in time, he shot his load there.

"Oh my, that's a lot of cum, Jason. Of course, it was a bit . . . hasty. But I think you're going to do just fine. All you need is to relax and enjoy yourself more. Yes, it was just fine for our first time together. Now why don't you grab a towel in the bathroom and get yourself cleaned up."

Cum was drooling down into Jack's pubes, onto the top of his thighs. He stood up, one hand covering his crotch and the mess around it, the other trying to hold off the underwear and jeans from his skin. He was trying not to trash his clothes, but after a few steps across the room, the movement began to approach something humiliating, so he stopped and let his waistband snap back into place, plastering the warm gunk onto his skin along with it. As he buttoned up his jeans, he looked over at O'Flannery who was busy tidying up the place—straightening pillows, picking up the wine glasses. He was whistling to himself.

Once inside the bathroom, the first thing Jack did was to lose the underwear. No way he was riding around town with those up against his skin. As to what to do with them once he got them off, that was another question. He wasn't about to just stroll out with them in his hand. Even if he managed to smuggle them out, then what would he do? Put them in his saddle bag where they would remain for the ride home. Suppose he got in an accident. He wouldn't want to be confronted with that kind of thing when the police arrived.

In any case, it seemed like an awful lot to go through to rescue a pair of underwear. He should probably just leave them there, wadded up and stuffed in the bottom of the wastepaper basket. Even if the priest did manage to sniff them out, who really cared?

Jack turned on the faucet and began to clean himself off. Looking at his reflection in the mirror, he was surprised to see how normal he looked—just another all-American guy washing his dick in the sink. He didn't feel normal, though, and he found himself looking closer into the glass, hoping to catch something he couldn't access from the inside.

What was the big deal, anyway? Getting sucked off in exchange for a lot of money. More money than he'd ever seen at the Cage. Money that it would have taken a full shift to clear at the fire department; he should've been happy he'd been able to pull it off.

Jack looked at himself again. He tried a smile. Felt better, seeing it there in front of him. He knew the mirror was a risky place to find his resolve, but it would have to do for now.

When he opened the door O'Flannery was waiting for him with the phone in his hand. "I've taken the liberty of calling for you already. Don't worry, I gave Benjamin a good report." He handed the phone to Jack.

"Benjamin, it's Jack. I mean . . . *shit* . . . it's me. Look, everything's fine, I'm leaving now . . . Yeah, I'll give you a call tomorrow." Jack handed the phone back to O'Flannery.

"Well, I'm sure we'll be seeing you again soon. I've got your jacket right here."

"Thanks."

"I put a little something extra in it for your travels. I understand it's not easy to get out here."

Jack found his way back outside to where the bike was parked. He unlocked his helmet from the seat, then turned on the choke before putting the key in the ignition. A single press of the starter button brought the engine to life. He was grateful for the quick response, knowing how tough the cold could be on the starter. Then he noticed the red fuel light illuminated on the instrument panel.

He thought over his options. There had been that Shell station on the way in, but he was pretty sure it had been closed. There would probably be something by the airport, but he hated to take a chance on any exit at this time of night unless he was sure. He looked at his odometer, trying to remember how many miles it had been coming out. He didn't think it'd been more than twenty. Well, that should be all right. His reserve tank usually gave him thirty or so if he kept his speed close to the limit. He switched the reserve on, fairly confident it would be enough to get him back to the 24-hour Chevron on Van Ness.

Still, it would make for a tense ride, with any hesitation from the engine sending an extra pulse of blood through his body. He'd never run out of fuel before but he'd pushed it; he knew how it would go. He backed off the choke, then hopped on the bike and pulled out of the parking lot.

On the highway again, the moon hung out in full above him, its white light dusting the pavement as if a snow had just fallen, the thinnest sheer. He wouldn't have been surprised if it really was snow. The air had only become colder since he'd ridden out, the last warmth of the day escaping through a cloudless sky. Having already been chilled once, Jack's resistance was low, and he was shivering again before he'd even reached the stretch along the water. He tried to remind himself how much he preferred it this way—the cold to the heat—how it generally kept him awake. But there was always the danger of having it sink in so far beneath his skin that he'd become numb with it. He finally had to slow the bike. It was a concession to the wind rather than the fuel situation and would make the trip longer.

To pass the time, he tried to remember bits of song lyrics, which he sang to himself. The first two couplets of a poem, which he repeated to himself. Frost's "Fire and Ice." One of many he'd been required to memorize at St. Mary's. He suspected the poet of having made minor support of ending the world in fire mostly because it made such a stunner of a rhyme. *From what I've tasted of desire, I hold with those who favor fire.* God, what a line. As far as a practical matter, though, getting burned alive had always struck Jack as far more unpleasant than freezing to death. He was frustrated to find he couldn't remember the next line, though he kept repeating the opening stanza in the hope it would bring it forth. All he could be certain of was that those missing words led down to the conclusion that ice would handle the job as well. *And would suffice.*

When he became too impatient to repeat even these simple phrases, he began to eye the odometer. With increasing frequency. Something he usually did at the end of a long day of traveling, a sign that it was time to pull over and take a break for the night. The problem now was that he couldn't look down at the numbers without catching a glimpse of the fuel light beside them, a constant reminder of his poor planning. He thought back to his hypnosis session with the priest, and telling himself to relax, focused instead on the sound of his breathing inside the helmet.

Finally, he rounded the sharp jut of curve east that revealed the downtown skyline, small but unmistakable in the distance. The Transamerica building, the Embarcadero, all outlined in colored light. It was less than ten minutes away now, this flickering jewel, a straight shot through the darkness. Resuming full pressure on the accelerator, he imagined what it would be like to remove his hands altogether—to let go—the bike racing on toward the city, and his body sailing back, back though the air, arched to open like a parachute.

Not even 3:30 and I'm out of cigarettes. What a waste, I don't even remember smoking the rest. I crumple the empty pack, take an easy shot for the trashcan. Miss.

I never should have come out tonight. Just stayed on the couch, minding my own business. It was almost midnight. I could have said no. Even if the money was supposed to be good. Even if it was supposed to last through till morning.

I pick up the phone to try Carrie again. Dial her number and wait.

Dammit, why isn't she answering? I don't even care anymore if she can help. Just to hear her voice. Someone's voice I know.

I hang up. Rub my hands on the outside of my arms. Start to walk to get my blood moving, at least. Along the sidewalk and then into the park. Sprinklers pop up on timers, spraying low arcs of water onto the already saturated fields. I stay clear of those. Climb the hill behind them, to the fountain.

Man, I wish I had a bump. Or at least some more smokes. A bump is what I really want. Just one. So what if it'd make me a little crazy, it's not like I'm—are those footsteps? Or something else. Coming down the path.

I strain my eyes through the shadows. The wind is shivering the palms.

"**K**evin?"

"Yeah. Who's this?"

"Jack."

"Who?"

That sick feeling inside. Stupid idea to call.

"Uh, Jack. We went swimming together a few weeks back. . . at the beach . . . it was cold."

"Oh, hey. I thought maybe you lost my number."

He glanced over to where the piece of paper was still taped, shook his head. No, he hadn't lost it. "So, I was wondering if you wanted to shoot some hoops this weekend."

"Weekends are bad for me . . ." Jack held on hoping for the pause, not the period. "But I'm free early next week, if you wanna try to set something up for then."

"What about Tuesday afternoon?"

"Tuesday works. Where d'you wanna play?"

"I was gonna ask you that."

"Dolores Park's where I usually go."

"In the Mission?"

"Yeah, that too far for ya?"

"No, that's fine. I've been by there. I just don't remember seeing a court."

"It's between the tennis courts."

"Oh, okay. I know where you're talking about. You wanna say around two?"

"Sure."

"You got a ball, right?"

"Yeah."

"See you Tuesday, then."

Jack hung up, wondering how it would be to see him again. He'd made the call, that was the important thing. After looking at the number every morning, taped inside the cereal cabinet. Telling himself he'd follow through with it later. Tomorrow. A week passed. Two. When he noticed he'd started leaving the cereal out on the counter, he realized how scared he was. Not only of spoiling the memory of a perfect afternoon, but going forward, all the potential that went along with it. He didn't really know anything about the guy. Whether he had a boyfriend. A girlfriend. All he knew was how good it had felt to be around him that day.

He'd been making his way along the perimeter of the cove. A mess of dirty blond hair, jean jacket, sweats. Stopping from time to time to crouch, examine something in the sand. As he drew closer, Jack returned his attention to the book he'd been reading. Normally if someone approached him like that, he would've felt crowded; if he'd been into socializing, there were other beaches he could have gone to. But right away he felt something different. On edge but interested. At least until the guy spoke.

"Knock-knock."

What, was he kidding? Jack furrowed his brow, trying to concentrate on the pages in front of him.

"Hey, lanky, you see anyone else around here? I said knock-knock to ya."

"All right, who's there?"

"Kevin."

"Kevin who?"

"Kevin Jensen. You?"

"You wanna know my name?"

"That's the idea. You sure are awful serious for a day at the beach."

Jack took a long look at who he'd been speaking to. The sun was persuading the color of the ocean into his eyes. "Yeah, well, I'm really into this book."

"What is it?"

"*Notes from the Underground.*"

"Sounds pretty dark."

"It's Dostoyevsky, I mean, you're not gonna get a lot of rainbows and butterflies."

"Mind if I take a peek?"

Jack handed him the book. He glanced at the front cover, skimmed through the back, then returned it to Jack.

"No offense, but haven't you heard the term summer reading?"

"Well, technically we got another few weeks before summer starts. I figured I'd better squeeze in all the gloomy Russians before then."

Kevin returned his smile. Then reached inside his jacket pocket and pulled out a paperback. "Here, check this."

"*The Jungle Books.*"

"Yup."

Jack put down his own book and began flipping through Kevin's. "Good stories. Yeah, I used to read these to my girlfriend when we'd go camping." It was the first thing that had popped into his mind to say, but it felt like he was trying to put up a barrier.

Kevin plowed right through it. "What a neat idea. Sitting around the fire and all, I could get into that." His eyes shone. Jack thought he should be forced to wear sunglasses. "Hey, d'you care if I set up shop here. . . I won't be staying long."

"Go ahead."

"Great, thanks." He pulled the rest of the towel out that had been hanging over the waistband of his sweats, made a half attempt to spread it out evenly. Then took off his jacket, started to take off his shirt. "Everyone probably asks you this, but you play basketball, right?"

"Yeah, everyone asks me, and yeah I do."

"Glad to hear it. Maybe I'll get a chance to show you a move or two sometime."

Jack lay back in the sand. "Maybe you will."

Kevin was guarding him, down by four, when he'd made the suggestion that "they really should make a basketball musical." Then he'd stolen the ball. Kevin was down by three.

"What d'you think about my idea?"

"I think I can't dribble and discuss musicals at the same time."

"You don't have to worry about dribbling anymore, since I'm about to run this game out." At which point he faked right, pulled back, and swished the jumper.

"Nice shot."

"Thanks." He held the ball at the check line. "Let's say you *were* gonna make a basketball musical. What d'ya think you'd call it?"

"How about *Play Now, Talk Later*."

"How about it?" he asked, trying the same move, but Jack got a piece of the ball that time. Still, Kevin managed to recover it and power in for the score.

"Nice drive."

"Wasn't it?"

Jack stuffed his next lay-up.

"I think you were over my back."

"You see a referee around here?"

"I think you were over my back," he repeated.

"All right, fine." He handed Kevin the ball.

Jack stopped his next drive, definitely clean that time. Missed the lay-up but got the rebound. Then finished it with two consecutive hooks from the left post. "You wanna go again?"

"Nah. I wanted to win that one."

"Which ones didn't you want to win?"

"Not all of them."

"I don't believe that."

"Believe what you want," he said.

They walked off under the shade of some trees where they'd left their stuff. Jack picked up his shirt, mopped the sweat off the back of his neck. "So I don't understand how it is you can like sports and musicals at the same time?"

"What don't you understand?"

"Well, I don't see what they have in common."

"I never thought about what they have in common. Maybe 'cause they both have a lot of action. Always something going on. Why? You got some sort of hang-up with musicals?"

"It's not a hang-up, I just don't like them. The singing part anyway. I usually get all tense right when I get the feeling someone's about to bust out with a song."

"I've never heard of anyone getting tense watching a musical."

"It happens."

Kevin passed him the water. "Tell me, what else you do with your time besides avoiding musicals?"

"Well, there's other things I like to avoid. Certain vegetables for example."

"Cauliflower, right?"

"Yeah, how d'you know?"

"You don't look like a cauliflower kind of guy to me."

"What kind of guy do I look like?"

"Hmm . . . rutabaga, maybe."

Jack tried to figure out whether he was getting slammed; he couldn't get a clear picture of the vegetable in his head. "I hope you're not talking trash over there, the game's over."

"What makes you think I'm insulting ya? Besides, the reason I picked it was because I've never seen one before, but it sounds kind of interesting."

"I see."

"Plus, it's fun to say. Rutabaga."

"Yeah, well, however you want to get your kicks . . ." Jack took a swig from the water bottle.

"Anyways, what I was trying to find out about was what you do. You know, for a living?"

Jack wiped his chin. "Maybe we should stick to vegetables."

"Come on, it can't be that bad."

He was toying with the hesitation. It was only to his advantage to get the information on the table—it didn't necessarily say anything about him. Kevin's reaction would be more important. "I doubt you've heard of this place called the Cage?"

"Up in Nob Hill, sure."

"Well, that's what I do."

"You're their accountant, right?"

"There you go, you got me all pegged out." Jack passed him back the water. "So how about you, what d'you do?"

"Furniture maker by day, escort by night." And then he added thoughtfully, "Although sometimes it's escort by day and furniture maker by night."

"Oh, yeah . . . cool." A month ago, Jack might've been interested in this new information. Maybe he could've asked Kevin a few questions about what to expect before he'd met up with the priest. Now he wasn't so sure. "Yeah, you furniture-making escorts are a dime a dozen around this town."

"Not as common as you Doysto. . .vesky—" he mangled the name once more before giving up and starting again. "Not as common as you Russian-novel-reading strippers." Kevin blushed into a smile and Jack gave up trying to keep a straight face.

"Don't worry about it. It's not like I can pronounce a single other word in Russian." He thought it'd be a good time to change the subject. "So what d'you think happened with Golden State this year?"

"Same thing as always. Still out in the wilderness, although I couldn't say what exactly went wrong this time. I don't have much time for watching sports."

"Just playing them."

"Not as much as I'd like. I usually only give myself one day off a week, but then the rule is no work whatsoever. Just fun stuff."

"Like sweating your ass off and having it handed to you on a platter."

"Hey, I thought we were leaving that on the court."

"I'm just pointing out the facts."

"You fellas looking for a game?" A man had walked up to them, his buddy hanging back a few steps.

Jack looked to Kevin. "I think we've had it, no?"

"I could go again."

"You sure?"

He winked. "Yeah, let's see how we play together."

That was the problem with hanging out with another guy when there was a chance of something going on that went beyond friendship. Even innocuous sounding phrases like "play together" could take on other meanings. Jack wasn't opposed to plays on words, but he could see them becoming tiring in this case. He wanted things clear. Either they were talking about basketball or they were talking about something else. It wasn't that long ago that he hadn't had to worry about situations like this with his friends, and he realized how much simpler it had been then. He wished he could tune his brain out of stereo; it would be nice just to shoot some hoops and not worry about the rest.

He went into the game distracted, not expecting much, but it had gone smoothly from the start. A quick cut inside, and he found the ball in his hands, a perfect pass from Kevin easily converted. And they continued to read each other after that. Kevin had the ball control, Jack the size, and they won both tightly contested games before the other guys called it. They returned to their things, flush with the good feeling of having connected again.

"That was great."

"Yeah, we sure had 'em confused with those picks."

"Yeah," Jack agreed, "for a while. But once they started switching, I should've cleared out more. You had that older guy burned to the basket."

Jack sat down in the grass. Pulled a blade and stuck it between his teeth, content just letting the sweat cool.

Kevin spun the ball on his finger. After a while, he asked, "How'd you get here?"

"On my bike."

"Motorcycle?"

"Yeah, that's right. Most people think I'm talking about a bicycle."

"Well, I noticed earlier when you pulled off your necklace that—"

"It's not a necklace."

"What is it, then?"

"Never mind."

"Okay, well, when I saw your keys, I was pretty sure that's what they were for. I used to have a bike."

"You still ride?"

"I gave it up. Had a bad wreck near the end of high school. Came out better than I shoulda, so I decided no more after that."

"It seems like that's the first thing everyone wants to tell you about. You know, about the wrecks they've had or their cousin who got maimed or something."

"I was just tryin' to explain to you why I gave it up. I still think it's a great way to get around."

"Especially around here where you get to weave through all the traffic."

"And pull up to the front at red lights. Yes, I know. I don't like taking my truck out unless I have to. It's not nearly as much fun and gas is so expensive."

"See? Another good point. Saves on fuel." Jack felt like the matter had been settled in his favor. "Of course, not as much as a bicycle. Doesn't do much for keeping you in shape, either, but I wouldn't trade it in."

Kevin gave him the once over. "Looks like you're in pretty good shape to me."

Jack felt a flash of heat across his face, while his brain spun its wheels in a bunch of different directions, trying to crank out a response. Accept the compliment, return it, make a joke. And then it had taken too long to say anything.

"You know, you should think about coming by the agency where I work."

Damn. Jack felt like he'd tried to surface with this whole escorting business only to get knocked back under. It had to be Atlas—the only agency in town as far as he knew—and he'd sworn he was done with them. He hadn't even gone by to pick up the money they owed him. And they'd never called him back. Why Kevin would want to get mixed up with an outfit like that he couldn't understand. "I think escorting might be a little extreme."

"You think there's something wrong with it?"

"I mean, for me. You gotta pay the bills, right?"

"Right," he said, flatly. Then he brightened again. "But it's more than that. I think it's a really neat job in a lot of ways, and it's a pretty professional operation where I work. If you stopped by, you could see for yourself what—"

"What is up with you guys and your recruiting?" Jack's voice had far more of an edge to it than he'd wanted. In fact, he hadn't wanted to say anything at all.

"What are you talking about?"

"Forget it."

"Forget forgetting it. What d'you mean about recruiting?"

"You work for Atlas, right? Look, I already ran a call with them."

"Really!? When?"

"A little while back. Your guy Jonathan came by the Cage and suggested I go down there, so I . . . went."

"That's kind of weird you didn't mention it right away."

"Not really. It wasn't anything I wanted to talk about. Still don't." Jack had been planning on asking him out for a beer, but it no longer seemed like such a good idea. There'd already been enough to try to absorb for one afternoon. He started to gather his things. "Look, I've got some stuff I need to take care of."

"Oh. Well, I guess I'll see you around then."

He looked over at Kevin again. *Of course, he worked for Atlas.* Jack would've hired him in a second. "Wait. Uh, can you make it for next Tuesday?"

"I'll be here."

"Well, I'll be here too, so . . . all right, take care then." He walked back to his bike certain he'd said the wrong things, wondering if it even mattered.

It was a long week. Jack spent most of it replaying events in his mind. There was a part of him that had wanted things to go perfectly, and that hadn't happened. He remained less than thrilled with the news of Kevin's employment, most of his feeling mixed up with his own awkward experience, but still, he didn't see how anything good could come of it. It was one thing when he'd been trying to become an escort, himself, but another to like someone who already was. Besides, maybe Kevin would turn out to be just another scout. A friendly one to be sure, but who knew?

He tried to occupy himself with reading, but he kept picking up a book and putting it down again, unable to concentrate. The next day at the gym he strained his shoulder pushing too much weight and hadn't gone back. Riding seemed monotonous, no matter where he went, and he nearly called in sick to work. Then, when he did go in, he saw that he'd only been given two slots on the following week's schedule.

He hadn't been sleeping well, but Monday night was the worst. He woke up late the next day, and by the time he arrived at the park, a full court game was already in progress. Kevin was waiting along with a couple other guys. The four of them took on the winning skins team, and then kept rotating in until enough people had left that there were only two teams left playing. Finally, that game broke up.

It had been a good workout, but Jack was never able to find his rhythm and he knew it didn't have anything to do with his shoulder. His eye had been off, his footwork lazy. He wasn't the only one who'd noticed.

"You were really out of it today."

"No shit, Sherlock. I should've brought some goddamn mortar along for all those bricks."

"You're lucky there was a crowd, or I would've been forced to give you a mighty personal spanking."

"Yeah, I was lucky all right." Jack tipped back the water bottle, emptied it. "We should remember to bring more water next time. That coast-to-coast just takes it out of you." He crushed the plastic and tossed it aside.

"You are going to put that in the trash, right?"

"Apparently."

"Then I'll be happy to inform you there's a fountain across the park. Come on." Kevin grabbed the ball and started walking. Jack retrieved the bottle and stuffed it in the band of his shorts. Then he fell in step beside Kevin.

"Now, guess who couldn't help themselves from doing some Double-O-Seven type investigating over the weekend?"

"Oh yeah, about what?"

"I made some inquiries at Atlas."

"Funny, but I seem to recall mentioning I didn't want to talk about that." He tried to snatch the ball away from Kevin, but he shifted it to his other hand and kept spinning.

"Yeah, but you had to expect that would only make me more curious."

"So what should I have said to make you less curious?"

"You should've just told me what happened. I heard you got O'Flannery."

"You know him?"

"You could say that."

"You've been with him."

"Um, yeah. Me and the rest of the staff. Past and present."

He wondered what else Kevin knew. "So . . . what did you think of that whole hypnosis routine?"

"He didn't do it with me, but I know he's done it before. What'd you think of it? And be careful what you say here, 'cause I've been informed about a few other things."

"Like what?"

"Like I understand someone was a little Speedy Gonzales."

"Are you fucking kidding me? Did you hear I left my underwear in his trash, too?"

"No, but thanks for that additional detail." His smile broadened. "Thoughtful of you to leave him with a souvenir."

"It wasn't for his benefit." Jack shook his head. "Man, I am so glad I got out of there. What do you guys do, sit around in your skirts all day and gossip about other people's calls?"

"Relax, *man*. Benjamin only mentioned it 'cause I asked him. Plus, he gave me some money to pass along to you. I've got it in my pack."

"Keep it."

"I'm not gonna keep it. It's yours. I don't know what you think could've gone so wrong that you don't feel like you deserve it. O'Flannery thought you were nice. Well, he might not've exactly said that, but supposably he said you were smart. He really was hoping to see you again."

"Whatever, I don't care." Jack was embarrassed with the attention. The money. Everything. He wished he knew where the water fountain was so he could pick up the pace.

Naturally, Kevin chose that moment to hold up. "Well. You seem like you do. Why don't you level with me about what's bothering you? Something sure is, that's all I've been trying to figure out here."

"Why does it matter to you?"

"Because it matters to you."

That sounded simple. Maybe even true. "Okay, so I'm gonna guess Double-O-Seven here has already figured out it wasn't the most positive experience." Kevin didn't smile and Jack's gaze drifted down toward his sneakers. "The thing is, I never felt like I was in control of the situation."

"I hear you. But if you're looking for control, maybe it really isn't the best job for you."

"I suppose. But Atlas just made it worse. Like they'd set up a playdate for me, and I had to constantly check in to let them know how it was going. I felt like a kid practically the whole time I was there and then . . ." He glanced up briefly at Kevin before continuing. His concern still seemed genuine. "And then, on the ride home, I guess I got a little depressed about the whole thing. I—I don't know, it was just one more night that made me wonder what I'm doing here, that's all."

"Haven't you figured that out yet?"

"Nope."

"Well, for one thing, you're supposed to be keeping me company."

A hint of playfulness had crept into Kevin's eyes and Jack didn't know what to make of it. Until after the basketball had bounced off the side of his head. "Hey!" he yelled, but Kevin had already taken off running. Jack rubbed behind his ear, looked over to where the ball had rolled in the grass. He stared at it. Then scooped it into his arms, before chasing Kevin the rest of the way to the fountain.

He'd left footprints. With his sneakers. Along the beach, leading to and from the place where their towels had been. Before leaving, he'd scribbled down his number. His face, finally, shy when he offered it.

Watching him disappear around the rocks—his compact wrestler's frame, the slight bow to his legs—Jack thought maybe later he'd try and follow the tracks. For a little ways, at least. To see which direction they were headed.

From the shelter of the cove, they'd raced through crosswinds to the open sea, the frigid water seizing their breath as they'd gone in and under. Then just as fast, maybe faster, they'd sprinted back to the shore. Huddled their bodies next to one another there. Not quite touching. Christ, it'd felt so good—all impulse rushing nerves, adrenaline pure.

The buzz had been slow to steady, wearing down in waves. If he closed his eyes, he could still feel it wash over him.

They were walking out of the deli on Sutter, back toward the Missing Sock where they'd left their clothes spinning. Kevin was drinking a smoothie through the straw he'd pulled from his cargo pocket. "You know, I've been thinking I might have to start using my real name at work."

It was in no way a continuation of the conversation they'd been having. That had been about the usefulness of fabric softener.

"So this means you're conceding the fact that Downy is a waste of money."

"I'm not consneeding, or whatever, anything. I'm tired of talking about laundry. It's bad enough we have to do it."

"You're the one who was crying because you were out of underwear, yo. I could've gone at least another week, no problem."

"You're still talking about laundry. You see that, right?"

"Okay, what's the new subject again?"

"The subject is me, and me not using a made-up name anymore."

"So this is the end of the line for Stan, huh?"

"No, Truss. I've been using Truss."

"*Truss?* Since when?"

"Since . . . since just once. And I don't want to hear any crap about it, I'm serious."

"You're never serious. And besides, you're not gonna drop a name like Truss on me and keep walking."

"Terrence Russell, all right. It was my grandfather's name. There, now you have it. The T from Terrence and—"

"I thought you didn't even know who your real parents were."

Kevin blinked away an instant of hurt. "He wasn't technically my grandfather, jerk. But he was kind of like that. But, listen. I'm wondering if maybe the only name I should be using anymore is my own."

"So why don't you? That made-up name stuff is a hassle, anyway. I remember the night I was with O'Flannery, every time he said, 'Jason,' I kept thinking there was someone else in the room."

"It's never been a hassle for me."

"Then why the sudden turnaround?"

"Well. What happened was . . . are you sure you really want to hear this?"

"If you'd stop drawing it out, yes. Just tell me."

"Two nights ago this guy told me he loved me."

Jack felt a single, extra beat in his chest and swallowed down hard on it. "So what's that got to do with your name?"

"You don't seem very surprised."

"Were you? Don't you get that all the time?"

"No. No one's ever said that to me before."

"Hmm."

"It was a big deal."

"I guess so."

"Don't you even wanna know who the guy was?"

Jack shrugged. "If it matters to the story." And then feeling conspicuous in his little show of disinterest, he asked, "So is this someone you've known awhile?"

"No, I tried it out on a new guy."

"Not exactly a long-term romance, then?"

"Right, exactly. Anyway, we didn't even really have sex. I mean we were in bed but . . . Well, he just kept holding me and saying, 'I love you, Truss.' He said it like three or four times. I kept being afraid he was gonna say it again, and then he did. Like really emphasizing the love and the Truss part, and I don't know, it just made me feel like such a faker."

"Maybe he was hoping you'd give him a discount."

"Maybe you're not taking me very seriously."

"No, I see your point. But do you really think you would've felt better if he said, I love you, Kevin."

"You're mumbling. If he said what?"

"I love you—hey, I thought you were trying to be serious."

"You weren't cooperating. But now that I've got your full attention. Yes, I do think I woulda felt better if he used my real name. That's the point."

"Well, I don't know. How could it've made the situation better hearing your name attached to some b.s. like the guy telling you he loved you."

"You don't think he really did?"

"What, after twenty minutes?"

"Well, aren't you the one who said when people fall in love, it's all 'instantaneous, overwhelming and . . .' I forget the third thing, but you definitely said 'instantaneous.'"

It was a drag, generally, when people quoted Jack's own bullshit back at him. Especially when it went up against some current bullshit he was trying to spin out. It wasn't clear what had him thinking he had anything smart to offer up on the subject of love, but he'd managed to slur something about it the other night over last beers.

"Yeah, I might've said something like that. Happens at first sight or doesn't happen at all. But I had more in mind, you know, strangers on a train."

"What's the difference if he saw me on a train or at his hotel door?"

"You realize you're making this more difficult. Which I don't understand, because my guess is for some reason you don't want to use your real name, so you're looking for a little justification so you don't have to."

"Yes, but I want it to be a good justification."

Jack already had a theory but wasn't sure he was prepared to have it proved wrong. Still, he hadn't been the one who hauled his dirty clothes crosstown so they could spend time together. "How about this? The difference is what I was talking about was falling in love, and what you're talking about is infatuation. You need two people for the first one. You didn't fall in love with him, did you?"

"No."

"Well, there's your answer, pal." He gave a quick jab with his left fist. "The guy was infatuated with you, he got confused and thought he loved you, so you shouldn't feel bad. You both used a fake name for something so that makes it even. No harm done."

"Hey, I think you're onto something there."

"I usually am. But the thing is, I don't see how it's gonna help you to be able to salvage Truss. That's three names you'd have to keep track of. Old clients. New clients. I thought you liked keeping things simple over there at Atlas."

Kevin kicked at a rock on the sidewalk. "Rats," he said. "Daniel told me the same thing."

There was no getting around the crush he had on Kevin. Sometimes so strong, he could feel it walking between the two of them down the street. With legs of its own. With hands that might have joined them, clasped at the back. That's the nature of a crush. It's happy to chaperone your feelings along, whistle a pleasant tune, but at the end of the day, you're stuck with it, while the subject of your affections gives you the peace sign and heads off in the opposite direction.

There was so much about Kevin he liked. His looks, of course. It wouldn't be fair to leave that off the list, or try to slip it somewhere in the middle, when it was the first thing he'd noticed. And it seemed like that always had to be the first thing, something physical at least, even a voice or a touch. The starting point of every route that ever led inside a person.

Getting to know Kevin was easier because he didn't try to put up so many obstacles along the way. He didn't seem to mind the exposure. This meant there was a kind of continuity between him and the rest of the world that made him seem at home wherever he was standing.

He could be mischievous but was rarely unkind. Smart with his tongue. He'd argue about anything if he was in the mood. He had opinions—some more thought out than others—but in any case, you didn't get the feeling he was weighed down by them. He managed to be confident without being one hundred percent sure about everything.

He didn't smoke (*I don't care what the surgeon general says, it smells like crap*), didn't think much of drugs (*I still feel like me on them, only not as good*), and although he drank, Jack had yet to see him flat out wasted. Not that he needed another excuse to clown around. At times, he could be almost aggressively immature, but for the most part his approach served him well. And was just about the right speed for Jack, who had visited adulthood, once, and didn't see the big rush in getting back there.

"Hey, Kev. When you were younger, did you ever read *The Red Balloon*?"

"I don't think so."

"There's a movie based on it, too, maybe you saw that. It's French."

"I'm American the last time I checked."

"Is that why you keep all those red, white, and blue boxers? So you don't forget what country you live in."

"You sure are talking a lot about my underwear today."

"Well, I was trying to talk about classic lit before you got me off track. Now . . . aw, hell, I guess there's not much to say if you haven't read it. You remind me of one of the main characters, that's all."

"I hope it's a fun one."

"Definitely the funnest one."

It might not have gone over real well if he'd been told it was the balloon Jack was thinking of. But it was true, so much of the time he seemed to be floating. On the court, across the park, down the street. Playful, sometimes darting, he'd disappear for a moment, only to be waiting around the next corner.

Kevin wasn't in front of The Crepe Company, but after standing there for five minutes, Jack noticed a hand poking out from the side of the shop. It waved, then was withdrawn. He debated whether or not to ignore these shenanigans before walking toward it.

"How old did you say you were again?"

"Old enough to decide how I wanna act."

Jack shrugged. "So, what'd you think?"

"Of the movie?"

"Yeah, didn't you go?"

"Sure, but I thought you mighta been asking about the whole experiment."

The "experiment" had been set in motion by an invitation from Kevin to catch a matinee. Jack had been forced to explain his position on tandem movie watching. He'd taken a hard line, while omitting the flagrant violations he'd committed, up to and including the film festival with Skelly. Kevin was mystified with his reasoning, but mostly disappointed, so Jack thought it through some more and came up with a plan as to how they could go together without actually going together. Kevin would arrive fifteen minutes early and sit on the right side of the theater. Jack would come later and sit on the left. Then they would meet up afterward for a drink. The more he thought about the plan, the more he liked it. He would have the feature to himself, and then, right afterward, someone to analyze it with. Kevin thought it was a weird idea but agreed to give it a try.

"Now that we did it, I think it's even weirder," he said.

"Really? I thought it worked out okay."

"Yeah, but wasn't what you wanted was for there to be no distractions?" Jack nodded.

"But I couldn't concentrate. I was thinking about you on the way over there because I was a little late and worried I was gonna bump into you in line, and then I was thinking about you when I walked in 'cause I could hear your voice telling me, 'make sure you stick to the right side.' And then when I sat down, I accidentally looked across the theater and saw the back of this tall guy's head, and I thought that might be you. Then I got to figuring you'd probably sit in the last row, but I stopped myself from looking back there."

"Wow, you really went through it, didn't you?" Jack wasn't exactly unpleased with this information. In fact, he'd had a somewhat similar experience on his end, but he didn't see the advantage in mentioning it. "All right, but once the film got going, then wasn't it great?"

"I guess. I don't know, maybe the whole thing was just a tad too much. Like I woulda been able to concentrate better having you right there beside me."

Kevin had just finished brushing his teeth and was about to turn out the light in the bathroom. Looking over at Jack, he didn't appear the slightest bit happy. "Hey, what are you doing with all the covers?"

"What I'm doing is, taking them all for myself because you stole them last night and I froze my ass off. Payback's a bitch."

"Couldn't you have just gently woken me up and told me?"

"Hell, no. You were making that strange clicking noise which I've now established to mean you're in a deep sleep and completely non-responsive to external stimuli. Like getting whacked with a pillow."

It was night three of a seemingly endless ordeal of a week, where he'd agreed to temporarily take in Kevin as a roommate. Part of Kevin's ceiling had collapsed due to termites, and his landlord suggested he find somewhere else to stay while they did the repairs. Kevin liked his apartment and didn't want to make a big fuss. Jack thought it was a lowdown deal and said so. He'd also been a little suspicious of the story. Not like Kevin would be lying, but maybe exaggerating the living conditions. So he'd suggested they go take a look so he could see the full extent of the destruction.

Sure enough, the place was trashed. "Wow, you weren't kidding."

"Why would I be kidding? You think I'd otherwise volunteer to shack up with the likes of you?"

Jack had told himself no matter what else happened, he was absolutely, positively not making a move on Kevin. He wasn't sure how it would be received, first of all, since he'd been unable to rid himself of the suspicion that Kevin was a professional flirt, just waiting to catch him looking so he could call the strikeout. And if there was more to it than that, well, he didn't want their first experience to be the result of some termite infestation.

Lying in bed with Kevin, he realized this approach seemed both prissy and unreasonably demanding, but he didn't care. He'd made up his mind.

"Too bad I don't have a couch."

"You said that the first night. Now how 'bout giving up those blankets."

"On what basis?"

"Well, don't I get any credit for all the truly excellent things I've done for you lately. Like . . . going to the movies with you. Alone. Most people probably would've told you to take a flying. How 'bout if I agree to go again? Or how 'bout I just start punching you?"

Jack considered these options, then unrolled out of the covers which he'd surrounded himself with, mummy style. "Okay, have at it."

Kevin got in. The mattress was big but not big enough. Kevin's elbow was just barely touching the side of his stomach. He felt increasingly poised for trouble. "I've got a confession to make," he began. Talking was usually an effective way to kill his sex drive, and though the results so far that week had been mixed, there had been some measurable successes. "To be honest with you, that movie experiment didn't work out all that well for me either."

"What d'ya mean?"

"I mean, I got distracted thinking about you when I walked in and . . . during the movie too."

"Gosh, staying over here I'm learning all sorts of stuff about you. How come you really only tell the truth when you're in bed."

"Leaving out information doesn't make me a liar. This is like the fuller version."

"Well, I'm glad to know it. It was kinda giving me the creeps that you could be sitting fifty feet away and just tune me out."

"That's funny because it was bothering me that I couldn't tune you out."

"Really!? Why?"

"Because I went to watch the movie, how difficult should it've been."

Kevin didn't respond right away. When he did, he'd lowered his voice. He said he wanted to tell a story about his Aunt Margaret.

"Hold on. You're starting in with something sentimental, I can just tell."

Kevin frowned. "If you're going to make a judgment about it maybe you better wait till you actually hear it."

Jack waited.

"Once upon a time, I lived with my Aunt Margaret. And of all the people who took care of me, I liked her best. Do you wanna know why?"

"Sure."

"Because she loved me. And, if you must know, because she made really tasty oatmeal cookies.

"Now, one night I was lying in bed and thinking about how much I loved *her* because she'd just tucked me in and I could still feel her hands on the covers, warm and soft. Like she was all but practically right there, okay?"

Jack nodded.

"Then I decided I wanted a glass of milk. So I got out of bed and walked down the hall. It wasn't like I was sneakin'—not trying to be quiet or anything like that—but I walked into the living room and there was Margaret and she didn't hear me. And she was knitting, which I'd seen her do before, and she had on the news, which I'd seen too, but never the both together. And right then, I knew she wasn't thinking about me at all. Like between the knitting and the TV there was no room for me, not even a little bit. That was the first time I ever imagined what it'd be like to be dead."

"Wow, I was wrong. Your story isn't hokey. It's depressing."

"I'm just sayin'—"

"I know what you're saying, but you can't go around thinking about people all the time. Even people you care about."

"But then it's not really true what people say about your never being very far from their minds. Margaret said that to me before I left, 'You'll never be far from my mind,' but I knew it wasn't right. Because it's like you're either there or you're not. And I don't like being forgotten so quickly."

"Yeah, but don't you find yourself doing the same thing. Meeting people and then forgetting about them. With your clients, don't you sort of have to?"

"Yeah, I do. I know it. Sure, there's been a lot of awfully nice people, and I think about them sometimes but . . . it's better to be the one doing the forgetting. Besides, there's never been one of them I really wanted to remember before."

Jack turned over on his side and faced the wall. "Maybe you'll get lucky and meet someone."

"I'm not planning to lose any sleep over it. G'night."

Jack was woken the next morning by a loud rapping on the floor by his head. He opened one eye, then the other.

"Looky there!"

"Look—" Jack cleared his throat—"Looky where?" He bent his chin forward to peer down, but he already knew what Kevin was pointing to. The tent pole he'd raised from beneath the covers.

"See. You want me. Admit it." Then Kevin busted out laughing, scrambled up from beside the bed, and began to get dressed.

In fact, Jack had been dreaming about water-sliding, after having waited in line with a large group of people, not one of whom he could recall having the slightest interest in. "Those are related to REM sleep, dink. Not the company in the room."

"Well, I'm leaving now, and I can see it's going down. Think about it." Then he pulled on his sneakers and was out the door.

Kevin was busy the rest of the week, gone all day and for large chunks of time during the evening hours. Saturday night when Jack got back from the Cage, he wasn't there at all. Jack had expected this, the guy was just doing his job, and he did his best to be comfortable with it. What he hadn't expected was not to hear from Kevin once he'd relocated back to his own apartment. It was one of those goodbyes where no one said they'd call, and then no one did.

Jack's buzzer rang just after dark.

"Hell-lo."

"It's Kevin."

"Kevin who?"

"Jack, this isn't a knock-knock joke."

"Well, what kind of joke is it?"

Kevin usually used the intercom to make a delivery announcement. *Sushi on a Bicycle* or some other lame claim. This time, Jack was happy just to hear his voice.

"Hey, come down here for a minute, will ya? Actually, it'd be better if you came down here like you might be going out."

"Well, am I going out?"

"That depends."

"On what?"

"Do you think you could just please come down here?"

"Okay. Give me five."

When he got down to the lobby, Kevin was sitting on the steps. He jumped right up.

"Nice shirt."

"Thanks. I don't know. Carrie picked it out for me."

"Of course she did. Okay, I need to ask you something. You remember Matt from Atlas, don't you? You met him the night we went bowling."

Jack nodded.

"Well, er, he decided to get all messed up about an hour ago, and there's no way he can take this call with me now. And I'm late. And I tried calling like three other people and I can't get anyone to go. I didn't wanna get Matt in trouble and I knew you weren't working tonight, so—"

"So you thought you'd call in second string off the bench. This is what I get dressed up for?"

"Just hear me out on this, okay? Now, I know you said you were through with the agency, but you'd really be doing this for me. I've been with this guy a bunch of times and he just likes having someone else in the room. He'll be so disappointed if it doesn't happen. His wife only gives him a few times a year to do this, and I'm sure she's split already, and—"

"You just want me in the room with you, that's it."

"That's it. You don't even have to be naked. Okay, it'd be nice if you could be enjoying yourself, too, but that's entirely it. Nothing else."

"You sure Matt can't make it?"

"Not a chance, he's crazy messed up." Kevin proceeded to twirl his finger around the outside of his ear to emphasize the point, a gesture that managed to make the whole proposition seem more innocent than nuts.

"All right, where we headed?"

"Hey, great, Jack, I really appreciate it. We're going to Marin."

He followed Kevin out onto the street. There was a Lincoln town car waiting.

"So this is how the other half lives," Jack observed, opening the door and getting in.

"Don't cry poor. Didn't you say you were from Connecticut originally?"

"What do you know about Connecticut?"

"Enough," he said. "Now scoot over."

Jack slid across the seat. "Like what?"

"Like it rhymes with money."

"You mean like a slant rhyme."

"Whatever." Kevin shrugged. "So why don't you tell me something about Connecticut? You hardly ever talk about when you were a kid."

"What's there to tell?"

"That's what I'm asking you. Just tell me something fun you did when you were growing up. At school or whatever. Anything."

"All right, let's see." A series of incidents came to Jack's mind but none of them seemed to meet the fun criteria so, one after another, he rejected them. "There was the first time I snuck into the city. That was definitely fun."

Kevin smiled, "This sounds like a good one. Wait, what city?"

"Hartford."

"Hartford? I haven't heard anything about that."

"New York. New York City, all right? Jeez. So this is in junior high. Eighth grade, I think, a couple months into the school year. Anyway, I got off the bus in this foul mood. I had to drag myself up the stairs when the first bell rang. Then I reached the double doors and I said to myself, screw this, why should I even bother going in here."

"This isn't very fun so far."

"Give it a chance, will you?"

"Okay, why were you in a bad mood?"

"Because . . . there was a situation at home."

"With your parents?"

"Kind of."

"So you do have parents. I was beginning to think you were raised by a pack of wolves or something."

"Yeah, I had parents."

"Something happened to them?"

"Listen, Kevin, I'm not trying to perk up your interest here, but I really don't want to talk about it. What d'you say we start this whole story over. This was back in junior high, and I got to school in this tremendously happy mood. The best mood ever, in fact. It was April and spring was in the air—no wait, better make that May—and I was so frigging excited I knew I couldn't contain myself inside a classroom all day, so I had to do something brilliant like steal into the city. Nod along if you're with me on this."

"Got ya. But we're coming back to your family another time."

"Okay, so the school sat directly across from the train station. You'd look at those tracks every day, knowing they led into the city, that you always had somewhere to go if you needed to, so this one day I walked over there and bought a ticket. Things were pretty quiet on the train, nestled in among a bunch of briefcases, but when I got off in Grand Central, man, it was intense! All the stars stuck frozen on the ceiling, with the crowds of people below moving in every possible direction. It wasn't like I hadn't been there before, but it was completely different, being on my own. No one to distract you from the energy."

"I've been wanting to get to New York for a while now."

"You should go."

"Maybe we could go together."

"Sure. So anyway, after I got out of the station, I decided to duck inside some sporting goods shop. Looked at sneakers for a while until I got myself together, then I started wandering around everywhere. The East Side, downtown. Places I'd never been before. Everyone seemed so vital, you know, it was like a privilege just to be able to stand there and look on. I kept asking myself why I hadn't done this sooner.

"The whole day was amazing. Plenty of adventures, but by the end I was getting pretty worn down. It was close to dark, but I wasn't ready to go home yet, so I went back to this park I'd been to earlier. Bummed a cigarette, thinking that would help me get back in the swing of things, but after the first couple hits I got so dizzy I had to sit down on one of the benches.

"Next thing I knew, there were two guys coming toward me, one of them pushing a shopping cart filled with cans, and the other holding a couple of paper bags. The one guy parks the cart, and the other one hands him a bag, and they both sit down on the bench next to me. The first guy pulls out a sandwich, unwraps it, and starts to eat, and the second one pulls out a sandwich, too, but then he starts looking for something in the bottom of his bag, turns it upside down, shakes it, but all that comes out is napkins. All these napkins blowing through the park and he says, 'Hey, they didn't give us any condiments.' And the other guy goes, 'Whadaya think this is, fuckin' Connecticut?' "

Kevin seemed to be waiting for more.

"Uh, that's it. The End."

He nodded. "That's funny. Now did he say fucking, or are you saying fucking."

"He did. I liked Connecticut. A lot, actually." Jack looked out the window.

"So what did your parents say when you got home so late?"

"No one said anything."

Kevin wasn't quite ready to let the subject go. "You know something?"

"What?"

"You're more of a tease than I am. It's not like you won't talk about yourself at all, but you drop these little hints."

"I'm glad you noticed. That you're a tease, I mean."

"See, you're doing it again. Trying to wiggle away."

"I don't think I am. Anyway, it's not like there's anything all that earth-shattering that I'm holding back."

"If you really believed that you wouldn't be so hush-hush about it. Did you ever think maybe by keeping things to yourself you're actually making them seem more important than they really are?"

Jack eyed him sharply. Then softened when he saw how earnestly Kevin was looking at him. "Look, I'm not trying to put you off, but I don't know what else to do when you ask me questions I'm not willing to answer. If talking about anything makes it so I have to talk about everything, I'd rather keep my mouth shut."

"But you could ask me anything, and I'd tell you."

"We're just different that way." The car had brightened considerably, and Jack realized they were already crossing over the bridge. The shadows of the cables were crisscrossing over them in odd patterns. "All right, why did you ask me to come tonight?"

"But I already told you that. Circumstances."

"That's all you got?"

"I could tell you a little more about what I was thinking. But when I'm done you better tell me why you agreed to come."

Jack nodded. "Fair enough."

"Okay, this goes back to when I was staying at your apartment. Well, the thing is, I was there for a week—one whole week. And I kept thinking for sure you'd try for something, you know, even a kiss. Even maybe just holding my hand when we were going to sleep. But you never did. Nothing."

"You didn't try anything either. You could've made the first move."

"I *did* make the first move. By coming over in the first place."

"I invited you in the first place."

"You didn't exactly throw out the welcome mat. Want me to replay the conversation for you?"

"No, I remember. You said your landlord had offered you a motel room, but you didn't want to stay there because it would remind you too much of work and you liked to keep work separate. And then I said you could stay at my place."

"What you said was, 'It's too bad I only have one bed, or you could stay at my place' and then I said . . . Do you remember what I exactly said?"

Jack exhaled loudly before he spoke. "You exactly said, 'That's fine by me.' "

"Not only that, I gave you a smile when I said it. Like a real big smile. There was no way I was gonna put any more pressure on you after that. That wouldn't have been right.

"And so I've spent the last few weeks coming to terms with the fact that you really weren't very interested. It's not like I ever thought you were completely straight, but maybe you were mostly straight and you weren't feeling straight with me and you didn't like that feeling, so you were keeping me at arm's length. Or maybe it was me. Maybe I just wasn't your type. I went round and round but all I ended up feeling was bad about myself.

"I've spent these last few weeks trying to figure out whether I could still be friends with you or not. It's not like I planned on Matt getting messed up, but when it happened, I said to myself, maybe here's a chance to find out.

"Now that's the whole truth that I can think of, so why did you agree to come?"

"I was so damn happy it was you ringing my buzzer, I would probably have done anything you asked." Jack got it out as fast as he could and then tried to retreat. "I think that covers it."

"What kind of happy?"

"Like as happy as I get about anything."

"And how d'ya feel now?"

"Honestly. I've been a little on edge since we got in the car, and now I'm kind of dreading this whole thing."

"You don't have to do it, you know, you could wait in the car. Why don't you wait in the car?"

"I didn't say I wasn't going to do it." Jack wanted time to think. About everything Kevin had just said. About what he'd just said. How in the world had he let himself get talked into coming? At times—critical times—he seemed utterly incapable of thinking things through in advance. Now, he was trapped between not wanting to let Kevin down, and afraid that, by the end of the night, he wouldn't feel the same way about him if he didn't. They were pulling into the driveway.

"Okay, maybe I'm not gonna do it. I hate to put you in a bind now, I should've figured this out earlier."

"You didn't put me in a bind. I was out of time and I had no one else anyway, so it didn't really matter if you'd said no then or now, I'd still be in the same position. This way we at least got to hang out."

The driver put the car in park and kept the engine running. Kevin hadn't made a single move to try to get out. The universe was surely testing him on this, and he wasn't confident he could say the right things with the audience up front. Jack leaned toward the driver. "Hey, would it be all right if you turned up the radio a little."

The driver turned it up.

"It's worse than all that. What I've been saying. Because I'm afraid if you go in there, I'm gonna get cold on you. And I don't want to get cold on you. Don't you understand that about me? That I really like liking you and I'm . . . I want more. I do. Like there's no question in my mind. But I'm not sure I can handle this." He waved his hand toward the house.

"This call?"

"No. All of this."

"But you'd have to."

"I know. I know that." He glanced at the front door of the house where he could see the guy had stepped out, shielding his eyes from the headlights, trying to peer out into the darkness. "Could you please not go in there tonight?"

"Oh my gosh, did you just say please?"

"Yeah, and look out, because I'm gonna say it again. Could you please come back to my place instead?"

Kevin rubbed his hands together. "Oooh, I think I like where this is headed."

"So, do you really think you'd be able to get out of this? Let me rephrase that, you better get out of this. But can you, seriously?"

"You're only asking me not to do this once, right?"

"Only this time."

"Promise?"

"Only this time."

"I'll be right back."

Jack watched him jog toward the house. He could see him talking with the guy at the door. He tried to tamp down on all the thoughts rushing in to tell him he'd been too quick. *Just wait*, he told himself, *don't think*. After a while, Kevin give the guy a quick hug and then he was back in the car.

"That looked like it went well. What did you tell him?"

"The truth. Short version."

"And he didn't get mad."

"He's been telling me since forever I should meet someone. He did say he wished it hadn't happened on his night, but he knows I'll make it up to him."

Jack let the comment go, taking Kevin's hand in his own. He ran his fingers along Kevin's knuckles, his thumb pressed into Kevin's palm. Then he dug into the flesh, kneading it, and didn't let go the rest of the way back to the city.

It took nearly two days before either of them managed to leave the apartment.

Lying in bed that first morning, Jack was relieved to find he wasn't the slightest bit interested in getting up, getting dressed, or even getting coffee. He rubbed the back of Kevin's head, and kept rubbing until Kevin turned toward him.

"What are you thinking about?"

Jack shook his head, smiling. "I thought only women asked that."

"What!?"

"Nothing. I'm being stupid. Happy stupid." It wasn't that being with Kevin had given him much new insight into the mechanics of sex with men. But what he was experiencing were the romantic feelings that he'd thought would only be possible with women, and it was in the warmth of those feelings Jack had been basking when Kevin asked him the question. Still, it was easier to talk about sex. "What I'm thinking about is, I can't believe I let you sleep here for a whole week and didn't lay a hand on you."

Kevin shrugged, indicating this clearly wasn't his fault.

Jack laughed, "So were you the one who planted those termites in your ceiling?"

"No. But I can't say I was all that upset when it happened. At least, at first."

"You've got to be the only person I've ever met who could see the upside in termites."

"There's always an upside. Now. About that week. Don't ya get how it woulda made more sense to see how you actually felt about being with me before you worried about everything else."

"I already knew it was going to be good, that was half the problem."

Kevin smiled. "You don't even know how good."

Kevin was born in Orem, Utah, and spent his early years being shuffled among the factions of an extended family that had settled on the outskirts of town. They were hardworking and tight-lipped. When pressed, they provided conflicting stories as to his origins.

A week before his ninth birthday, Kevin was placed with a middle-aged couple in Provo, and for a while he held out hope that their house would become a home for him. But the longer he stayed, the more he sensed he wasn't quite fitting in, and then one night he overheard his foster parents talking, going over expenses and complaining about cuts to their reimbursement payments. He hadn't realized how much it cost to look after him and promised himself he'd stop asking for that one extra thing every time they went to the store. But no matter what measures he took, he never grew to feel loved, and eventually accepted that his foster parents were doing the best they could with what they had.

A few months into his sophomore year, Kevin received permission to use the old shed behind their house for a wood shop. Shop was the only thing that interested him at school, and he found himself with a natural ability to shape the wood, to see the lines and to follow the cuts with the tools as if they were extensions of his hands. The projects in the classroom were limited, but at home he found ample opportunity to challenge himself. He began with the shed itself, buttressing the sides and putting on a new roof. It was a far from perfect job, but he was able to eliminate the leaks and considered it a minor success. He constructed a worktable, then set about to fix things around the house to help offset the cost of the tools that had been purchased for his use. His first effort was to replace all the kitchen cabinets with a riff off a design he'd seen in a catalogue.

Initially, his foster parents were pleased with his hobby. But then his grades, which had been for the most part average, began to slip. He dropped off the basketball team to free up more time for homework but ended up spending most of the extra hours in the shop. His senior year was a battle to keep his marks in line with expectations so he wouldn't have to close it.

After graduation, Kevin took a job at a construction site, staying around long enough to save up the money to buy a truck. Then he packed his tools and bandsaw into the bed of it and headed out to begin his new life. He was confident he would find someone to apprentice with, a craftsman who would recognize his talents and take him in, helping to bring his work up to the next level. It was an old-fashioned idea, and as he moved northward—through Pocatello, Butte, Missoula—it became clear that his plan was far-fetched. He ended up in Coeur d'Alene, Idaho, where he took a job at one of the plants that produced furniture veneers—figuring he would at least be in contact with wood, that this would help motivate him as he continued to forge ahead on his own.

"Idaho? Isn't that Neo-Nazi territory?" Jack had asked him.

"If you wouldn't interrupt, you'd soon be hearing that it has some trouble spots. Like everywhere."

His first job had been a fiasco. He was assigned to pull the freshly cut veneers from the machines and stack them while using scrubbed, bare hands to keep the material as free from smudges as possible. He worked the graveyard shift, and each morning when he would return to the cabin he was renting on Lake Pend Oreille, he would pull the splinters from his fingers, trying to rid himself of the experience.

But he wasn't able to do it. With the job being so tedious, most of his coworkers got by on one opioid or another, and they spent breaks blaming their lot on pretty much every minority group in the country. Sometimes, one group received more criticism than the others, but it was rare when they didn't all make at least a brief appearance on the list. It wasn't that Kevin hadn't heard this kind of thing before, but the consistency and intensity of hatred in that tiny breakroom was alien to him and became impossible to shake off whether he was on the plant floor or in his bed at night trying to fall asleep. He quit before he'd completed a month on the job.

Soon after, he got hired on at a mill less than ten miles down the road from where he'd started but it might as well have been on a different planet. Like the veneer work, pulling dry chain was repetitive, but he liked the fact that it was labor intensive—that he would break a sweat— and he noted with no small pleasure that everyone wore gloves. The job consisted of pulling boards from a conveyer belt and stacking them on the skids beside him. One day he might have the eight and ten footers, the next the twelve and fourteens. He started as a temp on swing shift but was quickly given a permanent first shift position. Like Kevin, his co-workers were dependable, and they showed up sober. During meals, they ate quietly. When they talked about anything beyond the weather, it was to share an anecdote about a newborn daughter or irritable in-laws. He did say there'd been a few off-color jokes, but even those were recounted with a certain shyness, the teller of the joke as likely to get red in the face as everyone else.

Jack raised his hand.

"Okay. But only 'cause you're being polite."

"What do you think made them so different from their neighbors?"

"Gosh, I don't know." Kevin scratched his head. "Maybe it was because management was so much nicer. I bet they just attracted nicer people."

His first week when he'd gotten caught, literally, with his pants down in the bathroom, the buzzer ringing and the conveyer belt started, Susan, the tiny but able-bodied woman who was working the piles next to his had grabbed his boards—in addition to her own—until he came running out and was able to take over. In time, Kevin grew to have a very strong feeling for her. She was always asking how he was getting along, rarely complaining herself though she had to have been struggling as a single mother. When she brought in the cookies she'd baked with her kids, she came with two bags: one for the crew and one for him. Not as good as his Aunt Margaret's, Kevin said, but they were close. He didn't socialize with Susan or anyone he worked with outside the mill, but there was always a friendly hello when they would run into each other at the grocery store in town.

For the most part Kevin was comfortable in his new job, his mind at peace when he finished his shift, his body sore but feeling properly used at the end of the day. Still, he was usually too exhausted to even think about working on his own projects. That first winter he left for the mill in the dark and returned home with the sun already setting. When he walked in the door, he never once sat down until he'd filled the stove with wood, showered, and had dinner made, since he knew once he planted himself in the chair in front of the fire—plate on his lap, sketch book on the armrest—he wouldn't be getting up again until it was time for bed. His days off he split wood and caught up with the dirty dishes, clothes, and other odd chores that had accumulated during the week.

In the summer months, with more daylight and no longer needing to worry about heating the cabin, he found himself with the extra time and energy needed to start up his bandsaw, which had sat untouched in the woodshed. Progress was slow, but he was glad to be making it. He built kitchen cabinets again, this time for his landlord's wife in exchange for a reduction in rent, and he found the job went much easier this time. He also began work on an elaborate dresser, not quite sure what he'd do with it, but he liked the largeness of the project, the amount of detail he would be able to put in. It would take plenty of time to finish.

The summer passed quickly, and autumn barely made a stand against the coming winter. Kevin found himself back in the same position, essentially having to abandon his shop work, and in reflecting on his situation, he knew he would have to make a change. He'd seen a glimpse of what the future might hold for him there in Coeur d'Alene, watching the men and few women who'd been at the mill for years, a number of them well into their forties now, bodies breaking down after so many years of strenuous work. They had little choice but to keep trying to push what was hurting harder. When one of the few management positions needed to be filled, people were generally brought in from the outside, leaving little hope for a cushioned landing as they approached retirement.

Kevin said he couldn't shake the image of himself as a tired old man, sitting in front of the fire in a rocking chair he'd built, surrounded by the few other pieces of furniture that he'd managed to eke out. Everything gathering dust, like in the closed, darkened wing of a museum. He made up his mind he would finish this second year into the next fall, and in the meantime, try to come up with another plan.

The following September, Kevin became involved in a relationship with a co-worker who'd just been through a divorce. Although it was primarily a sexual connection—they would meet in one of the rail cars behind the mill after shift—it was a powerful one, and Kevin realized the effect he could have on someone simply by sleeping with them. This man had been struggling for months at the mill and the affair seemed to have breathed new life into him. He came to work with a smile and left with an even bigger one.

As winter approached, Kevin did have second thoughts about leaving, But in the end, he couldn't help but feel he'd be failing to follow through on the life he'd set out to make for himself; that he'd be giving up something without ever knowing exactly what it could have been. Kevin was nervous about explaining this to the man he'd been spending time with, but after he did, he realized he'd made the right decision. The man held him close, and instead of pleading with him not to leave, or telling him how much he was going to be missed, simply said, "I'm really glad you came to work here. I mean that." Then he wished him good luck.

The morning of his last day, the landlord helped Kevin load the dresser into the back of the Chevy. It was ornamented and polished to such a point of pride that Kevin had tears in his eyes as he made his way carefully down the road, alternately checking in the rearview and glancing down at the directions in his lap. After following a series of branching dirt roads, he finally arrived at Susan's.

When she first saw the dresser, she kept shaking her head as if she couldn't believe it was sitting there in front of her, but ultimately accepted the gift in the joy it was given. With her kids pitching in, they rearranged the bedroom to make a place for it, and then, after glasses of lemonade, said their goodbyes. Kevin was just pulling out of the drive, when Susan came running out of the house waving at him.

"Here," she said. "This was my husband's and I want you to have it."

Kevin told her he couldn't take the pocket watch she was dangling in front of him, but she insisted. "Don't you worry, he had a bunch of 'em. Always collecting things, he was. But a good man. Like you are, Kevin, and no matter what happens in your life, I don't want you to forget that."

"Wow," Jack was a little in awe of the story. "I bet you were really crying on the way back."

"Bawling."

That night he packed up his truck and headed for San Francisco.

"Did you think about going anywhere else?"

"No, I was sure this was the right place."

"Because you knew I was gonna show up here eventually, right?"

"I had a feeling."

Kevin rented an apartment a few blocks from Dolores Park, then spent a day in the Castro where he pulled every newspaper and magazine he could find and took them back to his place. There he scoured the ads, a little overwhelmed by the sheer number of escorts advertising their services.

"Wait. Wait a second." Jack couldn't help interrupting again. "You just *knew* you wanted to be an escort? Like it was a childhood dream?"

Kevin smiled. "Not exactly. But I knew by the time I reached Eugene. See, I saw this cable movie at the hotel I was staying at in Salem. I only turned it on 'cause it sounded like it was gonna be all about my life in Idaho, but it was more interesting than that. There were a couple guys around my age who were hustling, and I'm not trying to brag, Jack, but I just knew I'd be good at it. That guy at the mill really did seem like a happier person after we got together and I thought to myself, there's gotta be a lot of other people out there who I could make happy."

"So you just thought you'd do this as some sort of public service?"

"Now you're being cynical."

"Maybe a little. But it's a legitimate question. I mean, you're not *that* bighearted, are you?"

"Well . . ."

"Well, what?"

"Well, I'd be lying if I didn't tell you I thought the hours would be good. To give me the maximum amount of time for woodworking. And it was a lot of money for short hours."

"That's the part you're ashamed about? Making money? But no concerns about, I don't know, selling your body?"

"That's just so wrong, Jack, I really should make you take it back. I'm selling my time—time with my body, I guess—but isn't that what everyone else does to make money?"

Jack thought about that for a moment. He couldn't find anything to argue back with. "Did you think it was gonna be exciting, at least?"

"In the beginning. But after the first few calls, it gets to be kind of ordinary, I think."

The mystery of how Kevin had gotten hooked up with Atlas wasn't all that hard to understand once Jack heard the story. He'd been one of the first escorts back when the agency was in its infancy, when Daniel himself was still taking calls. Kevin considered him a friend—even though he allowed for the fact that he could be "snotty" at times—and while Daniel couldn't wait to get behind a desk, Kevin considered the actual escorting with the agency an ideal set up. He wouldn't be marketing himself. He'd be leaving the choice of his clients to someone else. And he'd be able to focus on making furniture.

Within a month, he was renting regular workshop time in the Navy Yards on Hunter's Point. He was able to keep his truck parked there for running supplies, and he'd bus in on the 24 each day, with a notebook in hand, making sketches along the way. He met a number of other craftsmen in the building, and soon they were sharing tips and ideas over lunch. Compared to his previous constraints in Idaho, he felt he'd been given an almost excessive amount of time to pursue his work, and not taking it for granted, his productivity soared. Within a year he was selling pieces at the Fences flea market, and then, last November, he'd gotten a corner in the Everything Handmade store in the Mission just in time for the holidays. He'd finally been able to price items to reflect more than just the cost of his materials, and even if he wasn't fully recovering his labor, he was certain his skills were improving and that he had a future in furniture making.

"I'm still not at the point where I'm better in the shop than I am in bed. But as soon as it happens, I know everything will work out money-wise, and it'll be time to switch over completely."

"So you're not planning on doing this forever, huh?"

"You can't do it forever. Daniel says you should've already started planning for a career change by the day you find your first grey hair, but I don't wanna wait till then. But I'm not quitting tomorrow, either, so don't get your hopes up."

"I'm pretty content at the moment." Jack smiled slyly. "We'll see how long that lasts."

"Another five minutes?"

"Give or take."

"Then why don't you tell me about *your* plans while we're patiently waiting. From what I've heard, The Cage isn't exactly known for low turnover."

Jack shrugged.

"You think you'll ever try firefighting again?"

"I don't know." Jack had been trying to keep that possibility on the back burner, but it hadn't been easy with all the nearby fires he'd been hearing about recently. "I can't say it hasn't crossed my mind. Why, what would you think about it?"

"I think I'd be a little scared for you. Well, for me."

Jack shook his head. *Unbelievable.* Skelly hadn't had those concerns, but it wasn't like she hadn't had any. It sure was different being on the other side of things. "And I'm not supposed to worry about you? I mean there's the obvious stuff, but you're not exactly built like a security guard, you know. You never had any trouble?"

"Never." Kevin squeezed his arms, making his biceps pop out. Then he looked critically up and down each, before giving a quick nod and grinning liked they'd checked out okay. "I wouldn't mess with me."

Somewhere in the middle of all these conversations, Jack had managed to get comfortable with the idea of escorting again. Seeing as it was impossible to predict when Kevin's hair would turn grey, Jack thought it might make sense to give it another try. It still sounded more interesting than any other job he could think of to do in the city, and with Kevin worried about him joining up with the Forest Service, he didn't feel like he had a lot of other good options.

After Kevin's early attempts to recruit him, naturally he'd turned around and given Jack a hard time when he mentioned the idea.

Someone seems to have come down with a case of If You Can't Beat 'Em, Join 'Em. Jack had repeated the phrase back in an obnoxious voice, but he couldn't claim there's wasn't a competitive element to it. After hearing how smoothly Kevin seemed to run his calls he didn't see why—with a little more practice—he couldn't do the same. But what he really needed to prove to himself more than anything was that the relationship could be kept separate. That being with other people wouldn't get in the way of his feelings for Kevin. And in that way, he could imagine Kevin doing the same thing and holding the same space for him.

But first he had to figure out how he was going to break back into the business. He couldn't see himself going back to Atlas. And even if there had been another agency in town, he wouldn't have tried it. It had been too much of a group effort before, and Jack wanted to succeed or fail on his own. That would mean no more tag team calls with Kevin either, which was a good thing since he didn't want to share that part of their lives with anyone else.

After grudgingly purchasing a cellphone, Jack put up an ad on the Rentguys.com site, using the computer Skelly had left him. He checked the boxes indicating he was available most hours, excluding two to eight in the morning, and not on Tuesdays, the day he and Kevin had agreed to avoid working.

Once he'd been notified his ad had been approved, he waited expectantly for a call, but the phone wasn't having any part of it. So he decided to go to the barber shop around the corner and get his hair trimmed. Then, as soon as the guy had put the smock over him, the phone buzzed, and he had to jump out of the chair and rush out into the street, where he failed to get the call in time. Private number, no message. A good indication of how things would go for the rest of the day. Having done little to prepare himself, he managed to flub every single one of his first calls.

He'd been a little too candid.
When are you available?
My schedule's wide open at the moment.
I see. Good luck with that.

Ignorant
Are you verbal?
I like to have a good conversation, yeah . . . Is that what you're asking?

Ill-equipped
Do you like to give head?
Not especially, no.

Unaccommodating
I have to meet you out, can we use your place?
I don't take calls at my place.
Couldn't you do it just this one time?
Like I said on the site, I don't take calls at my place.

Indecisive
Would you consider giving a discount to a medical student?
Uh, I'd have to think about that. Can I get back to you?

And just plain confused.
Do you have big feet?
What?
How big are your feet?
You want to know how big my dick is?
No. I want to know how big your feet are.

After that last one, he'd suspended his ad while he tried to assess
what had just transpired. Making a list of all the calls—he'd gone zip

for six—to see what he could do better next time. He'd have to do better. Where possible, he wrote down more reasonable responses to the questions he'd been asked, so if they came up again, he'd at least be able to give the impression he knew what he was doing. In the future, he would make sure he didn't appear too available, but he probably wouldn't want to come across as too busy, either. Most importantly, he'd have to change his overall approach and tone, which had bordered on "Why are you hassling me about all this stuff?" If he couldn't be pleasant on the phone, it didn't bode well for the rest of the operation.

Kevin tried to convince him this was the perfect reason to come back to Atlas, where he wouldn't have to field the initial calls, but after Jack made it abundantly clear that wasn't going to happen, Kevin agreed to practice with him.

"You're lucky I ran the desk when Daniel was out with appendicitis. I've heard pretty much everything."

"Could you just not make it too wild to start out?"

"I'll see what I can do."

Kevin stepped out into the hall, and Jack remained inside the apartment waiting with the phone in his hand. *Shit.* He'd forgotten to ask Kevin how many times to let it ring. Jack opened the door again.

"Hey, Kev, I was wondering about the rings. What d'you—"

"No less than two and no more than three."

"Got it."

Jack had been steadily losing confidence in his scheme, but Kevin had made it seem like a good idea again. He was obviously a master. Jack was bound to learn something. He let the phone ring twice.

"Hello. This is Jack."

"Hey, handsome, I really liked your pictures."

"I . . ."

"Jack? Jack, you need to say something here."

"Hold on. I'm just looking over my list and I don't seem to have that comment."

"Oh boy. Let's try again. I say, 'I really liked your pictures' and you say . . ."

"Thanks. Thanks, I'm glad you liked them."

"And?"

"And . . . I'm even better in person?"

"No."

"And . . . you sound really handsome, too?"

"Better. But suppose the person doesn't have a good body image."

"You sound really nice? You sound like someone I'd like to spend time with? You sound like my boyfriend."

"Okay, that was funny, but we're trying to stay in character here."

"You're not staying in character."

"And I'm not the one who's having trouble getting clients, am I?"

"Fine. Keep going."

"So, what do you like to do?"

"Well, play basketball for one. And poker. Reading, and uh . . ."

"Seriously, Jack?"

"What? I like to do those things."

"They're gonna wanna know what you like to do in bed."

"Oh. Well, I like to do pretty much everything we do."

"I don't think telling them what you like to do with your boyfriend is going to clinch it for ya."

"How about . . . whatever you want . . . within limits."

"Okay, I don't want you ever to use the phrase 'within limits' again."

"I'm just telling it like it is."

"Didn't you put down a bunch of restrictions?"

"Yes. But I don't think everyone's paying attention to them."

"That's too bad. All right, start again."

"From the beginning?"

"Yup."

"Hey, this is Jack."

"Now I want you to remember how great you sound when you first pick up the phone. I was already standing in a puddle of my own drool by the time you got to your name but something's gonna happen shortly and I don't want you to get upset."

"What do you mean something's gonna—"

Kevin burst through the door, grabbed the phone out of Jack's hand and snapped it shut.

"You're really bad at this."

"I know. I hate the phone. That's why I asked for your help."

"Just be glad you don't have to use a pager like I did when I first started, those were a real pain. Now, I am gonna help you. You said you checked the boxes for email and instant messaging and phone, correct?"

"No, not for chat, I didn't want to have to sit around the computer all day."

"Okay, you're gonna need to uncheck the box for phone, too."

"But the site said that was the best way to get clients."

"I'm sure it is. *If* you're capable of having a halfway decent conversation. Just start with email, for now. There's gotta be someone out there who's just as uncomfortable as you and not wanting to talk on the phone either."

That someone turned out to be a businessman from Japan. He was staying at the Marriott downtown, and when Jack knocked on the door to his room, the guy opened it, took one look at him, and burst into tears.

Jack didn't know what to do—the man's sobs growing louder, head shaking violently in his hands. *Where was the goddamn training manual for situations like this?* The last thing Kevin had said to him was "just be nice." He waited with his hands in his pockets.

When the man's eyes finally popped up from the tops of his fingers, it was only for one wide-eyed moment, before they disappeared again like he was playing peek-a-boo. Continuing to shelter his face, he backed up slowly, until his legs hit the bed—at which point he sat down, hiccupped, and resumed crying.

"Listen, buddy, we don't have to do this. It's not a big deal."

The man looked up again, his eyes lingering this time. Jack could see that he wanted him to stay. He took a deep breath and walked into the room, closing the door behind him. Then he grabbed the chair from the desk in the corner and pulled it up beside the bed.

"Hey, so I know I'm not everybody's type, but I don't usually get a reaction like this." The comment struck hollow. He didn't even have close to enough experience to be making it, and the guy didn't look the slightest bit more at ease. "Okay, look, I haven't done this very much before either . . . if that helps."

"Yes," he nodded, "it does." Then he sniffled. "Maybe you can get me something to blow my nose."

Jack went and pulled some TP from the bathroom and gave it to him.

"Thank you." The man took off his glasses, blotted around his eyes, and blew into the tissue, before folding it and placing it in his shirt pocket. "Excuse me," he said. Then he put his glasses back on. "Your name is Jack?"

"Yeah."

"I'm Tom."

"Hi, Tom."

They shook hands.

Then sat there, silent and uncomfortable. Knowing what the goal was, more or less, but not quite sure how to get there. "So, uh, is there something that you were interested in doing . . . in particular." *That just wasn't sounding smooth.* "I mean . . . Hey, you don't have a bar in here by any chance, do you?"

"Yes."

"Maybe we could have a drink."

"Good idea."

That got some conversation going, at least. Tom gave a rundown on all the hottest talent coming from the baseball leagues in Japan. Who might pick up a contract in the States, was it really worth coming over. When he finished his drink, he placed it on the table, then spoke earnestly with his hands folded in front of him. "I just want a break, you understand. One hundred employees under me. I'm in charge of two divisions of my company. I take care of everyone, my son to school in the morning, money for my wife to go shopping. I walk the dog when I get home." He seemed to convince himself more as he went along. "I just want a break. That's not so bad, I don't think."

"No, it isn't," Jack agreed, standing up. He walked over and put a hand on Tom's shoulder.

When Jack got inside him, the man let out a cry, a final tear running down his cheek, but he kept on repeating how happy he was, so Jack stayed inside him, trying to be as gentle as possible.

Taking the elevator down to the parking garage afterward, he decided Kevin was probably right. Being with the guy had felt like a lot of things, but none of them felt like cheating. He wasn't feeling any differently toward Kevin than when he'd taken the same elevator up, and, in fact, could hardly wait to see him.

A few weeks later, and Kevin was getting frustrated. "What is it you don't understand about being nice?"

"It's not that I don't understand. I'm looking for some more detail, you know, if you could expand a little bit. I mean, it worked great with the first guy, but he was cool."

"See, that's your problem right there. Everyone's cool."

"Everyone is most definitely not cool."

"But everyone can be cool. It's your job to figure that out with every client. What makes them cool? Then you'll actually enjoy being around them and they'll notice that. They're paying you to make them feel good, not judged. Duh."

"Duh, huh?" Jack smirked but knew the gist of the advice was good—to be focused on the other person rather than himself. To have something to go in on besides the cash.

It didn't have be much. A star shaped mole on a guy's back, his leg tapping nervously in front of the television, the gentleness in his voice when talking about his folks. There was always something if he looked hard enough, and it was more a question of whether he had the desire or patience to find out. Sometimes he was lazy, or sometimes there wasn't enough time, and then he made a lousy job of it.

Given that he had essentially a single job description, Jack was surprised to discover how many different types of things different people seemed to want out of it. There were older men who wanted to indulge or, less often, be indulged, lonely joes interested in mostly hanging out and talking, seasoned, put-together professionals who didn't have time for entanglements; they wanted the physical contact like fast food, delivered with the guarantee you'd be out the door a few minutes later. And even if callers weren't candid about their fetishes, he eventually learned how to pick out these unexpectedly common types by the subtext of their comments, and if need be, direct them elsewhere without having to go through the awkwardness of meeting up. Or, at least, without any hard feelings. *It's a damn shame, guy, you'd look so good tied up. Call me if you change your mind.*

Not that these classifications were anything more than shortcuts referring to people who rarely fit neatly into any of them. There was one category, however, whose finer points Jack wasn't interested in pursuing. Guys to be avoided—either on the phone, learning to hang up sooner rather than later—or in person, he'd walked out once— when he had a bad feeling. It wasn't like he was under contract.

After months of more hits than misses, he developed enough

confidence to leave the Cage. Things had been pretty well played out there for a while, and he felt lucky to have gotten away with it for as long as he did. From early on, he'd suspected that once the novelty of having a former firefighter around wore off, people would realize he was an impostor, and he'd be out on his Fruit-of-the-Loomed ass.

"Guess who gave notice tonight?"

Kevin dropped into a boxing stance. "The cager. The cage man. Man in the cage no more."

Jack sparred a round before tackling him. "Okay, so now that I'm doing this full-time, there's something I've been meaning to ask you."

"Oh, no. Is it time for my advice column again? I thought you said you wanted to be independent."

"Come on, I've barely asked you anything."

"How 'bout you get off me so I can show you something that might help."

"All right. But you don't even know the question yet."

"It doesn't matter." He employed his recently released hands to make a circle with his thumb and pointer on one, and then using the finger from the other began to poke back and forth through it. He grinned. "It's really not that difficult."

"Look at you with your crude side and everything."

"This is what you drive me to."

"I need you to serious-up here, I'm looking for a professional opinion."

"Maybe I should get into my work clothes then."

"Okay, forget it. Just forget it."

"No, go ahead, I like watching you struggle. A little bit." Kevin drew his hand down his face, composing it in a mock solemn expression. "Proceed."

Jack had forgotten his question. "Oh yeah, so things have been going well, I mean, it's not like I'm on all the time, but no major problems or anything. But, uh, the one thing I haven't quite gotten a handle on is . . . what do you do when someone doesn't smell so good? I've got this one regular who's always wearing a garlic stick around his neck. To help ward off some exacerbation of a kidney condition or something, I'm cool with that, you know, it's medical. But then there's this other guy and it's just . . . a sour smell really shuts me down."

"That's a tough one."

"Indeed."

"Super tough. Yeah, you might want to say something, but you might not." He scratched his head. "I guess, I just try to think of it like it's something not permanent. You know, like someone's got a booger in their nose or whatever. It happens to everyone, it will go away."

"This doesn't seem to be going anywhere."

"Are we talking body odor here?"

"Let me put it this way. Your butt smells better than his mouth. Usually way better, and as far as—"

"That's because I have world class anal hygiene."

"Believe me, I'm clear on the fact that you've been spoiling me by now." Jack screwed up his face. "See, what happened was—I think it was the combination, really—but I pulled the guys cheeks apart and, as usual, it was pretty unpleasant down there and then I noticed this tiny piece of toilet paper stuck inside that I got kind of fixated on and— "

"You know what this situation calls for?" Kevin interrupted again, wagging his finger. "A very special piece of advice one of my possible grandfathers gave me many years ago. This is top secret stuff, now, I want you to treat it with the proper respect."

"What would the Elder recommend?"

"Deal with it," he said.

The duration of the calls helped. An hour usually, sometimes two. The short, intense bursts of experience suited Jack's personality, the time generally running out before his interest did. It reminded him of how he'd been on the ambulance, where he could immerse himself in someone else's life for an entire call knowing he'd be free to walk away afterward, while others would come along to take over. People who would be in it for the long haul.

He thought back to his ambulance work quite a bit, actually, making comparisons, even if they sometimes were a stretch. When he'd started as a street medic, it was like he'd suddenly had all these bodies thrown at him. This meant that by the end of his first tour, he'd already had more intimate contact with people than in his entire social career up to that point, and it was difficult to ignore the fact that he wasn't quite comfortable with it. Not a great characteristic for a medic to have, and he hoped the situation would improve with increased exposure.

He was able to make arm's length observations using the medical knowledge he'd committed to memory, but in fact, these were really no observations at all without the actual probing that was required to complete them. Of course he did plenty of touching, but combined with the urgency inherent in ambulance work, it meant he often rushed an examination in order to move on to implementing or helping to implement procedures. These were technical skills that he'd been trained to perform, but even here he tended to focus too much on his own hands and the equipment they held, making sure the cannula was placed just right, the IV needle held at the best angle. When this happened, it meant he was inevitably a step behind the constantly changing dynamic of the patient's body, and it prevented him from excelling at his job.

Being an escort, he was secure in the knowledge that the person requesting his services wasn't a victim. Of anything, likely, but loneliness. That the reasons for the call weren't dire. It took most of the pressure off, giving him the room to maneuver he'd never allowed himself before. What was the worst thing that could happen if he put his hand in the wrong place? He was told to move it. It wasn't going to ruin anyone's life. In this way, he was often able to forget his own hands completely.

To enjoy their exploring, the impression left by his fingers rather than the fingers themselves, and not only did he become more aware of the other person's response, but he was able to better anticipate what they wanted.

Not that he didn't have any other concerns about the job.

When he'd worked on the ambulance, even when a patient was a known HIV or hepatitis carrier, he'd never felt like he was in serious danger, figuring he was taking the extra measures that almost every member of every medical crew across the globe followed every day, usually without incident; to become infected seemed like a long shot and he continued to approach things the same way with his current occupation. If he raised the level of precaution to the level of risk, then that should bring him more or less back to normal.

In his more honest moments, though, he knew he was only practicing safer sex. That safe sex was a contradiction in terms, no matter who he was with. Kevin got tested every three weeks and Jack started going along with him, taking the same PCR RNA test the porn industry used. It wasn't cheap or anonymous, but it had the benefit of earlier detection since it measured the virus in the blood, not the antibodies that came later to fight it.

On the way to the doctor's office, they would talk about everything they could think of except where they were headed. In the waiting room, they would joke around, informing the receptionist they were there for another phlebotomy, the last one hadn't worked. Flopping down on the couch, reading aloud some headline from one of the tattered magazines on the table, "Wow, did you hear about this?" even though the news was six months old.

The Physician Assistant was current on everything, though. Easy to talk to, no nonsense with his advice. "If you're asking me if I know of any *documented* cases of HIV transmission through non-ejaculative oral sex, then you're asking me if I believe my patients, and the answer is yes. Absolutely. Lower risk isn't zero risk." Or his response when Jack had expressed his preference for using ultra-thin condoms. "You don't need me to tell you, you could be smarter about it." Not the answers he wanted to hear, but at least they were being provided.

Jack and Kevin went to the office together, they left together, but they got their results alone. Pieces of paper they would hand to one another without comment. Jack always called first before going down to pick his up. He couldn't stomach the idea of opening the envelope and staring at a result he couldn't blink away. Wanting the distance of the phone, just on the slim chance that somehow, something had happened. It wasn't particularly rational, but it was during those moments when he was dialing that he felt all the fear he'd been holding back grip him. When the receptionist would answer, there was a slight reprieve, saying hello, giving his name, and then the fear would grip him again, harder this time, while he waited for the result. Always his heart pounding. Always his body held crimped. He'd offer up most every supplication he could think of to have it come out negative, bartering with whoever might be listening.

The relief that came with hearing "Everything's fine" was fading by the time he'd put the phone down. Already having to face the fact that his results were never current. The best he could do was count backward. Five days, ten, twenty, toward both an older and younger version of himself that hadn't been infected. One who would wave across the distance between them, reminding Jack that if he'd only just stop what he was doing, it would give him a chance to catch up.

But he wasn't going to stop. That possibility was never put on the bartering table. He'd fallen for a guy who was an escort; he was sleeping with him. He couldn't see quitting until Kevin did.

One of the consequences of knowing Kevin's history was that, when they would venture out into the world, passing people on the streets, going to a concert or, occasionally, to the bars, Jack assumed he'd been with everyone. Which tended to push aside his feelings of possessiveness, if not knock them over entirely. He remembered how crabby he used to get getting introduced to old girlfriends' old boyfriends. Or even just their male friends, like that guy Skelly had student taught with. Just a couple of innocent giggles between them, and Jack had acted like a total ass that night at the campus barbecue.

With Kevin, it didn't make a lot of sense to be suspicious. Not that he wouldn't be capable of it, but for the moment, at least, Jack was feeling secure. It didn't seem naive, but rather a case of not confusing what was theirs with what wasn't.

Maybe it helped, too, that they talked about a lot of the calls. Put them out in the open. Put them in perspective by turning them into stories they could share. Jack wouldn't have felt comfortable doing it with anyone else. He'd witnessed the mean streak that ran through the city's queer community and that's why he'd mostly avoided it. The verbal attacks on strangers, the cutting down of a lover or supposed best friend when the other person wasn't standing even five feet away. In his own way, Kevin had agreed. "Yeah, I don't see the point of that when I can just go ahead and make fun of you to your face."

He seemed to like his clients so much anyway, it was hard to imagine him slandering one of them, and even if Jack didn't share his depth of respect for what they were doing, he tried to approximate it. Still, there were times when he worried he was selling out, highlighting something amusing that had happened while skipping over the more meaningful parts of a call. Or maybe it was more respectful that way, keeping those parts private; it was hard to say. In any case, whenever he'd get to feeling bad about it, he remembered they'd done much of the same thing at the fire department, when the circumstances were generally a lot more unpleasant. Any job where you've got bizarre stuff going down on a daily basis and you can't see the humorous side to it, you're going to be toast pretty quick—because if you don't laugh it out, or at least talk it out, all that craziness will go somewhere inside you where it's not so easy to get rid of anymore.

Eventually, their story swapping devolved into a game that Kevin named Top This. They flipped a coin to see who went first, and then each person had one chance to come up with their most interesting call. Whoever went second had the advantage since he only had to produce a story that was slightly more interesting than the first person's to win and could save more impressive episodes for later contests.

For the purposes of the game, Kevin agreed not to tap into any of his earlier experiences.

"A man walks into a crowded bar carrying a briefcase. Our hero is sitting at the bar with instructions not to recognize the man or the briefcase, even though he's seen them both before. He's supposed to accept a drink, play hard to get for no more than twenty minutes, and then walk out with him on the end of his arm."

Jack frowned. "That's kind of weak."

"Not really, we do it every month or so, different bar. I think it's kinda clever."

"Hmm. So part of the appeal of this story actually lies in the way it ties in with past calls you've had. Presumably ones that took place before I got mixed up with you and your deviant lifestyle. That sounds like a procedural violation to me."

"You're saying I can't use it."

"Why don't you take it up with the judge?"

"See, this is what I get for trying to go easy on you. I've got better stuff."

"Then bring it."

"Okay, our hero is led into the living room where he's told to take a seat on the couch. There's a parakeet in a cage in the corner. A parakeet that's really a red herring by the way, I'm just throwing that in to add some local color for ya."

"Don't expect to score any extra points with local color, why don't you stick with the essentials."

"Okay, there's a bunch of iced beer and a pitcher of water on the table. The man tells me I look thirsty and I should help myself to the beverage. I go for the water."

"Natch."

"Anyway. The guy disappears from the room and then a little while later he calls me upstairs. I find the guy in the bathroom, in the bathtub. The bathtub's got no water in it and he's wearing nothin' but a snorkel and mask, and he says, 'I hope you had enough to drink, cause I wanna get good and soaked.' "

"You're lying."

"Okay, he didn't have a snorkel."

"You're still lying."

"I'm not, Jack."

"Was he wearing flippers?"

"Don't be ridiculous."

On the whole, it seemed like Kevin got the better calls.

"Okay, our hero walks into the hotel room and there's a certain someone from a certain semi-professional hockey team waiting and—"

"No kidding, which one? Who, I mean?"

"Relax, I'm not giving you his number."

"Wait a second, I don't think there's even an ice rink in this town."

"He wasn't here to play hockey. More like hooky. With me."

Jack groaned. "That's cute."

"Why does cute never sound that way when you say it?"

"Because it's the worst four letter word I know."

"You're just sore cause you know you've got nothin' to beat this story with even if I didn't give you any more details and you're about to lose."

"You're right. Okay, how about this? I walk into the guy's house and follow him into the kitchen where he asks me to get undressed. Fine. Then he tells me I'll be mopping the floors. He holds out this mop for me to take, and I'm thinking, there's no way in hell I'm doing this, but then I remember I'd driven all the way out to Marin. All sorts of traffic on the bridge and looking worse on the way back, and I think what a drag it would be to have to return empty-handed."

"Oh, come on, you were excited."

"Anyway. I do notice the floors are pretty much sparkling clean and that helps so I squeeze out the mop and get started. He sits down at the table, picks up the *Wall Street Journal* and starts to read, tells me to keep to my business and he'll keep to his, which turns out to be getting his jollies under the table. Dude, I was out of there in less than fifteen minutes, and he tipped me way too much, seriously. So I went back and knocked on his door and asked him if his garage needed cleaning or something."

"What did he say?"

"Maybe next time."

"Okay, our hero has a midday appointment with this very sexy older woman."

"What do you mean woman? Since when do you do women?"

"We get the occasional female calling in. See, if you'd stuck around the agency long enough instead of putting your ad on Rentguys. What d'you expect?"

"Let's see. Cash only. All the payout for myself. No one babysitting me."

"I don't even have much interaction with anyone over at Atlas anymore. They learn to trust you. And I happen to like the fact that Daniel screens my first-time callers. He tried to get this lady to pick someone else, but said she wanted me and only me."

"Okay, what was the story with her?"

"That's it. I was just happy everything turned out all right. It's not like I have a ton of experience in the area."

"Meaning how much."

"One girl in high school, I told you that already. I've gotten better."

"Okay, real short one here. I walk into the guy's suite at the Windsor and there's a line of twenty-dollar bills leading from the door to the bed. That's it."

"Rose petals would've been nicer," Kevin suggested.

"From you, maybe."

Without fully consulting with the other founding member of Top This, Kevin had declared himself Official Honorary Judge for Life (Not to Mention the Possible Hereafter). Jack had let him keep the title because he was usually pretty fair in his decisions, and anyway, if he didn't agree, he just told him he'd been overruled. At which point, Kevin would remind him the judge couldn't be overruled, and they'd proceed to hash it out further until one of them caved or they called it a draw.

"I've reconsidered the merits of your appeal, and even though you've made a very long-winded presentation, I think I can see your point."

"How couldn't you?"

"Don't talk back to the judge. He's considering being lenient in this case."

"He'd better be considering."

Each of Jack's suggestions for stakes had been rejected. A six pack (boring), doing the other person's laundry (cruel and unusual). Kevin decided the winner should get a backrub. Which sounded good on paper, but when it came down to it, Jack realized he still wasn't all that comfortable getting a massage from another guy. Even if that guy was Kevin. Sure, it always felt good, but it just wasn't good enough to overcome the discomfort Jack felt being in a prone position. He always looked forward to the contests, though, because no matter who won, it inevitably led to their getting sidetracked into better things. If Jack was getting the rubdown, he might last five, ten minutes tops. If he was giving it, he usually made it no more than two, but either way, the result was the same.

They were in the shower when Kevin first brought up changing the rules.

"You know what I'd like to do?"

"How about you keep soaping my shoulders for the rest of the afternoon?"

"That's not a problem, but what I'm talking about is something else."

"Like . . ." Jack felt him press in from behind. "Uh, did you just grow a third hand there?"

"Something like that. Give you any ideas?"

He sensed trouble but wasn't quite ready to be with the program. "What, you got a stiffy, you want a medal for it?" No response, so he turned around. "What is up with you?"

"Come on, you know—"

As quick as he felt it hit him, he threw it back. "You mean fuck me."

Kevin nodded his head up and down, with that cherry-sweet smile not doing a thing to help his cause this time.

"Why d'you make this into a guessing game? Why didn't you just ask me straight up?" The sound of the water running was almost enough to cover the fear in his voice. He toned it down a notch. "Do you really think it's necessary?"

"No, it's not necessary, it's just somethin' I'd like to do, is all. You think you could be a little excited about it."

"What, exactly, am I supposed to be excited about?"

"You fuck me all the time, Jack."

"Man, you don't have to say that. You really don't, you make it sound like a goddamn punishment."

"It sure seems like that's your take on it."

This was going to be it. Their first real argument and he didn't want any part of it. Not even one. He stepped out of the shower and reached for the towel, trying to figure out where all this had come from.

"Hey, you still got soap on ya."

Jack stepped further away. Dried off quickly and put the towel around his waist. "Look, you're gonna have to give me some time on this one, all right. I mean, I can see where you're coming from, it only seems fair, but I'm not about to just . . . you know, spread 'em because you're suddenly feeling all frisky."

Kevin stepped closer to him, grabbed onto the top of the towel and held it. "I want you to know something. I can put this aside, no problem, but I'm not sorry I mentioned it. I'd like to do it and that's all." He paused. "Anyway, just so you know, it's not my most major fantasy."

Unmistakable setup there, and hearing it Jack wanted to, well, he just wanted to pull him down onto the tile and be inside him again. To thank him for throwing down a line to help pull them out of the situation. There was no chance of his not taking it.

"So what would that fantasy be, 'scort?"

"Well, I don't wanna give too much away, 'cause that might keep it from coming true, but what I can tell you is, it involves a 1970 Chevelle, convertible, of course, Nutella, and about five singing mermaids."

"Don't you mean mermen?"

"Hey, whose fantasy is this? And no, I didn't say anything about Ethel Merman. You can be such a homo sometimes."

He called Kevin when he got home. Something had been really bothering him on the ride back.

"Do you mind if I ask you a question? Because I'm having a hard time in even trying to think this through because . . . All I'm wondering is, has this been on your mind? Like the whole time, from the beginning have you been thinking about this because, I don't know, I was thinking everything was so . . . perfect, and looking at you and thinking that's what you were thinking, too, and now I'm worried I made that all up in my head and that—"

"Jack."

"I was obviously missing something, because I never felt—"

"Jack, you weren't missing anything."

"Are you sure?"

"Maybe it was in the back of my mind, somewhere, but I never really considered it till today. It's just that when it came up, it came up something fierce, as you may have noticed, and how was I not gonna say anything. But like I told you, it's not that important. I can move on."

"Yeah, but who knows when it might come up again."

"Well it probably won't . . ." Jack felt some potential amnesty, ". . . as long as I don't soap your back any more in the shower . . ." *Damn!* ". . . or don't ever give you a massage or—"

"Don't ever look at my ass again. Okay, I get the idea. You're walking two feet in front of me from now on."

A couple of days later Jack showed up with a bottle of Ultralube and what he considered to be a short speech. "Okay, here is my list of concerns about your fucking me."

"Are you gonna let me do it or not?"

"Don't be so impatient. What I should have done was make you buy me dinner first."

"I'll buy you dinner afterwards, how's that?"

"Fine, but there's still some things I want to explain to you." Kevin rolled his eyes. "People are always rolling their eyes at me, why don't you come up with something more original?"

"Why don't you stop saying things that make people want to roll their eyes at you? Believe me, I'd rather be putting my energy into more important matters."

"If you're gonna be all cute about this, it's not gonna work."

"No, go ahead. I'm curious, actually. I'm just giving you a hard time 'cause you make it sound so gosh darn serious: Following are the reasons why Jack has decreed he is willing to—"

"All right. All right, already. Look, this *is* serious. Just let me get through my list, okay?"

"Fine."

"Okay. First thing, as far as the physics of it go, I'm prepared. I mean, you know I'm on record for not liking a finger up my ass, so it's hard to be optimistic, but you also know I'd take all sorts of bruises for you, no big deal. Oh yeah, by the way, you're definitely facing me. I want you looking at me."

"I don't remember asking for your input on that decision, but lucky for you that's how I was gonna do it anyway. What else?"

"Okay, well, it's just that it's got all these negative connotations. And I'm not saying I don't understand that you already put up with all this. I'm just saying for me, okay. It's been a lot of years of hearing getting fucked like it's pretty much the worst thing that can happen to you. Like, you never hear anyone say, I just won the lottery. Yahoo, I really got fucked there."

Kevin looked dubious.

"Point is, there's not much positive spin on it."

"I don't see how there's much positive spin on the word fucked period, even if you're the one doing the fucking. What about when you fuck something up? You're the one doing the fucking, you're not telling me that's positive. I just ran over the dog, I really fucked up. Not exactly a good thing."

"True. But, at the moment, I'm more concerned with the person getting fucked."

"You mean, the fuckee?"

"Right."

"Okay, how about this? I got fucked up last night. People say that all the time when they get all messed up, drunk or whatever, like they did a good thing. Like they really had a good time."

"Well, there's a difference between getting fucked up and getting fucked."

"I guess you're about to find out, aren't you?"

"Fuck off. All right, let's move on to the third point."

"Which is?"

"Which is, I just don't like the idea that I'm doing this with someone younger than me."

"That's silly, Jack. I'm two years younger than you. We're in the same marketing demographic."

"Yeah, so are a lot of other people. Besides, you're two-and-a-*half* years younger and, I don't know. I can just tell that's bothering me somehow."

Kevin raised his eyebrows.

"Am I reaching here?"

"You've been reaching since you started with all this nonsense. Are you through?"

"Okay, I think that's really it. Other than my fear my y chromosome is going to be flushed down the toilet along with the condom, which you will obviously be using. But yeah, that's all."

And so they did it.

For a little while, anyway. Kevin was considerate and kept it short. When he pulled out, his eyes remained fixed on Jack, managing to both hover over and weigh down on him. "I know it's not polite to ask right afterwards, but I can't wait. What'd you think?"

"Christ, Kevin, you mind giving me a minute to collect my thoughts here."

"Oh, come on, you know already. Just tell me, what did it feel like, just say whatever you felt."

"Well, it was . . ." *a little uncomfortable, a little pleasurable . . . humbling.* "It was nice, thanks for asking." Then he couldn't help adding, laughing from relief as much as anything else. "Although I couldn't tell much difference from when you gave me the finger."

Kevin shook his head. "You're impossible," he said, but he was grinning when he flipped the bird.

Happiness is kind of dull in its own way. What can you really say about it? I shared a laugh today. I had an adventure. I made some money. I was happy. Happy people were generally annoying. Especially when they were ragging on about how wonderful their condition was.

Annoying to themselves, too, Jack realized while he was trying to explain how things were going to Bishkey at the start of a spring training game between the Mets and the Yankees.

It'd been more than a year now since Jack had made of point of catching the occasional game with Bishkey, the sport less important than having New York in at least one of the team's titles. Some of it was simply checking up on him, although seeing as he had to constantly remind himself Bishkey was positive, Jack had to believe the main reason he liked hanging out was because it just seemed like a good way to spend time. Bishkey remained the most grounded person he knew in the city, and even if they were different in a lot of ways, he was the closest Jack would likely ever get to having someone like Ren around.

Jack had given him what he thought was a restrained version of what was happening in his life, but some of his feeling had obviously slopped over the sides—Bishkey's eyes were starting to glaze—and as soon as Jack noticed it, he drew his story to a quick close. ". . . anyway, that about covers it. What about you, what's been going on with you?"

"Na much," Bishkey cracked his knuckles. "Gotta promotion at the end of the year. Paper pusher to people pusher. An upgrade, I take it, they give me a raise." Bishkey had really pulled his life together since he was diagnosed. Since his girlfriend left him. Got a nine-to-fiver downtown. Started volunteering after work for an organization that helped homeless kids with HIV. "Don't even know what to do with the extra dough. Figga that! Rather have the extra time to put in at the shelter, but that's like, no money so, this or that. Tryin' to keep things balanced."

"Seems to be working, you look great, man."

"Yeah. Yeah. Yeah. Sometimes I think so, too." Bishkey's expression was a tough read. "So tell me somethin', you missin' the chicks, yet?"

I don't feel like I'm missing much, Jack thought, then scowled at the fact he'd almost said it. "I don't know. I mean, I was flirting with my favorite librarian the other day. Ended up behind her in the stacks, she turned and kind of caught my nose in her hair, you know, I got a little turned on. But it's not like you stop checking people out no matter who you're seeing. It was a nice moment, that's all."

Bishkey nodded. "You're lucky, man. I haven't been able to be around anyone like that. Even just to lock eyeballs. I'm still shut to it . . . can't seem to—there's this girl at the office, right but . . . dunno, gonna be a while."

"When you're ready, I bet there'll be someone."

"Just so's you know, those whiskey specs are gonna have to come off before you check the score at the end of the game. Let me ask you somethin' . . . you spend the winter deluding yourself thinking the Mets have a chance this year?"

"Come on, it's springtime, everyone's allowed to be optimistic."

"Foolish. People are foolish in the spring."

"Well, maybe I'll just get drunk and keep those whiskey goggles on."

Bishkey smiled. "That's what I like to hear. Mo-de-ration and everybody takes the night off as far as I'm concerned, that's what I like about meetin' up with you. Once in a while, anyway."

"You sure about that, we could still switch up to soda."

"You kiddin' me? You goin' chince on me here? It's gonna be your night to pay and it ain't gonna be soda on that bill. See, unlike some other overpriced outfits, winning *is* integral to the Yank's front office strategy."

It had been a great game. Error free, smart plays on both sides. But after holding the lead for most of the game, the Mets couldn't find anyone in the bullpen to close with, and the top of the lineup on the other New York team had taken full advantage. Jack had been pretty devastated with the hit that ended it, but by the time he was paying the tab that play was already well on the fade, and he was almost enjoying listening to Bishkey gloat.

Stumbling home, he got to thinking. First of all, how his tolerance had gone increasingly to hell. It was funny, here Bishkey was implying he was this lush, and practically the only time he ever got plastered was with Bishkey. The last time had been for an Islanders game, but New York had gotten blanked and what else were they supposed to do?

Sometimes, it seemed like being drunk was the best time to analyze things, like you cut through all the bullshit and faced things for what they really were. And then other times, it was like being crocked just created all the bullshit, and it was a bad idea to spend much time reflecting on anything important. Still, once you started doing it, it wasn't simple to turn off.

He hadn't thought he'd been missing anything with Kevin, but maybe he was. Maybe their relationship lacked depth. After all, this was the easiest part, now. The early innings. Their only responsibility seemed to be to enjoy it. They didn't have to worry, yet, about where it was going. What, if anything, they might build on it. He tried to remember what they'd been up to lately. The previous night, for example, he'd looked forward to what? Having dinner with Kevin. They'd had chicken and rice. Cantaloupe on the side. Fascinating. He'd forgotten to put the silverware out and Kevin had asked, "Where's the spork and foon?" Stupid shit. That only sounded stupider when you mentioned it.

There had been a pretty heated political discussion while they were eating. That counted for something, didn't it? In fact, he could barely recall what it had been about. It just didn't seem that important.

Maybe it wasn't them. Maybe it was happiness, itself, that was shallow. With the way things were going in the world, maybe it bordered on being rude, if not downright offensive. Like even if there was enough to go around, it wasn't getting spread evenly, and he didn't want to be greedy. But he didn't want to be miserable either.

He wondered how much time Kevin spent thinking about it. Probably not much, he had his projects in the woodshop to concentrate on. The only thing he seemed stressed about lately was the fact the Navy Yards where he rented space were going to be shut down, and all the tenants kicked out to make room for toxic waste removal. *Do you know how much toxic waste there is around this state and they gotta pick the one place to clean that people are actually using?* He didn't see where else he was going to find such a good set up for a buck a square foot, but Jack was sure he'd find something. That it would work out. Which seemed to pretty well sum up his philosophy on everything these days, and he didn't want to analyze it any further.

They were lying on the bed, on their backs, arms resting against one another. Jack had been enjoying the whole tabula rasa thing going on in the ceiling and didn't have any other plans. "Did you just rip one?"

"Maybe."

Jack waved his hand frantically in the air. "Damn, man, that was sure world class. You suppose you could take it outside?"

"It's my apartment."

"True."

"So, Jack. I've been thinking—"

"Now why would you wanna go and do a thing like that?"

"That sounds like something I'd say to you."

"Well, all that thinking stuff's supposed to be my department. Believe me, it's overrated." Jack attempted to resume his contemplation of the ceiling. Problem was, now he could make out some shadows up there. "So you done thinking yet?"

"No, it's still happening."

"Does this mean I have to start thinking, too? Maybe I should get a cup of coffee."

"Maybe this should wait till later."

"Uh-oh, it is serious."

"No, it can wait."

"Fine."

He lasted about two minutes. "All right, what is it?"

"What's what?"

"I knew you were going to say that." He rolled over onto Kevin's stomach, wrestled with his hands until he had them pinned above his head. "Now spill it."

"You know violence never solves anything."

"What about tickling?" he suggested, shifting his hold to one hand, then getting his other under Kevin's left pit. "I hear that's a proven problem solver."

Kevin tried to curl up in defense but didn't look all that happy while he was laughing, so Jack stopped.

"Some people consider that a form of torture."

"Well, some other people feel the same way about conversations that get started and dropped right afterward."

"But now whatever I gotta say's gonna sound like a bigger deal than it was to begin with."

"What do you want me to do about it? The suspense is growing by the minute."

Kevin closed his eyes. "What would you say to moving in with me?"

Jack felt his body stiffen. He got up to make the coffee. "You want any?"

"That's going to make you edgy."

"No, it's going to make me awake." He opened the cabinet and took out the box of filters. "Okay, left field, you wanna tell me why you're bringing this up now?"

"Okay, avoiding the question, what does it matter? Haven't you thought about it before?"

"Yes."

"Well, what did you think?"

"I thought of it as a definite possibility."

"And that works how?"

"It means it's more possible than if it was just hypothetically possible, but it's not definite either. Follow?"

"I think I feel a headache coming on."

"Too late, I already had my way with you."

"Don't I know it. I'm wondering if I'll be able to walk straight when I get up."

"Why don't you just stay right where you are." Jack left the water to boil and came back over to the bed. "So what were we talking about again?"

"What a dork you are."

"Now there's a subject I'm comfortable with, why don't we stick with that one?"

"Because there aren't enough hours in the day. Now, here's what I'm thinking. If we moved in together it would be a really good way to save up money."

"What would we be saving for?"

"Something good. I don't know exactly."

"So is this about finances or living together?"

"No, it's not really about the money. . . I don't know why I said that."

Jack was getting confused and more uncomfortable. Kevin popped him on the forehead with the heel of his hand.

"Ow. What's up with that?"

"That means you should cool it."

"Some pacifist you are."

"I couldn't help it. You were making that expression."

"What expression?"

"The one that means you're getting all worked up for nothing. Why don't we talk about this another time? We could play some Top This instead, we haven't done that in a while."

"All right, but I don't have any good stories. Things were kind of routine while you were gone."

"That's all right. I do. It all starts with our hero standing in front of his apartment when a guy pulls up in a limo . . . and the next thing you know I'm on a plane to Montreal with a stopover in New York."

"You bastard." Jack kind of meant it, figuring him for true right away. It was the longest Kevin had ever been gone and he'd been sketchy about the details. "Okay, game over. I'm not gonna compete with that."

"Hey, I'm the Official Honorary Judge for Life Not to Mention the Possible Hereafter, and I'll let you know when the game's over." Jack frowned. "Now there's no reason to be—"

"Jealous? No. I get to stay here and help entertain the American Dental Association while you're gone. That's evens for sure."

"Maybe we should stop keeping track of score, loser. You know, not every single thing between us has to be a competition that you have to win."

"You're not gonna tell me you've got a problem competing."

"I don't. But the reason I like doing it is to bring us closer together. If it's too much, it's no fun."

It seemed like he'd managed to make another point. "Why don't you go stitch that on a pillow."

"I would, if I thought it'd help you remember it. You know, if you're looking for an excuse not to trust me, you've got plenty of opportunities."

"Maybe too many."

"Yeah, but it's been that way right along. For both of us." Jack couldn't think of anything to say. "Well, anyway, you should be happy for me. I had a really good time. One of the best of my life, actually, but that's just the point because I missed you the whole time I was there, and it made me think that . . .well, it made me think I wouldn't ditch you just cause you don't own a plane."

"You're telling me you took a private plane to Montreal?"

"No, but the man I went with has one."

Jack went back over to the stove and turned off the water. Kevin was right, he didn't need the caffeine. The whole thing was a mess. His not mentioning he was going to Montreal before he left, then bringing up this whole living together thing now. What was the connection? Had the guy liked Kevin's company so much he'd offered him some sort of houseboy position and Kevin was trying to press him with it. This was the guy who had a place in Palms Springs, right? The place Jack assumed they'd be going. Kevin had referred to him as an "older, older man," but whatever his age, he'd gotten to show Kevin New York and that was really bothering him. Too many things to think about, and the more he tried to untangle them, the more tightly wound he felt. He knew he couldn't spend the night.

At the door, they kissed, hard, but it was quick to feel forced and Jack pulled away.

"Was it the trip or the moving in that did it?"

"Both."

Kevin nodded. "You should know I've been waiting almost a week to fall asleep with you again."

That was almost enough to keep him there. "I've been waiting, too. Look, why don't we make up for it tomorrow night, okay?"

Kevin hesitated. "I can't tomorrow."

"Fuck, well, the night after, then. See if you can manage not to schedule any more international travel."

As he headed down to his bike, Jack thought how this was how it went with him. Growing up, he'd tried to temper the intensity that he had, by all reports, been born with. Cultivating a more laid-back attitude, and generally choosing not to deal with subjects that might otherwise bother him. And for the most part, he'd gotten away with it, because so many times things that looked questionable in the present moment turned out later to be nothing, and he was glad not to have wasted the energy worrying about them.

The problems began when something didn't turn out to be nothing. Because, in fact, he'd never really let go of his concerns completely. Yes, he'd gotten quite good at tossing them aside, into the trash bin, even. Except they continued to accumulate in there, and he didn't always take the trash out right away. That meant if something *did* happen to cause him to question his approach, it was a little too convenient to grab hold of the bag and start shaking. And suddenly he had a real mess on the floor.

Jack hadn't thought twice about anything that'd happened with Kevin while he'd been away, but he'd thought once about everything. He'd been gone a long time, with a man Jack didn't know. Something hadn't felt completely right about it. Jack wondered if he shouldn't have spent more time talking it through with Kevin before he left. If he'd known there was even the slightest chance of Kevin ending up in New York, maybe he could have prevented the whole thing. The trip. The discussion about moving in that'd come out of it.

Maybe he wouldn't be out on the street right now, waiting for a light to change.

When it did, he entered the crosswalk. He'd been planning on taking the bike for a spin, maybe down to the water to watch the sun set, but as he approached it, he noticed a piece of paper sticking out from under the rim of the fuel tank. *What a lousy time to get a ticket.* He hurried over, remembering the backlog of fines he still needed to settle with the city, thinking how long it'd been since he got busted in front of Kevin's. Double checking the signs, he couldn't understand what he'd done wrong; it should have been good till Thursday morning.

Then he realized the piece of paper wasn't a ticket at all. He shook his head as he scanned down the advertisement for one of the gentlemen's clubs nearby. Two-for-one admission.

While he was looking around for a place to toss it, the wind whipped up and blew the paper out of his hand. He watched it sail away from him. Then the wind died out as abruptly as it had come, and the paper floated down, back and forth like a leaf, landing with the blank side facing up. He was tempted to leave it there.

But then he thought better of it. He walked over and pulled it off the pavement. Brought it over to the bike and laid it on the seat. Then he began to fold it. It took a couple of tries to make the plane he had in mind, but other than a few telltale creases from his first efforts, it came out pretty good. He pulled a pen from his pocket and drew two stick figures, one tall, one not so tall, in the place where the cockpit should be. Then he wrote a message on the side. *Forgot to tell you I've got a plane too*, signing his initials below it. When he was finished, he ran back across the street, back up to Kevin's apartment, pressed the plane flat and slipped it under the door.

It wasn't until he was almost back down in the lobby that his thoughts turned against him. What a sap he was becoming. Origami now, what next? And why was he even acting so chummy when the whole Montreal story stunk, when he'd pretty much had his face rubbed in the entire trip. His gesture had weakness written all over it, and besides, Kevin would be sure to take it wrong. That he was somehow ready to move in together.

He tried to remember how far he'd slid the paper under the door. Maybe Kevin hadn't seen it yet, maybe he could get his fingers under there and pull it out. He hurried up the stairs.

Rounding the third-floor landing, he slowed, then stopped. This couldn't continue. His thinking was all over the map, and he needed to get control of himself. Nothing bothered him more than not being able to think clearly, and he'd never been able to think clearly about relationships. Not past a certain point, anyway, they were just too complicated. Why did he think this time was going to be any different? Because Kevin had a penis? If only it were that easy. He knew how the story was going to turn out, because this was how it always turned out, and it was just as much a trap for Kevin as it was for him.

Jack was going to have to talk to him. Right away. Let him know things between them were getting a little too close and they should probably take a breather. Spend some time apart. That was it, that had to be it, it was the only thing that ever made any sense. He could feel his mind calming with the simpleness of the solution. All the questions, all the confusion cleared away, replaced by only one action that needed to be taken.

Kevin was grinning when he opened the door, the plane in his hand. "Now is this your way of suggesting we need to spice up our sex life? Because if you wanted me to come with you to Lust and Lace or wherever, you coulda just asked me."

"Yeah, that's it."

"No, really, thanks for the note."

Jack stared at him.

"If you came to get it back, you can't have it."

"No, you can keep it. Listen, I need to talk to you."

Kevin's eyes filled with tears. Instantly, like a button had been pushed.

"Kevin, relax. What are you crying about?"

"I'm not crying. I just have an irritation that seems to be occurring simultaneously in both my eyes."

Dammit, he didn't want him making light of the situation either. "Look, I doubt this is what you're going to want to be hearing at the moment, but I've thought about everything and I'm just not sure—"

"Jack, either come inside and say what you gotta say, or come back some other time when you can. I'm not getting a speech from you while you're standing in the hallway." He choked back the tiniest sob when he added, "That's bullshit."

Jack felt the clench in his hands tighten. And then, against the tide of raw hurt in front of him, it began to give way. He glanced behind him, both ways over his shoulder, before stepping into the room.

"I'm awfully mad at you right now, Jack."

"You, mad at me?"

"Yes. Were you really, truly thinking about breaking up with me when you came back up here?"

"I don't know what I was going to say, exactly."

"But you were thinking about it."

"A little, I guess."

"You were gonna do it. I can't believe it! And you don't even know the whole story. Well, you know what? You don't deserve to hear it."

"Hold on there, cowboy. Taking a break's not the same thing as breaking up, and even if I'd gotten that far, I probably would've been right back on your doorstep with my tail between my legs in a matter of hours. I've got a history of panicking in relationships going back to when I was like fifteen."

"But you're a man now."

"Yeah, I'm working on it. What I don't understand is how this is about me all of a sudden. Like, how am I suddenly the bad guy."

"You weren't. Until you left."

Jack searched for a way to end the silence, the comment sinking in deeper than he was comfortable with. An apology seemed to be the only way out of it.

"Okay, I'm sorry I left. But I needed some time to think. I still do. Where was I supposed to go?"

"Why do you have to *go* anywhere?" Jack didn't know what to say. He looked to Kevin for help. "Okay. How about you stay here, and I'll go."

Jack brightened. "Yeah, that's gotta be a better idea." If he left now, it would be too easy to keep walking.

"But before I leave, I think we should clear up what happened. 'Cause otherwise you're gonna be thinking about the wrong things."

"I thought I didn't deserve the details."

"You didn't. But apologies go a long way with me."

Jack was leaning back against one wall, Kevin the other. Somehow, it seemed like it was up to Jack to begin. He held up his foot and briefly picked at the bottom of his boot where the tread was starting to peel. "Okay, for openers, you could have told me where you were going. Before you left."

"He didn't tell me anything I didn't tell you. Just be at my apartment with my bag packed."

"And a passport?"

"No, that's just the thing. He hadn't asked me about a passport because he wanted the trip to be a surprise. He was all worried when he got there."

"And you just happened to have one handy? Even though you've supposedly never been out of the country."

"Dang! Do ya think you could hold up the inquisition for a minute and I'll tell you why I was lucky enough to have it?"

Jack sighed and gestured for him to continue.

"Okay then. About a year ago this guy was supposed to take me to Europe. And I was so excited about going, I really was, but then I remembered I didn't have a passport, so I told him, and he said he could wait, just get it as quick as I could. I tried pulling all that documentary stuff together and it was a disaster. I had problems with my foster parents, my birth certificate, all that stuff. It ended up taking nearly eight months, and by the time I got it the guy had disappeared."

"It figures you'd have some sad story to make me feel bad."

"You asked for it."

"Okay, fine, you had your passport. But we're getting off track here. I mean, can't you see that if our positions had been reversed, you would've found this bothersome."

"I thought about trying to call you, but then what was I supposed to say, 'Hi. I'm in Montreal.' I thought that woulda been worse."

"It would've been worse." Jack looked down at the floor. "So what did you think of New York?"

"All I really saw of it was through the taxicab window. Back and forth to the airport. I could've met him for an early dinner after his business meeting, but I asked if it'd be okay if I just stayed in the hotel."

"And he agreed to that?"

"He said that was the best place for me, anyway."

"You could have told me that to begin with." Jack stood up away from the wall. "That really changes things. Shit, I might even be starting to feel guilty."

"You should. Room service wasn't very good."

"So, you're suggesting I got bent for no good reason?"

"I think 'overreacted' is the technical term." Kevin was looking a little too sure of himself.

"Don't think you're getting off scot-free, here. You could have helped me not to overreact, you know, by presenting your story a little differently. I mean, you were so coy about the whole thing. More than usual, anyway. Like you were really trying to put it in my face."

"I wasn't . . . okay, maybe I was trying to put it in your face. I did have a talk with myself about it after you left. I guess I didn't want you getting it all big in your head about how much I missed you. I . . ." He was trying not to tear up again and Jack had to look away. "I couldn't stop thinking about us. Like what it'd be like to travel together. Like what it'd be like to have our own place. I guess maybe it was staying at that house in Montreal, but whatever it was, I started really wanting it bad, and then I got worried maybe you wouldn't want it. And that made me feel nervous." Kevin hugged himself. "And that made me act weird. So you're right."

"For the first time this afternoon."

"See, what I shoulda done was tell you the whole story first. And how it made me feel inside before I said anything about moving in together. I blew it."

No, I blew it, Jack thought, but he couldn't handle any more of the blame right then. "So what'll we do?"

Kevin shrugged. "I was gonna get us a pizza, how about I go ahead and get it."

"Yeah, maybe it's a good time for intermission. It's funny, I couldn't wait to get some time by myself before and now I'm . . . I'm pretty hungry, I guess."

"I won't be long."

The door closed, and he was alone in Kevin's apartment.

The smell of wood again. Usually most noticeable when he first came in, although he could always detect it if he was paying attention. In the air. On Kevin, at times. It was a clean smell, natural. Coming strongest from the direction of his latest creation.

Jack walked over to the oak table—rectangular, simple, massive— and ran his hand along the top. After he completed a piece, Kevin liked to take it home with him and let it settle in for a bit before trying to sell it. He said you couldn't really tell exactly how it would look until you got it out of the shop, and sometimes he brought it back there again to make changes. Jack hoped he'd be satisfied with this one. He'd helped drag it up from the truck. They'd had to turn it six different ways before finally getting it through the door.

What little other furniture Kevin had, he'd made before they met. A cedar chest he kept his clothes in. A kitchen table, two chairs. The chairs were of the same light pine as the table, but there were slight differences between them, the curves of the arms and the designs carved into the backs. Jack liked that he'd taken the time to distinguish them. The way he liked so many other things about him.

He'd wanted this relationship to happen, and then, when it finally did, it turned out even better than he'd imagined. But as soon as Kevin mentions moving in together, just like that, he's nervous, thinking the guy's rushing things, getting too attached. But wait, give it another two minutes, because after hearing about the trip, he's suddenly worried that maybe Kevin's not attached enough. Why anyone would want to live with someone so shifty was beyond him.

But this was how it went when you fell for someone. Things seem perfect so much of the time, but when they're not, you knock yourself out worrying that the other person's either too into you or not into you enough. And either way, it can throw things off.

When it came down to it, though, didn't you want someone in your life who cared about you too much? To try to live up to the feelings they had for you—so you could almost believe you were worthy of them. But if you had to push yourself too hard, it could become a burden.

They sat on top of the oak table, the pizza box open between them.

"Good pizza, man. Greasy but good." Jack grabbed another piece. "I've been thinking through this whole Montreal trip and I've gotta admit, I was bound to have been uncomfortable even if I'd known before you left. So I was trying to think of ways to avoid something like this in the future and—well, it's not like anyone's ever asked me to go anywhere before, but—couldn't we keep it to, I don't know, shorter term regional travel?"

"Hey, I came up with almost the same thing! No more than one overnight in a row."

"Okay, then." Now came the harder part. "Any chance we could run with your thoughts for a while? I'm not necessarily accusing you of anything, here, but I noticed the box was down a slice when it arrived, and I really am hungry." He allowed himself a larger bite.

"You want me to try to make it easier for you about the moving in part?"

Jack opened his mouth full of pizza. "Uh, yeah."

"What I decided was, it wasn't fair to expect you to be thinking like me because you weren't on that plane, and you weren't in that house in Montreal. Therefore . . . I was gonna try to give you a chance to digest everything and wait for you to bring it up again when you were ready."

"So you're giving me a pass for today?"

"Yes."

"Hmm. But I bet you'd rather I didn't use it?"

"Yes."

"You sure you still want to do this after what happened earlier? Because now we're faced with the prospect of talking about moving in together on the same day I nearly suggested taking time apart."

"Which is why I decided I must have popped you on the head harder than I thought. See, it had to be a case of temporary insanity for you to have been thinking about leaving me."

"All right then, housing arrangements, here we come."

Kevin made a drumroll sound on the table while Jack finished off the rest of his slice.

"It's probably worth mentioning here that I've only lived with one person before who wasn't a roommate, and that didn't turn out so well."

"Skelly, right?"

"Yeah, Skelly. You're not thinking about having kids, are you?"

"Well, sure, someday. But not anytime soon."

"Good. Okay, so here's the problem the way I see it. Most of my . . . reluctance, I think, has to do with the fact that until you asked the moving-in question everything seemed to be going along really smooth. We're over at each other's place all the time, anyway. It's just been, like, easy. But the fact is, since you did ask the question, and if I did say no, then it's not likely things are gonna be as good as they were before because some part of you will probably resent me for saying no. Even if you're trying to be patient."

Kevin didn't step in to contradict him.

"On the other hand, something's still gnawing at me about moving too quickly. I can't put my finger on it, but I know I was already a little skittish before you mentioned anything about Montreal, and I feel like if I said yes right now, then I'd probably resent you for pushing me."

"A real pickle."

"I thought so, too. But it's one we could potentially get around if—" Kevin raised both fists in the air and gave a silent cheer—"I based myself out of here. You know, moved all my stuff over. But I kept my place a little while longer."

"You don't have stuff."

"I've got some stuff."

"So kinda moving in."

"With the idea of fully moving in at some point soon. How's that?"

"Good."

"Good? What about great? I thought I'd found a nifty solution to this conundrum."

"That's because you didn't think about what would make the plan even better . . . that we start planning a trip to New York."

Now, it was Jack's turn to cheer. "Of course. Yes. How could we not with the way you managed to save it for us and everything?" He gripped his hand on Kevin's shoulder and shook it. "Like the champ that you are." Kevin blushed.

"It kind of astounds me that there's anything left for you to blush at." Jack picked up the pizza box. "You want any more?"

"Nope, full here."

He put the leftovers away, then closed the refrigerator door behind him. Kevin was still sitting on the table, one leg swinging under it, his face turned toward the window. *Such a good guy. Such a good-looking guy.* Jack hitched up his pants. "So have you recovered sufficiently to go back to bed?"

Kevin turned toward him. "I think so. But I've got one additional request, having to do with a somewhat unrelated matter. Are you ready?"

"Possibly."

"I was wondering if you'd be able to tell me you love me three hundred and seventy-five times in a row."

"That's all?" Jack grinned. He couldn't have picked a better moment.

"Don't even think this is gonna be difficult for me. Except maybe the three seventy-five, you know I gotta ask about that."

"Thought you might . . . Three hundred and seventy-five is the number of days since we met. And seeing as you forgot to mention it that day—and every day since—I'm giving you a chance to get current."

"You really counted?"

"It was a long flight back from Montreal."

"I see." He walked over to Kevin and put his hands on his knees. "Do you think we could do a factor of three seventy-five? Like five is a factor."

"One is a factor, also. I bet once would do it."

"And you're planning on saying it back?"

"Of course. I've got some catching up to do, too."

Jack shook his head and held his finger over Kevin's lips. He looked into his eyes, the one part of him that would never grow old, and said it. Kept saying it, meaning it more every time, until he lost count.

"I'm really sorry I acted like that earlier. When I came back up the stairs. I just . . . I don't want to be like that with you." Kevin slid Jack's finger into his hand and held it there. Jack took a long breath, then let it go. "Don't ever let me leave you, will you promise me that?" He lowered his head. "Please."

"You realize you're hogging the covers again." Jack gave another tug but couldn't get them to budge. "Hey, what's going on over there?"

"What's going on is, you stopped cuddling."

"That's because I lost circulation in my arm. I was worried about gangrene setting in."

"You've got another arm, don't ya?"

"Yeah, I guess."

"Then let's switch places."

"All right, hold on." Jack crawled over. They re-situated themselves. "That better?"

"Way better."

They lay there for a few minutes without speaking. Jack thought the best approach would be a roundabout one. "Hey, so have you ever noticed how many different places you've, uh, visited before. You know, different buildings. Because I was out on the bike the other day and it was like, damn, I can't even ride ten blocks without passing some apartment I've been into. It's like I've got x-ray vision and I can see inside. Who lives there, what their bedroom looks like, what they look like. Naked. What they like to do naked. Everything so transparent. This town's getting smaller, I swear it is . . .

"Or something else that's been kind of bothering me. This is maybe worse, actually, I don't know, but it all started when I wanted to get us tickets for that Country All-Stars concert Thursday night. I was planning to surprise you, but they ended up being sold out, so . . . Anyway, point is, I was thinking about getting them, and then I started to add up how much the whole night was gonna cost, and I figured it would equal about one and a half hours of work—one and a half fucks, that is— and then I said to myself, wait a second, I don't know if that's the kind of calculation I want to keep making on a regular basis.

"I just think it might be time to start exploring some other options. Looking ahead to the summer and everything. I know you're gonna say I think too much, but don't you even think about it at all?

"Hey, Kev, you still up?

Kevin?

No one's there.

And no one's going to be there and the moment you realize that is the moment . . .

5:27

I climb higher up the hill. Above the playground. Pause to catch my breath, then turn around. There's usually an amazing view of the city from here, but now it's mostly hidden by the fog, the lights outlining the bridge disappearing into nothing.

I don't know what I want anymore. A place to lie down. To stop thinking. I'm running out of stories to tell myself, but I can't stop. I need to stay awake.

Jack could never fall asleep afterward. He might nod off. Five minutes. Ten minutes, tops, if given the chance. But Kevin made some of his best tips that way, attracting kindness when he could have been taken advantage of.

He slept like an angel.

If you give yourself the benefit of the doubt—that you know something about the nocturnal habits of the divine—it makes for a generous compliment. One you might bestow upon a child, but Kevin appeared all the more devout because he wasn't one. That he'd lived this long and still let his guard down in the company of strangers.

Once, he said, he'd awoken to find a client staring at him, from the foot of the bed, kneeling. Other times, he'd found himself alone, in a hotel room, with far more than the required amount of cash on the table. He seemed humbled by these tributes, but they shouldn't have come as a surprise. Beauty tends to get rewarded. To be in the presence of it is to be convinced there's something right in this world. But if beauty is the easiest good to recognize, it is also the easiest to mistake for something else. The last to be resisted and the first to be resented. The most vulnerable to malevolence.

If a man comes to believe he is cursed in life, he may eventually decide that his only recourse is to push himself harder and faster in the direction of his perceived future. Toward the ugly and the unpleasant. Toward the cruel. But faith in salvation can be stubborn. And no matter how far he might go, he will rarely go so far as to believe he is beyond saving.

Still, he might try to push it further.

The fog hadn't quite lifted the morning that one such man, determined to escape into his own fate, used Kevin's blood to try to seal it. Cut him badly. Deep and many times.

The first moment when Jack walked into the hospital room and didn't recognize him, made the second, when he did, even more excruciating. He couldn't see Jack, though, his eyes were closed. The nurse stood over him saying he was lucky to be alive, but he wasn't looking so lucky that day.

He had survived. Came within a pint of losing his life, but he was hanging in there. Doing his best to eat the food they were serving him. Trying to make small jokes with the staff. He refused to give them his foster parents' number until they promised not to call it. Jack tried to convince him to call, and he assured him that he would, once he began to heal up better. He didn't see the point of subjecting them to his present condition, and it was hard to disagree. He didn't allow any other visitors.

It was a long week before they let him come home, of watching out the hospital window and telling him not to speak to conserve his strength. Kevin hadn't wanted to go back to his apartment, so they'd gone to Jack's. There wasn't much more than a mattress there, and once Kevin sat down on it, he started talking and didn't stop. He was still trying to understand what had happened. He hadn't seen it coming at all.

I mean we were having a really nice time, Jack. Really nice, and then . . . I guess I must have fallen asleep and I woke up and he was yelling—I put up my hands—he was yelling, Faggot! Faggot!

Jack didn't know what to say. The man had turned himself in to the police, but what did that mean? There weren't any answers, and he didn't want any. Not to those questions, anyway. What was really plaguing him was why he still felt cut off from Kevin, even though they were finally by themselves. Why the apartment felt like an extension of the hospital. When Kevin lay back on the pillow, Jack wanted to put his arms around him, but instead he continued to listen while Kevin spoke in increasingly smaller circles, the words soon replaced by the moist, clicking sound in the back of his throat that rarely lasted more than a few minutes after he'd fallen asleep. The room was nearly dark, and there was finally some solace in it, listening to the rhythm of his breathing.

Four o'clock in the morning, moonlight pressing through the blinds. Kevin was still curled up on the mattress. Jack covered him with an extra blanket, even though it wasn't that cold. Hoping there was something, still, to protect.

He didn't see how he could have been out for more than an hour. The sun was just a possibility facing the horizon when he turned off the Great Highway, having just cruised the longest, flattest strip of road he knew inside the city limits—mostly without red lights, where he could build up some speed. He was still trying to shake off what had happened, but it stayed with him the whole time. And even if he wasn't feeling ready to go back, he knew he had to.

As soon as he turned away from the ocean, he knew he should never have come out. Nothing gained, and he'd left Kevin alone his first night back. *How could he have left?*

He raced through the streets, but by the time he arrived at the apartment Kevin was gone.

No note. No sign he'd even been there besides the crumpled blanket on the mattress. *Where could he be?* Jack was trying not to panic. Maybe he went back to his place to get some of his things. No, that didn't make any sense. He would have waited until . . . Jack checked his cellphone. Three missed calls. Lost in the noise of the engine, what had he been thinking? He pressed through to his voicemail. There was only one message.

Jack, I don't know where you are, but . . . I'm not feeling so good so I'm gonna grab a cab back to the hospital, just to have them take a look. I'm sure it's nothing. I'll try you again soon. Don't worry, okay?

Sprinting out the door, down to the street, to his bike where he'd parked it. Jumping on, the key rammed in, revved, and then finally, riding, his body leaned all the way forward *please just let me get there* the wind blurring his eyes *please don't let it be that bad . . .* he turned up toward the hospital, laid his horn out against the oncoming cars, kept it blaring until he reached the emergency entrance, dropped the bike, ran toward the double doors, toward the empty gurney coming through them, then over to the receptionist's desk. "Do you have Kevin here? Did he just come in?"

The receptionist looked up from the computer screen. "Okay, first thing I need to happen is that you slow down. Can you do that for me?"

He just looked at her, pleading.

"Now what was the name again?"

"Kevin. Kevin Jensen."

"Are you a member of the immediate family?"

"No, I'm a friend of his."

"Sorry, but I can't give you any information unless—"

"I'm his best friend, for Christ's sake. I—he—was just here. I picked him up from you guys yesterday. Yesterday afternoon, you released him to me."

She got on the phone. Jack bit his lip. Held onto it to keep the room from disappearing. The faint taste of blood in his mouth. The fluorescent bulbs above him. The buzzing filled his ears.

"You sure you're going to be all right?"

A man was holding out a cup of coffee in front of him. Jack took it. "Me? I'm fine."

"We've already notified his parents."

"He doesn't have any parents."

"They'll be coming in this afternoon, maybe you want to wait for them. Or come back later and meet with them."

"No, I don't think so."

"Do you want to talk to someone?"

"Who?"

"We have people here you can talk with."

"A doctor you mean?"

"A kind of doctor, yes."

"I wouldn't mind knowing from a doctor how you managed to release him yesterday. He had to have been feverish, you know, even then." *And how had you taken him, so wanting to get him, to get you both, the hell out of there.*

"His doctor is with another patient right now, but you can speak with her when she's through."

"Do you think it was because he didn't have any insurance? That you were worried about getting paid?" *Do you think you could have taken his pulse before you walked out the door, that you could have taken the six seconds to get a pulse? Do you think you could have felt his forehead? Or touched him at all?* "You're not answering the question. And you should, you know, because it was you guys that poisoned him. You don't just get sepsis without a little help from the hospital."

"I really think you'll need to speak with his doctor. Would you like some more coffee?"

"No."

Jack put down the cup and left.

For the first few days, lying beside the mattress—ceiling dark, ceiling light, ceiling dark again—he tried not to tell himself apart from the floor. But when he shifted position, he could feel an ache pressed into him like he'd been under furniture. The stiffness. The lurch of trying to overcome it, standing up, lightheaded, stomach empty. When he'd finally taken a shower, it wasn't so much a revolt against the dullness as a continuation of it. He turned on the water hot enough to singe his skin, cold, cold, it felt the same, going through the soaping motions.

He hadn't gone there with the intention of picking a fight. He wouldn't have guessed he had the energy for it. He only wanted to follow through on a plan he'd found the resolve to carry out. Donating blood, a procedure he'd been doing, sporadically, since high school.

He took the bus over to San Francisco State. Stood in line for his paperwork, then got the number for his screening and looked around. Hundreds of chairs were spread out in the auditorium, about a third of them full. He went to the back and started filling out the forms. He should have known what to expect. The questions hadn't changed.

Still, seeing them printed there, set in type, his anger was quick to surface, and he felt strengthened by it. Yes, he'd had sex with another man. Whose business was it, anyway? When his number was called, he went up to the flimsily partitioned row of tables. The nurse waiting for him wasn't unattractive, dark hair pulled back in a braid.

"Hello," she said.

"Hi."

"Do you have your questionnaire with you?"

He handed it to her.

"I just need to go over your responses, and then we'll take a little bit of your blood to check for iron deficiency. Are you all right with that?"

"Fine."

"Let's get started then. Are you feeling well today?"

"Great."

"Have you ever—"

No. And so it went, down the list, till they reach number twelve.

"You checked here that you've had sex with another man. Did you mean to check that?"

"Yes."

"I'm sorry, but you won't be able to give blood today."

"What about tomorrow?"

"I'm sorry, but if you've had sex with another man you can't give blood then either."

"Why not?"

"This is our policy."

"But why?"

"Because it puts you at a higher risk for HIV and you could infect someone else with your blood."

She was trying to talk with him. *Why was she doing that?* He wanted some vacant face he could yell into. Vacant eyes. But it didn't matter, he wasn't going to stop now. He'd finally found something he wanted to say.

"Do you know I had an HIV test last month and it was negative? Do you know I get tested regularly and that I always use a condom and you're not willing to take a chance on me?"

"We have to try to minimize the risk."

"You're rewarding ignorance is what you're doing, you see that, right? You'll take a chance on every motherfucking frat boy who—"

"Sir—"

"Walks in here having boned half the chicks on campus, doesn't care about safe sex, doesn't get tested, but just so long as he tells you he hasn't slept with another guy, tells you he feels all chirpy inside today, then that's it. You're all set, good to go with that."

"We test all the blood that's given to us."

"Then what do you have to worry about, lady? Come on. You're not going to tell me there isn't someone out there who wouldn't be willing to take a chance on my blood. Someone who really needs it. How about someone who's already positive that's just been in an accident. Or you could put it on ice for six months or whatever, you know, hold it and retest it again, just to be sure."

She didn't say anything.

"I just don't understand how you can sit there and turn me down. How you can face yourself when you know there's a shortage."

"And could you face yourself if you ever infected someone?" She held his gaze for a moment—Jack tried licking his lips, his tongue dry—then looked behind him. "Sir, you're holding up the line. People are waiting to give blood. If you feel this is so important . . ."

"Listen, just one more thing and then I'll go." He stood up, his legs wobbly. "What would you do . . . what would you do if you had someone in the hospital right now who you loved and had lost a lot of blood and they needed you, what would you do then?"

"You can make arrangements to give to them directly."

"Boy, you've got an answer for everything, don't you? Okay, suppose you don't have someone in the hospital right now because they're dead. Because they died from complications from blood loss and suppose you were going crazy inside from missing them and you didn't know what to do with yourself anymore, so you came down here."

"I'm sorry. Maybe you could make a donation to blood services to help pay for our work."

"No!" He slammed his fist down on the table. "Not money."

As he was being led out of the auditorium, he thought how patient the woman had managed to be with him. How she'd stuck with him the whole way through. "Pamela" read the scripted name on her tag. He couldn't help despising her.

Back in the apartment, he remembered everything.

Returning late from a call, Jack had tried to open the door as gently as possible, but he could barely get it to budge. Kevin was on the other side. He'd propped himself up against the door and, sounding half-asleep, told Jack not to come in.

Kevin had gotten sick. Awoken in the middle of the night with a fever, sweats. Chills that continued through the next day. Jack had never seen him with so much as a cold and he was scared. He wanted to ask if anything unusual had happened on the job—anything whatsoever—but all he said that night was that he hoped he felt better.

Kevin recovered twenty-four hours later. He'd traced his condition to a carton of Thai food he let sit out too long, but he took off from work and fourteen days after that he took his blood test early, just to be on the safe side. It was clear, as he'd expected.

While they were waiting for the results, though, something had changed inside Jack. The doubts he'd been having had reached a tipping point. And when he realized they weren't going to tip back, he decided to talk to Kevin.

He said that he'd had enough. That he was sick of worrying every time he didn't feel altogether well. Sick of worrying about condoms breaking or where cum was landing. Sick of having to feel through the wasted muscle of someone's ass, trying to find that healthy person underneath who wanted to be held. He was sick of the endless treadmill of tests, of never knowing for sure. He didn't want to do it anymore. And, this was the hardest part, he didn't want Kevin to do it, either.

Couldn't they try something else for a while? It probably wasn't the best time for him to mention checking in with the Forest Service again, but there were plenty of other things he could do in the meantime. He had his bike, he knew the streets. All those new delivery startups were looking for drivers. Or he could go back to bartending. Both, if necessary. Whatever it took to give Kevin a chance to finally establish himself as a furniture maker. It just didn't make sense to keep on the way they were going. They had something good—really good—why look for trouble?

Jack listened to himself talking and he didn't recognize himself at all. He tried to make a joke, saying this might be the first sign he was a latent conservative, but he wasn't kidding. It wasn't until he'd rounded the corner of his final point that his voice sounded like his own again . . . *and I don't want to have to wear a condom, anymore, when I'm inside you.*

He was sure, at best, Kevin would have to think it over. But Kevin surprised him. He said he'd known this day would come sooner or later;

he just hadn't known what he'd say when it did. But now he knew.

The rest of the afternoon was spent adjusting plans. They would move in together and no more escorting after that. Jack would give notice on his lease, and that would give them nearly six weeks to look for other work, taking every possible call in the meantime to save up. Kevin thought they should consider skipping the New York trip for the time being, but Jack had insisted, no, they were going to do it anyway. First class all the way. And so they'd come up with one final game. They opened an account together and competed to see who could put in the most money. Jack had never had such an easy time with his clients, knowing it almost over, sprinting toward the finish line. Checking the deposits at the two-week mark, he could see that he was winning.

Got what he deserved for going down to the Embarcadero. A bunch of tourists and a run-in with an old friend. He'd gone there to visit the sea lions, but they weren't around. Only the chattering crowd. It didn't really surprise him to see her standing in the middle of it, just registered vaguely as something to be avoided, so he threw down his cigarette and turned to walk away.

Jack?

How quick it happened, hearing his name through her voice and like that getting hooked back up in time. To a past he'd been carrying around like a pack on his shoulders, separate and balanced so he'd barely been aware it was there anymore. But he'd just felt it slip, and with the sudden weight he was already tired of the encounter before he'd even said hello. It was Skelly's first roommate from college, and he couldn't remember her name.

Jack, it's Kate.

He'd barely acknowledged her with a hello when the questions began.

So what are you doing here, and weren't you fighting fires in New Mexico, and wasn't Skelly living with you, and . . . he was trying to think of the least number of incidents he could describe that would still connect together and create a semi-coherent story about his life. Even with all the details it wasn't a simple operation, but Kate didn't push him to fill in the gaps. She told him some things about herself, her job, and then started to go through the list of people they both had known, a little blurb accompanying each name, all of which failed to make an impression. The wind was loud and lashing her hair across her face. He was having trouble concentrating, blinking in the sunlight.

". . . and he was talking about how wild you always were. Have you talked to him recently?"

"Who?"

"Steve."

"Steve, uh, gosh, no I haven't. Have you?"

She was looking at him funny. "Well, anyway, it's just great to see you."

"You too."

"You look really good, Jack." *That's not true*, he thought. The possibility disturbed him.

He nodded when Kate said they'd have to keep in touch, hoping she'd leave it at that. But then she reached into her purse, pulled out a card and handed it to him. "Everything's current," she said.

He stared at the card.

"Why don't you call me right now, and that way I'll have your number."

"I can't. I mean, I don't have a cell."

"My God, how do you live?" She seemed even more shocked about this than running into him in the first place.

He raised his finger to his lips, as if it were a secret she shouldn't be sharing with anyone, but realized, holding it there, what he really meant was for her to stop talking. "Actually, I do have one, but I don't have it on me right now. Because it's not working very well and . . ." He could see she was finally losing patience with him. "But, here, let me give you my home phone." He scribbled down the number and held it out to her.

She hesitated before taking it. "Even if you don't call me, you really should get in touch with Steve. I know he'd love to hear from you. Goodbye, Jack."

Steve had been Jack's roommate during their first two years of college. A good-natured kid who came from one of the tinier towns in Kansas. That someone both as smart and naïve as Steve could still exist had been a revelation to Jack. He envied him the easiness of his world view, and whenever he found himself getting in hot water, he would make a point of spending more time with him. They always managed to have a good time together: playing cribbage, half studying, and generally staying out of trouble.

Freshman year, Steve had asked Jack to edit a science paper for him. Jack marked it up as requested, but seeing as it was the only paper Steve had ever asked for help on, he suspected the real reason it had been given to him was so that he might get something out of the content. If that was the plan, it worked, because not only had Jack read it with interest, he'd made a copy for himself, underlined it in places, and kept it along with a number of his own assignments.

When he got back to the apartment, he dug it out of the box that Skelly had left him.

I have chosen to do my paper on the topics of sensation-seeking and the theory of the optimum level of arousal. These two factors can be used to explain the various behaviors and characteristics of all people.

An individual's optimum level of arousal depends upon that individual's rating on a sensation seeking scale (SSS). Scores on the SSS reflect the extent to which an individual seeks out or alters his or her state of being for excitement and pleasure. From the SSS, people can be judged to be low sensation seekers or high sensation seekers. <u>Although it may seem that high sensation seekers tend to do things which are riskier than what low sensation seekers might do, both groups are actually acting within their optimum levels of arousal due to their self-appraisals of risk.</u>

Let me briefly define high sensation seeking. It is <u>a trait defined by the need for varied, novel, and complex sensations and experiences and the willingness to take physical and social risks for the sake of such experience.</u> The high sensation seeker is sensitive to his or her internal sensations and chooses external stimuli that maximize them.

One factor that distinguishes high and low sensation seekers from one another is the <u>want for novelty</u>. Novelty can be defined as the maximal unpredictability in a sequence of events. To achieve this novelty, the highs will vary their routine, in contrast to the lows, who are less distressed by an unvarying routine. The lows cannot avoid novel situations completely, however, because no matter how rigid a routine they may create, novel situations are inevitable. In addition, low sensation seekers may even, without outside prompting, seek novel situations (though less often than the highs). For example, at one point last summer I felt that I was playing too much baseball, so I looked for something else to do and came up with horseshoes.

This example also serves to demonstrate that not all novel situations need to be inherently risky . . .

The image of Steve playing horseshoes used to entertain Jack. Reading it now, he couldn't remember why.

Another way high sensation seekers distinguish themselves from low sensation seekers is their <u>desire for complexity</u>. Complexity refers to the number of stimulus elements and their arrangement. Not only do high sensation seekers prefer more complexity in their lives, but they conceive of their social acquaintances in more complex ways than do the lows.

Highs tend to be impulsive. Some classifications of impulsivity according to Wangeman et al. are: acting without thinking or adequate reflection, reacting quickly to a first impulse on the spur of the moment, and taking risks and chances. This impulsive behavior occurs in individuals who find the attractions of the promised reward both strong in absolute terms and relatively stronger than the deterrent effects of potential punishments. Also, highs have difficulty in tolerating boredom. This difficulty may express itself in many forms: gambling, mobility and traveling, amount of acceptable life stress, sexual activity and attitudes, drug and alcohol use . . .

He flipped through the remaining pages, skipping down to the end.

I have written mainly about the negative applications of sensation seeking. From the information I have given, one might conclude that there is no way for high sensation seekers to get out of the destructive realm of risk-taking that high sensation seeking places them in. To think this, however, would be a mistake. The reason for this is that sensation seeking is a displaceable motive. This means that activities required to meet an individual's "pleasure requirements" are interchangeable. For example, a person could take up rock climbing or scuba diving. Or, professionally, she or he could take up an occupation that would be useful to society, such as becoming an astronaut. These activities could help maintain optimum levels of arousal, while, at the same time, subjecting the risks inherent in them to oversight and safety rules. Also, one should realize that there is a relationship between high sensation seeking and achievement strivings, and that highs, when put in the right environment, are particularly well suited to getting the job done.

What is important to recognize is that there isn't anything inherently "wrong" with either high or low sensation seekers. Rather, you should try to recognize the type of individual you are, and then try to use your optimum level of arousal to optimize your life!

I hope that I have properly depicted the subject and made the application of the topics interesting.

Other than the dim recognition of Steve's voice behind the words, he realized the paper meant nothing to him anymore—taking risks, not taking risks, what difference did it make? —the hope he'd once seen for himself in it was gone. It was time to get rid of the paper. The whole box, in fact. What was the point of holding onto all the old stuff? He wouldn't be staying in the apartment much longer, anyway; he'd have nowhere to put it.

The handwritten notes from Liz continued to pile up under the door and he continued to ignore them. He'd run into her a few times, but she'd never said anything to him directly. About the rent. Until, coming back from the library one afternoon, he passed her in the lobby, vacuuming, and she held her hand up for him to stop. He hurried up the stairs.

A couple minutes later she was standing outside his door.

"Jack, I know you're in there and I know that you're . . . having a hard time right now."

He winced. He couldn't stand the fact she knew, but she'd been there the day they'd gotten back from the hospital. She and Kevin had always been friendly, and when she kept asking how he was coming along and wouldn't stop, after telling her again and again everything was fine, he'd finally given in and told her it wasn't.

"It's okay if you don't answer me, I know you can hear me. I wanted to tell you, if this was only up to me, I'd give you more time. I really would, but it isn't. I can't give my boss any more excuses and I can't cover for you myself. You've been a great tenant, Jack, I'm sorry, but it really complicated things when you gave notice and your last month's rent is about to run out. If we don't get something from you soon, we're going to have to start eviction proceedings."

He hoped she was through.

"If you can come up with anything, anything at all, just let me know. We can make arrangements. All right?"

He didn't want to make arrangements. He wanted to be left alone. Of course, he had the money. More than he'd ever had since coming to San Francisco. But the reason he had it sickened him, and he didn't want to touch it.

When he finally heard her footsteps withdrawing, he turned to his pile of books. For the first time in his life, he'd taken an interest in science fiction. He'd never understood the appeal before, it seemed too far removed for him. But that remoteness was what attracted him now. He started with Vonnegut, indebted to the author for being so prolific. Plenty of books, and he knew this was only the tip of the iceberg. An entire genre to discover.

The hardest part was approaching a book. Opening it. The idea of reading was difficult for a number of reasons, but once he was doing it—working his way through the early pages—one world gave way to another, and he was belted in for the ride. Then he tried not to put the book down, often finishing in one sitting. A short break and he was ready to begin again.

When the final knock came, this time he did open the door. But only after listening to Liz grow increasingly flustered on the other side, explaining the kind of trouble she'd get in if she didn't hand him the notice personally. He took it from her and shut the door again. Glancing over the information, he saw that he'd been given some additional time to comply before the courts would get involved, but he didn't expect he'd be needing it. He should have already left.

Realizing there was, in fact, something he wanted to negotiate, Jack brought the paper down to Liz's office. He told her that while he didn't intend to drag out the proceedings, he wondered if she'd let him hold onto his parking spot behind the gate. He hadn't touched the bike since that morning, when he'd driven by Kevin's one last time on the way back from the hospital. He wasn't sure what he was going to do with the bike now, but he knew he didn't want to take it with him.

Liz agreed to let the bike stay. She said she didn't think her boss would find out, and, besides, the space wasn't big enough for a car. If someone else came along with a bike, they'd worry about it then. She never asked him how long it would be for, and by the time Jack got back to his room, he'd mustered the proper feeling to try to show his appreciation.

"Hey, sorry to bother you again, Liz." He put the laptop on her desk. "I don't know whether you need this or not, but . . ."

Liz looked at him closely.

"I mean, for all the trouble I caused you. I cleaned up the hard drive and everything and . . . well, it's kind of old anyway, but I wanted you to have it."

Liz glanced down at the computer. "I'm not sure this is a good idea."

"But I wouldn't even be using it." Jack wasn't sure why this one thing had become so important to him. "I don't care if you sell it or anything, just please don't say no."

She nodded. "Okay, Jack. I'll take it."

The next day he put some clothes and a few other items into his pack. There was a zippered compartment on the inside that he'd never used for anything, it was too small. But that's where he put the pocket watch he'd taken from Kevin's place. He'd been keeping it wound every day, but the reason he'd started doing it eluded him now and he didn't want to look at it anymore.

He thought he was done listening to Kevin's message, too, but he couldn't quite bring himself to leave the phone behind just in case he wanted to hear it again. Once, playing it, he'd managed to find some hope in Kevin's voice, telling him not to worry, making it sound like everything was going to be all right. Granted, Jack had mostly been cynical about it, but there had been that one time. He put the phone in with his clothes and made a clean sweep of everything else.

The last thing he threw out was the mattress, dragging it down the steps to the bins in the basement, where he placed it off to the side. Then he went back upstairs, grabbed his pack, and took one last look around, before closing the door. Liz gave him a hug in exchange for his keys, and he headed out into the Tenderloin expecting to disappear into it. Thinking of all the people who made the street their home, he didn't see how it could be that difficult, but he quickly realized he'd overestimated himself.

A handful of nights out was all it took. Church doors locked, gates blocking steps, shards of glass, metal spikes on walls you might want to hop over or lie down on. Delirious from half naps, nudged awake by hands in his clothes or startled awake by the sound of breaking bottles, he'd slump back onto the sidewalk, wishing the sun would come up. And then, not long after it did, wishing it would go down again. The heat increasingly oppressive, his face burned red after the newspapers had blown off. Near constant vigilance was required; it was hard to make a point of not caring about anything.

There were people who would have helped him out, but the last thing he wanted was to be around anyone he knew. With the spare cash in his wallet now gone, though, he was either going to have to call someone, or he was going to have to make a withdrawal from the bank. Once he understood that was the decision, it was an easy one to make. Before hitting up the nearest ATM, he promised himself he would only ever touch half the money.

The first thing he did with it was to take the bus up to the aquarium to see Aqualung. Thinking it was the first Tuesday of the month, but he'd missed a Tuesday. So instead of going in, he wandered around the park where, finally, he felt something ease up inside him. He'd been too far out of his element before; he hadn't grown up in a city and had no natural instincts to fall back on there. He scouted out some spots in the trees, went downtown to get a tent and supplies, and came back before nightfall. There was satisfaction in having a part of him just take over and handle the situation. He'd been making campsites, forts, since he was a kid, and everything went up without his having to think about it. As long as he varied his location and moved early enough to avoid the park patrol, he believed he could make it for a while. He was able to relax, somewhat, with his books again.

If anything, it was too nice. The grass, the flowers. Being near the beach. Not that he ever went down to it. One morning after a light drizzle, he was breaking down the site when he remembered he'd left the bike uncovered. A kind of slight he had to admit, even though he didn't think he blamed the bike for what had happened. He decided to go back and take care of it. There was no way he was up for a ride, but at least he'd be able to run the engine, make sure the battery was keeping a charge.

The bus dropped him on O'Farrell, and as he walked down toward the apartment, he felt some apprehension. But when he slid the gate open, the bike looked the same as always. The cover was still stuffed inside his helmet, and he took it out, shook it, and spread it on the ground. Then chose the ignition key and inserted it. The bike stuttered on the startup, coughed up some smoke, but smoothed once the engine began to warm. He took the choke off and let it idle. Then he walked outside the gate and sat on the curb.

The neighborhood had its own kind of erratic pulse that Jack had always liked, but he couldn't feel it right then. It just looked filthy to him. Puke on the sidewalk. Someone down on their knees searching for their crack bag or God knew what else. Someone else screaming. People go crazy here, he thought, but at least they've got the right company to do it with. And they're always looking for more. You never had to wait long for someone to come up and talk to you.

The guy had passed him going down the street, and Jack recognized him when he returned. Tattooed arms, wicked looking scar on his face. He nodded. "Howdy."

Jack nodded back.

"You ain't gotten far, have you?"

"No."

He stopped. "You live 'round here?"

"Not really."

"Well, where do you live?"

It wasn't any of the guy's business. None of it was unless Jack wanted to make it that way. "The Sunset."

"Is that right? You don't look like you seen a shower in a while."

Jack considered, again, whether to continue the conversation; he hadn't had one in a while. "I've got outdoor accommodations at the moment."

"Uh-huh. How's that workin' for you?"

"Fine."

"Fine? Good." He produced a pack of cigarettes, unwrapped it. "Want a smoke?"

Jack stood up. "Yeah." He took one from the pack.

"So you got friends over here, you visiting your people?"

"I just came by to check on the bike." He pointed through the gate. "Long story."

"Oh, yeah. Bikes are some cool shit. Very cool. Takes guts to ride one a those, I 'magine."

"It doesn't take much."

"Uh-huh, so you don't think you're a big shot. I like that. You must be a good guy to pal around with."

Jack dropped the cigarette to his side. "Don't want to waste your time. I'm not looking to hook up."

"I ain't lookin' to hook up with you neither. This town is so fucked, man, you can't even say hello to someone."

"I'm just letting you know."

"Well, I'm gonna let you know how it is too. I just got screwed royally by two of my best friends. Former friends that is, and I says to myself, Darius, you know what, you might as well try your luck with a stranger. It can't do you much worse."

"You shouldn't trust me either."

"Yeah, but at least I know that already."

They smoked for a while without talking.

"You got a job you're workin' at?"

"Not right now."

"Lookin' for one?"

"Probably gonna have to before long."

Darius snapped his fingers, like an idea had come to him fresh. "You know, I could use someone to run errands for me. Just pick up some things at the stores from time to time . . .You look like you'd clean up pretty good."

The proposition had trouble written all over it, but Jack was drawn in. It was something to do, at least. Maybe he'd be useful.

"Would I need to use the bike?"

"Nah, it wouldn't matter how you got around. You got a phone I can reach you at?"

Jack nodded.

"Then I think we got ourselves a deal, here." Darius smiled, the scar jumping up his cheekbone. "You'll get some floor space out of it. And other benefits as well, Darius has access to things." He threw down his cigarette. "I'm just around the block here at the Pacific Bay, if you wanna come along."

"All right, give me a minute."

Jack went back to where the bike was idling and turned the motor off. Hung the keys around his neck, tucked them inside his T-shirt, then waited for the bike to cool a bit before covering it. Looking down at the concrete beneath his boots he thought, *this seems about right*. The park had been a refuge but a temporary one. Now that he was downtown again, he realized he didn't deserve to go back.

Darius had an ID made up for him that afternoon, and over the course of the following week, Jack picked up a handful of orders at electronic goods stores around town, under the name Tomlinson. His responsibilities didn't take but a few hours, and it seemed like, as much as anything else, Darius wanted him for the companionship. In the background, which was just where Jack wanted to be. They stayed in the room most of the time, rarely saying more than a few words to one another. Sometimes, Jack would put his book down and join Darius on the PlayStation.

Darius was big into credit card scamming and would probably have gotten rich between everything if he didn't have an extreme speed habit to contend with. It kept him constantly wired with plenty to spare, and after days of observing him from across the room, of seeing how awake, how engaged he looked while not seeming to care about anything more important than getting the highest score on *Grand Theft Auto*, Jack was reminded of how he felt the night he'd taken the drug with Carrie, and how that didn't seem like such a bad thing anymore. Before asking for a bump, Jack stepped out into the hall and erased Kevin's message.

A week later and Darius was starting to lose his cool. First with the computer, removing everything off his hard drive, program by program, in the hopes he was going to bring back some fonts that were somehow missing. Jack watched for a while, then went over to piss in the sink.

"When do you even use them?" he asked, tapping off.

"Use what?"

"The fonts you're looking for."

Darius considered this for a moment. "I just want them."

An hour later and still no luck. Darius was going to try to get hold of some computer helpline, but then his face paled with the phone at his ear. "Shit, listen to this." He handed Jack the phone and then, before Jack had a chance to listen, took it back. "It's the store manager at Electronic Express. They're onto us for sure." His mouth dropped open. "Shit, they got the address here, too." He was up in a flash, pulling clothes from the drawers, throwing them on the floor.

"You gave them the address?"

"I didn't give it, I got it. Came with Tomlinson's mailbox."

Darius disappeared from the room—leaving Jack to try to piece together the shady business he'd been involved with, wondering whether the guy was being perceptive or only paranoid—then reappeared a few minutes later with a luggage rack, lifting the corner where a wheel was missing to get it to roll. After filling it with the small fortune in computer hardware he'd accumulated, half the boxes not even opened yet, he asked, "You gonna help me or not?"

Jack called for a cab.

Next thing they were down in the lobby with all the gear piled up behind them. Darius was arguing for the deposit back from the woman who sat behind the front desk. Her voice was getting louder by the second, and when she started shouting in Mandarin, he was certain things were headed for trouble.

Jack watched the cab come and he watched the driver looking at them through the window like an accusation and he kept thinking, *Let's get the fuck out of here, Darius. Let's get the fuck out of here.* But Darius was oblivious to the whole situation. So, trying to stay calm, he grabbed him on the shoulder and put it as reasonably as he could. "Listen. Darius. Hey. We need to get going." When Darius looked at him like he was a stranger—started arguing with woman again—that's when he finally woke up to himself. *What in the world are you doing, you've got no ties beyond two weeks to this guy, get going.* So he left.

He had just started down the street when the cops pulled up. They could've been there for any number of reasons, but the only one Jack could think of at the moment was they were about to be arrested. He had to get away from there, far away. His bike was just around the corner.

He pulled through the gate and leapt out into traffic, feeling the determination set into his jaw, but still having no idea where he was going. Then as soon as he got an idea, about needing to get across the bridge, that's all he was able to concentrate on so the next thing he knew he'd swung full circle past the Bay again. Pathetic, he thought, unable to stop himself from staring at the entrance as he went by. The cop car was still parked outside, the lights spinning blue. He looked into the sideview mirror to see if he could pass for sober, but his eyes were pinpoint wild. He was terrified of himself.

That's when he asked the bike to take over. He didn't yell. Only said *please. Now. Please take me out of here now.* And it did. Somehow kept him steady, right through wrong turns, then dodging in between the hundred cars backed up to the bridge it hauled him out of there, clenching the handlebars at every cop passed, thinking he was being chased the entire way to Sacramento, fucking *Sacramento*, until he finally saw a sign for a motel, the very first one on the outskirts of town, and he pulled off, booked himself into a room, locked the door, bolted the door, yanked the curtains closed, and jerked himself off until he began coming down. His skin was raw, but he finally believed he was safe, still feeling the bike between his legs.

In the morning, he didn't want to move. He lay there as still as possible, hoping to find some way back into sleep. But there were retching noises coming through the wall behind the bed, barely muted, and they were getting worse. Sounded like some lady. An old one, it had to be. She couldn't even spew a cough, just dry heaves. He got up and walked over to the window. Pulled the curtains back, just a little way, and watched the highway traffic passing in the distance.

After checking out of the hotel, he'd walked up to the bike. Put his fingers, then his lips to the tank. Kissed it, apologizing. For having ridden it fucked up and he promised he would never do it again. A new promise to cover the break of an old one, but it felt genuine. *I can still take care of the bike, even if I can't take care of anything else,* he told himself.

By the time he was filling up at the gas station, he'd made a pretty good case. Recalling how he'd never once missed putting high test in, even after the prices started going skyward and didn't stop. All the repairs and extra touches. So there he was, all stuck in his head with his devotion, going over his measly sacrifices, meanwhile showing that he didn't mean them at all. Or didn't mean them enough.

He thought he'd gotten his head clear for the ride back, but when the oil light came on, he didn't see it. He noticed a smell, something like burning, right before the end, but it was too late. If it hadn't been for the congestion on the freeway, he'd likely have been dead or worse. The fact that he was barely moving, the fact that everyone else was barely moving, saved him. But not the engine.

It locked, like someone had slammed on his brakes, and he went flying over the handlebars, landing on the trunk of the car in front of him, then slid down. No one ran him over.

Later, he roll-called the excuses in his mind. He had an old Yamaha, and it wasn't the simplest procedure to check the oil unless you had someone helping you balance the bike or put it on the center stand. There was a muddied-up window to look through, but the bike had to be level for the reading to be accurate. Still, it was hardly that big a deal; he'd managed to do it for years. Usually by finding a flat surface and a wall to lean the handlebar up against. He did it regularly, and always before a trip. Point was, he'd never let the oil get low before, so how would he have known what to look for? Those indicator lights were impossible to make out in the sun, anyway, and besides, what would have been the point of surveilling them. There'd be no green halo to tell him the engine was in neutral, and as far as watching for the red, he'd just fueled up after leaving the hotel. He wondered what color the oil light was.

Maybe it never came on. Maybe he didn't even have an oil light.

He meant to ask Don about that when it got towed into the shop, but the discussion had centered on his drain plug and how that had gotten loose. Replacing the engine, was it worth it? He had to believe it was. The only bike he'd ever had, the one thing he'd managed to hold onto.

It didn't occur to him that maybe the soul had gone out of the bike and he was just looking to keep the shell.

For the entire day he'd been caught up in it. Talking to the bystanders, the police. Refusing the ambulance. Riding back with the tow truck guy to City Cycle. Then over to the library to get online. Finally, he found a guy in Oklahoma who had what he was looking for. He called to give the information to Don, who agreed to have the engine shipped in, to put it on the bill with the rest. Jack turned off the phone and it was over.

He walked into the room behind the reference section and collapsed into an armchair there. For the first time felt the soreness on him. The right side of his face. His back. His whole body really. He pulled up his T-shirt revealing a blackish welt across his ribs. He thought about going to the restroom to make a full inventory of the bruises, but decided it was enough just knowing they were there.

He was staring at the ceiling when Louise came by.

"I caught you!" she said.

"Hey, Louise."

"I don't think I've ever seen you back here without a book in your hand."

She had a smile on. As always. He found himself returning it. "You gonna take away my library card?"

"I'll let it slide this time." She pulled her hair back behind her ear. "But we are closing. Five minutes, okay, you must have missed the announcement."

She started down the aisle, then turned back around again. "Jack, is everything all right? I saw you when you came in and—"

"Everything's fine. Thanks."

He picked up his pack and followed her part way toward the circulation desk, then cut across to the exit. Outside, it was cooling. The streets subdued. He thought over his options again, which weren't many. There was only one he was interested in anyway.

He hadn't seen Carrie since her birthday party a few months back. Since she'd taken him aside and given him hell for being too wrapped up in his own life, for not hanging out enough. He hoped he wouldn't get another lecture. But when he called her up, told her he was in bad shape, she didn't ask why, just told him to come right over.

Carrie opened the door wearing a red-striped top hat. It shot up toward the ceiling, then sagged off, slightly, to the side. "Oh my God, Jack, did you get in a fight?" She looked more curious than concerned. A relief.

"With the pavement, yeah, I had a small problem with the bike."

"That bruise is really gonna bring out the color in your eyes." She brought her hand up as if she was going to touch his face. "Just give it a day or two."

"Well, I guess there's that to look forward to." Jack walked past her, then stood in the middle of the room while she locked the door.

"So you get in a wreck and you decide to call me. Where's your friend?" It was only a dull stab further blunted by his realization that she didn't know. He thought she would have heard something.

"That's finished."

"Really! I was expecting a wedding invitation any day now."

"Well, you can stop checking the mailbox."

"I'm sorry. I guess. Are you sad?"

"Sad." A strange sound escaped his mouth. It struck him as funny, and once he started to laugh, he had a hard time stopping. He wiped the corners of his eyes with the back of his hand. Tried to focus on Carrie, who, for the first time, was looking uneasy. "Sorry about that. I'm way out of it right now. It's been a long day."

"Do you want to take a nap?"

"Not really. I would like to do something, though."

He hoped she'd suggest alternative activities. When she didn't, he took the initiative. "I don't know if you've got anything stashed around here, but I could really use something . . . just to take my mind off things. I mean, the bike's totaled. Just totaled and . . . I don't have an apartment either, I got evicted."

She seemed impressed. "My goodness, Jack, so many life changes in such a short time. I don't think that's the recommended approach."

"Yeah, well, mine seem to come in streaks." He switched his pack from one shoulder to the other.

"Of course, you can stay here tonight. As long as you need to, even." She pointed her index finger in the air, swiveled her shoulders, hips. "Hey la . . . Hey la . . . Jack is back!" She squeezed him suddenly, released him just as quick. "I quit my job last week. Now we'll have two things to celebrate."

He wondered what the second thing was.

"Can you believe it, my manager said she couldn't keep letting me go through the clothes for myself first. I was like, hello, the best clothes want to be with the best dresser. It wasn't like I was stealing them. I did walk out of there with this hat though."

"Yeah, I noticed that."

"It's beyond, isn't it?"

"Dr. Seuss would be proud."

"Exactly." She touched her nose and pointed at him like he'd guessed a charade. "Do you know, right after I got it, I decided to do a little research on Mr. Seuss. And let me tell you something, *The Cat in the Hat* is all about drugs. I'm positively sure of it."

Jack yawned.

"Oh. We better get you something fast. Hold on, I'll be right back."

She returned hugging a fairly sizable toolbox.

Jack shook his head, "Are we doing drugs or home repair?"

"Ha, clever boy. If I hear any more jokes about this, honestly . . . Most people don't understand how important it is to keep things organized." She undid the latch and opened it, the three tiers of drawers rising. "Now, what would you like?"

"What would you recommend?"

"Well, I've already had some of *this*. But I know how you feel about it, so that's a big no- no for you. Now, let's think. You look like you could use something happy. Why don't we go with the happy compartment?"

He'd been hoping for the other but agreed.

"Do we want it right now? Because I'd anticipated having a quiet night in. Cleaning. This place is such a mess. I've been running around like a madwoman, but then I had to get my haircut—they took too much off, you'll be shocked and—"

"Why don't we go out."

"Why don't we." Without taking anything from the box, she closed and latched it again. "I'll deal with this later. Don't worry, I'll make sure we've got everything we need. Now you know I'll have to change."

"Not the hat though."

"No, the hat will be the centerpiece. I'll build around it." She was already looking lost in her plans.

He moved toward the couch. "Mind if I turn on the TV?"

"I didn't think you watched television. You never let me put it on when you were here."

"I've been re-evaluating a lot of things."

"I see. Now before I get ready, do you want anything to eat?"

"You have something?"

"Not really."

"That's all right, I'm not very hungry."

She retreated to the bedroom with the toolbox. Left the door open, that was rare. Talked to him through it. "I don't think I've seen you since my birthday."

"You haven't."

"You missed the best part. You shouldn't have left so early."

He clicked through the channels, the usual garbage. It was almost worse than nothing.

"We took over the whole fire escape, and it was like this vertical party, you know, people moving up and down. The crowd just got more and more appetizing."

He settled on an infomercial. Some former star from his childhood pushing product. Man, he was getting old. He turned his head, peered through the bedroom door. Carrie was in her underwear, bending over, picking something off the floor. She was skinnier than he'd ever seen her. He sat back on the couch and closed his eyes.

She startled him coming out. Black and white stripes everywhere. Thin vertical ones on her shirt, thick round ones looping around her legs. He felt his brain click past the joke, something about zebras colliding.

"I know you think this outfit is great now, but just wait till you see it later."

"So you're all set."

"Yes."

He stood up.

"Oh, Jack, look at you. You can't go anywhere. Don't you have anything else with you?"

He glanced down at himself already knowing he'd have to change. "Yeah, I've got stuff in my bag."

"Rips are so not in style right now. And you should shower, too. Trust me, the worst thing to have happen when you're trying to be happy is to look down and see how grimy you really are."

Inside the club, she slipped him a pill with a smile. Twenty minutes of expectations after that. Her watching him watching her. Until it started to pop. Carrie let out a scream and spun out and away into the crowd. Jack watched her disappear. The happiness welling inside him like a demon. He struggled with it, felt it trying to crawl up his throat. Walked over to the bar and took shots, neat, of whiskey, till he'd drowned the buzz sufficiently, then ushered it into the corner where he danced out a small square pattern and didn't look up at anyone.

He didn't know how many hours it was before she finally reappeared. "Bet you didn't see me, but I saw you. Lots of times." She leaned in toward his ear. "I forgot how low maintenance you are, Jack, I'm so pleased to see that hasn't changed." She seemed to be telling him something important. He bent his head closer to hers, but she pulled back.

"Here." She held out a scrap of paper.

He took it. "You wrote me a poem?"

She shook her head.

"A poem?" he shouted.

She shook her head again. *Just read it.* He unfolded the paper.

I found out what happened but I'm going to pretend too.

She was staring at him when he looked up.

Okay?

He couldn't even be sure she was talking out loud. Her lips weren't moving.

Okay?

He looked at her, hard, for one moment. *Okay.* Then looked away. People were still dancing but he couldn't hear the music anymore.

"Jack?"

Someone was tugging on his arm. It was Carrie.

"Don't get distracted."

He looked in his hand. The other. Both were empty. "What just happened?"

"Nothing happened. You need to focus on what's about to happen."
She was steering him toward the exit. He could see light creeping around
the crack in the door. "Don't worry, I've got something else for you."

A day and more later, strung out beyond speaking, they made it back to
the apartment building. The elevator was out of service; Carrie leaned
against him while they climbed the steps. At the door, she tried several
times to get the key in the lock. Watching the cheerless attempts, he
noticed her hat was gone. Maybe he'd noticed it before. But now,
without it, the stripes in her outfit reminded him of shackles. Shackles
restraining a skeleton. He tried to shake the image away, but it followed
him to the bed.

He checked the clock, again, to make sure the time was right. Tried to
sync his memory to the time. Then gave up, deciding it didn't matter.
He pulled on his jeans and walked out to the kitchen.

Carrie was making tea.

"Sleep well?"

"I guess." He felt more tired than when they'd gone to bed, but
definitely better. "So how do you handle this on a regular basis?"

"You get used to it."

She put two cups on the table and sat down. Jack took a seat across
from her.

"Now Jack. I don't want you to feel like I'm asking you this
because . . . that I'm trying to add to your problems in any way, because
I know you've been evicted and so I'm sure the answer is no. And that's
fine, that's completely fine. I'm just trying to get the facts so I can have
those clear in my mind. Now, do you have any money to contribute
to the rent?"

It wasn't the most pleasant question to wake up to, but he knew it
was a fair one.

"Yeah," he answered grimly, "I do."

She took a sip of her tea and swallowed. "That is the most wonderful news."

He wasn't sure where she was getting her funds from. He didn't ask, but one night she said she was taking him out to dinner. Carrie wore a polka-dotted scarf and this incredibly plush pink sweater. She never wore pink. He reached for her hand under the table and they closed their fingers around each other. They were tender the whole time like that, till near the end, when the waitress came by and asked if they wanted anything else. Jack ordered a fudge-topped brownie. It arrived with a flag on a toothpick, stuck in the center. He took a bite and left the rest. It was the Fourth of July.

He woke in the middle of the night. Pillow wet, he had an erection. He wished it would go away. He wished Carrie had been awake to conceal it. He wouldn't have to wait long. Sleep was a cloud they kept falling through.

The first really bad night for Carrie was the night she tried to lock herself in the stall at The Rexx. A shoulder to the door opened it, and there she was, crouched on top of the toilet, hands pressed against the walls, eyes shifting. She was rambling about three women who had just tried to kill her. Pure jealousy, she said. And she could still have had a point then, although the bathroom was empty when he walked in.

"I'm telling you," she insisted, "there were three of them with guns."

"Did they each have a gun?" he asked, not even close to striking the right tone.

"Fuck you, Jack," she told him.

When they came out, everyone was moving slowly out of their way. He led her over next to the drums beating in the back. They began to dance. At least that's what it felt like, although he couldn't be sure with the floor shifting out from under their feet. It reminded him of looking down the elevator shaft in Carrie's building. When they'd press the button and then peer through the window while the cage was coming up, feel a rush, like they were the ones moving.

The first really bad night for Jack was the one he started to draw down the rest of the bank account. Walking to the ATM, he could smell smoke. Wildfire smoke, probably, creeping ever closer. It had settled into the streets after the sun had set and he inhaled it greedily, like fumes from a cigarette. California was burning and he didn't care.

He didn't know who he was with. Some friends of Carrie's. They left the Five and Dime and headed over to Luna. Carrie talked their way in, even though the place wasn't quite ready to open. Notebooks and pens, cashbox and glasses of water at the bar, overhead lights on like some underground office. They hid in the back and watched the place fill up. There was a guy on the stairs doing a strip tease. Pants pulled to his knees, hands in front of his crotch. Then the full frontal. Brown eye for the encore, wagging his ass. His girlfriend giggling in Jack's ear. Jack stood there with his arms folded, waiting for something to have an impact.

Natasha should have been from Russia and she was. Big blue eyes, saucered-out, blond hair cut ragged and held up from her face by some kind of band or barrette. Jack told her he was as much Russian as anything else, which wasn't saying a lot. She told him she moved from Moscow to Barstow where she finished high school, the lone foreigner in a sea of rednecks that even just a few years ago were calling her a Commie. Even one of her teachers. So she learned quickly. Her English accented, but the diction flawless. He asked if she still had thoughts in Russian that she couldn't express—if she was frustrated by that—but she said it rarely happened. Almost never.

Natasha said she'd stopped taking the pills because she couldn't feel them anymore. It had been a while, and she thought she might like to try them again. It was supposed to be her quietly publicized welcome back party. He congratulated her. And her wannabe boyfriend, who'd just walked over.

"This is going to be even better stuff," the guy said.

Her eyes lit up, "I think so, too."

Then they got into a discussion about the pills. The pros and cons, ending in a debate about whether or not nerve endings regenerate.

"They don't come back," Jack argued.

The guy shook his head, "I studied to be a scientist. I know."

"Well, maybe you did, and maybe you knew, but not anymore. The only nerve endings that regenerate are the ones in your nose."

Natasha tried to bargain a peace. "The serotonin does come back. You're right about that," but the guy only glared. She looked to Jack. He had little else to say. She wanted someone who was committed. To leaving or staying, but he was neither.

The next time he saw her she'd become convinced. He nodded at her, then went to find Carrie.

Within a month it had become a routine. The same faces, the same darkness, the same music. And in the morning, the harsh light. They could usually keep it together through dawn, the sun filtering through the haze of the bar, putting off as long as they could that first step outside. If only they could have closeted themselves away, then, but they were always too edged out to go directly home.

In the back alley they'd cling together. Teeth grinding. The stench of gasoline leaking from their pores, like they might incinerate the next time someone struck a match. With no ideas of his own, he'd agree to go with her over to the flea market at the Fences. Carrie checking out the latest inventory, Jack slouched at her side. He only paid attention when it was time to move.

He could just start to see it then: the first cracks in the makeup. Fault lines spreading across her face, some likely hidden behind the enormous purple shades that wrapped around her head. An hour later, she'd begun to peel, flake. Pulling his arm with one hand, sequined pants draped over her shoulder, to the exit. In sudden need of a mirror and a sink, where she could wash the layers down and start over.

"You realize, you're the only one who's ever seen me like this," she informed him through the door to the Chevron restroom he was guarding. He waited there, privileged and guilty.

They'd gotten into an argument. The usual. He told her he had six pills. She told him she'd given him eight to hold. She was certain. He wasn't. He'd lost some before, but there was no way he was going through his pockets again. She informed him she was kicking him out. Immediately. They went back to her place so he could get his things.

Inside, she found the missing ones in the toolbox. They'd somehow migrated to a different compartment.

"Does this mean I get to stay?"

"Yes, but I wouldn't get too excited about it." Carrie had begun to reorganize the compartments.

"But I like being here."

"You're so full of it, Jack, truly you're worse than I am. You know what a bother the city can be, and here you are living right in the middle of it."

Jack shrugged.

"I just don't understand why you'd ever want to fit in here."

"I'm not trying to fit in."

Carrie sat back on the couch. "Do you see how much nicer these are going to look when I get them all grouped by color?"

"Much nicer."

"I thought so. Now, where was I? Oh yes, isn't there something better you could be doing with your recreational time?" Jack bit his lip. Carrie continued, unfazed. "Didn't you say you used to do a lot of camping back in . . .wherever it is you came from?"

He tried to remember back. "Yeah, I did. I guess, I did tell you that." His voice trailed off before rebounding a bit. "What about you? Weren't you the big outdoorswoman right after we met? Taking care of that park up in Oregon."

"I was. I wish I could've stuck with it, but I just get so tired. Of everything." She seemed resigned to it. "It's not fair that all the things that are good for me end up boring me in the end."

Jack pulled his hands from his pockets. "Hey, so as long as we're here, you mind if we do another bump?"

For a while, it looked like she was going to ignore him.

They didn't go anywhere right away. Instead, they played solitaire. Two decks, head to head, on the floor for hours. Looking over at her from time to time, he couldn't tell what she was thinking, but he saw her cheat. At least once.

And then that song she loved came on and she disappeared into the bathroom.

With most people he'd been getting high with like that, the room would have closed in around the place where they'd stood or smoked or even laughed, hard, and he might have forgotten they'd ever been there. But his mind never wandered too far from the close of that door. The light coming under it, a slit of blue-black carpet. Carrie was inside. The wick of a candle was burning next to him. Nothing else. No scream, no mirror smashed, not a sound until she walked out and there she was.

Jesus, Carrie.

Blood wasn't streaming down her face, it wasn't, just drying in trickles from the rake of her fingers.

"Don't hate me because I'm beautiful," she said. Giggled. He wasn't laughing.

She started to dance, her eyes catching him each time she spun around. Then she stopped. Resumed a slow swaying motion and she wouldn't take her eyes off him. "So what do you think, Jack? What. Do. You. Think." He looked away. "Jack, darling, you're missing the point. Look at me. Don't you see? This is as bad as it gets. This is as bad as it fucking gets!"

No, it isn't, he thought. *No, it isn't.*

He forced himself to look. Again. God, why couldn't he have kissed her then, all over, dragged his tongue along her skin and then in. Feeling out the gashes, spread his warm spit over her wounds. Why couldn't he have taken her in his arms, clenched her hands behind her back till the sickness had shaken itself out from both of them. But he couldn't get past it. She'd done it to herself.

"You're disgusting," he told her. And she stopped dancing.

There was no way to take it back. The betrayal. In her hands, his words. He tried to lessen a blow that had already been struck. "Come on," he said, nudging her on the shoulder, "Let's go out. Luna's still open. Or the End Up. End Up's definitely open." Her eyes squinted up at him, but he wasn't registering. "You just need to get yourself cleaned up. Come on, I'll help you." She let him take her hand and he led her back to the bathroom, where he sat her on the side of the tub. Rinsing a washcloth with warm water, he began to blot her face. It didn't look so terrible underneath.

After a cigarette, she recomposed herself. "If we're going out, I'll need to put some makeup over this."

"You're just going to infect it, why don't you leave it alone." She reached into her purse. "I've never understood why you put that stuff on, it's not like you're the only one out there with a few acne scars."

"Oh, I think you understand very well, Jack."

He waited for her to finish.

Then they left.

Time to get moving again. Back down the slope. Thinking what a good thing it was that Carrie didn't answer the phone. How it would only have led to trouble for both of us.

Reaching the bottom, a smattering of raindrops. I angle toward the MUNI stop on the edge of the park. Dimly lit. But glowing brighter—ethereal, almost—as I approach. Fifty yards, forty, the sky opening up, and I jog the rest of the way in.

There's no competition for space beneath the plexiglass, and I lean against the back of it, coughing. Phlegm comes up. I spit to clear it. Twice. Then pull down the middle slat and take a seat. Upright at first, looking out into the darkness. Then elbows on my thighs, chin in my hands. Then lying down, trying to stretch across the other slats. I end up having to turn on my side, body pressed to the thin back railing, arm wrapped around it, to keep from falling off.

Closing my eyes, I listen to the sound of the drops on the roof. And the final words of Carrie's poem, the one she whispered to me across the pillow that first February, when the city nearly drowned in it.

The rain can't wash the streets from your skin.

Maybe Carrie started needing more, or maybe people stopped feeling so generous toward her, but she wasn't in a position to be keeping up with her wardrobe and paying for her party favors, and before long she'd placed herself on the arm of a dealer. The guy was slime, but she said she knew what she was doing, and at first Jack wasn't feeling the most argumentative with the trickle-down benefits. When some of the more relevant contents of her purse mysteriously disappeared—a lot of crystal, a few pills, and, depending on which version you went with, eighteen or forty-two dollars in cash—he thought she'd pink slip the guy for sure, but she couldn't prove it was him, and she wanted to believe it wasn't. He asked if she'd like him to talk to the guy, and she said, not even trying to disguise her annoyance, "Like that would really help. You know how much he respects you."

It was right around then that Jack had been effectively squeezed out of the apartment. The guy wasn't even there half the time, but he didn't want to share, and Carrie was tired of getting into it with him. Jack was also out of money. He'd emptied the account, borrowed off people he sort of knew, people he didn't know at all, borrowed off whatever charm he could force up, but it had spent quickly.

He wasn't sure what to expect when he called Bishkey.

"Hey bud, long time, no talk. I left a couple messages. What, no callback?"

"Yeah, sorry about that. I had a lotta stuff going on and—"

"No worries, I was just planning to try you again, myself. Big games. Big games. For both teams. Coming down to the wire, I can't believe it. A subway series with actual ramifications."

Subway?

"Friday won't work. Catch the second game Saturday?"

"Yeah, sure. I, uh . . . actually, I was hoping I could talk to you about something."

"Everything all right?"

"Yeah, I just need to talk to you."

When they sat down, Jack didn't waste time starting in. He'd already distilled everything he planned to say down to four sentences, and he mostly stuck to them.

"Jesus H. Christ, you gotta be shittin' me."

Jack waited for the words to sink in. Bishkey shook his head.

"Not good. Not good at all. Fuck, when did this happen?"

Jack was briefly tempted to say more but that wasn't why he was there. *Bring it up and then shut it down*, he reminded himself.

"The thing is, I'm not really up for talking yet."

Bishkey looked further surprised and maybe even hurt. But he recovered quickly.

"No sure, sure. I get it. Still raw." He held Jack's gaze for a moment, then looked down at the table and pushed at some crumbs with the back of his fingers. "Anything I can do."

It didn't sound like a question, but he'd said it. Jack made his request. When it was met with silence, he added, "It would just be for a little while."

"You plus my couch? I don't think you'd fit so good."

"If it's too much trouble, then . . ." he didn't know what.

Bishkey squinted, rubbed the bridge of his nose. "All right, Jack, we'll try it. I can't say no. But let's get one thing straight. You're lookin' a little hopped up at the moment."

Jack didn't know how to respond. When he first walked in, he'd been sure Bishkey would notice, but then he told himself, no, he was pulling it off. "What makes you say that?"

"Everything. Come on, buddy, what d'you take me for here? No beans in the coconut? Whatever it is, I'm just telling you, I don't want any of that shit in the apartment. Zero. Dig?"

"Yeah, sure, man. You don't have to worry about that with me."

"Uh-huh. When you needin' to come over?"

The night he got there, Bishkey added more conditions. He said he wouldn't take any money himself for rent, but he'd appreciate something regular so he could donate it to the shelter. He said Jack could use his computer, but he didn't want to know what Jack was doing on it, and if he was thinking about doing something stupid, he should think again. He said there'd be no coming in at odd hours, specifically between midnight and seven, weekends included. And of course, he said there'd be no smoking in the apartment.

Jack wasn't about to argue with him. About anything. So after a few days of pacing and puffing in the hallway, the near constant nodding at various neighbors, their looks equally disapproving whether going in or out, he decided he might as well try to go along with the clean air initiative while he was on the premises. He stepped out into the hall less and did his best to keep up with the regimen of vegetables, vitamins, and news programs on the inside.

The fact was, he hadn't been able to spend much time there.

But he knew how important it was to him, so he always checked himself before going back, and if he didn't like what he saw, he'd wait: forcing more water down, sitting through back-to-back matinees, or just walking the streets for hours.

He didn't just think about trying to take the bike. He made specific plans, and then headed over to City Cycle with his keys in his pocket.

Not his originals—Don had those—but his spares. To make room in the shop, they pulled out all the bikes they weren't working on during the day and lined them up along the sidewalk, and he knew his would be there. He said to himself, *hey, it's my bike.* And not only that, but weren't they the ones who'd let it get stolen originally?

So there he was, scheming his way along Valencia, when he saw Don come out of the shop. Don smiled at one of his customers coming in. Shook hands with him. And just like that, Jack knew he'd been walking down the wrong street. Had no business being there except to confirm how lost he was and left to wonder where he might end up next.

He turned to go, his fingers clenched around the keys, the grooved metal digging into his palm.

He always saw her on the same corner. He saw her there and never anywhere else. How much bleach in the blond and it took barely any imagination at all to subtract the lines off her face and figure her for beautiful. He'd seen her eyes behind the sunglasses—blue, naturally. The one time he tried talking to her, when she was quick to name a price. She was gaunt by way of cigarettes, bottles in paper bags, and being knocked thin by too many men. He was sure she could trace it in her own mind. The one or two missteps that led her down there.

He told himself he had to go back to work so could get the bike out of the shop. He told himself he had to go back to work so he could get some money to Bishkey. He told himself a lot of things.

When he started taking calls again, he didn't have any expectations, even low ones, but when the first door opened, there was an unmistakable desire waiting for him on the other side, and he realized it was his own. This made him all the more revolting to himself, and he was oddly reassured by it.

As he was by his customers. The clients. The not so subtle hatred he felt toward them, all of them, and each of them. He'd already lost his regulars, but there were others waiting to take their places. Calls he would have turned down before, but what was there to fear at that point, really? He was confident he could overwhelm any darkness they might be harboring so they'd be afraid to show even a shadow of it. Maybe they smacked their old lady around, maybe they'd screwed some homeless kid the previous week instead of handing him a few bucks for breakfast; it wasn't difficult to imagine. That they deserved their feelings of worthlessness. He wanted them to feel lonelier after he left, and in that way, he was determined they pay twice.

It had always been a struggle for him to be warm, anyway. Why not go with his natural inclinations? The meth made it easier—a lot easier—to be distant, and he looked down on what was happening not from above, but from away. He tried to keep the speed separate from the calls, but occasionally they crossed, and even when they didn't, he could still feel it in his system. For him, there was nothing erotic about it; it was just fuel for the machine. Contaminated fuel, to be sure, that made his performance unpredictable. So he had to take more drugs— legal ones—to keep on top of it.

The calls were a blur, one smearing into the next. He'd run a handful, hand some cash to Bishkey. The rest going for the bike-fund under the couch, where it was just a little too handy. Then he'd turn off his phone and go out. Disappear for a few days, a week, until he was broke. Sleep it off. Then run another set of calls.

Early morning. City Clinic. A line of people waiting outside. Sunglasses. A bottle of water protruding from a purse. Not so different from the clubs around the corner. The last one closed an hour ago, it was possible someone had wandered over. No one looked real excited to get in here, though. Guys with hands in their pockets. Couples whispering. A man at the end of the line talking too loudly on his cell. Something about upholstery covers.

Across the street, Bessie Carmichael school. Through the windows, kids in their tiny chairs or running around the cafeteria tables. They didn't look out.

Eight o'clock. The unlocking of the door. Everyone filing in behind the heavyset woman who opened it. When it was his turn, he answered some questions, got a number and took a seat. There were low budget videos reeling on the front monitor. People in various STD predicaments. Potentially dire, but they only showed the ones with cures. The chlamydia diagnosis seemed like a godsend. Everyone got a lesson, a happy ending. It was depressing.

He'd had a condom break. Ultra-thin, ultra-stupid. The guy said he was negative, but he'd also said he was thirty. It had been a vigorous session and he figured he should probably get checked. He hadn't gone back to the Physician's Assistant. Too expensive. Besides, no one expected it of him anyway.

When he saw Matt walk into Underbar, his hand started to shake. He snuffed out his cigarette, wanting to leave, but his dealer was supposed to be there any minute. He nodded at Matt as he approached. He could keep it friendly just as long as Matt didn't say anything.

"How's it going, Matt?"

"Good, you?"

"Good. Keeping yourself busy?"

"Same old." Matt was on his way to meet a trick but had a little time and a little Tina on his hands and was willing to share. Jack searched the bar for his dealer, again. Looked to the bartender, who was counting change. They didn't care what you did there. He grabbed his cigarettes and followed Matt to the bathroom where they did a bump together. When he tried for a kiss, Jack pushed him off. Then he asked for another bump.

"Sure thing," Matt told him, slipping the bag back in the leather pouch hanging from his belt. Then he took out a travel toothbrush and unfolded it. Took out a tube of toothpaste and squeezed, spreading along the bristles.

"You got a date with the dentist?" Jack put his hand in his pocket to steady it. "Because I think that convention pulled out of town a long time ago."

Matt made a thorough job of it, rinsed. "You better watch your mouth, man. No one's interested in meth rot."

"Uh-huh. And brushing your teeth's a good idea right before a call. You should maybe floss, too, cut up those gums."

"You giving me a hard time?"

"I'm just saying it doesn't make much sense."

"Glad to know you're looking out for me." Matt smiled into the mirror, a broad smile that he quickly retracted. "I only got a couple of guys I do it with now anyway. They're safe. They take care of me." Then he pulled out some pomade and unscrewed the lid. "I'm not even with Atlas anymore—I told you that, right? They tried to keep everything on the q.t., but even with their client list and connections they still had to shut down for a while. Just till the dust settled, you know. But that's when I realized I didn't need to be bothering myself with the middleman anymore."

Jack needed not to think about Atlas right then. He watched Matt closer while he worked the pomade into his hair. Eyes disconnected from the rest of him, grey face. Death with a hard-on.

And clean teeth.

Matt zipped up his supplies. Undid the bolt, then turned before walking out. "You know, there are a lot of guys out there who miss him. It's a shame about that."

Jack had hesitated—*hesitated*—before lunging toward the door, then cracked his head against it, closing. He slumped down in the corner. Touched his hand to his forehead and came away with blood. His cellphone started to ring. He tried muting it but couldn't find the right button *dammit!* someone was trying to get in. He grabbed the knob and held on—"Give me one fucking minute!" He pulled himself up, threw some cold water on his face. One thing he was certain of: he wasn't done with Matt.

Jack pushed his way out, scanning the crowd as he went. Past his dealer standing by the entryway, outside, where he saw him getting into a cab. He ran up just in time to get the door shut in his face again.

"Hey!" He pounded on the side of the cab. "Hey, why didn't Daniel screen that call? WHY DIDN'T HE SCREEN THE CALL?" The cab was pulling away and he kept after it, "HE SHOULD HAVE GIVEN IT TO YOU, YOU FUCKING PRICK." *He should have given it to you.* Jack felt tears shot into his eyes. He glared through them at the cars, horns beeping. Too many, he needed to get off the street. He reached the curb and waited for his breathing to slow. Then he tucked his shirt into his jeans and began to walk.

Jack knew Bishkey was a light sleeper, that he needed his rest. He knew he'd be breaking his no re-entry rule, but he had to get himself onto that couch. Thought he'd been so quiet slipping in the door, but there was Bishkey, two minutes later, standing over him. "As God is my witness, next time I'm changing the locks, you won't get a key." Jack told him it wouldn't happen again, but Bishkey wasn't through. "You know how hard it is having you around? You have any idea, with the way you're living your life? And look at me, man, look what happened to me."

"I thought you were on a good treatment."

"Yeah, I'm gonna live, Jack, but that doesn't mean it still doesn't suck. I gotta watch everything I do. Every hour of sleep I get. Everything I put in my body. And sometimes I still feel like shit, and stuck half the night in the toilet and for what?"

"I was out of line, I get that."

"You bet your ass you were outta line. You're outta line every time you walk in this door."

Jack raised his voice to match Bishkey's. "Then why did you let me stay?"

"Because you were the one . . . the fuckin' *only* one who didn't bail on me last year. I owed you, but the way I see it, that debt's been paid. Over. Done."

He watched Bishkey switch on the light above the stove, then pour himself some water. "I thought you might get it back on track here but—fuck—what the fuck do I know?" Then the light was turned off again, and Jack was left alone. He was up the remainder of the night.

When Bishkey came through in the morning, Jack closed his eyes and kept them closed until he heard the front door slam. Then he got up and went to the bathroom. Took his clothes off and looked in the mirror . . . for a long time.

He was probably down twenty pounds. His chest sunk, cheekbones sticking out. He didn't look much better than Matt. How was that possible? It had just been a few months for him and already . . . No matter what substances he'd put in his body, he'd always felt like he was in control, but the speed was running him. Right into the ground, and he wasn't sure he liked it.

He looked at himself again. Wondered what he was getting so rattled about. Wasn't this what he wanted to happen? Maybe he didn't have the guts to finish the job.

Bishkey had been ignoring him, but on the second night when he came home and found Jack in more or less the same position, he tried breaking the ice.

"Whadaya doin', making sure nobody steals the couch?" Jack smiled inside, but it didn't quite make it up to his face. "Cause the way you look, even my sister, you couldn't stop her."

"Yeah, well, if she tried to carry me off with it, I'd probably let it happen."

He nodded. "Sorry I blew a fuse the other night. I know you gotta be hurtin'. But, come on, Jacky boy, why you still here? I woulda been back in the Bronx so fast your head would spin, except my family won't have nothin' to do with me. Think I'm a fruit loop. Even my cousin won't take my calls anymore. Like a beggar, I'm tellin' ya. Don't act like you care but, hey, I'm just sayin'."

"What makes you think I have anywhere to go?"

"Well, look, then why don't you stop makin' things worse while you're here?"

"I can't make it worse."

"You can make it worse. Wait till the trap door opens . . . you think this is the basement? And what d'ya think your buddy would say about all this if he could see you now?"

"He can't see me, okay? He can't see me at all, that's the fucking problem." Jack could feel his emotions getting away from him, but he let them run a little further. "Besides, I already started down that path the other night and I couldn't take it. What, you think I've got a high opinion of myself right now and I can just add the weight of what he might think on top of everything else? I was getting crushed out there, man, that's why I came back early."

Bishkey stuck out his chin and nodded slowly. "You're a sucker for making me feel sorry for your ass. But I do. You know, I got ears if you wanna talk."

"I think I've already taken you up on the offer." Jack sighed. "Somewhere in here I'm grateful to you, Bishkey, you gotta know that. You're the only sane person I know right now."

"Then you really are in trouble." Bishkey walked into the kitchen. "You want some mushroom tea?"

"Dude, that stuff is heinous."

"But it's got properties. Special properties."

Jack just shook his head, but the next day after Bishkey left for work, he'd snuck a glass. Got halfway through it, before gagging and pouring the rest down the drain. *Let's take things one step at a time here.* He made a bowl of oatmeal instead. By the end of the week, food had started to seem like a legitimate idea.

He went back to the library for the first time since the bike had gone down. Flipped through a few books, realizing he wouldn't have the patience for them. Checked out some poetry instead. The volume of Dylan Thomas's work looked plenty dense.

The following Tuesday he took the bus to see how Aqualung was making out at the aquarium.

Jack was rereading *The Seed-at-Zero* when his cellphone rang. He put down the book, glanced at the number. He didn't recognize it, that was a good thing. Since turning the phone back on two days before, he'd ducked a bunch of calls. He decided to try this one.

The guy got right to the point.

"Sure, no, don't worry about that," Jack assured him, scribbling down the address, "I know the neighborhood."

Bishkey waited till he hung up before pitching a piece of popcorn at him. "Returning to duty, huh?"

"Looks like it."

"Kinda late."

"The guy says he wants a sleepover." Jack got down on the floor and scrounged under the couch for cab fare. "If it turns out to be a crank, I can still get back here by midnight." Then he searched his pile, hoping for a clean pair of underwear.

Bishkey turned the volume back up on the TV. "Don't forget your pajamas."

When he got out of the shower, the room was empty, the door to Bishkey's bedroom closed. An intermittent beeping sound was coming from the vicinity of the table, traceable to his cell. He checked it one last time, then turned it off and plugged it into the charger. He shouldn't need it tonight unless . . .

He glanced at his backpack before walking over to it. He hadn't touched the pocket-watch since the day he left his apartment, and for a moment, he was afraid that it wouldn't be inside. Or worse, maybe, broken. But it was there, all in one piece. He gave it a test wind and listened for the ticking before springing the cover. Staring at the Roman numerals, he wasn't sure what he should be feeling. What he was feeling.

Finally, he pulled the knob and set the time. 11:00. Close enough. Then he closed the cover, put it in his jeans, and headed out the door.

Let the hero seed find harbor, Seaports by a drunken shore, Have their thirsty sailors hide him

Our hero steps into the foyer, the first in a series of candles flickering on the long, mirrored table inside the door. Chill Mix 5 thousand playing somewhere in the background, he knows the tune. Where every beat goes bump in the night, but he isn't getting rattled. It's been twelve days since he saw Matt at the Underbar—twelve respectable days—and he's determined to keep going. Still, he hopes the guy won't offer him anything.

The man's name is Carter, and he's just arrived from Minneapolis. He seems nice. Normal even. His opening gambit is an explanation for why he called. "I've been so busy with work, I just haven't had the time to make friends."

It wouldn't be that hard for him, Jack thinks, and then says aloud, "There's a bar not too far from here where you wouldn't have any trouble . . . a bunch of them, actually, you could save your money." The guy probably knows this, and he could definitely use the cash, but he's glad he said it. There's something in his voice he hasn't heard in a while. Some kindness.

"To tell you the truth, I almost did go out. I got ready and everything and—I realize I'm not all that much to look at, but—I thought I could, well, try. And then I got to the door and I decided I just couldn't face all that cruising. I wanted . . . you know . . . a sure thing." Carter looks down at the floor. "I hope that doesn't offend you."

"Why should it?"

"I don't know. I don't know if I'd want anyone to call me that."

"You're just as much of a sure thing tonight as I am."

"Yeah, I guess you're right about that. I guess what I'm trying to say is, I'm really glad you're here. Thanks for being here."

"No problem, I'm glad to be here." Jack takes off his jacket, throws it on the back of a chair.

"Would you like me to hang that up?"

"Nah, this thing wouldn't know what to do with itself on a hanger."

"Oh. Okay." Carter seems hesitant about something. "You know, they said it was supposed to rain earlier."

"Yeah, I heard that. It's been a couple months since we had any."

"None at all?"

"That's pretty typical for the summer here. But now that we're moving into the fall, especially winter, we'll make up for it."

"I missed the nice weather, then?"

"That all depends on what you mean by nice."

Carter nods. "Well, we won't have to worry about all that. Like I told you, what I'd really like to do is sleep in tomorrow. Not go anywhere. No alarms, for once no alarms. I've been getting up so early trying to get ahead at work. I feel like I'm the only one at the office who's stressed out about it, but I can't help myself. That's just how I am."

"You'll probably settle into it. That's how it goes when you start somewhere new."

"I hope so, but—I should probably stop talking about work. Would you like anything to drink?"

"Yeah, water would be great."

Carter goes to the kitchen. "Ice?"

"A little."

He returns with two glasses.

Jack takes one, downs it. "Nothing worse than kissing with a dry mouth."

Carter blushes. "I like kissing."

"Then we got that in common. See how easy this is gonna be." He knows he's making a play at being cool, but at least he's got his lines down.

"So, do you have a partner?"

"Nah." Jack tips back the glass again, begins crunching the shards. "I'm not equipped for the long-term stuff."

"But you've tried the 'long-term stuff.' "

"Yeah, enough to know better. It's much easier to be a nice guy for an hour or two."

"In Minneapolis, you have to be nice pretty much all the time or people think something's wrong with you."

"Ha. That's gotta suck."

"You get used to it. Being in a good mood's not so difficult once you set your mind to it. So where are you from?"

"Back East, originally."

"And you went to school there. I mean, did you go to college?"

"Yeah. I went to University of New Mexico."

"Why there?"

"I wanted a change."

"And you liked it?"

"Yeah, I did."

"So why did you come here?"

"Oh, I don't know. I guess I made a wrong turn at Albuquerque."

Carter looks disappointed. "You wish you'd stayed in New Mexico?"

"No, I'm kidding. I was just quoting Bugs there. No, I came here because I wanted another change. Seems like it's easier to switch location than anything else."

"Not for me. I really didn't want to leave Minnesota. But then I really didn't want to lose my job with this company either, so I had to make a decision."

Jack nods while stifling a yawn. Stretches his hands over his head.

"I don't know why I put this music on, it isn't very good. It's like I've got this recipe in my head, you know, put on lounge music, light some candles, add guy."

"Yeah, right."

"I think I'm going to change it."

He goes to the bedroom, puts on something classical. Jack follows him there, feeling more and more comfortable. He grabs Carter from around the back, kisses him behind the ear. Turns him around and presses his tongue through his lips. Then he pulls him onto the bed. Clothes slide off. A light sweat seals their skin.

"Hey," Carter whispers.

"Hey."

"Could we hold up for just one second? I want to tell you something."

"Sure."

"Well, people might think this or that, but, it's like they don't always take the time to learn about someone, and . . . I just want you to know there's a beautiful man inside me."

Hearing the sense of discovery in the guy's voice, Jack feels inexplicably happy. Like Carter's just figured out something about himself or shared it for the first time. He squeezes Carter's hand. "And I'm lucky to be with him."

Jack leans in for a kiss, but Carter is shaking his head. "No, I mean you."

Jack freezes. Trying to grasp at the meaning, letting it sink in. He can feel a wave of sadness about to wash over him but he has to duck it. A bigger one is building up behind, and that's the one he'll ride until it crashes.

"What is it?"

Jack pulls out of him.

"What is it? What's wrong?"

"*This* is what you think is beautiful?" He hits himself on the chest. "You don't even know, you really don't."

"I don't understand. You said this was going to be easy. You said—"

"Don't look at me like that." Jack rips off the condom, scrambles off the bed. "Don't look at me at all."

"Oh, my goodness, you must be on something." Carter reaches for his phone.

"Don't touch that phone, Minnesota."

"I'm sorry."

"What d'you have to be so goddamn sorry about?"

Carter looks around the room in search of an answer. "I don't know." Then he wipes his eyes with the back of his hand. "I don't even know who I was going to call. I—"

"Do not start crying, you understand me?"

Carter nods rapidly but the tears keep flowing.

Jack grabs him by the arm. "What did I just say?"

Carter is sobbing now, and Jack can feel everything spiraling. The more fiercely he grips him, the harder the sobs. Jack's hand is clenched in a fist, his body tensing to strike. He just wants to obliterate the tears in front of him, spilling from eyes that hold no confusion now, only fear. Staring deeply into them for the first time, Jack hesitates *How much easier it must be to hurt someone when they're asleep* then stops, suddenly nauseated with himself. He gives Carter's arm a final squeeze, but the fight has gone out of him and he turns to find his clothes.

Yanking on his underwear, his pants. *How did I get here?* His shirt, socks, boots. *How did all this happen?* He glances at Carter who is cowering on the bed. He looks as helpless as Jack feels.

"It wasn't your fault. I shouldn't have come here tonight."

Out through the living room, his coat off the chair, the foyer, fumbling with the door, the fucking locks on the door, then down the stairs and out into the street. Running. With the rain above, in front, behind, rain falling down and he's going to get drenched. He turns the corner and looks around wildly. There's a ledge coming off the building ahead.

A horn held in the distance, carries with it the sound of the rain it's pierced. Then cut, leaves only rain. Cramped in the cradle of seats. A turn of the shoulder, a slight unbending of knees. Clothes damp, chilled skin. Eyes open. It's gotten lighter. And getting lighter, it seems, by the minute.

I think I'd keep lying here if it wasn't so cold. Or maybe a little colder. But it's just enough to get me to sit up, so I swing my feet around onto the ground. Blood drains in, legs tingle, and I try to massage some more feeling into them.

I wonder if people realize how shaky their identity is. How much of it is tied up with their friends and family, pets, even the furniture in their homes. Daily reminders of who they are and what they're responsible for. They might have an idea, vaguely, that all this could be lost. But they might not have considered how much of themselves would be lost along with everything they cared for. No one there to recognize you. Having to construct yourself from near scratch every morning. Hard to pretend you're doing anything more than making yourself up as you go along.

Standing now. Traffic's picking up. Cars no longer strays on the prowl but blending together. The flow and lull of their engines.

Losing myself didn't always feel like such a curse. I looked forward to it, being out on the bike. Whether bent into the shape of a curve or launched out along a straightaway, refusing to blink at the blur of the world, just pushing through it, pushing luck a little, because when it felt right like that, nothing could touch you.

In the rain, though, it's always been different. Adjustments have to be made, extra care taken, starting down the road in front of you. Check six times before crossing, prepare to brake at ghosts, then take a deep breath over cable car tracks and swallow tasting metal. No, it wouldn't be a joyride out there now. I'd need to know where I was headed. Take it slow, steady. One mile at a time. Keeping my eyes on the road and the blackness buried in the pavement.

BIRD

A **single highway ran** through the heart of Copper County, so that's the one you traveled on. Beside it, the railroad tracks, abandoned. The only light for miles a blinker. Cars passing under with a sluggishness suggesting traffic that wasn't there. Locals mostly, checking up on friends and relatives. Borrowing supplies or returning them, in broad view of the hardware store and its dwindling inventory. The post office worked, people went there. To the grocery store, six aisles that had moved into the back of the filling station. Across the street, the school, shut, the few kids that were left bussed away—older ones in one direction, younger in the other.

Still, the residents kept up a modest effort against the decline. Dusty vehicles getting a soap-down and wax in the drive. Talk of today's weather, tomorrow's. Heads shaking, nodding at what had been seen via satellite TV. Shiny dishes perched on rooftops with shingles warped, torn, missing. Commiserating about it all over beers at the Rusty Nail. The most stubborn rumors there concerned the barber, said to be an old Mafia boss from back East, the visitors he had, where he went Wednesdays and Thursdays when he closed shop. No customer was willing to risk a shave, but five dollars a head is what he charged for a buzz cut and a chance to maintain a low profile, although I'd already heard about him the week after I arrived, a stranger to the town but not the landscape.

The mountains of northern New Mexico. Rising up out of the desert. Their peaks inclined to catch clouds drifting by. Enough, sometimes, to turn a storm over the forests that grew up in their shadows, making them fresh, verdant, alive. No smell could match the sweetness of an approaching rain on dry, desert air, and when I caught wind of it that first day riding into town, I felt a sentiment, at least, of coming home. Early April when the sun was still shy enough after dawn, letting the chill from the night air linger.

The turn-off to the ranger station wasn't well marked but led easily enough to the small compound of buildings that comprised it, a number of which had been put up by the Civilian Conservation Corps in the 1930s. They were still manned because the forest that surrounded the town, crept down from the mountains and into it, had flourished against the decay, and in the heat of summer when the grasses were brittle and the color had gone out of the earth, the dry lightning would strike down like match to kindling. The thinking went it was best to catch the blaze here, before it spread to someplace it could do some real damage.

It was a big canopy of trees, and not many to watch over it. An old navy captain who left his wife for the summer and lived up the thousand spiral steps to the lookout tower with maps and books and compass for companion. Frank Belin, in charge of operations, more or less. Eli, whose health no longer permitted him to go out on fires and whose position I'd taken, now the part-time mechanic. One ailing pick-up. Two rigs, and enough guys to fill them. Ortega the foreman of one, Garrity, the other. Both solidly into their thirties. Ortega's kid brother, Lando, a wisecracker with a jittery leg. Ramirez was a loner, held forth on UFOs if you pressed him. And then there was Boker. Come up off his reservation the previous season, and my showing up should have meant he was no longer low man out.

We rubbed each other the wrong way almost immediately.

"Ay, another gringo," he complained. The only one not to shake my hand when I'd tendered it around the circle of them, playing Hacky Sack in front of the bay. "The rest of us will be gone by the end of summer, just you watch." He looked to Ortega for approval, but Ortega ignored him.

"Put down your gear, *ese*," he told me. "We're on break now."

In the early part of the season, the job kept pace with the town. Not enough work to push myself into, so I took to getting up at daybreak and heading over to the dirt track behind quarters. Cleared of cactus and scrub trees, something like elliptical, although no one seemed to know how long it was. I guessed a quarter mile. Interspersed along the perimeter were a couple of chin-up bars, a plank ramped onto piñon stump for sit-ups, some old tires set two across and twelve deep for high stepping through. I'd stretch, jog a few miles, do some rotations on the equipment, then jog a few miles more, sprinting the last time around. That was the best part, everything into it, the one sure thrill from having quit smoking. Legs giving way before lungs, knowing I still had room to breathe.

Otherwise, there wasn't much excitement in it. The occasional rattlesnake to dodge, still thawing and too slow to be much bother. The last lone yelps of the coyotes, close and then farther away, fading. A tranquility to things I was comfortable with, but that was soon disrupted by Boker, who showed up after a few days with no other apparent purpose than to badger me.

"What d'you think you're doin' out here? Getting yourself all tired before the day's even started."

That was the first time he'd come, when I'd been disoriented enough by his presence to be genuine with my answer.

"Wanna be ready when the fires get going."

"So you can run the other direction?" He snorted. "Fear'll make you move fast enough, you don't need to be in shape for that."

I sped past him, hoping that'd be the end of it, but he continued to stand there. Arms folded, watching my progress around the track. Coach short a whistle, except he'd just as soon the team quit.

"Think you're gonna score points with Belin being out here. That man doesn't care what you're getting up to. He's asleep himself."

I kept my pace steady after that, and eventually Boker wandered back the way he came.

He was there again the next day. I couldn't understand it. That he'd drag himself awake just to come down and get his two cents in. Wasn't it enough we had to work together, share quarters together? But I didn't want to give him any easy sign he was unsettling me, so I tried to resign myself to the company.

"Mornin'," I said.

He nodded. "Jackrabbit's out of his hole again, I see."

That almost got a grin out of me. I slowed as I went by him, turned and pedaled backward.

"Why don't you do a few laps yourself?" I suggested, patting my stomach. "You might be able to lose some of that gut."

"What gut you talking about? This here's pure subsidized Indian muscle." He jiggled it for emphasis.

"That's just not healthy," I told him, facing forward again, muttered back at him, "You're not gonna live long hauling that around."

When I approached him again, he was hooting and hollering, slapping his knee, like someone had told the funniest joke. Then he stopped abruptly and spit. Not quite at me.

I've been reminded lately how much easier a time you had making friends than me. I mean, you never seemed to have a problem with anyone. Almost anyone.

I'm not sure it's a good idea to be trying to connect with you again, but I suppose there's only one way to find out.

Testing. One. Two . . . Testing.

With the rest of the crew, things were going along fine enough. No one asked me too many questions, and I didn't ask many in return. As far as protocols went, there'd been none discussed in any sort of official way, everyone having worked out a routine among themselves, my job being to figure a way into it.

The first few days were spent inspecting equipment and counting supplies, which was helpful by way of becoming familiar with what they had and what they didn't. The hose pack tie Ortega showed me was new, the hose itself whiteish and much narrower than the one we used on the engine back in Santa Fe. Presumably, I'd have a chance to employ it on a regular basis.

There was a heap of chainsaws in the storage shed, but only two Stihls, one of which Ortega handed me the day we went to take down some dying cottonwoods for an elderly neighbor friend of Belin's. "Might as well enjoy it now," he explained. "Seniority gets those for the fires."

The cottonwoods were tough on the chain, and when we got back from the job, the first thing I set about doing was filing mine out. Meanwhile, everyone else dropped their saws off with Ramirez. I was curious, so when I was through, I walked over to stand behind him while he worked on the others. He had a near perfect touch, light, even, shaving just the right amount of steel. Myself, I tended to hack off too much to get the point I wanted, and my angles weren't always consistent. I kept watching him, hoping to learn something.

That day was the only one we'd actually left the property. Mostly, there was tinkering with the equipment and the trading of mild insults over Hacky. When lunchtime rolled around, Ortega would hop in his Bronco along with his brother and head over to their mom's, since, he claimed, the only thing his wife hadn't figured out how to burn was toast. Garrity went home to his wife, and Ramirez left in the company of a stray dog that had adopted him. With Eli up in the office eating with Belin, that left only me and Boker. Along with a quickly dissipating spirit of camaraderie that, one afternoon, made me reckless.

"So what'd you bring me for lunch today?" I asked him.

"Buffalo turds."

"I suppose you made those yourself." I looked over in time to catch a sparkle in his eye snuff out.

"Maybe another time I would have brought corn and squash. But my grandfather's grandfather told him the white man just used that to stuff himself so he had something in his belly to kill the Indian with." He held a long, dignified face, then burst into laughter, riding the mad stallion of it, trampling over any chance of a retort. I waited until he appeared to have exhausted himself.

"You know what my grandfather's grandfather said to him?"

Boker raised his eyebrows high. "This oughta be good."

"He said he was crawling around the dirt in some remote burg in Russia, looking for a turnip for his stew. I doubt he had much occasion to be harassing your relations."

"He was biding his time is all."

"You don't know my family, Boker," I snapped. Suddenly no patience for him.

For someone convinced the world was badly intentioned toward him, Boker spent an awful lot of time laughing. In his bunk with the sunrise, going to sleep, in the dark getting up to take a leak. I'd even caught him once in a dream. At least, it seemed that's what it was, in between the snores that came through the holes of his giant nostrils. Even then, I didn't trust what I was hearing. Could sense a hatred in him trying to shake itself loose. In a crowd, he tried to overcome it, which meant he always laughed later than everyone else, and then, as if to make up for the delay, kept laughing long after the rest had stopped. When the two of us were alone together, he was more forthcoming with his bitterness.

"Lookit what we got here. The white man's still running in circles." He let me get another lap in before continuing. "Always making sure they're big enough so he can't see he's gettin' nowhere."

When I came around for the third time, he was standing in the middle of the track, his back facing me. "White man thinks he's moving forward but then—whoop!—that straight line circles around and bites him in the butt." And then he pantomimed the whole scene, jogging in place, grabbing his rear, turning around in wide-eyed startlement. He was directly in my way, and I'd just as soon have knocked him over, but I'd been keeping my impulsiveness in check and I wasn't about to let him set me back. I adjusted a few inches to make room for his ridiculousness and kept running.

Boker didn't come every day, and he rarely stayed for long, but he normally stood in the same spot, behind the tires, and he staggered his arrival time, sometimes not showing till near the end, so that I kept anticipating him. And in that way, he'd be standing there even when he wasn't. His face stretched wide. His dark hair pulled back in a braid. His dark eyes resting wounded or blinked to violent. Not the pair I wanted watching over me.

It seems like I've been thinking about you more and more instead of less and less. The letter I wrote you before I left San Francisco was supposed to be a goodbye, but that hasn't worked out on a number of levels. Try not to be too smug about it. I remember heading out to the beach with some vague idea about how I was going to rip it out of my notebook when I was finished writing. Toss it in the sea, bury it in the sand, I don't know, something deeply symbolic and meaningful, no doubt. It sounded good until I actually got out there and finished. Then I could hear your voice in my head, ragging on about littering and all that. There was no way I could just trash it. There was just no good place to put it, so I kept it in the notebook and took it back with me. That should've been my first clue I'd be checking in again.

Don't think I'm unaware of the fact I might not be reaching out like this if I'd already found my footing around here. I hope that doesn't cheapen it too much. Knowing you, I don't think you'd hold it against me.

After a while, Belin wised up to the fact there wasn't much happening down at the bay beside Hacky. Garrity said it happened every year like this. That Belin didn't care what was getting done until it'd been brought to his attention that nothing was. Typically, by Eli, this time annoyed at Lando for playing with his welding tools, running around with the blowtorch and goggles like he was some kind of alien. So we had a meeting that afternoon and Belin divided us into teams of two, each with our own set of projects to accomplish. Boker and I were assigned together, the tension between us having been noted and encouraged to be gotten out of our systems.

Our first task was to take the saws along the handful of trails that led up from the sprawl of state park that contained the ranger station, clearing them of debris, fallen trees from the winter storms. We hadn't had a single visitor to the place that I'd seen, but apparently by Memorial Day hikers would start to straggle in, strays among the otherwise sedentary users of the campsites and barbecue pits scattered throughout the park.

The next morning we headed up the Pass, and when we came to the first downed limb, I suggested Boker take care of it, I'd move further up the trail and get the next. "Sure thing, Boss," he said to me. I shook off the attitude, reassuring myself it was a one-man job, and we could accomplish more by leapfrogging ahead of one another.

An hour later and still no sign of Boker. I should've known better, I suppose, even though I swore I'd heard his saw start up not long after we separated. I was conflicted between not wanting to continue doing the work for him and wanting to get the work done, but ended up pressing on until the trail ended, opening into an alpine meadow. I put the saw down, unhooked my pack and placed it alongside. Thought I might lie out in the sun for a bit, but I couldn't get comfortable, so I got back up and looked around. Spied a nest of hatchlings in the crook of a piñon. Examined a cluster of shrubs and speculated as to what kind of berry might be coming onto them.

When I came back down the trail, Boker was right about where I'd left him, sitting in the shade of some scrub oak.

"That limb get the better of you?"

He bent over to untie his boot lace. Then retied it again, same as it was. "As a matter of fact, I couldn't get the saw to catch."

"As a matter of fact, huh? Seemed fine this morning when we tested 'em."

He shrugged.

"Well, why didn't you take it over to Eli?"

"You know, I was thinkin' right before you came up that I prob'ly just flooded it. I bet you it'll work fine by now."

"That's a bet I wouldn't take," I told him, dropping the choke on my own saw and holding it between my knees. "This mean you're ready to get some work done?"

He stood up. "Just waitin' on you, Boss."

"Hey, Boker, you wanna cut the crap. I was only making a suggestion about splitting up. It didn't amount to anything, I think that's clear enough."

So we stuck together after that. Both of us inuring ourselves to the kind of profitless exchange our conversations resulted in. Taking our turns with opening remarks that were merely the lighting of fuses, all of them generally short.

Not like I really had anyone else to turn to. Skelly had been quick to suggest a hope for renewed friendship, but I was in no position to be evaluating the offer. Coming on the heels, as it did, of her announcement that she was five months pregnant. I was trying to understand how I could've been surprised by it, why it seemed to matter, but in the end, it was only another dull pain settled over me, like I'd bumped into something and just needed to draw back to be able to absorb it.

I'd been in touch with Ren on a semi-regular basis, but he was busy with union negotiations, and as far as the rest of my old buddies from the fire department went, the closer I'd gotten to being able to see them, the further away they'd seemed. Boker was the person I seemed destined to spend the most time with, but I obviously wasn't keen on pursuing that any longer than necessary. So after shift, after making myself dinner, I took to meandering around the grounds with a field guide I'd dug up from Belin's office, where I'd been helping out with paperwork a couple times a week. The book I'd found smelled as old as its copyright, but wasn't any less valuable for it, advancing my knowledge of the local trees and flowers and plants—which were edible, which were reputed to have medicinal purposes. Even simply identifying the ones I hadn't been on a first name basis with before gave me a feeling of accommodation.

When it became too dark to see—and if I wasn't too tired—I'd take my bike over to the Rusty Nail. Driggs served the best root beer I'd ever tasted, and he had a barman's natural sympathy for the outsider. Along with a natural suspicion, and I felt worthy of them both.

"So ye been to California. Seems like every man's gotta take hisself there sooner or later."

"You been?"

"Naw, plenty enough come back as go. I can git my fill standin' right here."

Right here being behind his counter where he'd been pouring drinks for nearly sixty years. He possessed a trove of information about the history of the area and seemed pleased to bend a fresh ear toward his stories. Mining stories, stories of outlaws and politicians, traitors and double-crosses. The way he told it, it was like the posse had just pulled out of town, hooves pounding at the sunset, and if you hurried outside you could still catch it.

Returning to quarters afterward, I'd always find Boker up, hair down, his six-five frame bent over the pottery wheel he'd brought along with him. A joint at his side. He'd been kneading that clay for hours into familiar shapes with no edges, which his girlfriend would come to pick up every other week. Paint and then sell in the city. I admired his work, but the more I watched, the more it brought out a loneliness in me that I didn't want to grapple with.

"Ever notice how that pottery wheel of yours is always turning circles? Round and round, never going anywhere."

"The wheel's turning," he answered, "but I'm creating something."

"What, a bowl?"

"People have to eat."

"Aw, come on, that's just for pretty the way Malia paints them up. Just gonna sit on a shelf somewhere on Canyon Road."

He took a hit from his joint. "If people can't figure how to use a bowl properly, that sure ain't my problem."

You'd probably be feeling some sympathy for my archnemesis by now, but I'm having a hard time coming around. It's like, what does he have to complain about? He's got skills, a job, a girlfriend. Maybe it's just low-grade jealousy talking, but it makes me nervous that he could have all these things and still be such a pain in the ass.

The only time Boker seems content is when he's on his wheel. Pedaling, whistling to himself. Nothing seems to rattle him then, and I wonder if you were different when you were in the shop, too. Maybe in reverse, with you constantly dissatisfied and chucking stuff around and then acting like such a nice guy the rest of the time. Somehow, I doubt it.

I know what your shop meant to you and I bet if something had happened to me, instead, you would surely have gone on building things. Maybe even more impressive than they otherwise would've been. But I'm not talented like that. Probably the best I can hope for is to save some trees from being charred. Trees that might one day be harvested, not losing their strength, their beauty, their usefulness, but being transformed by someone's capable hands. They won't be your hands, though. That's the crime of it.

We were patrolling deep in the woods. Middle of the afternoon, and my energy was flagging. I fidgeted with the radio.

Boker squirmed in the passenger seat. "I'd like to know what kind of good's getting done scoutin' around this early in the year. There's still snow drifts up top of Baldy."

"Yeah, but there's no fires to worry about up there."

"There shouldn't be no fires to worry about anywhere near here, if the Cap'n can't spot 'em from the tower."

We both knew it was the captain's day off, and Belin's niece was on lookout. She wasn't supposed to have the sharpest eye.

"So you're saying you wanna be through?"

"Doesn't matter to me. You're drivin'."

By which, he meant it was my responsibility if we got busted for cutting out early. We were approaching the turnoff for 112, an eighteen-mile loop of narrow, rutted road.

"You know we're supposed to finish up with the loop."

"Man, I don't like going back there. I didn't sign up to be no private investigator."

I didn't like it myself. We'd be passing into marijuana territory, a well-tended stash of crops staked out in the national forest. It was common knowledge you could get your land taken if you got caught growing on it, so people figured it was better to grow on the government's, since the government wouldn't have much interest in seizing property it already owned. Still, any encroachment on the plants was taken very personally, with some of the meanest kind of traps you could imagine being set: traps to snap your leg, rat traps baited with shotgun shells and trip wire, barbed hooks strung along fishline to snag your flesh. You risked those, not to mention potential encounters with the occasional firearm if you were foolish enough to venture away from the truck. Or even if you weren't. Garrity had been the victim of a couple of potshots when he'd pulled over to piss, told of other run-ins that were best avoided. Theoretically, we were supposed to report violations.

I looked over at Boker. "You just don't want to disturb your suppliers, is what it is."

"They ain't my suppliers, shit, those people are crazy. I don't recall being issued flak jackets with my gear . . . course maybe you got one."

The engine idled in the road.

"What the heck, let's go back. We gotta fuel up anyhow."

"Whoa! Captain Jack's gonna break a rule. Better call the papers."

"Hey, cool it, Boker. Before I change my mind."

The thing was, I'd hardly taken the job with the idea of becoming some sort of model employee. Yeah, I'd been wanting to do things right, but I didn't think I was trying to cram it down anyone else's throat. Between Boker and me, though, we'd started to take on roles, with what might have been minor variations in character getting exaggerated. I came off like a workhorse next to him, and yet I was straining against my own weaknesses, trying to rein in my tendency to drift. But Boker just seemed to see the rules I'd set for myself and not the reasons behind them. When I asked the other guys about his habits the previous year, they said he'd definitely been more with the program. Garrity suggested it might've had something to do with his grandmother passing, but then Ortega reminded him that'd happened the winter before. Privately, he told me that if Boker didn't step it up, he was in danger of being let go at the end of the season.

We'd gotten called up for a job up in Colorado. After midnight, flashlight on my face, Ortega telling me to get ready, I was going with him and Lando. I scrambled out of bed while Boker pretended to be asleep, the only attention I paid him. While I gathered my things, Ortega's walkie talkie crackled in the background, and by the time Belin's voice came clear through the radio wondering how long we were going to be, I was already at the door. Ortega told him five minutes.

"Should be big money," Ortega predicted, walking over to the office. I kept up alongside, thinking about that first paycheck before I'd folded it into my pocket. A glimpse of understanding as to why crews had a reputation for starting fires, or at least taking their time on mop up.

Colorado meant travel pay and overtime pay, and likely night pay and hazard pay all added in to our salary. But it also meant big adventure, and I couldn't wait.

We got cancelled not even twenty miles outside of town. I was in no mood for it coming back, but Boker was still awake and gloating now.

"Didn't quite make it to the state line, I see."

I threw my crap down on the floor, away from me.

"You shouldn'ta even got to go at all," he continued, angry he hadn't been picked. Some chore he'd neglected to do for Belin is what I'd heard. As long as he was yapping, I figured I might as well turn on the light, which I did, trying to organize the stuff I'd left on my bed. Then gave up and pushed it onto the floor with the rest, flopped down on top of the covers and stared at the ceiling.

"I don't know which is worse, you goin' or Lando. That kid isn't accountable for a thing around here besides his last name." Then he quieted his voice. "Sure must be nice to have family around to help your situation along."

That was possibly an opportunity for me to jump in and criticize along with him, Us vs. the Ortegas, but we weren't brothers and I wasn't interested in what anyone else was doing right then or saying anything about it. I reached over and turned out the light, hoping he'd get the message.

"Just so you know, that counts as your turn. Hope you enjoyed your little vacation, cause I'm up next."

"I don't make the decisions around here, Boker." I raised my head off the pillow, turning toward him in the dark. "And you don't either."

Probably a full minute passed before he began to giggle.

I slept miserably that night. Didn't feel like getting up at all the next morning, never mind to run, but I did anyway. *Just keep going like you been going*, I told myself, but didn't make a good enough case of it, because when I got down to the track I proceeded to yank the muscle in my calf while I was stretching. I felt my temper flare, and then got to moaning about my predicament, hearing my old man's voice, *watch what happens when you get a few more years on you, my boy*, him complaining about his aches and pains when he'd always seemed healthy enough to me. I hadn't been drawn to be around him when he was talking like that, but sitting on the ground, trying to rub the kink out, I wished he'd been there to share condolences.

Instead, I had Boker. Who, for whatever reason, must have followed me down from the bunkhouse. He hadn't been by in a while and had never once gotten there before I was done warming up, but there he was. Behind the tires, hands on his elbows, looking cold.

"Why you gotta be out here?" I finally asked him.

"I hear it's a free country."

"Who told you that?"

"An eagle whispered in my ear. Then shit on my shoulder."

"That's deep, Boker," I told him, hobbling up. "Why don't you take your lazy ass back to bed where you know it wants to be."

I cursed my leg, determined to run on it anyway. That cost me the next day out. And the one after.

I've been going a little stir crazy since they put me on light duty. Too light, it feels like, I've been in quarters most of the day. Wish I could read the way I used to, but I don't seem to have it in me anymore. Still managing to do some thinking, though. Mostly about the past, not my favorite subject, generally speaking.

Remember how you were always hounding me to tell you a story about my family? Well, maybe it's a case of better too late than never. I thought I might give one a try.

Once upon a time, there was a young woman who was the first in her family to go to college. She had the full package: brains, looks, and a sly sense of humor. She chose a decent sized school near Cleveland, and when she got there, she discovered a lot of things about herself, one of them being that she was pretty good at tennis. (Stick with me here.) So one day she's out playing, and her opponent knocks the ball over the fence and out onto the grass where a young man who happens to bear a striking resemblance to yours truly is strolling by, and he picks up the ball and returns it to her.

The young man and the young woman were inseparable after that. Or as inseparable as you can be when you live in separate housing.

One night, the young man picks the young woman up at her dorm room, takes her out to his car, and just before closing her door, tells her he has a surprise for her. And then instead of heading toward town, he drives through campus and somehow manages to make it out onto the football field. It's the middle of winter and there's snow on the ground. He stops the car, briefly, and then he begins to drive again. Forward. Backward. Looping around in a circle. And for like the third time the young woman asks him what in the world he's doing, and for the third time the young man says, "Just wait." Finally, he puts the car in park and turns toward her. He looks in her eyes and says, "I just wanted to write I love you *in the snow." (I didn't ask, but I'm gonna guess it was cursive.)*

Anyway, fast forward a number of years. Dad driving me home from basketball practice, cranking up the volume and singing along with "Maggie May" (I wish I'd never seen your face) and Mom, "He should have just let me be, I was winning that match until he came along," and what was I supposed to be left with but a kind of cynicism about the possibilities of love.

Except I didn't have to be. It wasn't my story.

It probably wouldn't have made any difference, but I should have told you that one. You were right. Keeping things inside really does make them seem like a bigger deal than they really are.

Skelly called up to the ranger station today to see how I was coming along. She's a good friend, she really is, and I bet she'll make an even better mother. You can just tell she really cares about you.

I told her about how I'd messed up my leg, and that led to me recounting a few of my other anecdotes about Boker. She laughed quite a lot, and that made the whole thing seem less onerous, right there. It was going really smooth until she interrupted one of her own stories with—"Jack, do you mind if I ask you something?"—and that's when I knew I wasn't gonna be long for that conversation. Even if she probably deserved an answer to any question she might've been interested in asking.

What she wanted to know was what my time in San Francisco had meant to me.

I told her something cute. Like the short answer is there is no short answer. Which naturally I followed up by saying I had to go, but the truth is, I didn't have a good enough answer.

I look at my life right before I met you and, I don't know, you might as well have asked a pinball what it meant to be bouncing off the next bumper. Anything to keep rolling, light up the machine, set off as many chimes and bells as you could while avoiding getting drained. Which is where you knew things were headed, anyway, so why not make the most of it while you were still in play.

It sounds good, the way I've written that, and it was, to a point. That was the point when I kept wanting to restart everything mid-game anytime I ran into trouble.

Left Connecticut at seventeen. Left school. Left the fire department. Left Skelly. All bad practice for the night I left you alone. It's easy to recognize the pattern now. Even if I had to leave San Francisco to fully admit it. I wish I could say that's what my time there meant. That I was finally done with leaving.

Light duty ran straight into my two-day break, and I decided to follow through on my plans to take the bike further north to do some camping. I was tempted to get in a quick workout at the track first, but even though my body was willing, my heart wasn't in it, not fully prepared for another encounter with Boker. I put the field guide in my pack along with a few other items, then headed over to the gas station to fill up and get some groceries. Passing out of town, a number of people waved and I waved back.

I got to the trailhead and parked. Hiked up along the stream bed, the spring runoff already coming down off the banks. Nothing like what it must have been, but still, growing wilder and stronger as I went. When I reached a small cascade of falls, I dunked my head under, then took the cold, clear rush of that up higher still, the forest thickening with fir and spruce. The trail peaking, and I climbed up an old ponderosa and looked out over where I'd come from.

It really was quite a sight. Some of the prettiest country I'd ever set eyes on, a vast swath of green hemmed in by sky and mountain. Partitioned by old logging roads, darkened in spots where they'd done some prescribed burns the previous season. I could even make out the faint trace of a switchback on a far ridge, one I was pretty sure connected back with the ranger station. It came to me how with all the trails around, it didn't make much sense to be sticking to the track in the morning. There were plenty of options for more interesting runs. I'd still be coming back to the same place at the end, but I knew there were a lot worse places to return to.

At the end of May, a couple of college kids showed up, sent over from NMSU's forestry program. Summer credits for Chris and Jeff. Both appeared undernourished and had a whiff of questionable hygiene about them. They set themselves up in the middle of the bunkhouse between Boker and me, and out of their bags came laptops, music players, game players, and other assorted electronica. The first thing one of them wanted to know was if we had an internet connection, and while I was in the process of explaining that Belin had a satellite feed in his office, the other one cut me off.

"Don't even tell me cellphones don't work here."

He was holding his phone at arm's length, then stuck it in the air and began to follow it around, chasing bars. Boker walked out of the room, leaving me to entertain questions.

"I think you can get reception on that little hill behind the office."

"By the entrance?"

"Yeah."

"Nowhere closer than that?"

"Not that I know of. Maybe."

The hill was the one place I'd seen Lando chatting, but it wasn't as if I'd made a thorough investigation. The last I'd seen of my cellphone was the day I left California when I ran over it with my bike. Even then the only result had been the quiet crush of the screen, but it was an improvement.

"Anyway, like I was saying, Belin's got times posted when you can get online."

"You have to sign up or something?"

"No, it's usually available."

The next morning over coffee, the two of them were bleary-eyed and sullen, like they were trying to comprehend how and why they'd ended up here, and after a week's time, it looked like they still hadn't figured it out. They'd cut a conversation when you came into the room or stumbled on them in the field, likely having persuaded themselves they were making observations about things the rest of us couldn't see. The first time they did share their views, it was to point out how Boker and I had failed to properly place the limbs we'd cut along the trail for erosion control, and Boker spoke what was on both our minds when he said, "We just do what they tell us."

"Besides," I added, "then there wouldn't be anything left for you to do." Despite these grumblings, I had to admit they made excellent additions to the Hacky circle.

One evening, I came in with a bag full of Cota leaf I'd been collecting and found them sprawled on the living room couches. They were pressing buttons furiously on their gaming devices and narrating their accomplishments to one another. Without warning, Chris jumped off the couch, apparently having beaten a high score. He held out his hand for the high five, but Jeff just nodded at him. *Whatever*, I thought, turning to walk into the kitchen. That's when I noticed Boker in the corner. He was sitting in front of his pottery wheel, but the wheel wasn't moving. His roach clip was in the ashtray beside him. He looked as if he might be ready to pull his hair out. It was odd to be in a position of feeling sorry for him, but I did. So much so, that I didn't think it through very far when I asked if he wanted to come along with me to the Rusty.

His initial response was an expression I'd never seen before. "No," he said finally. "No, I'm not goin' with you."

"Suit yourself," I said, putting the herbs in the back of the fridge. Then I went into the bathroom to wash up.

When I came out again, Chris and Jeff were still going at it, but Boker was gone. He reappeared outside while I was wheeling my bike off the front porch to tell me he'd changed his mind.

"I'll go," he said, "but you can't be breathing a word about this to Malia."

"Why would I say anything to Malia? I don't think that woman's said three words to me since she's been coming up here."

"I'm not askin' you about why you would say something. I'm askin' you not to do it."

"Well, I'm telling you I won't." I was about to suggest he reconsider and stay right where he was. "Meet me at the end of the driveway, then, I don't wanna mess around with the two of us on all this gravel."

It was awkward as hell with Boker getting on. I kept my feet bolted to the ground and a white-knuckled grip on the handlebars while the seat sank heavy with the planting of his ass, trying to telegraph to the bike that it was going to be a short trip. Taking off was a challenge with the extra pounds, but I trusted him to cooperate because we were both at stake. We wobbled at first, trying to stick inside the tread lines from the trucks where the dirt was compacted, and then finally caught a bit of speed, kicking up a small trail of red cloud as we went. He could barely get his legs around me enough for his feet to reach the side rests, giving him little choice but to hang over me like a coat. It was only four miles from the ranger station to the highway, and another half mile to the bar, but by the time we'd pulled up in front of the Rusty, it felt like twice that.

I hadn't attracted much attention myself when I'd visited before, but when Boker and I walked through the door we copped more than a few stares. I can't say Driggs looked uneasy about us being there, but he didn't seem all that excited about it either.

I turned to Boker. "What, you've got a reputation around here?"

"Not that I know about," he answered.

The pool table rarely saw much action, and we settled in there. Played a few games with both of us being pretty well matched. After a while, the alcohol started to work its alchemy, and we sat back up at the bar.

"It's interesting how you don't seem to do much racial baiting around Garrity," I pointed out. "Looks like his parents raised him Caucasian."

"Garrity wouldn't get ticked off the same way you do. That'd take half the fun out of it."

"Uh huh. Might also have something to do with the fact he's assistant foreman."

Boker grinned. "That might be another factor." Then he took one of his elbows off the bar and turned a few degrees toward me. "So how is it you ended up comin' out here?"

"I wanted the job. And I wanted to be back in New Mexico."

"Can't understand that at all. You're not married, are you?"

"No."

"You got a girlfriend?"

"Nope."

"Why not?"

"Lots of people don't have girlfriends."

"True. But you look like the type that should have one." He eyed me suspiciously. "Whadaya suck dick or somethin'?"

"Wouldn't suck yours."

"Well, I sure as shit hope not." Boker didn't seem quite sure how to proceed. "Whose would you suck?"

"Aw, I don't know. My own, I suppose. If I could reach it."

"Yeah, it's too bad about that."

"It is. I worked with a guy in California who could do it. He wasn't even that big, or anything. Just flexible."

"I don't suppose I'll ask how you happened to come upon that little demonstration."

"You could. I don't care."

"Naw, I don't think I'll pursue that line of inquiry any further. Still . . ." Boker seemed to contemplate the possibilities. "That sort of thing could make a man keep to himself."

"Could. Have to be careful not to let yourself get carried away." I nodded Driggs for another round. "So how long you been seeing Malia?"

"A long time."

"She sure doesn't say much."

"She's like that with most people she don't know. With most people she do, too. Don't be fooled, though, she can cuss up a storm when she wants. And she ain't real shy in bed, either, I can assure you of that."

I didn't doubt him, having almost stumbled in on the two of them a couple weeks back.

"Yeah, she's a real wild woman. I can't take it all the time. I really can't, but then again I sure do like . . ." he threw back his head, "Oo-whee, I sure do like takin' what I can handle."

And for the first time his laughter caught, and when Driggs dropped the beers in front of us, I raised one of them in salute.

I was a chicken tonight. Or at least half a chicken. I meant what I said, I really don't care what Boker might suspect about me or what he thinks about it, but I could have been more forthcoming. Maybe one day someone will ask me if I have a boyfriend, and I can tell them, "No, but I did"—I'm pretty sure I'd say that, even though it's kind of an abyss thinking about what I'd say next—but until that day comes, and let's face it, that day's not likely to come, I've gotta figure out how I'm going to handle myself around guys again if the conversation turns personal. I'm supposed to be seeing Ren before long, and what am I gonna say?

It's like how do you explain just because you fell for one guy doesn't mean you're gonna fall for any guy who happens to be sitting on the next barstool. There's sure a long way between knowing you're capable of getting together with someone and wanting to do it, and with Boker, I've already got enough strikes against me without him worrying about whether or not I want to get in his pants. He'd probably find a reason to be offended either way.

I guess Boker and I were learning to get along all right. There were certain things we couldn't help sharing. Being outsiders for one. Being the same age, for another. Closing in on thirty and not so young anymore. And here we were spending our time with the same job, crummy as it was in some ways. We were no fire jumpers, no hotshots, just line diggers with shovels and two hundred fifty gallons of water to piss when we got the opportunity, and there hadn't been many.

We'd had some small turnouts, all lightning strikes in the backcountry, but it was just a matter of the captain radioing in the coordinates, and us busting over there in the trucks to get them. A couple hours' work, and it was over.

In the middle of June, we started a thinning project in a ponderosa stand about an hour's drive from the ranger station. It was the best work we'd done all summer. Good for us, good for the health of the forest. Removing the weaker trees. Leaving the dominants and co-dominants to thrive. A number of them were towering and gave a satisfying thunderclap when they fell, and, after our haranguing by Chris and Jeff, we were sure to get them turned parallel to the hill slopes to benefit the soil. The crew finally seemed to have found a rhythm. Getting up in the morning, we knew exactly what we needed to do and did it. After a couple of the shifts, Boker and I went into the Rusty together, but things were basically peaceful. That lasted almost two weeks.

Belin had called us into his office for a meeting. He was standing behind his desk, looking more aggrieved than usual to be there; you could tell it wasn't going to be good news.

He told us the Soltano family was selling their land, near countless acres that shared a border with the park. The title company had required a survey for the buyer since it hadn't been updated since the 1800s, and when it was completed it showed the original markers to have been skewed. The Forest Service fence was impinging on their land. It was going to be our job to move it.

No one was happy about the situation. Lando was the first to scrap about it. "That fence is their problem."

"Not that side. We put that up in the late fifties."

"Now, why would we have gone and done a thing like that?"

"Because we did. Because this is a fence-out state, as you all better know. Because we didn't want cattle mingling with the visitors to the park. And before you go asking why we put it where we put it, I'll tell you right now we were only following the same markers that have been there since before we became a state, mostly along the arroyo. No one's ever questioned them until now."

"Who in their right mind's wanting to buy land out here," Garrity wanted to know.

"Developer from Dallas is what Eli told me. Paying a pretty penny for it, too. He's got plans to parcel it out with view spreads."

"With views of what?"

"With views of—hell, I don't know, with views of the views. Point is, there's a lot of talk running around on account of the railroad starting up again; they say you'll be able to get up to Albuquerque in under an hour. Folks wanting to play weekend rancher and such is what they're counting on. This town might not be finished yet."

Ortega took his hands from his pockets and crossed his arms. "Town's fine like it is."

"I'm not here to argue that point. Just so long's you're all clear that the south fence needs moving."

"The whole south side?"

"The whole south side."

"How far we movin' it?"

Belin scratched at the back of his neck. "Not far."

There were plenty of rotten posts that needed replacing, and we cut fresh ones by the truckload, the juniper that ran rampant through the forest offering wood to spare. The barbed wire we wound up in sections, the sole purpose of which was to be able to unroll it and use it again. Then the reality of the job set in like the headache that it was. The ground was typical mountain desert—dry, rocky, with pockets of caliche, and unyielding to blows against it no matter how strong. We'd already broken two post hole diggers and we were just getting started.

Above the rest of us, Boker was furious. Of course, he saw fit to save up the worst of it to convey to me. In the middle of the afternoon, edging toward ninety degrees, my shirt soaked through.

"I can guarantee you it's some white man who went and caused this. It's the stupidest thing I ever heard of, moving a perfectly good fence twelve feet."

I was trying my best not to put the job in a poor light, and we'd all rehashed the thing a hundred ways to Sunday. He'd barely done any work, and I was sick of his whining. I threw down the post hole digger beside me.

"In the first place, it's not a perfectly good fence, it could use some attention, so now's probably as good a time as any to move it. In the second place, you don't know who's behind all this. Just as likely some tribe of Indians all awash in their casino booty. Probably'll have billboards posted up and down the freeway advertising for it like they put every other goddamn place. Probably put up another goddamn golf course in a few years and suck off whatever water's left around here." I reached up with the back of my hand and wiped my mouth.

Boker seemed to be weighing his next words. "Whoever it is, it's white man's ways, I can assure you of that."

"You can't assure me of nothin'. If it was your extra twelve feet, you'd want it."

"It isn't nobody's twelve feet, you think God himself put down these markers?" He shook his head. "Nobody knew the difference a thousand years ago, and nobody's gonna know the difference in a thousand more."

"In a thousand years, the white man will be brown, and then who are you gonna blame for all your trouble."

"In a thousand years, I'll be surprised if there's any man left standing."

Boker didn't seem the slightest bit upset about it. And with that heat pouring down, relentless from the summer sky, I couldn't help but agree with him.

With Garrity and the Ortega brothers leading the way, we all started going down to the Rusty after shift. To shoot pool and have a beer. Beer always talked about in the singular but guaranteed to be in the plural. When you'd look down those miles of fence with no end in sight, you needed to know there was at least something on the horizon waiting to spell you. But while a group of us went, it was Boker and I who stayed. The drinking wasn't doing either of us any good. I'd stopped getting up to run in the morning, blaming it on my not wanting to be outside any more than I had to. But with Boker, it was becoming increasingly evident that he had a problem with the alcohol. In retrospect, I suppose he'd showed some telltale signs before, but the fact he'd kept his consumption reasonable had served to obscure them. Besides, we'd been having a good time then and I hadn't been looking for trouble.

The first beer would usually come off fine enough between us, good feelings all around, finished for the day. But as the night progressed and the other guys went home, an eerie expression would come over Boker's face, one that could be mistaken for desire but never contentment. That is, it wasn't at all how he seemed when his foot was pedaling the pottery wheel. Instead, it was a slightly manic look, anticipation shining through his eyes, so that no matter how easygoing he might be acting, if you saw real close, you'd know he was already thinking ahead to that next drink.

And so the point would inevitably come when it was useless for us to be around each other anymore; he'd just say I was full of white man shit and offer to kick it out of me whether we were talking pool or politics or what flavor the rain was. I'd tell him it was time to go, I'd be waiting for him outside. And I did wait. Repeating to myself how senseless this all was, how we wouldn't be coming again. Nearly convincing myself of it before Boker would stagger out from the bar, slurring one thing or the other.

"My grandma would never treat me like this," he'd say.

"Your grandma? What the hell are you talking about, Boker? Treat you like what?"

But he wouldn't answer, just reluctantly got on the bike, soon complaining about my erratic driving when he was the one slumped over me and causing it.

Same story, night after night, and yet I continued to drink with him. And him with me. Picking at the same scab, and it was only a matter of time before it was going to bleed.

"Chalk up another one," Boker proclaimed, leaning his stick against the table.

"Yeah, for me. You lost."

The stick clattered to the floor. "I won."

"That was a foul."

"The hell it was."

"Come off it, Boker, you managed to hit my three first. The thing moved a foot across the table if it moved an inch."

"It was a clean shot."

"You had to've had your eyes closed." I looked to one of the guys slouched on a stool beside us. "You musta seen it."

He sat up a bit. Adjusted his hat. "He mighta hit it."

I glared at him before turning my attention back to Boker. "I'm not about to pay for the next game. Why don't you re-strategize while you're racking 'em." I started toward the bar, then turned back. "And you might wanna pick up your stick while you're at it."

While I was waiting to order, Boker hit me so hard across the back with the stick that it knocked tears into my eyes. Somehow, I wasn't expecting it, and it took a moment of recovering before I turned around and clobbered him. Kept clobbering him, his arms fat and slow and weak toward his defense. But he wouldn't go down. Just kept listing there, a battered, defiant mess.

Word got back to the station by lunch the following day. I was thinking we would've lost our jobs if we had a different boss, but Belin had other ideas. He said while we were on the clock we were to keep out of each other's way. And he said if it happened again, it better not happen again in town.

"If you can't keep your hands to yourselves, there's plenty of room to tussle around here," he told us. "Assuming you got energy for that sort of thing at the end of the day."

When we were walking out of the office, Belin held me back by the shoulder. He waited until Boker had exited. "I have to say I didn't expect that out of you."

"Yeah, well, I didn't expect it out of myself either."

"Maybe you haven't picked up on this, but people in town don't think all that highly of us as it is. Even though we're trying to help out around here, a green fire truck is still a vehicle that works for the government."

"I wasn't thinking about the job when it happened."

"I know it. And it's too bad because by not thinking you might have messed things up for yourself in ways you don't even realize." I wasn't sure what he was referring to but figured the ways I already knew I'd messed up were enough to think on. "It doesn't take but one person to stop something like that. There's times when you need to control yourself, which is all the time when you're in Forest Service attire, and you're old enough to know how to go about doing it."

"I realize that. It's just . . ."

"Go ahead, speak your mind. There's no point in you standin' here otherwise."

"Well, the thing is with this fence job. I mean patience was never my strong suit to begin with, but I've got none coming to me at the end of the day."

He nodded. "It's not work I'm proud to assign, but it is work that needs to be done, regardless of how it came about."

"I've told myself that a bunch of times, I guess it hasn't sunk in yet. It just isn't what I pictured myself doing. Coming here to fix someone else's mistakes. I came to fight fires."

"And you will. Besides, you don't think the intensity and scope of many a fire we face today is the result of mistakes made, or at a minimum, poor planning? Same as plenty of work that goes on in this country and the whole world over. I can guarantee you there'll be someone comin' along after you to fix yours."

"Not every mistake can be fixed."

"True, but most can. And as far as fires go, you need to stop being pig-headed about it. This season's off to a slow start, I'll give you that, but it won't last. I've been here a long stretch, and I'm sad to say I've never seen a summer without one. If it's not in our backyard, it'll be someone else's. The season's getting longer, the fires bigger, not enough bodies to fight 'em, not enough money to pay for the bodies. You'll have your hands more than full up. And then you'll think back on our little chat and remember what I said. Now, do I need to connect any more dots for you?"

"No, sir."

"Good. Just be thankful you got your health and aim to keep it that way."

Hopefully, you've got better things to do than cheer or hiss every move I've been making down here, but I can't help evaluating, and I'm not real pleased with myself at the moment. It seems like the more transparent I get, the more I've got to face up to what I see. And the way I see it, no sooner do I tell myself I have to be one hundred percent committed to staying here, than I go and do something that almost gets me kicked out. Pretty sneaky, huh? But not real smart, since I should've considered the only thing worse than me packing my own bags would've been someone else packing them for me. I'm not sure what the point of figuring all this stuff out is, after the fact. When it feels like it's too late to do anything about it.

We had the fence finished by the end of the week. Belin and Eli came down to help out and that gave things a boost. It also kept Boker and me on our toes, although I don't think we needed any assistance with staying out of each other's way. I'd hardened myself against the bruises and swellings in his face, figuring at least he'd finally have a legitimate excuse for slagging off, though the few times I saw him he didn't appear to be, and of course it was my knuckles that were sore and kept me from working at full tilt. The one time I saw him taking a break, he was a ways down the fence line, staring off at some point known only to him, and I thought about the distance between men, and how little of it was going to be bridged with a drink. A fist or a kiss. Just forgotten for a while, maybe that was the best that could be done about it.

Boker and I hadn't spoken to each other, but I knew he was getting a ride to the bar every night with Ortega, who dropped him off on his way home. Boker must've walked back or maybe bummed a ride. The first night he stumbled in late, I lay in bed thinking what an idiot he was being for going back there, wondering if Belin had talked to him. If he had, it wasn't doing any good, he couldn't seem to quit it. In the morning, I found a blanket thrown over the pottery wheel.

On my next day off, I decided to go into Albuquerque. The plan was to sit inside the air-conditioned movie theater all afternoon and catch whatever was playing, but on my way out of town I had to pass by the bar. A couple of guys were just coming out, and I pulled into the lot beside them. Then waited for them to get into their truck before I hopped off the bike.

Driggs nodded at me when I walked in. Pulled some mugs from the dishwater and set them on the rail. Then looked up at me again when I reached the bar.

"Just stopped by to tell you I was sorry about what happened."

"Sorry for what, gettin' yer back broke? I saw the whole thing. I saw it comin' through the front door before you even showed up that night. Imagine you prob'ly did, too."

I nodded. "Yeah, so I was wondering if I owed you anything damage-wise."

"Lessee. No, I don't believe I'll need to charge ye for havin' to turn a couple a stools back on their feet. But there is one favor you can do me."

"Sure."

"I don't want yer friend comin' in here alone anymore. That man can't handle hisself."

"Did you tell him that?"

"I did."

"When?"

"Every time he come in this week, but he ain't in no condition to be rememberin' it."

"So what d'you want me to do about it?"

He didn't answer right away. Finished wiping down the mug in his hand, put the towel over his shoulder. "If he's gotta come, I'm suggestin' you might want to come with him."

I stared at Driggs. "You really think I can control him?"

"Not much. But if he gets ornery, he'll take it out on you. See, right now he's takin' it out on the rest of my customers—little comments and such—and I can't have that. Can't have everyone on edge when they comin' in here to relax."

"You could just call Appleby and be done with it."

"You could have yerself a seat, yer makin' me nervous standin' there."

I sat down. Driggs poured me a root beer and set in on the counter. "Now, you gotta know I don't like trouble in my bar. But I don't like callin' the police neither, that messes with my idea of my place. My daddy never called the police, they never was no police to call. Anymore, I'm too old to be wrestlin' with my customers, and I'm too smart to be pullin' out my shotgun less I really need it. In my time, I hadda remove exactly two individuals from this establishment and I'd just as soon git to my grave before I make it three."

"Okay, but what about just not serving him at all."

"Let me ask you a question, son. Have you ever given money to a man on the street? I betcha you have. And have you followed that man around afterwards to see what he does with that money. I betcha you haven't. Hell, you can sniff what he does with it right there in front of you. See, that's between him and God, that's not yer business. Yer business is to decide whether or not to give a man what he asks for."

"Even if it's just enough rope?"

Driggs didn't look up. "I told that fella he should take a break."

The barkeep sounded sincere as always, but the more he talked, the less convinced I'd become of what he was saying. It seemed like an awfully tall order to fill: Sure, to try and make a clean swallow of this world you ought to have a taste for poison, but not so much you ended up choking on it. Boker had made it plain that he'd had more than enough, and I couldn't see how he was in need of any more temptations.

"I think it's best if we both stay clear of here for a while. I'll talk to him."

In the theater, I couldn't sit still and left while the previews were still running. Drove around for the rest of the day, not sure what to make of anything, past or present. It was only on the ride back up the mountain that I finally began to get clear on my thoughts, and then, just outside of town, pulled over to collect them.

You know who I've been thinking a lot about today? And not for the first time, either. Bishkey. Yup, the Bronx Bomber, himself, and how I don't even want to take a guess as to how things would've turned out if he and I had been doing bumps together on his kitchen table instead of drinking mushroom tea. He not only took me in but encouraged me to get my act together (well, technically, he yelled about it). It doesn't seem like you always have the chance to pay people back directly, but that doesn't mean you don't owe anything. I had a chance to start paying down a little of that debt with Boker, and I didn't take it.

I think the hardest part about trying to be a decent person is accepting the fact that you're going to come up short sometimes. It's easier, in a way, once you've given up on yourself. Convinced you'll never amount to anything good. Then you can feel like you're getting ahead of your mistakes. You make another one, and it's like, "See, just as I suspected." They don't even feel like mistakes anymore, really, they just feel like what you're doing and who you are.

I didn't consider myself especially angelic before we met, but it wasn't like I thought I had horns growing out of my head either. I knew I didn't like to cause trouble for people, but, as you discovered, the way I generally handled those situations was to try to back out of them rather than trying to work them through. You didn't seem to have a problem calling me out on that. And I suppose I listened, for once, because I liked the man I was becoming when I was with you. I know it's not possible I could ever be that person without you here, but it was like I threw the whole prototype overboard.

I did keep your pocket-watch, though. You know that, right? Finding it at the bottom of your cedar chest is the last memory I have from that morning. I wasn't really thinking when I took it. I just knew I wanted it.

Then, in the beginning, when I'd wind it up, I'd think about what the woman who'd given it to you had said. About what a good person you were, and how right she was about that. But somewhere along the way, I started to believe that the only goodness left in this world was under that cover, and I couldn't stand to look at it anymore.

I was trying to remember what made me take it out again that night at Bishkey's. There was something in my mind about wanting to run that call right—the way you would've—and I guess I was hoping for some luck. Holding it in my palm on the cab ride over, pressing my fingers against it, I thought back to the first night we got together, returning to the city in that Lincoln town car, and how I'd held your hand so tight, and how I wished I could hold it that way again.

But it was more than luck that I was looking for. I held onto your watch hoping a part of you might rub off on me, too. Somehow get through my skin. Like I didn't have a single decent bone left in my body.

I did, but you wouldn't have known it from the way things turned out that night. Not my finest hour. Not only was I unable to pull off a Kevin, my behavior seemed out of character even for me. But you know, I'm not really sure we get to pick and choose which of our actions define us. Just try not repeat the ones we're not proud of.

It was my last call, true. But it wasn't my last screw-up, and even if I can't stop myself from doing wrong, I don't think that's going to let me off the hook from trying to do better.

I was late getting back. Passed Ortega's truck coming down the road with only the Ortegas in it. I parked the bike outside in the gravel and cut the engine. Faced with the opportunity to talk with Boker, I was losing my nerve and told myself I had no business doing it. Like Driggs said, he was the one who'd taken the first swing; it wasn't likely he'd be seeking me out.

I walked over to the office and let myself in. Turned on the light, not really sure what I was doing there. Shuffled through some papers. Then turned the light out again, locked up, and made my way back to quarters.

Inside, Boker was sitting in the corner gazing out the window. The blanket was off the wheel. He turned toward me. I tensed when he spoke.

"Thought I heard you pull up a while ago."

"I did. Had some things to take care of. You stayin' in tonight?"

"Looks like it."

"Gonna run the wheel?"

"Might."

I nodded. "Where's Mutt 'n' Jeff?"

"Out cradle robbin' again. Went off to some local's party. I'll tell you, those girls keep gettin' younger and younger."

"Sure seems that way."

Boker was staring at the pottery wheel in front of him. He looked worn out. "Malia's coming up tomorrow. Not gonna have any pottery for her. Not sure what I'm gonna tell her."

"You'll think of something."

"It won't matter what I say, she'll figure it out. She's smart like that. Smarter 'n me."

"She's not that smart, she's with you."

"Might not be after tomorrow."

"She doesn't seem like the type to cut and run."

"No, she prob'ly would've done it by now if she meant to."

I figured I'd stalled long enough. "Hey, so I saw Driggs earlier today."

Boker frowned. "What'd he have to say?"

"Said to say hello."

"Ha. Goodbye's more like it. I believe I was told I needed some time off from the Rusty. It occurred to me today the man might be serious."

"I gather he probably is. Listen, Boker, about that night . . . I just wanted to say I could've handled things . . . from the beginning, I . . ."

"Why don't you make like a good gringo and speak English?"

"I'm sorry I hit you, all right? I mean, not the first punch, but the ones after that."

"What punch? I didn't feel a thing, first or last . . . I'm not sorry I cracked you with that stick."

Why the hell not? I just about snapped but I knew. "What I really want to say is I'm sorry I kept taking you to the bar. Drinking with you, like that. I had my suspicions, and then that first night after the fence job started, I could just tell it was a bad idea."

"Leadin' a horse to water's no felony. I don't recall you pourin' anything down my throat."

"Doesn't matter, I still shouldn'ta done it. A friend shouldn'ta done it."

"A friend, huh? Well." He considered this for a moment. "Maybe a friend woulda thought twice." When he looked back at me his eyes were wet. "Man, I don't know what's got into me this year. Somethin' sure ain't right. Even before you showed." He shook his head. "The thing is, I don't feel at all connected to what's happening around me. Not a bit."

"Well," I said carefully, "there's advantages to that. Not being connected, I mean."

"Not so many."

"Yeah," I nodded to myself. "Not enough." Then I looked at Boker again. "Any idea why you've been feeling like that?"

"What's it matter why?"

"It doesn't matter, I guess." I pulled out the chain from under my shirt and began tugging at the keys.

"It's hard with just the two of us. Malia's the best thing I got goin', but it's hard. I don't like what's happening on the rez so I come here, don't like what's happening here makes me want to go back to the reservation. Just collect my check and be done with it." He reached over to the table and picked up the lighter, sparked it a few times. It didn't catch, and he put it down again. "I hate feelin' stuck. And even if gettin' drunk's the one sure way to guarantee I won't get unstuck, I can't help myself, you know, it feels like I am for a while." He nodded toward me. "Must be nice you can hop on that bike whenever you want. Just go."

"Too easy, sometimes. Nothing usually gets better while you're gone." I tucked the keys back under my shirt, forced out the last words. "It can get worse."

"Things'll get worse anyway if they want to."

"I know that. But what's the point of helping them along?"

Boker sighed, a rueful smile crept onto his face. "Malia would say something like that."

"I bet she would. Listen, I don't know what else you got going on, Boker, but it sounds like you know how lucky you are to have her. I'd be sure I wasn't risking that."

We held each other's eyes for a good while after that.

Then he reached over and picked up the lighter. Sparked it until it caught. Picked up the joint from the ashtray and lit it. I shook my head when he held it out for me to smoke, but he kept it held there, so I reached over and took it from him and took a toke off it and handed it back, and then he took a toke and placed it in the ashtray again. He sat back on the chair and I slid down onto the couch and closed my eyes.

I was almost asleep when I heard him start up the wheel.

All's been quiet on the western front for a while now. I almost started talking about you the other night, but I didn't. First off, when it comes to someone else's trouble, it's usually not the best time to start swapping war stories. "Well, sonny, that reminds me of the time when . . ." You know, like your problems are fine but let's go ahead and compare and contrast them with mine, which are even more interesting. It wasn't like Boker told me much, anyway. But I felt like I knew where he was coming from, even if I'm not sure how he got there.

It's like if there's only one cure you can think of, then that's the one you take.

When I lost you, that's all there was. The loss. It seemed as if I was in the middle of this ocean, and all I could do was keep drinking from it, no thirst or quench to it, no taste of anything else. Just spluttering and trying to keep my head above water. But you can only keep treading like that for so long before you start to become disgusted with all the commotion you're making. You've got to be alive to be making it, and you weren't the one who needed saving. So you tell yourself you better sink or swim and be done with it one way or the other.

I know I had to push down everything that'd happened to take those first strokes. But then I just kept taking them, even though I knew I wasn't getting any closer to shore. Sure, those pesky feelings of rage and guilt would surface every once in a while, but I felt detached from them. Just like I felt detached from everything else. I wasn't quick to realize the cure had become a sickness of its own.

You know what struck me most about Boker the other night? It was the way his tears brought something humble to him. Something that was asking—not me—but someone, for forgiveness. He just seemed so innocent of any crime he may have committed, and I thought to myself, if only I could have one moment like that.

Well, I got a bunch of them. You oughta know when I woke up on the couch and went stumbling out into the woods, it was because I thought I was going to throw up. That's not what ended up happening, of course. I'm pretty sure there was some howling. I can't say if there was a moon. I'd always been afraid if I let the waterworks get turned on, they'd never stop—and for

When the fires finally came that first summer, they burned hot, igniting the trees and all the pent-up sap under their bark. Watching a forest go down in flames was tougher than I'd imagined, but it seemed like it was happening everywhere at once and there wasn't much opportunity to step back and take it all in. We felled snags and humped hose and sprayed water, but mostly I put my shoulder to the shovel with the rest and dug line. Removing combustibles from the fire's path, exposing the mineral soil, trying to contain the fire.

Digging line requires a certain mindset. It doesn't really matter what kind of shape you're in, or how strong you are, or what your technique might be. Working alongside inmates from the State Pen led me to believe they understood this better than anyone. You weren't going anywhere, so might as well put your head down and keep digging. Not quite a futility to it, although there could be, at times. When you've seen a blaze jump across eight lanes of highway, you're not likely to overestimate the power of your little bit of scratching in the dirt.

It was the last day of the Valle Grande Fire and we'd fought it hard. A dozen crews. Without any air support, there was none to be had, all the slurry bombers tied up further west. Aided by the wind, which had lain low for us. Led by bulldozers that had halted the head of the fire, our lines holding against the flanks.

We were returning to base camp. Pockets of smoke steamed around us, the blackened ground at our feet, the same black we'd be blowing from our noses. I could feel the back of my throat dry and tight, and having tamed my thirst those past days, I finally let loose the full force of it, chugging from the canteen. Then I handed it back to Boker. He took one last swig and poured the rest over his head.

Ortega nodded as we approached, and after the group of us conferred for a while it was decided that Ortega would stay with Garrity and Ramirez, while Lando would return with Boker and me to the station to get one of the trucks back in service.

We drove back to Copper Canyon talking about the fire. About how lucky we'd been with the weather, how the teams had worked well together. We talked all the way home, with Lando between us, passed out on Boker's shoulder.

Late that afternoon we pulled into town, and after dropping Lando at his house, went down to the bay and got the truck in order, cleaned the equipment, and refilled the tank. Then we went up to quarters to get ourselves cleaned up. When I got out of the shower, I was still wired. I knew I wouldn't be able to sit around and dressed quickly.

When I passed Boker on the living room couch, pulling on his socks, I nodded at him, then walked out onto the porch where the bike was waiting. The screen door smacked shut behind me. I hesitated. Turned and poked my head back inside.

"Hey Boker, man, let's get out of here."

"I know I don't wanna go to the Rusty."

"That's not what I had in mind," I told him. "I was thinking we could just take a ride."

It was less than a week before Boker would get shipped out to Washington State with Garrity and Ramirez for a monster fire that would eat through scores of acres its first night, with no sign of abating—a fire that would converge with two others and occupy them for the rest of the summer. It was before Boker would meet up with some cousins there and decide to stay on. Send for his girl. Malia coming by quarters to pick up his pottery supplies, reserved as always, but sure to pass along to Boker the good luck I'd wished for him.

It was before me and the Ortega brothers would work a bunch of medium-size blazes around the state, in Lindrith, Las Barancas, and finally finishing up the season in Questa. Before I'd accept the offer from Belin to caretake the ranger station for the winter—him finally following through on a promise to take his wife somewhere warm.

It was the close of the day when Boker climbed onto the seat behind me and we started down the five miles of washboard that led to the highway. A steady rumble beneath the wheels, the faint smell of singed cedar, the heat peeling off us as we pushed through it. I was trying to figure out which direction we should go, when I felt his knees tighten, and a moment later, his arms ease themselves from around me. He lifted them, spreading them wide until they were fully stretched. Then he began to move them. Up into the air and down. Up again. The late sun behind us. And now the shadow of enormous wings cast ahead.

LAST TIDE

I **walked all the way** *from Union Square. Maybe just to prove to myself once and for all how small this town really is, I don't know. It wasn't that far. Looking around this empty beach, it's hard to believe you were ever here. But I know this is where we met. Near these rocks. And even if I couldn't find the exact spot, I feel like I'm close.*

Me and the bike are leaving tomorrow. Got a firefighting job back in New Mexico and they want me there by the start of next week. I'll be in the forest again, I'm looking forward to that. Working with Bishkey these last months has been good but it was never meant to do anything more than get me back on my feet and I've been on them for a while now. Maybe you already know all this. Because if there is a heaven then you've got to be in it, looking down and following the action. Probably had to cover your eyes there, for a while, I know it got pretty grim, and I know you weren't big on horror flicks.

I've been trying not to think about it too much. Any of it, really, but I didn't want to take off without offering you an apology. You always said they went a long way with you, and even if you're not in a position to forgive me, I hope you can hear me out.

When I left you to go out on that ride, I was just trying to clear my head. I never even paused to consider you might not be there when I got back. I'm sure there's a bunch of someones out there who, if they'd been in my place, felt about you the way I did, would never have left your side but none of those someones is me. Or wasn't me.

I'm sorry, Kevin. I wish I could've been there. I wish I could've held you better when you were in the hospital. I wanted to, but it was hard enough just looking at you, all those scars, and trying to fathom how there could be that kind of hatred in the world. I couldn't see past the ugliness of it, and that left you fighting for your life, alone. I just have to believe I would've come around if there'd only been more time.

I realize I didn't know you that long, and I might not have known you that well. I'd like to think I did, but who's to say anymore. I do know I had more confidence in you than I did in myself, but that still doesn't mean things would have worked out between us. Nothing ever did with me before and besides, I never got to see what it'd be like to hold your hand walking down the street—any street—not just these rainbow-colored ones. But boy, what I would have given for the chance to find out. And without that chance, it's too painful to keep thinking about all the potential you had, with or without me.

You know, I'm going to have to shut down on you again after this. Otherwise, I'm just going to be in a bad mood for the rest of my life, and who's going to be around to pop me on the forehead and snap me out of it? I wish I could think of something more to say besides goodbye, but I'm running out of words and I need to get a grip on my feelings before they run away with me, too. Holding them back doesn't seem like much of a strength anymore, but I haven't figured out another way.

ACKNOWLEDGMENTS

Special thanks to early readers Michael Denneny, Jessica Kubzansky, James Saidy, and Erika Atkinson. Thank you Paul Cox for Bronxing it up, Thor for the risk paper, and Alison Callahan (I'll tell you why if we ever run into each other). Thank you Elizabeth Hatlett, Kimberly Hitchens, and the whole crew over at Booknook.

Finally, thank you Rachel Stout. For helping convince me the story still was still worth telling, and then helping me tell it.